M

CW00385907

Also by Emma Stirling

A Field of Bright Poppies
The Cockleshell Girl
Clover Blossom

MARIGOLD SUMMERS

Emma Stirling

HEADLINE

First published in 1994
by HEADLINE BOOK PUBLISHING

10 9 8 7 6 5 4 3 2 1

British Library Cataloguing in Publication Data

Stirling, Emma
   Marigold Summers
   I.   Title
   823.914 [F]

   ISBN 0-7472-1029-2

Typeset by Keyboard Services, Luton

Printed and bound in Great Britain by
Mackays of Chatham PLC, Chatham, Kent

HEADLINE BOOK PUBLISHING
A division of Hodder Headline PLC
338 Euston Road
London NW1 3BH

MARIGOLD SUMMERS

Chapter One

It was a day at the beginning of April, 1934. A bright day at a bright time of the year. Easter was just around the corner and the summer holidays a time to look forward to. The countryside was at its best; the spring foliage of the trees hazy against a blue sky, the sun beaming down like a genial benefactor. The grass beneath the trees in the grounds of the Convent of Our Lady of the Rosaries was a picture with the brightness of daffodils and the purple and yellow of late crocus.

Kate Linley was playing hooky, perched high in the branches of a tree, sketch pad in hand, pencil busy transferring to paper the lovely scene before her. What better way to spend such an afternoon than this, instead of wasting it in the classroom, having drummed into one's head dates of boring old battles of Cromwell and the Roundheads.

Sister Devota thought differently. Kate's absence from her class had been noted. It wasn't the first time it had happened. Mother Superior had been informed and had acted accordingly.

The middle-aged sister had been sent to investigate. She waited at the foot of the tree while Kate, showing an inordinate display of navy-blue knickers and black cotton stockings, but not a hint of dismay at being found out, scrambled down to stand beside her. At sixteen she was already taller than the nun who waited with such a grim countenance.

Somehow, this girl intimidated Sister Devota. Her quiet way of talking, her ease at making friends, the way her hair, almost silvery in its blondeness, swung like a silken curtain about her cheeks as she moved. All served to make the nun more aware of her own lack of beauty, the swarthy complexion and lank hair concealed by the black habit.

Her thin lips tightened. What a delight it would be to shear those golden locks, as her own had been shorn, to swathe that slender figure in the all-concealing guise her chosen life had forced her to wear . . .

With an effort she brought her thoughts under control as she heard the clear voice of Kate Linley say, 'Well, what has Mother Superior in mind for me this time? She must be running out of punishments.'

'Never that, young lady,' the nun answered with smug satisfaction. 'The Mother Superior will never run out of punishments for such as you.'

1

In the office with the almost life-size statue of Our Lady in her blue robes, her feet bare and standing on golden plaster roses, Kate faced the woman behind the desk. Her own gaze fixed intently on the picture of the Sacred Heart in its place on the wall behind the large desk, she tried to answer the demand for an explanation of yet another of her wayward caprices.

'I thought an afternoon spent in the sunlight and fresh air would benefit me more than one spent in a closed room learning about things that will never be of the slightest use to me. I took my drawing pad and was able to sketch views of the valley and hillsides. It's not often you get that certain light and today it was just perfect. See, Mother . . .' and she opened the large pad she had held tucked under her arm, offering it for the woman's inspection.

Mother Superior's small eyes, set deep in her plump face, studied Kate from behind thick wire-rimmed glasses. They rested briefly on the open pad, on the lifelike drawings of trees with their delicate spring foliage. She turned a page and caught her breath as her eye fell on a black-and-white drawing of Sister Hosea. Sister Hosea was the youngest nun in the convent and a great favourite with the pupils.

Slender and fragile-looking, the sweet face peered out from under the black cowl, as though startled by Kate's request to pose. The long sweeping lines of the habit were pleasing, hinting at the slim body beneath.

Mother Superior's lips firmed. She closed the book quickly and said, 'Often in this life we have to put aside such temptations and concentrate on what is important. You remember why we are put on this earth, Katherine – to love and serve the Lord.'

'I know that, Mother. But can history, things that happened hundreds of years ago, make me serve our Lord any better or be more important than the thing I love best: sketching?'

The Mother Superior sighed. The girl had talent. But she must not be allowed to waste one talent for another. History was part of their curriculum. Her parents had placed her in the care of the nuns on the understanding that she received the kind of education a young lady deserved. It had been clear from the start that this child, a beloved only daughter, had been spoiled.

Samuel Linley and his wife, Monica, had sought a new life in India nine years ago and had lived in New Delhi all that time. They loved its spacious tree-lined streets and had been very happy there. Samuel was the manager of a large engineering project. At first, Kate had attended the small local English school. Their decision to send her home to boarding school had cost her parents sleepless nights, but it was finally decided that school in England would be in the best interests of the child. Kate was twelve, precocious and already exhibited an unusual talent for drawing. An English education would bring out the best in her.

There were sketches all over the Linleys' bungalow; water-colour impressions of ruined temples, of wine-red bougainvillaea cascading over white walls, of Kate's cherished small black poodle, dancing on her hind legs in a foolish attempt to catch a butterfly.

Samuel declared firmly that Kate must have her chance. 'If she chooses to join us after she's finished school then I shall be delighted,' he told his wife. 'But she must be given the choice.'

Letters had been exchanged between the Linleys and the Convent of Our Lady of the Rosaries situated outside a tiny hamlet in Kent. Monica had spent some years there when her own parents were abroad and had in turn been both miserable and happy.

Kate immediately fell in love with her new surroundings; the lovely countryside; the hillsides glutted with their carpet of ferns, the tender new shoots curling fascinatingly below your feet as you walked.

All so different from the hot dusty land where she had spent the formative years of her childhood. Her memories of India were of hot bright sunlight, of her ayah in her white sari going everywhere with her, tears running down her cheeks as she waved goodbye to the girl she had cherished as her own child.

Kate remembered the cook, of being smuggled into the hot dusty cookhouse at the end of the garden and being given chapattis, thin and crisp, straight from the pan. Sometimes there would be a fresh mango to follow, causing the ayah to tut-tut with her tongue and bathe her before her mother had time to notice the sticky juice that covered her face and hands.

The sweetest of her memories was of her poodle. What a handful she'd been, so energetic it defied one just to keep up with her. Kate had named the enchanting little creature Paloma, causing her father to laugh and comment, teasingly, 'You can't call a black poodle Paloma. It means white dove.'

Kate had smiled. 'So? What's wrong with having a black dove? There must be black doves about – somewhere.'

'I don't think so, my dear. None that I've heard of, anyway.'

He'd given her an affectionate smile and Paloma the poodle had stayed, fast attaching herself to the family, being treated more like another daughter than a dog.

It had been heart-wrenching to leave Paloma behind but Kate's parents wrote often, relating all the news, the mischief the little dog had been up to. Kate would laugh and read the letters aloud to her friend, Julie Johnson.

Mother Superior sighed again, then looked at Sister Devota for guidance. At times she was forced to admit that Katherine Mary Linley was a sore trial. The dear Lord had given her the gift of capturing on paper the very soul of her subject, but that could never excuse the lack of conscience she showed for her misdemeanours.

'I think, Sister Devota,' she began, 'an afternoon displayed in front of her class would be sufficient punishment. Reading about the history lesson she has missed.'

Sister Devota nodded. 'As you wish, Mother Superior.'

She had escorted Kate back to the class, where she was forced to stand in a corner, her back to her classmates, the heavy history book in her hands open at the page she was to study. The final indignity was the pointed paper dunce's cap placed on her head, causing smothered laughter from the girls who thought this a great joke. All but Julie, who bent her head over her book, wretched at her friend's embarrassment.

Meeting Julie later in the common room, Kate said, 'Honestly, you'd have thought I'd committed a mortal sin instead of skipping one class. What a palaver!'

'I always get the feeling that everything Sister Devota doesn't approve of is a mortal sin,' replied Julie caustically.

Kate reached over for the exercise books that contained her unfinished homework. 'Bloody dates of King Charles and Oliver Cromwell! I bloody ask you!'

Julie looked round at the groups of girls busy with their homework. 'Don't let old Devota hear you swearing. I shudder to think what the consequences might be for *that* little lapse from decorum.'

'To hell with decorum,' said Kate, and they both laughed. Her voice lowered, Kate went on, 'Have you ever thought of running away?'

Julie grimaced. 'Constantly.' She gave her friend a sharp look. 'Why, you're not thinking of doing anything foolish, are you?'

Kate reflected on the thick woods that surrounded the convent school. Narrow paths meandered among the towering trees, making everything spooky and alarming even in broad daylight. Ingenuously, she pictured herself with food salvaged from the dining room, wrapped in a large white handkerchief. She would creep out when everyone was asleep and make her way to the nearest station. She had a few shillings, saved from the pocket money sent regularly by her parents. Enough to buy a ticket to where her aunt lived in Buckinghamshire.

Aunt Norma was her mother's sister. She lived alone in a thatched cottage in a tiny hamlet miles from anywhere. Kate had spent every Christmas and summer holiday with her since she had become a boarder at the convent. She and other girls who were going home on holiday were escorted by train to Victoria by Sister Hosea and there handed over to their waiting relatives. But she could find the hamlet by herself if she had to. She was a growing girl, not helpless. Hadn't Amy

4

Johnson flown solo all the way to Tokyo just two years ago? It showed what a girl could do if she put her mind to it.

Aunt Norma, from all accounts, had made a disastrous marriage, frowned on by the family. On the mantelpiece above her large old-fashioned grate, a silver frame held the sepia-tinted photograph of a young man in uniform. Good-looking in a flashy kind of way. Kate didn't think one would trust him with the family silver. There was something about the eyes, a shifty look that she didn't like. Her aunt never spoke of him and Kate often wondered about his whereabouts.

Kate enjoyed her visits to Aunt Norma, though in a contrary way she missed school and was glad to get back when the time came.

Realizing that Julie was waiting for an answer to her question, Kate said, 'Don't worry, I'm *not* thinking of doing anything foolish. My parents went to a lot of trouble and expense to send me here. My father, especially, expects great things from me. I wouldn't let them down.' She smiled. 'Anyway, my aunt would pack me off again as soon as she saw me, so it would all be a waste of time.'

'Is that where you'd go if you did run away? To your aunt?'

'Who else?'

Julie was as dark as Kate was fair, and she tossed that black mane of hair now and laughed.

When the summons to present herself to Mother Superior came the next time, Kate cast her mind back to her recent activities. But there was nothing that came to mind, nothing she had done to incur the Mother Superior's wrath.

A sharp rapping of the flat ruler on the desk top alerted Kate to the fact that Sister Devota was waiting. Aware of the curious gazes of the other girls, Kate followed the nun from the classroom. Since the episode of the afternoon spent perched in the tree she'd been on her best behaviour. She racked her brain for some reason for yet another summons but could come up with nothing.

Mother Superior was seated behind her desk, her hands tucked out of sight beneath the starched white bib of her habit. When Kate entered the room, she leaned forward and reached for an envelope that lay on the blotter before her.

'I have just received a communication from your mother, Katherine. I think you had better read it.'

Kate was suddenly, vividly, aware of the small room, the whitewashed walls, the colourful pictures of suffering saints and martyrs, all seeming to accentuate its starkness, the sense of impending bad news.

'Has something happened to them? Oh, tell me, Mother, are they all right . . .'

Even as she reached for the letter she was praying that her fears were groundless. Yet why should her parents write direct to the Mother Superior and not to her?

Perhaps they were coming home on leave! Were already home! Her hopes soared as she saw the postmark: London.

Her mother's handwriting seemed to leap out at her, explaining to the Mother Superior that an accident sustained by her husband had made it necessary for them to come home. They were staying, temporarily, in a small hotel in Victoria but were looking for a house to buy in the suburbs. In which case, seeing that they intended to make England their home again, Mrs Linley felt Kate would, eventually, be better back with them. She was in the middle of writing to Kate and would be in touch again with the convent.

Kate felt sick. Her father ill! What sort of an accident? It must have been a bad one to have made them decide to leave everything and come back to England! She looked up, meeting the Mother Superior's eyes, compassionate for a change.

'What do you think could have happened to him, Mother? And why didn't they write to me from India, when it first happened?'

The elderly nun took the letter and slipped it into its envelope. 'They will have their reasons, my child. You must not worry. The good Lord will take care of it. Wait and see what your mother has to say in your letter, and in the meantime you must pray to our blessed Lord for comfort.'

Following an impulse she couldn't resist, Kate didn't rejoin the class but went instead to the dormitory she shared with seven other girls. Chaste white-covered beds stood, four on each side of the room. Long narrow French doors between each bed were open to the sunshine. She sat on her own bed, her hands slack between her knees, eyes staring unseeingly out on to the emerald green of the gardens.

A new house in an English suburb! It would mean a new school, new friends. A whole new way of life. She hoped it would be near a river. How Paloma would enjoy the walks along the river bank, delighting in chasing rabbits across a common . . .

Then, like a lump of lead sinking in a grassy pond, she was reminded of the six months' quarantine period required for animals entering the country. Paloma would pine and it would be costly. But her parents would manage the expenditure somehow. And she believed that visiting was allowed. Six months would fly past . . .

She stirred, suddenly aware of her surroundings as soft footsteps echoed along the highly polished corridor leading to the dormitory. Sister Devota appeared, hands tucked under her white bib, alertly examining every inch of polished surface for dust or polish smears as she passed. Kate jumped to her feet as the nun approached, unable to suppress the flush of guilt that crimsoned her cheeks.

Sister Devota stood looking at her thoughtfully. 'So, Mother Superior gave you permission to miss the rest of your lesson, did she?'

Kate's flush deepened. 'No, Sister Devota. I just wanted to be alone – to think . . . In any case, I don't imagine I would have been able to take any of the lesson in . . .'

'Allow me to be the judge of that, Katherine Linley.' She came closer, her black eyes dropping from the pale gold hair to the slender ankles in their black stockings. 'What makes you think you have the right to shirk when the rest of your class are so studious? You know full well you have absolutely no right to be in the dormitories at this time of the day. Unless you are ill. And,' peering into Kate's face, the thin lips curling in a sneer, 'you appear perfectly healthy to me.'

'I am. I'm sorry, Sister. I just felt that a moment on my own was needed. I'll rejoin my class now . . .'

'How gracious of you!' There was no attempt to conceal the taunting emphasis of her words. 'It would be better for your soul if you were made to spend the rest of the day weeding the tennis court.'

As the girl turned on her heel to walk away, Sister Devota watched her, and around her mouth was a self-satisfied smile; she was getting her own back for the feeling of insecurity the presence of Kate always gave her.

Chapter Two

The letter from Monica Linley reached Kate the very next day. Vague in the extreme, her mother wrote of an accident sustained by her father injuring his leg which had entailed him having to take time off work.

> I was so worried, Kate. You know how he enjoys his work, hardly ever takes time off. He brooded the whole time he was home, driving me to distraction. I couldn't get him interested in anything. He is so used to working that he really doesn't know how to handle leisure.
>
> Sadly, complications have set in, your father's job was affected and we have been forced to return to England. Not wanting to worry you sooner than I had to, I purposely didn't write to you before. I know you were leaving at the end of summer, dear, but now I'm afraid it will have to be earlier. Probably Easter.
>
> We are staying, temporarily, in a small hotel near Victoria station, but we hope to begin looking for a house when your father is feeling better. I will keep in touch and look forward to seeing you at Easter. Try not to worry; I am doing enough for all of us. Everything, I'm sure, will be all right.
>
> Your loving mother.

Kate passed the letter to Julie to read. Julie sat, head bent over the page, then looked up into Kate's worried face. 'Tch, look at you! Your mother said not to worry and already you're imagining all kinds of terrible disasters.' She clicked again with her tongue. 'And don't argue. I know you well enough to recognize that expression. Admit it, you're worried stiff.' She flicked the page with one finger. 'Although why you should be I can't imagine. It all sounds pretty straightforward to me. Pity about your dad, though.'

Kate shook her head, the worry still clouding her eyes. 'It's not straightforward at all. If it was, why didn't they write and tell me before they left India? Why wait until they arrived over here and then write first to Mother Superior? And if they intend to get a house then they must know they're not going back.'

Julie folded the letter and passed it back. 'I thought you'd be delighted at the news. Just think, a chance to leave this place and enter the free world again. And the way old Devota's been at you this last month, well – I wish someone would give me the chance. I'd be off like a shot.'

Kate gathered a handful of the pine needles that littered the ground and let them slide slowly through her fingers. She looked thoughtful. They were sitting in their favourite place, hidden beneath the concealing boughs of an ancient fir tree. Its branches bent to the ground, affording a wonderful hidey-hole for the two girls.

'I shall still have to make new friends.' Kate wrinkled her nose. 'It won't be easy.' She remembered the way the other girls at the convent used to tease her when she'd first come here. They'd gather in a circle about her, jeering, saying things like: 'I thought it was hot in India!'

'It is,' she'd answer, and the jeers would grow, girls taunting, 'Why aren't you brown, then? I mean, all that sunshine . . .' and, 'Let's see the jewel in your tummy button.' A hoot would go up when Kate blushed. 'Go on, we dare you . . .'

Julie had soon put a stop to that. Julie had been her faithful ally. And now they were to be parted. She felt her eyes smart and stood up quickly, thrusting her mother's letter into her gymslip pocket. Julie followed suit, dusting the clinging pine needles from her skirt. The bright sunlight filtered in through the overhanging branches, creating a secret cave of olive-green light.

'I wonder who'll discover this place after we're gone?' Julie murmured, gazing about her. 'I always thought it such a pity this wasn't a mixed school. Wouldn't it be just perfect for a date with a boy?'

Kate laughed. 'It sure would. Anyway, you'll still be able to come here.'

'It won't be the same. Not without you.'

Again Kate felt the smarting in her eyes. 'Oh, Julie . . .'

The sound of a bell ringing from the tower built on to one corner of the convent reminded them that it was teatime. Julie took Kate's arm, hustling her across the grass. 'Nothing will ever be the same again without you,' she said.

'As soon as I know where we're living, I'll send you my address,' Kate promised. 'You can come and visit. Spend a weekend with us. Do say you'll come. I'd love you to meet my parents.'

Julie laughed. 'Just you try and keep me away.'

Easter Sunday, and the church was filled with Easter lilies and maidenhair fern. Sunlight sparkled on the polished brass candlesticks, stray beams resting on the heads of the girls as they knelt at prayer. The coloured glass window behind the altar that depicted Saint Christopher carrying the baby Jesus on his shoulders cast warm shades of reds and blues over the congregation.

The pupils were allowed to wear their Sunday-best frocks for this occasion, and floral patterns in bright colours predominated. Further letters had arrived from Kate's mother, and Samuel and Monica Linley had promised to be present. 'And it will be your last gathering, I'm afraid,' her mother wrote, 'for I have informed Mother Superior that you will be coming home with us. We feel, now that we are in England, that your duty is to be with us. I shall need help in starting this new life, Kate . . .'

The mass was nearly over and still they had not arrived.

Kate had felt excitement at the thought of seeing her parents again after the years apart, and she surreptitiously watched the entrance, turning every so often to peer along the pews filled with kneeling girls. Father McLeary was on the point of blessing the congregation, bidding them go in peace, when the sound of high heels on the stone floor echoed through the hushed church and Monica Linley made her presence known.

Although she seldom attended church these days, she remembered to observe the formalities, bending one knee and making the sign of the cross before joining Kate and Julie in their pew.

'Where on earth have you been, Mummy?' Kate hissed through clenched teeth. 'I thought you weren't coming.'

Her mother frowned, shaking her head slightly to indicate that one did not talk in church.

Aware of Sister Devota's rebuking frown, Julie muttered from the side of her mouth, 'Hey, you two, watch it! The dragon's got her eye on you.'

Monica raised plucked eyebrows. 'Dragon?'

Kate laughed. 'I'll explain later, Mum,' she said.

Father McLeary's thumb traced a blessing and the congregation filed out. A number of the girls had been allowed home for the Easter break: the ones who were still there had parents visiting for the day. Kate's own mother embraced her, remarked on how much she'd grown and then spent the next half-hour in uncomfortable silence, obviously trying to think of something else to say. This wasn't unusual. Most of the parents acted this way.

Kate overheard the conversation of one family group, seated on a decorative stone bench. The mother, dressed in a silk frock, white gloves and hat, was suggesting they drive into town, take lunch and visit a cinema.

Sister Devota, walking slowly past, stopped to listen. Kate and Julie suppressed a giggle at the look of horror that came over the nun's face.

11

The cinema! On a Sunday! And an Easter Sunday at that! What wickedness was taking over the world?

Julie's own parents had not been able to come that year, being abroad. Her father was the managing director of an international company. When they did come, they made up for their omissions, the back seat of their car piled high with presents.

Mother Superior waited in front of the convent to say goodbye to Kate and her mother. Monica Linley looked attractive, earning many an admiring glance from visiting fathers. She wore a beige dress, a fox fur draped casually over one shoulder. The head of the poor animal, complete with glass eyes, hung down over her bosom. Kate shivered. She remembered this as a prize possession of her mother's, something she had hung on to in all her years in India. A small felt hat, trimmed with brown corded ribbon, was tipped provocatively over one eye.

The two women shook hands formally and bade each other goodbye. Then there was nothing left but for Kate to say goodbye to Julie and a few of the other girls who had been her friends.

She threw her arms about Julie, not caring that Mother Superior shook her head at such a blatant display of emotion. Pupils had been taught that shows of emotion, especially in public, were to be frowned on, being a sign of weakness.

Kate didn't care. She was going to miss Julie and although she was glad to be free from the restrictions of the convent, happy to be going to live with her parents again, she dreaded to think of days without her friend to confide in.

'Goodbye, goodbye!' whispered Julie, tearfully. 'Don't fret, we'll be seeing each other again before you know where you are.'

Kate sniffed. 'Promise?'

Julie sniffed too. 'As if I'd lie to you.'

Walking beside her mother from the carved stone porch of the church, Kate looked eagerly for the sight of her father. She'd imagined that, with his bad leg, he would be waiting in the car.

Seeing the disappointment on her daughter's face, Monica experienced a slight pang of guilt. She thought: sooner or later, she's got to know.

'Daddy didn't come, then?' Kate asked in a bewildered tone.

'No.' Monica opened the door of a black Austin for Kate to clamber in. 'I feel I should warn you, dear. Your father has become very reclusive. A changed man.'

Kate settled in her seat. 'Because of the accident? I'm sorry. It must have been bad.' When her mother didn't answer, Kate looked at her. 'Come on, Mum, I'm a big girl now. You can tell me.'

Her mother's lips pursed. How did one handle such an inquisitive sixteen-year-old? She blurted out the first thing that came to her mind.

'He fell and broke his leg, Kate. It was all very worrying at the time. All right? No more reminders.' Monica eased the car through the wide gates at the end of the drive, pausing briefly to make sure the road was clear. 'Don't let's spoil a perfectly nice day by talking of depressing things. I'd rather talk about my good news. Yes,' turning to smile into Kate's eyes, 'I think we've found the perfect place in which to live. It's in a suburb to the north-west of London, new, modern houses with every facility, gas as well as electricity. Nice houses, Kate, built of red brick with fair-sized gardens at the back and a tiny square at the front. We can start planting things.'

'I've always thought how wonderful it would be to pick your own strawberries,' said Kate, feeling some of her mother's optimism rubbing off on her. 'And tomatoes. And those lovely white roses they grow in front of the convent.'

Monica Linley thought of the round patch with the statue of Our Lady in the centre, the sweet-scented white roses growing all about Her. She gave her daughter a shrewd look. 'To remind you of your happy times here?'

Kate smiled. 'Something like that, Mum.'

They stopped in a small village for lunch. The tall steeple of a church, glimpsed through magnificent beech trees, a public house that looked as if it had been there since Tudor times, a small general store doubling as a post office. Across from pleasant public gardens ducks floated on a round pond.

Monica Linley parked outside a tearoom. They crossed the pavement to the low arched doorway. A bell jangled as they entered.

Immediately a woman appeared from a curtained recess. Round and homely-looking, her rosy cheeks creasing in a smile, she showed them to a table in the window, handed them menus, then waited for their order. Monica said she'd just have a cheese and tomato omelette and a salad. With a pot of tea. Kate said she'd have the same. Still smiling, the woman disappeared into the kitchen.

They were the only customers. Kate spread yellow farm butter on to the slice of brown bread at the side of her plate and watched as her mother poured from the shiny brown teapot. Sipping her tea, Monica sighed. 'Ah, that's better! The first decent cup of tea I've had since we left India. The tea on the boat was atrocious and the stuff they serve in the hotel where we're staying isn't much better.'

'What sort of an hotel is it?' Kate lifted her own cup to her lips. It was clear that her mother felt awkward in the presence of a daughter she hadn't seen for four years. It was natural, Kate supposed. She must seem like another girl. The years between twelve and sixteen wrought changes that alone would make Monica uncomfortable.

'It's just a small hotel. Bed-and-breakfast residents mainly. Most are single men who are at work all day, so your father is able to get his rest.' She looked away. 'Although it can get noisy at night.'

Kate frowned. To her, the hotel sounded awful. Not at all the sort of place in which her parents would choose to stay.

'Can't you find somewhere else, Mummy? London's a big place.'

'An expensive place. A really good hotel would be well beyond our means.'

This was news to Kate. She'd always thought that her parents, if not wealthy, were at least able to afford better things than those her mother was now describing. The boarding fees at the convent, for instance, must have been considerable. If things were as bad as Monica had just hinted, then no wonder she'd insisted that Kate should leave.

Kate felt a warm glow of compassion. She reached across and laid one hand on her mother's.

'You should have stayed with Aunty Norma.' The suggestion seemed the most logical to Kate. 'She would have been pleased to have you. She was always so happy to see me when I went there on my holidays. Until you found a house, I mean.'

Monica lifted the spring onion from her salad with fastidious fingers and laid it on the side of her plate.

'I couldn't do that.'

'Why not?'

'We never got on as girls, and I don't think we'd be any different now.'

'But . . .'

Her mother's lips pursed in a tight bud of obstinacy, her face arranging itself in her subject-closed expression. 'Get on with your omelette, Kate. It will taste like leather if it gets cold.'

The light meal finished, Monica opened her handbag and to Kate's surprise took out a packet of cigarettes. She hadn't known that her mother smoked. She never used to, eyeing the women who did as though they were trollops. She fitted the slim white tube into a long ivory holder and snapped a small silver lighter. Then, picking up her handbag, she looked around. 'I wonder if there's a ladies' room here?'

'I'm sure there will be.' Kate spied a discreet sign in one corner of the room. 'Over there, Mummy.'

'Do you need to go?'

Kate shook her head. She watched her mother, slim and still pretty, cross the room. Her dress of beige linen had a collar of white organdie. The collar crossed at the front, the two ends finely pleated, flaring out across the bodice. Nice! thought Kate. She noticed things like that. Brown crocodile-skin shoes and matching handbag completed the picture of refined elegance. When Kate had last seen her, Monica had refused to conform to fashion and wore her long hair coiled in a smooth chignon at the nape of her neck. Obviously, with the advent of the thirties, she had kept up with the times, and now, a couple of shades darker than Kate's, her mother's hair lay about her head in deep waves and pin curls.

Instinctively, Kate reached for the menu lying to the side of her plate. The pencil she always carried was produced from her blazer pocket. With a few swift strokes she had the likeness of her mother on the plain back of the menu: the narrow calf-length skirt hinting at the long line of her thighs as she walked, the merest suggestion of the rounded buttocks. A truly elegant picture.

But for all that air of calm gracefulness, something was wrong. Kate could tell. By the time her mother reappeared she had finished that first cigarette and was fitting another into the ivory holder.

She had renewed her lipstick and powdered her nose. She stood behind Kate's chair and looked down at the sketch on the menu. 'Really, Kate.' Her voice held displeasure. 'You should ask permission before you use somebody else's property to scribble on.' The woman had appeared behind them, the bill in her hand. Monica felt in her handbag and produced a ten-shilling note which she handed to the cheerful soul.

'I'm sorry, defacing your menu like this. But no piece of paper is safe with my daughter around.'

The woman accepted the note and felt in her apron pocket for change. 'That's all right, dear, don't give it a thought.' She picked up the menu, holding it to the light coming from the window. 'It's very well done, isn't it? The young lady must be gifted, to draw like this. Goin' to be a fashion designer, are we?' She smiled at Kate benignly.

'My daughter's too young and immature to decide yet what she wants to be.' Monica gazed loftily at the woman. 'Although every now and then she sees the sense in what her mother tells her. In any case, it will be up to her father and me to decide.'

The woman held the sketch out to Kate. 'Here, take it, miss. It's worth keeping.' Her voice held sympathy.

'You keep it,' said Kate. 'I have no use for it. Maybe you can use an eraser to get the pencil marks off.'

Back in the car, Kate asked the question she had been dreading to ask all morning.

One hand resting on the partly wound-down window, she said, 'How is Paloma? How is she taking to the kennels?'

And her mother's answer made tears stream down her cheeks, longing for the comforting presence of Julie.

'I should have known,' sobbed Kate, tears dripping off her chin on to her cream blouse. 'I should have known you wouldn't bring her with you.'

The heart-breaking sobs started again. Kate lifted her tightly clenched fists above her head, startling her mother by her wails of anguish as she shook them. As though denying the truth of the thing she had heard.

'Really, Kate, there is no need to be so dramatic. It was, after all, only a dog.' Her mother sounded weary, as though the whole thing was much too much for her.

Kate remembered the sketches of the little dog she had loved doing. She'd shown them to Julie. 'Not bad from memory, eh?' she'd challenged. 'I bet she hasn't changed a bit. Not in four years. Not in a dozen years.'

'Wishful thinking there, old girl. She'd be an old granny with a stick and spectacles if she was human.' It was the sort of reply guaranteed to bring Kate down from her flights of fancy.

'Of course, you're right,' Kate laughed. 'Proper little know-all, aren't you?'

And now the fun-loving little dog was no more . . .

Kate turned in her seat to face her mother. Her voice quivered as she said, 'Couldn't you have met the quarantine fees?'

Her mother pursed her lips. 'If we couldn't meet the fees for your continued education in the convent, my girl, we certainly couldn't afford the quarantine fees for a dog.'

Kate wiped her eyes, drew a deep breath and gazed straight ahead through the window. Her mother's tone had said that the subject was closed; there was nothing left to talk about.

Even though the sun shone on the roads, which were busier than usual, being Easter Sunday, Kate saw nothing of the beauty of the lovely day. Bicycles were everywhere, their riders enjoying the fine weather, the men clad in khaki shorts and open-necked shirts, the girls in cotton frocks, converging on the road in groups of twos and threes.

Which didn't help Monica's mood at all. She let Kate know in no uncertain terms that she shouldn't be doing this. Driving a car was a man's job. Ignoring the fact that Kate was sitting beside her, listening to her every moan, she said, 'Useless, he is, that father of yours. Absolutely useless. Won't do a thing for himself. Expects me to run around after him . . .'

Monica broke off to swerve sharply to the middle of the road, narrowly missing a car that was parked on the grass verge with its bonnet raised. Steam rose from its engine and in spite of Kate's agony, she had to smile at the two girls who sat on the grass at the side of the road, hugely enjoying their boyfriends' confusion in trying to ascertain what the trouble was. How free they must feel; what fun to be able to escape the eye of busybody adults for a whole day!

The carefully selected newspapers the nuns allowed them to read related how Mr Roosevelt's New Deal had brought the Americans hope of recovery, but how England still had to regain the pre-eminence it once had in industry. Gazing at the happy faces about them, one would never have guessed that the country was caught up in the throes of a depression. But Kate supposed second-hand bicycles were cheap to come by and the cotton frocks the girls wore were probably home-made.

She sighed and said appeasingly, 'I'm sure that once we've found a place of our own everything will be back to normal.' Or as normal as it would ever be, she thought.

'Then you're easily satisfied if you think that,' replied Monica scornfully. 'My God, what a country! We have to come back now, smack in the middle of a depression, your father hopeless and thousands of men out of work! The savings we have aren't much, barely enough to make a deposit on one of those houses I told you about and buy some furniture. But we have to make an effort. I shall go crazy if I have to stay in that hotel for much longer.'

She thought of the conversation she had had with Samuel. It had been her suggestion at first that they rent a house.

'We could buy our home with a mortgage instead of paying almost as much each week in rent,' he had explained. There was a boom in the construction industry as housing of many types was built for the different social classes. The new suburbs springing up all around London boasted fine examples of large detached houses with garages at the side, built for prosperous sections of the upper middle class. That, of course, would have been Monica's choice, but needs must and in the foreseeable future something smaller and more modest would have to do.

Monica had looked sceptical. 'And how much would that be?'

'Weekly payments of twelve and sixpence will secure a two-storey semi with three bedrooms.'

The scepticism remained. 'Hmmm. What about the deposit? We don't want to leave ourselves with no money at all.'

'A deposit of five pounds is all they are asking for. The house costs five hundred pounds. How could anyone better an offer like that?'

She said now to Kate, 'You'll have to get a job, you know. It won't be easy. School-leavers don't get paid much but it will be better than nothing.'

'But I wanted to go to art college . . .' Kate bit her lip. 'I thought you and Daddy understood all along I wanted to go to art college.' She gazed at her mother's profile. 'Does Daddy think the way you do? About me leaving school?'

'Your father doesn't think at all. That's his trouble. If he'd thought what he was up to we wouldn't be in this state of near-penury.'

'But it can't be that bad.' Uncomfortable at the way her mother had spoken about her father, Kate tried not to show it. 'I could probably get a scholarship in art. I'm sorry, Mummy, but Mother Superior did say that in her opinion I was sure to . . .'

'There's no money in art, Kate. Not the kind you do. And I can't see you becoming a famous portrait-painter.' She gave her daughter a sharp look. 'Can you?'

Kate nodded and folded her arms about her breasts as if she was hugging her dreams to herself; departed dreams that were doomed to failure . . .

Chapter Three

Kate could feel her mother's tenseness increase as they approached the outskirts of London. It was so busy, cars and tall red buses everywhere.

She remembered how, when they had arrived in England four years ago, she had thought she'd never seen so many cars. She and her parents, there to see her safely into boarding school, had stayed in quite a nice hotel overlooking Green Park. It had been wonderful. She'd walked with her father every morning in the lovely park, breathing the cool fresh air, laughing at the antics of the ducks on the tree-fringed lake. They had stopped to have a mug of tea at a roadside kiosk, her father joking with the workmen who stood about, swapping insults about the government.

Kate's thoughts were drawn back rudely to the present when a blare of horns signalled that Monica should have given way on the busy crossing. Her mother slammed on the brakes, her lipstick standing out starkly against her suddenly pale face. The car shuddered to a halt and Monica leaned forward, her knuckles white on the steering wheel.

'Are you all right, Mummy?' There was concern in Kate's voice.

'Yes. Are you?'

Kate nodded.

'That idiot came out of that turning without even slowing down. I ask you, this country . . .'

Looking pointedly at the sign ahead of them, Kate said, 'I think you should have given way, Mummy.'

Monica sniffed and bent to release the handbrake. 'I give way to no one. I'm not used to giving way. Neither should you be. Your father does enough of that.'

Every time Monica mentioned her husband in those scornful tones Kate cringed. Besides the broken leg, what terrible things could have happened in their lives for her mother to speak of her father like this!

Her imagination ran riot, reaching its height when they stopped at last outside a dingy-looking hotel in an equally dingy side street. The huge busy railway station was nearby, resulting in everything being covered in a fine layer of soot and grime. The black iron rail that ran the length of the stone steps leading to the front door was evidence of this

19

when Kate examined her hand after climbing the steps.

The tiny foyer – a hall, really, but given the grand title when the three-storey house was converted into an hotel – boasted a small counter on which a jug of wilted flowers stood. Kate's nose twitched at the smell: a mingling of the stagnant water from the jug, soot and something she thought with distaste could be mice.

Poor Daddy; to be a virtual prisoner in such a place! She thought of their lovely spacious bungalow in India; the gardens with their beds of bright canna lilies, the lawns kept green by diligent gardeners. Inside, the bungalow was cool, the coolness enhanced by the pale pastel colours of the walls. Delicate sun-filter curtains fluttered at the open windows. Here, if anyone dared leave a window open, Kate thought, everything in the room would be covered in soot in next to no time.

In her eagerness to get to see her father, she took no particular notice of the man who followed them up the narrow staircase. On the upper landing she turned to ask Monica which room was theirs and saw the man's hand on her mother's arm. She saw Monica shake it off angrily and heard her mutter something under her breath. Then she was smiling at Kate, saying, 'Meet Mr Patrick, dear. It's his car we've been using. He was so kind, letting me borrow it like that.' She smiled again, turning to the man. 'And this is my daughter, Kate, just home from boarding school. Say hello nicely, Kate.'

Kate said hello as nicely as she knew how, trying to avoid the knowing eyes that appraised her. Mr Patrick was slim and his suit, a nifty brown pinstripe, looked too big for him. His dark hair was slicked back and his eyes crawled over her like two slugs. Though he was handsome in a Clark Gableish kind of way, still Kate felt an instinctive aversion. How could her mother bear to accept the loan of *anything* from a man like that?

She heard her mother's voice: 'Your father's in number twenty-five, dear. Just along the landing.'

Kate couldn't wait to get away. Number 25 was at the rear of the house, which was back-to-back to other tall buildings. They would obstruct the sun and block out most of the light even on the brightest day. She tried not to let her feelings show on her face as she stood in the doorway, gazing at her father.

He was sprawled on an ancient velvet couch drawn up to one side of the window. He looked tired, frustrated. The deep suntan that Kate remembered was no longer in evidence, replaced by a wan look that in repose added years to his age.

Although a book lay open on his knees, he wasn't reading. His head rested against the back of the couch, his eyes closed. Doubtfully, Kate stood silent. It broke her heart to see him like this, the strong, ebullient man who had made her early years so memorable. If he was asleep she didn't want to wake him. There would be plenty of time to talk later . . .

As though aware of her presence, his eyes opened and gazed straight at her. 'Kate! My own little Katie!' He struggled to raise himself, his hands reaching out for hers. 'How are you, child? My goodness, how you've grown. Quite the little woman, eh! And so pretty with it.' He smiled. 'I was worried about your mother driving all that way on her own, but she insisted and you know your mother once she's made up her mind. Nothing is going to change it. And I – I didn't really feel up to it. But you're here now and nothing else matters.'

The smile had lightened his features, making him seem more like the man Kate remembered. 'Cook wept buckets when we were finally ready to go. We had an awful job convincing him it wasn't possible to come with us.'

Kate approached the couch, bending to kiss her father's cheek. 'Yes, we're all together again. Hello, Daddy. I'm sorry to see you like this. Mummy was telling me about your bad luck.' She smiled. 'We're going to work hard, have you back to rights in no time.'

A guarded look clouded his face. 'What *has* your mother been telling you about me?' Then he smiled again. 'All the wrong things, I bet,' saying it as though it was a joke.

Kate thought back to her mother's answers to her questions; hedging, cautious. 'Well, not much really. Except that you'd hurt your leg.'

Her father looked away, unable to meet her eyes. 'She blames me for all that happened. Treats me as though I'd done it all on purpose . . .' He sighed. 'But I've gone through all that and come out the other side. All I want now is to see us safely settled down and me working again.' With a quick change of mood he seemed to brighten, patting the side of the couch, inviting her to sit. 'Did your mother tell you about our plans? The new house she's seen?'

'She did, and it sounds wonderful.' She also told me about having to leave school and get a job, thought Kate. Not so wonderful!

'It will be a whole new way of life for us, Katie. A whole new way.' He picked up the open book, a novel by someone she hadn't heard of, marked his page with a turned-down corner then laid it on the small table beside the couch. 'Of course, we'll have to cut back at first. It might be a bit of a squeeze but we'll manage.'

Saying one of the two things that were uppermost in her mind, Kate murmured, 'And I'll get a job soon and that'll be even better.'

He couldn't meet her eyes. 'I'm sorry, Katie. I know how much you wanted to go on to study art.'

'I don't mind, Daddy. Truly I don't . . .' What harm was there in a white lie if it eased her father's conscience? 'Let's talk about that when you're better, eh?'

'You're such a dear, sensible daughter. I can't think what I've done to deserve you.' He reached for the cup of tea that stood on the table. Kate quickly forestalled him, leaning over to get it first. It was cold, a skim of dark brown on its surface.

She grimaced. 'You can't drink this. I'll get you some fresh.' She rose, holding the cup and saucer in front of her. 'Daddy, do you mind if I ask you something?'

'You know I've always answered your questions whenever possible.' He smiled. 'Fire away.'

'Did you really have to get rid of Paloma? Couldn't you have found some way to bring her over . . .'

She couldn't conceal the bitterness in her voice and Samuel, hearing it, felt as though a knife had just twisted in his guts.

'If there had been any way possible, my darling, any way at all, you can be sure we'd have found it. We left with very little money and the quarantine fees would have been enormous. And you know poor Paloma would have fretted.'

She was old enough to understand that the balancing of having money and *not* having money was all-important. But they had never lacked for anything in the past. How could things have changed so dramatically now?

Whenever her father had been sick before – the odd touch of malaria when he shivered and was ragingly hot in turns – the company he worked for had always been understanding, giving him as much time off as was necessary. 'I'll just get the tea,' she said and went out to look for the kitchen. This was downstairs at the back, and was inhabited by a surly-looking woman who listened to Kate's request for hot tea with a grudging air, intimating that this was a bed-and-breakfast establishment and that she wasn't at the beck and call of residents. Kate lingered just long enough for the kettle to boil and the tea to infuse before climbing the stairs back to her father. Passing along the landing, she could hear her mother humming in the room she surmised must be her parents' bedroom.

Placing the tea within Samuel's reach, Kate sighed and seated herself again on the couch. 'How did Mummy take it? Was she upset about Paloma?'

'Well, of course, dear. We both were.' Taking her hand, he added softly, 'There really was no other way, you know.' It had been like getting rid of a beloved child, he thought. A mischievous bundle of naughtiness that had enchanted them since joining their little family as a tiny puppy.

'Did Mummy go with you?'

The questions were disturbing. Surely they would be better forgotten? He released her hand and picked up the cup of tea, sipping it experimentally. 'No. She had invited someone to tea that afternoon. She said if she kept busy it wouldn't seem so bad.'

He looked at her. 'Better not to dwell on it, Katie. For your own peace of mind. We can get another puppy when we're settled in our new home.'

She shook her head, and was about to say she never wanted another dog in her life, when the door opened and her mother came into the room.

'Ah, here you are, Kate. Come along, now. I'll show you your bedroom.'

It, too, was at the back of the house, overlooking a scrubby piece of ground that had once been a garden. She could see where rose bushes had grown wild and a gnarled apple tree had dared to throw out pink blossom. She turned from the window and surveyed the room. The walls were papered in an unpleasant shade of green, reminding her of the pine disinfectant Cook had used in the kitchen. There was a wardrobe and a chest of drawers and the narrow single bed. She tested the springs, bouncing up and down a number of times until they creaked. The bedspread was of rough textured cotton, a dingy white. A good blowing in the sun and wind on that washing line Ayah used in the back garden would have done it the world of good.

She didn't like the idea that her parents, who had always seemed so upright and honest, were holding things back from her. Why should her father be so reluctant to talk about Paloma, about the real reasons for their move home? She resented the air of mystery with which they surrounded everything. Why couldn't they be like she remembered them; ordinary, caring parents? She'd listened with a breaking heart to her father trying to justify the fate of poor Paloma. Even though she might not agree with it, it was, as Mother Superior had drummed into her pupils, a daughter's duty to try and understand.

During the days that followed, she was further surprised to see that her father walked without the slightest sign of a limp. So the broken leg couldn't have been so bad after all. Certainly not bad enough to mean him leaving his job.

She sighed. Maybe, one day, the mystery of it all would be revealed to her – even at sixteen, her parents still treated her like the child they had seen into the convent four years earlier.

One morning, Monica collected the keys for the house from the estate agent, and Mr Patrick once more offered the use of his car. Her parents had seen the house, of course, but Kate hadn't, and she sat in the back seat of the car, staring with eagerness at the streets through which they drove. The bustle of London was soon left behind and they emerged into what the newspapers were calling the 'Green Belt'. A bit of country where Londoners could walk their dogs and watch their children play.

They turned off a busy High Street into an avenue of newly built houses. Monica drove almost to the end of the road and then pulled up.

For long moments Kate sat in the car, letting the novelty of the idea seep into her consciousness. Only now was this new life taking on a feeling of reality. Samuel stood with her mother on the pavement, gazing about him. He turned to smile at Kate. 'Come on, slow coach, I thought you were keen to see your new home.'

Kate pushed open the car door and scrambled out. There was a large bay window with diamond-shaped leaded glass and a 'sunrise' theme in the coloured glass on the front door. Samuel dug Kate slyly in the ribs with his elbow, saying, 'Look at that! The rising sun! A token of good luck, eh?'

Numbly, she nodded. The white bungalow in New Delhi might have been in another world, another life. Although if she closed her eyes she could still visualize it, set in its green lawns, its beds of bright orange marigolds, with their strong, piquant scent, gleaming in the strong sunshine.

Feeling in her handbag for the keys, Monica pushed open the gate, which they saw also displayed the sunrise theme carved into the wood, and said, briskly, 'Well, come on. Let's see what sort of a job they've made of the decorating.'

'I'm sure it will be very nice, my dear,' said Samuel.

'Well, for what we're committing ourselves to, it had better be,' said Monica in her not-to-be-argued-with voice.

The front door opened up on to a narrow hall from which a staircase rose to the bedrooms. The front room would be the sitting room, giving a view of the street through the bay windows. There was a kitchen and, on the other side of the hallway, another door that led to the dining room. This had long French windows and Kate imagined them in another month, when summer was really here, standing wide open to the garden that Daddy would create out of this rubble.

The rooms were decorated with pale distemper, with a narrow, patterned frieze along the walls under the picture rails.

After a tour of the house, which didn't take long, Samuel said, looking at Kate, 'Well? Do you approve?'

Monica answered for her. 'I suppose one can get used to anything – in time.'

Meanwhile, as they waited for the negotiations for the purchase of the house to go through, Kate used the time to wander round museums and art galleries, exploring London as she did so. Oxford Street was so busy, with its tall red buses and traffic that crawled along. You took your life into your hands just trying to cross from one side to the other. She walked the length of Regent Street and was quite exhausted when she arrived back at the hotel. It would have been more enjoyable if she'd had money to spend – all those gorgeous clothes she had seen in the windows! She sighed, promising herself; someday, someday . . .

On the last day but one, emerging from her room on her way to the bathroom along the landing, she came upon her mother and the man she had introduced as Mr Patrick the day they arrived. There was a scuffle, she heard her mother's voice in a low, angry tone, breathe, 'Don't, not now, Gerry,' and the man grinned and pushed past Kate on his way to the stairs. Kate couldn't repress a shudder as his shoulder brushed against her. Horrible creature! How could her mother even *talk* to him?

Monica Linley seemed flustered; uncharacteristic of her mother, who was always so calm and collected.

Kate said, 'I don't like that man. He's creepy.'

'Nonsense. You're imagining things, dear. You're far too young to make judgements, anyway. Mr Patrick is perfectly all right.' Her mother frowned. 'Have you finished helping Daddy with his packing yet?'

'Yes, it's all done.'

'Don't forget, we have to be up early tomorrow and at the house. The removal van will be delivering the furniture before lunch.' And as Kate walked away she was aware of the man standing at the top of the stairs, his eyes on her.

Chapter Four

Kate was glad to see the back of that hotel. She couldn't wait to inspect the new furniture they had bought. That had all been done while she was still at school, stored in the shop until it was needed. Suddenly, she tingled with the adventure of it all. She thought of the brand-new rooms, smelling of new wood and paint, of clean shining windows after the depressingly soot-stained ones of the hotel, and the thought was bliss.

Although the garden had been a wasteland of builders' rubble, she could see in her mind's eye the way it could be. They, she and Daddy, would get stuck in to it and soon it would be like their own patch of paradise. She smiled, thinking the phrase extravagant, but really, it said it all.

She helped the next morning, carrying things from the van to the house, putting them down in the rooms indicated by her mother. Small things like lamps and kitchen chairs. Getting her parents' big double bed up the staircase proved to be tricky. Monica stood at the foot of the stairs, exclaiming sharply every time the two men who came with the van scraped a corner against the wall.

'Orlright, missis. Keep yer 'air on,' one answered back when they'd had enough of her fault-finding. 'If you think you can do better you're welcome to try.'

Kate heard her mother's outraged gasp and caught Samuel's eye. He raised his eyebrows comically and made a clown's face, and Kate had to bite her lip to repress the giggle that threatened.

'Steady on, old girl,' Samuel said soothingly to his wife. 'The men know what they're doing.'

'Do they? I very much doubt that.' Monica gave a little scream as the bed tilted, leaning over the banister rail at a drunken angle.

The men battled to right it, their sighs audible. 'If you want to do something constructive, lady,' said the older of the two, 'why don't you go and make a cup of tea for us all. I reckon yer 'ubby and the little girl could do with it. I know me and me mate could.'

Monica turned a thunderstruck face towards Samuel. Reading her mind, he gave her a little push in the direction of the kitchen. 'Go on, there's a love, and do what the man says.' Thankfully the water, electricity and gas had been turned on earlier by the appropriate authorities.

Monica Linley went. But she didn't like it and Samuel knew that later he would be on the carpet for daring to side with someone other than his wife.

The tea revived them. Monica took her eyes off the men long enough to write a list of groceries and Kate was given a ten-shilling note and dispatched to the High Street at the end of the road. The men got on with the job they had been paid to do.

Kate memorized the short list and thrust it out of sight in her coat pocket. She felt nervous as she walked up to the busy High Street. No ayah to help her now. The street was fascinating, with its rows of shops on both sides. There was a Woolworths and a Marks and Spencer, looking very new, and in between there were all manner of small shops, selling everything a person could possibly need. What a vast difference to the bazaars in India where she and Ayah went with her mother to shop. There had been so many people, hordes of them, seeming to appear from nowhere. All talking nonstop, laughing and cheerful, the women peering at her and Monica from the folds of their colourful saris. Kate knew she would remember the smell for the rest of her life; the piquant aroma of curry and sun-baked earth and orange marigolds.

Even so, she decided, this new suburb had a charm all of its own. On her way to the High Street, she'd seen where some of the roads leading to the new building sites were still unmade: a sea of mud and rain puddles. Despite the talked-of depression, there were workmen everywhere; digging, pushing wheelbarrows, climbing ladders to the roof of a not yet completed house. So much activity. It was going to be exciting, living here.

To make her purchases, she chose a small grocery store where a genial-looking man in his shirtsleeves, a large white apron tied about his waist, stood beaming behind the counter. Beside him, a young girl, obviously his assistant, stood with drooping shoulders.

A well-polished kitchen-type chair placed before the counter was filled to overflowing with a stout woman who was obviously catching her breath after her walk to the shops. A shopping basket lay on the linoleum-covered floor beside her. Standing politely to one side was a youth, obviously waiting his turn. Kate got the impression of height and slimness and dark eyes under thick brows.

As Kate entered the shop, she heard the seated woman say: 'Phew, I swear that road gets longer every time I come shopping.'

'Why don't you send your daughter, Mrs Wells?' The shopkeeper smiled at Kate. 'She's big enough now to be trusted with a bit of shopping, in't she?'

28

'Our Sarah?' Mrs Wells's whole body shook as she laughed. You'd have thought it was the funniest thing she'd ever heard. Turning to look at the girl behind the counter, the woman said, 'Just you keep a sharp look-out for the next pig to fly past, ducks. My Sarah's as likely to offer to shop for me as that to 'appen.'

'Don't ask her, tell her,' advised the shopkeeper. 'Young people today need telling.' He turned his head to look at the girl assistant. 'Ain't that so, Ruthie?'

Ruthie blushed and looked down at the floor, murmuring something indistinct beneath her breath. Kate guessed that she would be the perfect target for her employer's witticisms. She couldn't have been much older than herself, and Kate felt an instant rapport with the timid-looking girl.

'Anyway,' the shopkeeper turned back to Mrs Wells, 'what can we do you for this fine day?'

The stout woman made a gesture with one hand, waving at Kate. 'See to your next customer, Mr Shipton. I'm in no 'urry.'

The beam widened as the shopkeeper bent over the counter towards Kate. 'All right, love, what's it to be?'

He seemed to have forgotten his other customer; the youth standing so quietly beside the open door. Kate murmured a thank you to Mrs Wells, then said, 'The young man was here before me.'

'Was 'e, now? Well, 'is kind can wait, while I serve their betters.'

Mrs Wells joined in his guffaw and Kate blushed at the blatant sarcasm in the shopkeeper's voice. Flustered, she said, 'No, really, he was here before me . . .'

The youth moved the cloth cap he held from one hand to the other, shuffling his feet. 'Go ahead. I can wait. I am in no hurry.'

'Well, if you're sure . . .'

'I am, miss.'

She gave her order in a clear voice. Half a pound of tea, ditto butter, a loaf of bread, two pounds of potatoes, sugar, cheese, eggs: all the things Monica had thought necessary to start a new life in a new house. She had said they would have a makeshift meal of chips and eggs tonight. Something at which she would normally have turned her nose up. To Kate and, she suspected, her father, it sounded like manna from heaven.

'All right, you 'eard what the young lady said.' Mr Shipton gave the girl, still goggling over the exchange of words, a little push. ''Op to it.'

'Yes, Mr Shipton.'

She scuttled over to where a sackful of potatoes stood open beside the door. Shovelling them out with a large scoop, she weighed them on a scale that required much ingenuity, adding and subtracting various loaded weights until she got the correct amount. Then it was over to the side counter where a large white china basin filled with eggs stood. Carefully she put six in a brown paper bag. Mr Shipton meanwhile was shaping a slab of butter, expertly, diligently patting with his wooden utensils until satisfied with the result. The final touch, a firm press with a wooden stamp, fashioned a cow in a field.

He wrapped the slab of butter in greaseproof paper, folding the corners neatly, then looked at Kate. 'What about some lard or dripping?' Seeing Kate's frown, he sighed. 'Well, are you goin' to boil the potatoes or make chips?'

Kate clicked her tongue. 'Of course. I didn't think.' Monica hadn't put lard on her list. Kate wondered if she even knew how to cook chips after all those years of old Cook shooing her out of the kitchen whenever she poked her head inside the door.

'I'd better have some.' She didn't think she'd enjoy chips fried in dripping. 'Lard, please, Mr Shipton.'

Her purchases complete, she watched while the girl hunted for a paper bag large enough to put them all in, and reminded herself that a shopping basket similar to Mrs Wells's would be her next priority.

Mummy would never think of such mundane things.

Thanking Mr Shipton, smiling at the girl, once more slouched behind the counter, she passed the youth waiting so patiently just inside the door. Suddenly shy, she gave a little nod of acknowledgement and saw the lid of one dark eye come down in a wink.

The shopping was heavy and she hurried, feeling her tummy begin to rumble at the thought of the delicious egg and chips with bread and butter and lashings of tea that would be her feast tonight. How did one cook chips? she wondered, striding along the newly made road that led between the semi-detached houses. But then, her mother must have cooked before she left to live in India, when she and Daddy were first married and Kate was a little girl! Surely it couldn't be that difficult? And Daddy was there to help . . .

She gave a little skip, and heard a voice behind her say, 'Mind the eggs! Don't want to break them before you get home, do you?'

Startled, she turned to meet the amused gaze of the youth from the shop. Without so much as a by-your-leave, he reached out for her packages, taking them from her and cradling them in one arm. 'We seem to be going the same way, so why don't I carry them, hmmm?' His own packages appeared to be stuffed in his bulging jacket pockets.

Unable to help herself, she blurted out, 'Why did you let them get away with being so horrid to you? You should have been served before me. It wasn't fair.'

'Oh, I'm used to it. I decided long ago that very little is fair in this life. People's attitudes don't bother me any more.'

30

'But it *wasn't* fair. And why do you buy from that shop when the man is so rude to you?'

'Because my mother rents a shop down the road belonging to Mr God-Almighty Shipton and he lets her have a discount on everything she buys.'

'It must be a hefty discount to make you even want to set foot inside their door.'

'It's enough. Over the weeks it adds up.' She eyed the grey flannels and tweed jacket that seemed too big for him and didn't really go together, and was aware that he was inspecting her too. The day was warm and so she'd set out without a coat. In her plain cotton dress, the colour of old wine, with its crisp white pique trimmings, she knew she looked good and smiled widely at him.

'What sort of a shop?'

'A small dress shop. Her idea was to stock it with dresses she would design herself and eventually hire women to sew them for her.'

Kate's attention was caught. Her steps slowed and finally she stopped, turning to look at him. 'How absolutely fascinating!'

He laughed. 'And how absolutely non-profit-making. So far it hasn't caught on. Women around here, housewives and teenage girls, are used to running up their own frocks on the family Singer machine.'

Kate nodded. She could see why the discount he mentioned was so important, worth risking the shopkeeper's infantile ideas of humour for.

'I can understand that. But there must be occasions when they want something – well, something different. For a dance or a wedding?'

He grimaced. 'A few.'

They commenced walking again. 'So how does your mother manage?'

'My mother is a very clever woman. She is a trained couturière and worked in Paris before her marriage to my father. But she's never really had the chance to put her talents to the test. As it is, she makes every penny do the work of two. She's acquired a small number of customers who ask for something different, as you put it, but she must acquire a lot more before she can call herself a success.'

Kate said again: 'How absolutely fascinating,' and he turned and said, with a directness that left her blinking, 'How old are you?'

She didn't think it was considered polite to ask someone's age, but she answered, truthfully, 'Sixteen. How old are *you*?'

'You look older.' He smiled. 'I'm twenty.'

They walked in silence past the unmade gardens, the houses that were, in the main, still empty. Then he enquired, 'Have you just moved here?'

31

'Yes. Just this morning. In fact, we're *still* moving in.' She nodded towards the parcel of groceries he carried. 'That's for our supper. Isn't it lovely moving into a brand-new house?' She pointed. 'See, that one, the third from the end of the road.'

'They're all nice houses along here. You're lucky, too, it being a dead end.'

'Why is that? A dead end? Isn't that the name of a film? I saw it advertised in London.'

'A cul-de-sac,' he explained. 'Only cars that need to come down here do. Where we live it's like a madhouse. So noisy my mother prefers to stay in the shop for as long as possible. Even after it's closed.'

'I thought you said you lived down here?'

'I said we were going in the same direction. I take a short cut through the playing fields and cross the footbridge over the railway lines. We live in a block of flats that have definitely seen better days. My mother was horrified when we first moved in but she's coming to grips with it. It's quite an experience, really. Although some of our neighbours would be more suited to a cage in the zoo.'

Kate laughed. 'Can't you find something better?'

'Oh, yes, we could. It just takes a bit of money, which, as I pointed out, unfortunately we do not have.'

She frowned, gazing at his profile as he walked beside her. 'I'm sorry. I shouldn't be asking all these questions. Mother Superior would have ticked me off if she could hear me. It's rude to ask personal questions.'

'You go to a convent school?'

She sighed. 'I used to.'

About to explain about India, she decided against it. She didn't want him to think she was bragging when his family were so obviously hard up. Not that there was anything wrong in being hard up. Her own family were on the brink of being that . . . There came a mental vision of her own mother, a scarf tied about her head, a wrap-around pinny covering a rough skirt and blouse, taking in washing or scrubbing floors for some old biddy.

Her mother would starve to death before she descended to that. On reflection, she couldn't see her mother doing any kind of job.

She said, 'When you finished school, did it take you long to find a job?'

'I work for my mother. You'd be surprised just how many jobs there are in a dress shop that a mere male can do.' He shrugged. 'I augment my earnings by working part time at whatever I can get.'

'I admire that.' About to blurt out her own disappointment about not going to art school, she decided not to.

This boy would know her whole life history if she was not careful.

Funny, he was so easy to talk to. Educated in an all-girls' school, mindful of the warnings dished out by the nuns about the opposite sex, and how all they were out for was to get their wicked way with girls, she had always been a little timid of boys, never knowing how to act in their presence. But with this boy – well, that was exactly what he was – easy to talk to.

They were almost at her gate. Remembering what he'd said about the short cut, she gazed about her, saying, 'What playing fields? You said you crossed the playing fields.' All she could see were rows of houses while at the bottom of the road a copse of birch trees, their silvery bark gleaming in the sunshine, hid what lay beyond.

The playing fields, he told her, belonging to the Railways. 'You can only see them when you get beyond the trees. Part of a sports club. It's pretty there. There's tennis courts and a green for bowls and a pavilion where they have dances and social gatherings.'

'Do you ever go?'

He grimaced. 'Me? No. You have to work for the Railways to be eligible to join. And I live on the other side of the railway tracks, which practically makes me an outcast.' He smiled, taking the bitterness out of his words. 'What does your father do?'

She looked down at her feet. 'Nothing – for the moment. Although he'll be looking for work as soon as we're settled.' She added proudly, 'He was a manager in his last job. But he . . .' She bit her lip. 'He had to leave. He had an accident.'

'I'm sorry. Jobs aren't that easy to get just now, with the depression. There's a lot of good men on the dole.'

She didn't like to ask what the dole was and said instead, 'What does your father do?'

It was as if a dark curtain came down over his face, masking all expression, his eyes suddenly blank. He turned away. 'He was a teacher. A brilliant man. But I don't have a father any longer. He's dead.' He looked at her. 'I'm a refugee from Germany.'

His pronunciation had told her he was foreign. Funny, he spoke English so well, too.

Kate flushed with embarrassment. 'I'm very sorry. Me and my big mouth. I shouldn't have asked . . .'

He lifted a hand, stopping the flow of sympathy. Most people didn't mean it; they expressed only words. But this girl sounded genuinely concerned.

From the lofty heights of his twenty years, he gazed down at her. He'd very nearly allowed the bitter sadness left by his old life to show. The wonderfully carefree life that had ended in January 1933, when Hitler become Chancellor of Germany.

At first, like many people, his father had followed the path of least

33

resistance, but going his own way. The Nazis didn't want that. They demanded absolute obedience. To try to go against them was like adding another nail to your coffin . . .

It had all started with the flag, that dreaded ensign of red and black with its obscene twisted cross, fluttering by the headmaster's command over the school . . .

He shuddered.

He'd promised himself he wouldn't dwell on it. Not ever. All that was in the past, forgotten. Here in England they were secure, safe from the strutting brownshirts of the Nazi party . . .

They had reached her house. The removal van was still parked outside, although it was obvious that the men had finished. Canvas sacking was being folded and placed in the back.

The men stopped to light a cigarette and then climbed into the front of the lorry. The oldest, the one who had been impudent to her mother, grinned down at Kate, giving her a thumbs up. 'Good luck in your new 'ome, ducks.'

'Thanks.'

They watched the van drive slowly away. The youth, whose name she had still to discover, relinquished the bag of groceries, and Kate was suddenly conscious of her mother's face behind the leaded pattern in the front bay window. Monica was frowning, wondering no doubt how her daughter could possibly have allowed herself to be picked up in the short time she'd been absent.

One hand on the gate, Kate turned to smile at him. 'Thanks for carrying my things.'

He shrugged, returning her smile. 'It t'weren't nothin'.' Imitating exactly the drawling tones of his favourite film actor, the cowboy Tom Mix.

She wished he would move on. Her mother was still glued to the window, probably making up all kinds of scenarios in her mind. Belatedly, he called just as she reached her front door, 'I'm Paul Konig, by the way.'

Before the door was jerked open and her mother glared out, she called back, 'And I'm Kate. Kate Linley.'

'See you sometime, eh?'

'You're bound to. It seems a small enough place.'

He gave a formal little bow, the quintessence of old-fashioned politeness. Then strode away.

Her mother fussed behind her, unpacking the groceries and laying them out on the kitchen table. 'You don't waste much time, do you? You're only sixteen, young lady. I should have thought the nuns would have taught you to fight shy of men who try to pick you up.'

Kate couldn't help but laugh. 'Mum! He's only a few years older than me. He didn't try to pick me up. He was in the shop where I bought the groceries and he came out behind me and offered to carry my packages.'

Monica grunted, then dropping a number of potatoes into a bowl of water, stood looking at them vaguely. 'They'll need peeling, I suppose.' It sounded like a task completely beyond her conception.

Kate silently blessed the training given by the nuns in domestic science, which had included simple cooking as well as making beds and mitreing corners of sheets.

She picked up the small knife that had come with the rest of the kitchen utensils. 'I think that's what you usually do with potatoes you want to use for chips,' she said lightly. 'Where's Daddy?'

'Battling with the beds upstairs. You wouldn't believe how difficult it is to fit the springs on the base.' Monica sniffed. 'I think it was disgraceful of those removal men just to walk off without even *offering* to put the beds together.'

'They're not paid for that, Mum, only unloading the van. At least they carried the beds upstairs.'

How long, Kate wondered, would it be before Monica realized that workmen here wouldn't rush forward to help whenever she clicked her fingers? Her mother had a lot to learn.

She said, 'Why don't you go and help Daddy and I'll get on with the supper?'

Her mother's sigh of relief was audible. 'Yes, you do that, dear. But I think if the water is hot enough I'll go and soak in a hot bath first. I'm sure Daddy is managing just fine on his own.'

Looking at the peeled potatoes, Kate tried to decide whether she should cut them thick or thin. Not *too* thick, she thought, but then not too thin or they would be hard. She compromised on a middle course and stood back, watching the chips turn a golden brown in the hot fat. The eggs and peas offered no problem. You'd have to be pretty gormless not to know how to cook eggs. The plates would have to be warmed, too. She'd better light the oven. From upstairs, Monica called, 'Samuel, can you remember which packing case the towels were in?'

Kate drained the chips and turned them from the wire basket on to a plate which she thrust into the oven. The peas were boiling nicely and the eggs wouldn't take a minute. She ran upstairs to find her father struggling to lift the top from the first of the half-dozen packing cases that littered the bedrooms and landing.

The rest of the evening passed in a flurry of sweeping bare wooden floors and deciding where to put the furniture they had bought. By bedtime they were exhausted. When Kate finally got to bed, she lay thinking of the young man who lived on the 'other side of the tracks'. He seemed nice, polite and not at all pushy. She wondered what Julie would have made of him. Lucky to have two brothers who were older than her, Julie knew all about boys.

And that air of tragic mystery about him – well, that made him all the more attractive.

Chapter Five

Over the years her father had sent cheques to cover the expense of new clothing. She and Julie, accompanied by little Sister Hosea, would go into Canterbury, the nearest large town, with Mother Superior's warnings about buying nothing frivolous ringing in their ears. They would spend an exhilarating afternoon touring the shops. Afterwards they rode the lift to the top of the big department store where waitresses in dark frocks and white aprons and frilled caps bustled, serving tea and cakes to weary shoppers. They ordered cream cakes and a pot of tea for three and Sister Hosea had been rendered speechless by the excitement of it all.

Now, diplomatically, Kate waited until her mother was in a good mood before broaching the subject of new clothes.

The move had been a big upheaval in their lives and her mother was finding it difficult to settle down. She was snappish and short-tempered, constantly harping on the fact that so much was expected of her. Kate helped all she could, in between seeking work. Being young and adaptable, she had quickly become used to yet another change in her life. Woven like a rich tapestry into her childhood was Ayah and the sights and sounds of India. But this new life was quickly taking on attractions of its own.

They sat at breakfast. The sun filtered through the net curtains Monica had insisted on hanging across the French windows. Kate had investigated thoroughly the various shops in the High Street, and mindful of the lack of money said, 'There's a shop opposite Woolworths that sells women's clothes and seems quite reasonable. We could try there.'

Her mother's attention was centred on a split fingernail, the result of helping Samuel shift the sofa for the umpteenth time. It still didn't look right. The room was far too small, that was the trouble. If only they had been able to afford something larger, for example one of those detached houses she had seen on their first visit to the new suburb.

She answered Kate's suggestion of new clothes with a vague, 'You've still got the things you wore on school holidays at Aunt Norma's. Won't they do?'

37

'Oh, Mummy, they're a bit tight on me now. I've worn them for the past year. I need new skirts and blouses. And jumpers, and, I suppose, cardigans.' Adding a sweetener. 'I'll need them when I get a job.'

Monica sighed. 'When! The crucial word. It could be weeks. Months. You won't have to be too fussy, you know. Not the way things are.'

'I don't intend to be too fussy. I'll take whatever comes along.'

Monica, sensing sarcasm, looked up. 'Within reason, of course.'

'Of course within reason.' She hadn't told her mother, but she'd even replied to an advertisement for factory work. In a chocolate factory, to be precise. Even that job had been taken.

Breakfast finished, Kate had been left to her usual task of washing up, while Monica went upstairs to apply her make-up. They had fallen into a routine; Kate did most of the housework while Monica shopped or popped in for a cup of tea and a gossip with the woman next door, often not returning until almost lunchtime. Or dinnertime as they referred to it around here. Alice Bennett was about her mother's age, a good-natured woman with reddish hair and a wide smile. She liked nothing better than a good gossip, and being new to the district, having moved in only weeks before the Linleys, she enjoyed the daily chats with Monica. Sometimes, Monica would even visit her in the evenings, when Mrs Bennett's husband wasn't at home. He was a shift-worker and often worked late.

Samuel would help Kate with the housework when he was at home, dusting, polishing, cleaning the windows.

But mostly his time was spent in looking for a job. He'd lost count of the number he'd applied for, being turned away when they learned his age. Despite his experience, a man over the age of forty was considered to be on the scrap heap.

Kate felt so sorry for him. She'd meet him at the front door, one look at his face telling its own story. 'No luck?'

'No, Katie. Not this time.' A fatigued smile creased his face. 'Never mind, someone, somewhere, must want a bright young forty-two-year-old, mustn't they?'

'Of course they must.'

She washed the breakfast dishes, then stacked them away in the scarlet-and-white-painted cabinet. It had leaded glass windows over its upper shelves where you were supposed to display your best Sunday tea set. As they still had to get round to such luxuries, Monica kept a spare tea pot and glass jug there, just to fill the space.

Kate hung the damp tea towel over the edge of the sink and turned to look at her mother. 'Isn't it a bit warm for your fur, Mummy?'

Monica ran one hand over the rich, glossy fox fur, with its glass eyes and plume of a tail. Kate could imagine the small wild creature scampering joyfully through the woods, unaware of the hunters lying in wait for it. Or, equally horrifying, the steel trap buried in the long grass, set by men who made their living out of such barbarities.

People seemed to see nothing wrong in killing a beautiful wild creature in order to make a coat or a neckpiece for some fashion-conscious woman.

No matter how wealthy she became – and she smiled at this flight of fancy – she would never resort to such an unwholesome practice.

'Not at all, Kate. In a little while it will be too warm and then I shall have to pack it away for winter. Until then, let me enjoy it. It's one of the few things I have left to remind me of the life I had to leave.'

Kate was becoming used to this air of martyrdom. Her father had already left for his various appointments. They were scattered far and wide now and sometimes it took most of the day, catching and changing buses.

And still there was no sign of work. Samuel Linley was merely one of hundreds, travelling wearily from place to place, constantly praying that this time they would strike lucky . . .

In the High Street they passed the shop run by Paul Konig's mother. On her visits to the High Street, Kate had lingered outside its one window, trying to summon up enough courage to go inside, to introduce herself to Mrs Konig and mention that she had met her son. The window display was tastefully done: one model, placed to one side, wearing a frock of pale-grey georgette with a white shawl collar draped alluringly about the neck. A long string of pearls hung almost to the waist. Kate had thought how much more attractive it would have been had the collar been a pale pink, or even the grey of the gown. With perhaps a pale-pink silk rose at the base of the throat, nestling in the filmy georgette.

She'd smiled at her own temerity. Who was she, sixteen-year-old Kate Linley, to query the taste of the woman who had fashioned the frock?

The name, in gilt lettering above the shop, was simply: Rosa.

The rest of the window was taken up by a small wheelbarrow, painted white and filled with an assortment of spring flowers. The wax model had been positioned bending slightly towards it, as though admiring the colourful blooms.

'Well, it's nice to see that someone has a bit of taste around here,' remarked Monica. 'Beautifully done.' She leaned forward towards the glass. 'But no price tag, I see.'

'They don't put price tags on goods displayed in windows in this kind of shop, Mummy.'

Her mother raised thin eyebrows. 'Oh, really!' The sarcasm in her voice was unmistakable. 'And since when have you been an authority on the subiect, young lady? I can hardly believe that sort of information would be contained in a lesson from the nuns.'

'No, of course not.' It was just something she knew, in a strange, instinctive sort of way.

The shop door opened and a woman came out. Elderly and very overweight, she carried a flat box under her arm. The stripes of lime green and pale mauve on a grey background were very effective. Before the door closed behind her, she turned to say, in a loud, gushing voice, 'Oh, by the way, I shall be requiring that frock before the end of next week. My husband has a very important dinner engagement and insists I look my best.' She simpered. 'But I'm sure, with your excellent reputation, Mrs Konig, you will be able to manage that.'

Another figure moved from the shadows of the shop's interior into the ray of sunshine coming through the door, and Kate looked on Rosa Konig for the first time.

Both she and her son had the dark hair and eyes that would not have been out of place round the campfire of a Hungarian gypsy camp. Although she looked more foreign than her son, the likeness was unmistakable.

The woman held the door until her customer had gone, then, catching Monica's eye, gave a polite inclination of her head. Then the door was closed on the treasure trove Kate was certain must lie within. She longed to take hold of a pencil and paper and begin fashioning other well-groomed models to join the one in the window.

'Doesn't that look interesting, Mummy? I'd love to work in a place like that.'

Ideas flitted about in her brain. Shapes and colours, silks and filmy chiffon. Hardly aware of her surroundings, she followed her mother along the road.

The shop Kate had described was busy and Monica disliked being kept waiting. Used to being served straight away, she moved about the crowded shop, gazing at price tickets, her frown telling of her irritation.

Finally the harassed little woman who, with one girl, made up the staff, served them. Monica dropped the change into her handbag and closed it with a snap. While the woman went to wrap their parcels, Monica said in a low voice, 'It will certainly have to do us until your father gives me more. Goodness knows what we're going to do for food and warmth. I tell you, Kate, it's going to take some getting used to, this new life of ours.'

Kate wanted to say, perhaps if you didn't keep harping on about the old life it would be easier. But she didn't. Her mother would have to settle in her own time, in her own way. As she herself was doing. And, once he was bringing in wages, as her father would.

Carrying their shopping, they began the walk back to the house.

Filled with an urge she couldn't ignore, Kate said, '*Why* is Daddy finding it so hard to get a job? I mean, with *his* qualifications . . .'

'Times are hard, Kate. You know that. We're in the middle of what they call a depression. I don't know how some people manage, really I don't.'

Kate wasn't going to be sidetracked. 'You haven't answered my question, Mummy.'

Her mother looked blank. 'Oh, what was that?'

'Why is Daddy finding it so hard to get a job?'

'I must say, for one so young, you have a very forthright manner, Kate. I'm afraid a lot of people might find it off-putting. I don't know whether I like it. Perhaps later, when you're older, it might be attractive, but not now.' She turned her head to look at Kate. 'I should have thought the nuns would have taken you to task over it.'

'Well, you couldn't fault them for trying,' said Kate, remembering the times her 'forthrightness' had got her into trouble. Then, persistently, she went on, 'Why are you so secretive about Daddy? Every time I bring up the subject, you turn to something else.'

'Forthright, as I just said.' Monica sighed, and her words fell like stones in the sudden silence. 'Well, young lady, if you must know, your father was sacked for embezzling – although they didn't use that word but were much more diplomatic – a considerable amount of money from the company. Accused of being a charlatan. I've never felt so ashamed in all my life. Although he declared himself innocent of any crime, he was most certainly guilty of fecklessness, of leaving important matters of finance in the hands of a newer, younger man.'

Kate looked stunned, wishing she'd never asked. 'Mummy . . .'

'The auditors had taken charge of the books and claimed they found discrepancies. Your father was called to account for the loss and couldn't, even though the book-keeping had recently been taken over by a younger man, a nephew of one of the directors. Your father was asked to leave, a euphemism for the sack.'

'How dreadful for Daddy!' Kate gazed at her mother, white-faced.

'Dreadful for all of us. But for his irresponsibility we wouldn't be in the state we're in now. But harking back to the past will do us no good at all. It's all gone and we have to make the most of what we have left.'

'So there was no accident? No broken leg?'

'No. We had to tell you something and when I suggested this your father agreed.'

Gazing at her mother, Kate was shocked by the eyes blazing with anger. In those few moments, she knew she had grown up. The innocence of childhood, like some bright phantom creeping away, dragged tattered dreams behind it.

'When I think of all the things *I* had to forfeit, Kate, I feel physically sick. I so miss all the social events we went to. Your father was never very keen, but then he always has been an old stick-in-the-mud.'

One gloved hand went to the fur across her shoulder, as though to reassure herself that it hadn't been a dream, that time of luxury and sweet living. The long fingers caressed the soft fur and Kate heard her sigh. The road where they lived stretched before them, her mother's high-heeled shoes wobbling on the yet unmade pavement, and although Monica Linley may have been there in body, Kate knew that her spirit was elsewhere.

'Do you remember, Kate, the dances and whist drives? It seemed there wasn't an evening when we weren't dressing up to go out. Remember how we took you to some of the dances in the officers' mess? You were doing the Charleston as expertly as any grown-up young woman before you were ten.'

Kate remembered all right. She remembered, when her parents had decided not to take her, Ayah sitting with her in the soft, warm Indian night. Ayah would tell her folk tales of her own country, rich in legend and colour, and Kate would recite old nursery rhymes. 'Humpty Dumpty' and 'Little Bo Peep' and the one about the little girl with the little curl who when she was good was very, very good and when she was bad was horrid.

Ayah would laugh and say, 'That is you, my darling!'

Kate was sure Ayah didn't understand half the things she told her. But she'd laugh and when Ayah laughed it was like little silver bells chiming in the moonlight.

Busy with settling in, Monica had little time for anything but her own problems. Samuel, to a lesser degree, was the same. But then, thought Kate, she couldn't blame Daddy for being preoccupied. His search for work continued. There was no money for buses, not every day, at least, and so Samuel was forced to walk.

Soon Monica began to complain about the number of times his shoes had to be sent to the cobblers.

'The amount of money we're spending having your shoes soled and heeled would *pay* your bus fares,' she pointed out.

When, at last, Samuel swallowed his pride and went to sign on for the dole, he was informed in no uncertain manner by the hard-faced man behind the desk that as he'd been living and working abroad for the past nine years, he could hardly expect the tax-payer to fork out for his keep now.

'Cheek!' exclaimed Monica when after supper one night they sat discussing money matters. 'So what did he suggest? There must be some way . . .'

'He mentioned that the Poor Law might be my only chance. Men in danger of destitution because they have no unemployment insurance cover can apply for that from the Public Assistance Committee. He said I could claim for twenty-six weeks but only after a stringent means test.' To Samuel, the message could not have been more forcefully or nastily driven home.

'And what does that mean? A means test?' They sat either side of an empty fireplace.

'It means an investigation of all sources of family income and the value of everything we have bought.'

Monica looked up, frowning. She had been stitching at a broken strap on a petticoat which she now let fall into her lap. 'You mean that they'll come into our house and poke about to see what we have that is valuable?'

Samuel nodded.

Monica's frown deepened. 'I don't think I want people digging into our affairs, Samuel.'

'We might not have a choice, my dear. It may be the only way, until I get a job, that we can keep our heads above water.'

Monica twisted the silken petticoat into a ball and thrust it into the sewing basket beside her chair. How could he sit there so calmly and puff away at that damned pipe, as though he hadn't a worry in the world? she thought furiously. As though they were not staring destitution in the face . . .

He made her so angry. If, for once, he'd lose his temper, tell those men down in the unemployment office exactly what he thought of them and their rules and regulations. Common sense told her that that attitude would get him nowhere, might even make things worse. But still, if he'd just do *something* . . .

Now, to take her mind off her worries, Monica discovered a brand-new way to pass her empty afternoons. The town possessed two cinemas. The choice of most people was the Dream Palace in the High Street, with its mirrors and chandeliers, the interior looking like some secular church.

Monica had gasped with astonishment when she'd first caught sight of the new building. It was like a fairground kiosk, with coloured lights all round the entrance. A queue of people stood patiently waiting on the pavement outside, the commissionaire in his gold-epauletted uniform shepherding them into straight lines as though he was a sergeant-major and they new recruits.

Plastered right across the front of the building was the biggest poster Monica had ever seen. She stood, lost in wonder at the beautiful girl with the impossibly jet-black mane of hair and darkly ringed eyes who languished adoringly in the arms of a deeply suntanned man. He looked as though he was going to kiss her and the sight of it made her go weak at

43

the knees. Monica had never been to the pictures – India didn't possess such luxuries – although she'd heard of them, of course. The glass doors were flung open as she watched and the queue began to shuffle forward. Hesitantly, Monica fingered the change in her pocket. Why not? she thought. Why shouldn't I treat myself to an afternoon out? The thought that the price of the ticket would more than pay for Samuel's bus fares didn't enter her head.

She joined the end of the queue and was soon sitting in the plushy darkness in a comfortable chair, being carried effortlessly away into a world of dreams. It was a South Sea adventure with the girl being rescued from a hurricane by the hero, who scooped her up in his strong arms from a palm tree that bent almost double in the wind. The girl, still with her hair immaculate and not a trace of the disaster on her flawless skin, lifted her face for his kiss and Monica almost swooned.

To think she'd been missing all this! She couldn't help comparing the handsome hero to her own husband and, sadly, Samuel dropped another notch in her estimation.

She walked home still wrapped in the fantasy of it all. After that first rapturous experience she went to the pictures three times a week. The programme at the Dream Palace changed on a Thursday and a Monday so she went then no matter what was showing. Matinées had an admittance fee of sixpence, and tea and biscuits were served in the interval.

For the third outing she chose the other place. Tucked into a side street, this had started life as a theatre, putting on obscure one-act plays. The elegance of the gold velvet curtains was now faded, the gilt paintwork badly needing retouching.

It was popular for its cowboy films, especially the Saturday-morning serials when the young audience raised the roof with their cheering of the hero and catcalls for the baddies.

Newspapers reported MPs bemoaning in the House of Commons that the cinema was the biggest drug of all time. If that was so, Monica Linley had certainly been hooked.

It took her mind off a distressing future in which, it seemed, men from the Means Test office would come barging into her house, demanding to search it for the few valuables they still had.

As for Kate, well, she missed her friends at the convent so much that it hurt. Julie most of all. She helped her mother with the housework and ran errands. But there was still a lot of time on her hands. She wasn't used to being idle, it didn't suit her ebullient nature. She would wash up after lunch and then go for long walks. The park was a haven of peace. She thought how Paloma would have loved it, all those enticing trails to follow, the smooth, emerald-green lawns to race across, and had to push the thought away before she wept.

Drawing soothed her, and she sketched to her heart's content. She still had all her drawing materials – pads and pencils and coloured crayons. Her biggest worry was what she would do when they ran out. Her mother reminded her incessantly that it was ridiculous for her to sit around and do nothing. Kate knew that. She kept her eyes open but even vacancies for school-leavers seemed practically non-existent.

Mostly, when she arrived home after those walks, the house would be empty. She thought she preferred that. Kate never minded her own company, enjoying the solitude, able to listen to Henry Hall and his Band on the wireless without her mother saying, 'Oh, for goodness' sake, Kate, turn that thing down. It's giving me a headache.'

She enjoyed the songs that were popular: 'I Only Have Eyes For You' and 'Painting The Clouds With Sunshine', among others. She would join in with the male singer, moving about the room with the steps the nuns had taught her at their dancing classes – always with Julie leading as she was the taller of the two, their faces devoid of expression. You weren't supposed to show pleasure in the dance. She wondered how she would feel with a boy's arms about her instead of Julie's, and a thrill of anticipation would come over her.

It really was lovely to have the house to herself . . .

Kate couldn't begrudge her mother this escape from the realities of her new life. Although, on a rainy day, when there was no money for a bus for her father, she did find it provoking.

This particular afternoon, walking back from the park, the road was almost deserted, as usual. Parked cars in Wesley Avenue were few and far between. Children wound their way home, glad to be free from the bondage of the classroom. Glad that it was summer and that the long school holidays would soon be upon them.

So when Kate saw the car parked outside their house she stopped in her tracks. She recognized it immediately. It was the car her mother had borrowed from that awful man who had been introduced to her as Mr Patrick.

And the worst thing of all, she saw as she drew closer, was that he was sitting in the front seat. Obviously waiting . . .

Her mother must still be out. Too late to retreat: he'd turned his head and seen her coming towards him.

Chapter Six

Mr Patrick smiled and opened the door, climbed out. Lifting his hat, he said, 'Didn't make you jump, did I?'

Stiffly, Kate answered, 'No, not at all.'

'Am I glad to see a friendly face. It seems your mother is out, my dear. I rang and rang but there was nobody home.'

Cheek! thought Kate. Surely her mother wasn't thinking of borrowing his car again! And yet what else could this obnoxious man be doing visiting Monica?

Today he was dressed in a plaid suit of light- and dark-brown checks. Loud and common. His hair was slicked back and a spot of egg yolk adhered to the yellow silk tie that was far too wide and showy. Kate thought his appearance repulsive. But it wasn't only his appearance; everything about him disgusted her.

She sniffed, feeling for the front door key in her pocket. 'My mother is often out at this time of the day.' She pushed open the garden gate. With its cut-out sunrise motif, it was a pleasing addition to the appearance of the house.

Daddy had already begun to lay the front path with crazy paving, and the handkerchief-sized pieces of garden each side had been turned ready for planting.

Reluctant to open the door under Mr Patrick's smirking gaze, Kate held back. Perhaps if she ignored him he would go away. 'My mother might not be back for ages yet,' she said, hoping she sounded sincere.

He grinned. 'That's all right. I don't mind waiting. Especially in the company of such a pretty girl.'

She felt herself flush and turned to look at him. 'What do you want with my mother, anyway?'

He wagged a playful finger, making her flush deepen. 'Now, now, I'm sure you don't really want to know that. Let's just say – well, for old times' sake.' Pointedly, he looked at the key in her hand. 'Aren't you going to open the door?' He flicked back the cuff of his shirt, glanced down at his wristwatch. 'It's four o'clock, y'know. Sitting there, waiting for someone I knew to come by, I was thinking how welcome a cup of tea would be right now.'

Kate's lips firmed. 'I'm not supposed to ask anyone in when I'm on my own.'

'Oh, come now. I'm not just anyone. You know me.' One corner of the full mouth lifted in a sardonic twist. 'Your mother knows me even better.'

'I'm still not supposed to ask anyone in. As I said, my mother might be ages yet. There's nothing for her to hurry home for.' Steadfastly, she stood her ground, determined not to be browbeaten by this loathsome man.

Recognizing the resolve in her voice, he shrugged. 'And as *I* said, I was hoping for a cup of tea.' He approached a step further, gazing down into her eyes. 'Pity, just when I had the feeling we were getting on so nicely, too.'

Jesus! he thought. How old was the kid? Fifteen? Sixteen? Whatever else that convent school she'd been going to had taught her, she knew how to stand out, firm as a rock, in defence of her mother. His lips twisted. If she only knew . . . !

'Well, I mustn't lead the young innocents astray, must I? I'll just sit in the car until she comes. Surely you can't object to that?'

Kate objected to everything about him. The way he spoke about her mother; the whole proprietorial attitude of the man.

She saw the twitching of the curtains where the woman next door had been attracted by the parked car. Mrs Bennett was the neighbour with whom her mother was friendly. Short of moving him forcibly, Kate would just have to ignore him. Perhaps if he sat long enough he would get fed up and drive away.

She let herself in, closing the door quickly behind her. She just hoped he'd be gone by the time her mother came home.

She put the kettle on the stove and set the table for tea. Monica liked afternoon tea to be served as it always had been; on a white starched cloth and with the small silver cake knives laid to one side of the plates. Kate added the sugar basin and milk jug and the teakwood stand for the tea pot. Then she stood back, before deciding to augment the scene with the small vase of anemones from the top of the wireless.

There were scones she had baked yesterday. She liked baking and her mother supported her enthusiasm, wrinkling her pretty nose and saying that she herself never was any good at baking. Or cooking or cleaning or ironing, thought Kate tolerantly.

Going to the bay window, she peered through, breathing a sigh of relief when she saw that the car had gone.

So he *had* got fed up waiting! Good! She'd know what to do if he ever came again. Then she sent up a silent prayer that he never would.

She was singing along with the wireless when the front door opened and her mother came in. The music was loud and she didn't hear Monica until she stepped into the room. 'Kate! For goodness' sake!' She made a gesture with one hand towards the wireless set. 'The music . . .'

'Sorry, Mummy.' Kate turned the wooden knob then looked up to smile at her mother. The smile faded when she saw the grinning face of Mr Patrick looking over Monica's shoulder.

Monica breezed in, pulling off her gloves, finger by finger, glancing in the oval mirror above the fireplace. One hand reached up to pat a stray curl into place. Then she was turning to Kate, saying in a slightly reproachful way, 'Mr Patrick tells me you refused to invite him in to the house. That you left him waiting outside. That you were, in effect, quite rude to him, Kate.'

For a long moment Kate was lost for words. Then, flushing, she said, 'You know you and Daddy said I wasn't to invite anyone in while I was alone . . .'

Her mother clicked her tongue. 'We meant young boys of your own age, dear. Not steady, upstanding gentlemen like Mr Patrick.' She turned to the man, who grinned, obviously enjoying Kate's discomfort. 'Young people these days . . .' she sighed. 'I don't know.'

Her eyes swept the prettily arranged table. 'Better set another cup and saucer. And a plate. It's just as well Mr Patrick was driving slowly up the road just as I was coming down it. At least his journey's not completely wasted.'

Kate drew a deep breath. 'Daddy will be tired when he comes home. He won't want a stranger sitting at our table . . .' She finished the sentence in a mumble.

Monica glanced sharply at her. 'What did you say?'

'I said especially someone we don't particularly like.'

With that, she turned on her heel and ran upstairs, shutting herself in her room. Retribution was not long in following. Her mother pushed open her door and stood, frowning. 'Kate, you were very rude just now. Now you march right down and say you're sorry.'

'I'm not sorry and I'd rather not lie.'

Her mother came further into the room and closed the door. 'Why are you acting like this?'

'Because that's the way I feel. Why did you ask him to tea?'

'Because he's a very good friend.'

'He might be your friend but he isn't Daddy's friend and he isn't mine.'

'Well, he's *my* friend and that's the end of it. Now go down and apologize and don't let me hear another word about it.'

Mr Patrick was very gracious. He patted her shoulder and, catching Monica's eye, smiled, saying he knew what it was like with teenagers. Samuel arrived just as they were pouring the tea. Hearing the front door open Kate went into the hall to greet him. He looked tired and at Kate's enquiring look shook his head. 'Sorry, love, no luck today.'

Quickly, she said, 'We've got a visitor, Daddy.'

Her father's brows rose. 'Oh, really!' Who could be visiting them? Being new to the town they still had to get out and make friends.

Moving closer, she lowered her voice and breathed, 'It's that man, that Mr Patrick, who lent Mummy his car.'

'And he's come to see how we're getting on?' Something in her father's manner seemed to change. Kate nodded. 'Well, I suppose I'd better play the genial host even if it is all a bit of a sham.'

She watched as her father shook hands with Mr Patrick then took his place at the table, accepting a cup of tea and a plate of buttered scones from Monica. Their visitor didn't even have the grace to look uncomfortable. He raised his cup as though it was a glass of beer and said, 'Cheers! How's the hunt for jobs going? Found anything to your liking yet?'

'It's not a case of to my liking. I've got to the stage where I'd accept almost anything.'

Kate felt herself cringe inside. Daddy didn't have to justify himself to this man!

'Hundreds like you, old man. At least you've got a lovely wife and a pretty daughter to comfort you. Not like poor old me. I've got no one.'

'Having a family makes it all the harder. You see, I'm used to giving them everything they want. My wife's been spoiled, I suppose, used to people doing everything for her. She never had to worry about a thing. Did you, my dear?'

Monica looked complacent and simpered, 'Not a thing.'

Although the newspapers had been full of the Wall Street crash in 1929, followed by world-wide economic collapse, to the Linleys, enjoying the easy colonial life in India, it hadn't meant much. Thousands had been made bankrupt, causing international repercussions. In America, men in threadbare coats waited on the breadline, shuffling forward to receive hunks of bread and hot soup. As the ticker tapes in every office spewed out their endless figures, businessmen who only minutes before had been millionaires threw themselves from windows high up in giant skyscrapers.

Samuel wondered if the craziness would ever end. The life to which they had become accustomed was over. It would never come again. He had to keep telling himself that everything would be fine as soon as he could get the job that somewhere, surely, must be waiting for him. And to do that he must be more assertive, push himself forward more. What sort of a man would force his wife to face the indignity of a means test?

He finished his scone then wiped his fingers on the damask napkin.

'What brings you this way, Patrick?' Although he tried to sound genial Kate noticed the faint air of tension in his voice. 'A bit off the beaten track for you, I should have thought.'

Kate saw the look exchanged between her mother and the man. A quick shake of the head from her mother and then she stood up, saying, 'Didn't you say this was just a brief visit? That you had to be back at the hotel before . . .' she darted a swift look at the mantel clock, 'before six?'

Mr Patrick grunted. 'I did, didn't I? Oh well, no peace for the wicked, as they say.' He rose to his feet. 'Now that the weather is nice, you'll have to allow me to take you for a drive to the seaside one Sunday. Brighton's always been a favourite of mine.' Looking directly at Kate, he added, 'You'll like Brighton. Gay and lively, it is. Plenty to do besides the sea and sand.' And to Kate's astonishment, he winked. Actually winked at her, right there in front of her parents.

She blushed a fiery red. Daddy, thank God, hadn't noticed. Neither, it seemed, had her mother. *She* was preoccupied in rubbing with a napkin at a small butter stain on her frock. Daddy was reaching for the box of matches on the mantelpiece.

The pipe he had recently taken to smoking lit to his satisfaction, he sat back and said, 'Yes, I always liked Brighton. We used to go there a lot when I was a boy. Swimming, making sand castles. Yes, Brighton's a great place.'

Daddy looked pale, tired circles underlining his eyes. The situation was bound to be taking its toll on him. Kate wondered if her mother ever noticed. If she did she never showed any compassion. Her voice was abrupt whenever she spoke to him.

Please let him get a job soon, Kate prayed. Then they wouldn't have to listen to Mr God-Almighty Patrick offering them days out at the seaside. They would have their own car and could thumb their noses at people like him . . .

Monica saw their visitor to the front door. Kate could hear their voices discussing something as they stood in the hallway. Low, soft voices that hinted of intrigue.

When she came back Monica glanced obliquely at her husband and then retired to the kitchen. Kate followed, helped with the washing up then went into the sitting room. Returning, her sketching pad under her arm, she said, 'I thought I'd take a walk to those fields at the bottom of the road, Mummy. Do a bit of sketching.'

'Well, all right. Only don't be too long. There's still supper to get and I'll need some help.' Monica peered into the brown paper bag of potatoes and a grimace crossed her pretty face. 'You know how I hate peeling those things.'

'I won't be long. Leave them and I'll do them when I get back.'

Kate felt that she needed to get out into the fresh air. Away from the memory of that flashy man who had sat opposite her mother, giving her knowing looks, patronizing her father.

Outside the front gate she turned to the right, making towards the green fields and trees that promised escape. At the bottom of the road were mounds of builders' rubble, dumped there with the intention of being shifted sometime in the future.

The tarmac ended abruptly and the last house in the row stood detached, alone, as though abandoned by its neighbours. Built of red brick that had faded to a soft rose colour, contrasting in an old-fashioned kind of way with the cream pebble-dashed walls of the new houses, it had a small glassed-in porch arching over the front door. The windows were large and square, antiquated compared with the fashionable diamond-leaded bay windows of the new houses.

And it was much more extensive than the new houses – Kate guessed at at least four bedrooms – with a big garden at the front. Sadly neglected, the rose bushes stood tall and gangly, bent by the wind, badly needing pruning. A large hydrangea that once must have been beautiful grew lank and ungainly in the centre of the lawn.

Passing, Kate wondered at the history of the place and stood for a moment gazing up at it. Her heart gave a little flutter of alarm when a curtain in an upstairs window was pushed aside and a face peered out. The paleness of the face seemed to merge into a mass of white hair, creating an overall impression of the supernatural.

Then the curtain fell. Kate shuddered and walked on, eager to get away from what her imagination likened to a ghostly apparition. She'd have to find out more about that house.

Stepping carefully round a small hillock of abandoned tar that glistened like black gold in the slanting rays of the sun, she walked on. The warmth of the summer's day had softened the tar. Its pungent smell mingled with the green of the nearby fields.

The short cut that Paul Konig had mentioned wound through birches and sturdy oaks before coming out on to the open spaces of the playing fields. It was the first time Kate had ventured this far. Now she was glad she had. It offered all kinds of pleasant surprises, away from the acres of raw new suburbs going up all around.

A white clubhouse stood to one side. This time of the week it was deserted but she imagined that at weekends in fine weather it would be crowded with people enjoying themselves.

To one end of the grounds there was a high brick wall beyond which trains thundered on their way north. The London, Midland and Scottish line, this was. It ran past the bottom of their garden, screened by a high wooden fence. Daddy had plans to train a climbing rose over the fence. A tea rose, he'd said, those small pink or cream flowers that did so well.

'I can remember we had one in our back garden when I was a boy,' he told Kate. 'It was always a delight to have tea on the lawn. I never could decide which I liked best, their perfume or the smell of my mother's baking.'

Kate began to walk, searching for a spot where she could sit and sketch. Suddenly she heard a voice behind her call: 'Kate! Hey, Kate!'

Her steps slowed and she turned to see Paul Konig coming towards her. She'd spotted him a number of times since that first time in the High Street, and they'd waved at each other. He was coming now from the direction of the railway bridge. His pace increased when he saw her stop and wait for him. His cap was on the back of his head and he looked dishevelled, as though he'd been hurrying.

She smiled, said, 'Hello, Paul. How's things?'

He shrugged. 'Not bad. I was just on my way to help my mother close the shop for the night. There's been a spate of burglaries in the High Street and she seems to think if I lock up it makes it so much safer.' He grinned at her. 'So, how are you settling in?'

'Fine. I love the house and my father has started already on the garden, and my mother has a new love in her life – the Dream Palace in the High Street. It's all new to her, being able to actually go to a cinema.'

He gave her a surprised look. 'Why, what remote part of England were your parents living in before you came here?'

'Not England. India. Although I was at school here.'

'My, my, now that *is* interesting. It must be a truly fascinating country. What on earth made them come back?'

He certainly was a great one for questions, she thought. But then, lately, she wasn't so bad herself. 'Oh, it's a long story. I'll tell you all about it sometime.'

He nodded. 'I'll remind you.'

It was like being quizzed by a genial uncle. As though he was years older than her and concerned for her welfare.

'You must miss your friends and your old life. What do you do with yourself all day?'

'I try to keep busy. This time of the year the park is very pretty. I love walking there.' Kate wrinkled her nose. 'But I *do* miss my old life.'

'I know. I miss mine. The Germany that was, not the one that is now.'

'You speak English very well. Did you learn it at school?'

'My grandmother was English, an indomitable old lady. She insisted we speak only English when we visited her. She died in 1930. You'd never believe how much I missed her. Last year my mother and I came over here.'

'After your father died?'

He nodded, looking away. 'Yes, after my father died.'

'I'm sorry. It must have been a sad time for you. I've read that some parts of Germany can be very beautiful. Where did you live?'

'We lived in Berlin. Berlin *is* beautiful. Or used to be. But not any more.'

Knowing she shouldn't pry but unable to help herself, she murmured, 'Was it something to do with your father's death? Why you and your mother decided to come over here to live?'

For a long moment he was silent, gazing across the fields towards the clubhouse. Then he said quietly, 'In that secluded place where you went to school, did you ever hear of the National Socialist German Workers' Party? Led by a man named Adolf Hitler?'

Her smile was impish. 'I wasn't interested in newspaper stories then and I don't think that came into anything the nuns taught us . . .'

'Don't joke about it. It is far from a joking matter. My father . . .' He stopped, glanced down at his wristwatch and went on, 'Look, I've got to go. My mother will be having cats . . .'

'Kittens,' she supplied lightly.

'So, you say kittens. Knowing my mother they are more likely to be full-grown spitting tom cats.' His gaze dropped to her sketch pad. 'And I've interrupted your drawing.' He smiled. 'Tell me, are you good?'

She lifted her chin. 'Not bad.'

'I wish I had time to watch you portray something of this green summer brightness. So, Kate Linley, what do you do with yourself over the weekend?' He sounded interested and she couldn't stop herself from blushing.

'We usually go to mass.' Sometimes her mother came, sometimes not. Daddy never went to church though. Theirs was a mixed marriage and when asked Daddy would say he belonged to the religion of life. Whatever that was! 'Then if it's nice I usually help my father in the garden or go for a long walk.'

'Of course, mass! You go to Saint Mary's, in King's Road?'

She nodded. 'Yes. It's a long walk but it's the only Catholic church here.'

'My mother sometimes goes. There is a short cut through those trees,' and he pointed to where, behind the sports fields, a narrow stretch of woodland remained. 'If you walk back to your road and take the other path leading to the left, you'll come across a shallow stream with stepping stones. Follow the path and it will bring you out behind the church.'

Kate thanked him, storing away the advice, and saw him again look at his watch.

'My goodness, just look at the time. I really must be going.' He waved and strode away, leaving her gazing after him, wondering at the dreadful things his background might contain.

And why should he be interested in what she did at the weekend? She had never been out with a boy, never had a date. He was twenty, a young man, while she was still only sixteen. She was really kidding herself if she thought for one moment he was interested in her. He was just being friendly, that was all . . .

She really mustn't appear too inquisitive about his father. Paul's whole demeanour had hinted at something tragic concerning his death. And what, for goodness' sake, was that German Socialist what-d'you-call-it he spoke of? She'd ask Daddy. These days, when he was home, he spent most of his time hidden behind the spread-out pages of a newspaper.

She didn't stay long. The mood for sketching had gone. She closed the pad and retraced her steps back home. Her gaze lingered on the upstairs windows of the red brick house with its sad, untidy garden. The lace curtains fell in smooth folds. Nothing moved there now. She must ask Paul about it when next they met.

Her mother opened the front door to her knock. She was greeted by: 'I hope you haven't been sitting on that damp grass doing your scribbling. You'll end up with a cold on your kidneys. And you know what happens to children who have a cold on their kidneys?'

Kate sighed and put her pad and pencils away in the drawer in the sideboard. 'No, Mummy. What happens to children who get a cold on their kidneys?'

'They end up wetting the bed.'

Kate followed her into the kitchen, reaching for the peeler and bag of potatoes. 'The trouble with you is you still see me as a child. Tell me, when was the last time I wet the bed?'

Monica lit a cigarette, and stood, one hip leaning against the draining board, watching Kate begin on the potatoes. 'Ayah would be better at remembering that. But I know it happened fairly regularly when you were growing up.'

'Pity Ayah wasn't here now, she could do these blessed potatoes.'

Monica frowned at the girl's flippant tone. She drew on her cigarette, tilting her head to watch the smoke swirl against the ceiling. 'Insolence is most unbecoming in a young lady, Kate. I hope you will bear that in mind. I trust that the hard-earned money spent on your education with the nuns has not been squandered.'

Kate's mouth tightened against the too-hasty answer that sprang to her lips. 'I'm sorry, Mummy.'

'I should think so too. Now, when you've finished I want you to go up to the spare bedroom, remove anything belonging to you left lying about there and take it to your own room.' Kate cut the last peeled potato into chips and placed them next to the small pile lying on a clean tea towel. She covered them with one corner of the towel.

'Why, what do you plan to do with the spare bedroom?'

Her mother smirked. 'I've had a stroke of luck. Seeing that your father shows little likelihood of bringing in any money, I've let the spare bedroom to a paying guest. I don't see why we should leave a perfectly good room empty when we can earn good money for it.'

Kate's heart sank at this news. A paying guest! Someone else in their home, using their bathroom, commandeering the wireless in the evening, perhaps wanting to listen to some other wavelength than the one Daddy liked!

'What does Daddy say about that?' she asked.

Monica shrugged. The hand holding the cigarette gave an elegant wave. 'Your father made no comment, but I'm sure he saw that what I suggested makes sense.' Another wave of the hand, as though dismissing the whole subject. 'Now, hurry up, there's a good child, and get that room cleared up. I've put clean sheets out for the bed. Mr Patrick will be arriving bright and early tomorrow morning and I want everything ready for him.'

Kate's heart sank. 'Mr Patrick?'

The tightness in the girl's voice made her mother direct a sharp glance at her. 'Yes, Mr Patrick. He's sick and tired of living in that awful hotel. And who can blame him? While we were saying goodbye at the front door he asked me if I could suggest alternative accommodation and immediately I thought of our spare room.'

Kate caught her father's eye as she hurried past the sitting room door on her way to the stairs. The look there told its own story. That her father felt as impotent as she against her mother's obstinacy.

Chapter Seven

Now only rarely did Kate have the house to herself in the afternoons. Often Gerry Patrick was there. Returning from her walks, she'd make her way upstairs to her room, and hearing her footsteps on the stairs, he'd appear at the open door of his own room, that insinuating grin on his fleshy lips.

'Hi, gorgeous,' he'd say, imitating his favourite actor currently showing at the cinema in the High Street. 'How's tricks?'

That particular day when he appeared, Kate froze, acutely aware that her mother was out. Demonstrating how much at home he felt, Mr Patrick was in his shirtsleeves and braces. His face was flushed as though he'd been drinking.

'Good afternoon, Mr Patrick,' she murmured, careful to avoid eye contact. Her face expressionless, she hurried past him on the narrow landing to her own room.

As he'd done before, he called after her, 'What's the hurry, then? Got time for a little chat, haven't you?'

'Not now. Sorry.'

Their lodger gave a gruff laugh. 'Well, that's frank if you like. We won't argue about it. I don't want to argue with you, Kate. But I would like to know what I'm supposed to have done to make you dislike me so much.'

Did you have to have a reason to dislike somebody? Kate wondered. Wasn't this instant distaste some kind of chemical reaction, like falling in love was supposed to be?

'What about a cup of coffee?' he urged, reluctant to give up the fight. 'I was just on my way down to make one.'

Coffee, alone with this man in the small cosy kitchen, was unthinkable. 'No thanks.'

'Well, if I can't twist your arm, I can't. Do come and talk to me when you've got your feelings sorted out, won't you. After all, your mother and I are . . .'

He left the sentence unfinished. His grin spoke for him.

Kate went red. 'My mother and you are – what?'

His grin widened. 'You don't really want me to answer that, do you?'

'Save your breath, Mr Patrick. I wouldn't believe a word you told me.'

57

Kate clutched her sketch pads closer to her chest and escaped into her room.

Spreading the most recent of her work out on the small table under the window, she tried to ignore the fact that they were alone in the house together. It wasn't easy, knowing that he was prowling about, might join her at any minute. What would she do if he did? The nuns hadn't prepared her for someone like Gerry Patrick.

When she tried to explain her feelings to her mother, Monica frowned. 'You haven't been rude to him again, have you?'

Kate sighed. 'No, I haven't been rude to him again. Although I'd dearly love to be. He's a real pain in the neck, Mum. I hate it when I come home and find you've gone out but he's here. He makes me feel . . .' She shivered, clasping her arms about her, 'all prickly.'

Surprising her, Monica laughed. 'You're growing into a very promising young lady, Kate. You must expect men to start taking notice of you. I'm surprised there isn't a boy – or a number of boys – hanging around. I'm sure Mr Patrick means no harm.'

Having safely diverted the subject, Monica turned to rearrange the Indian brass ornaments displayed on the mantelpiece: the set of three peacocks, tails spread and glowing with finely worked coloured enamel; the tall shapely vases that were useless for holding flowers because their necks were too narrow. 'Once you are working and beginning to meet boys you'll start to feel different.'

Kate sighed. It was no use talking to her mother. Mummy just didn't understand, could not see beyond the façade of egotistical self-satisfaction, so blatant it made her skin creep. So long as his rent money was paid in regularly each week, Mr Patrick could do no wrong.

'I suppose you're still a bit young to be thinking of dating boys, anyway.' Her mother turned to gaze at her, her mouth turned down at the corners. She almost resented the pretty young woman her daughter was becoming. Next year when Kate was seventeen would be time enough for boys. She wagged a parental finger. 'But you just be nice to Mr Patrick, try to get to like him.'

'Why? Why is it so important for me to like him?'

Her mother's eyes met hers in the mantelpiece mirror. 'Because it is. And because I say so.'

It was one of the times when Kate wished she had Julie to confide in. The two girls corresponded, but it wasn't the same. She would never have dreamed she would look back upon those meetings under the old fir tree with such poignant nostalgia.

And then the thing she most longed for happened: her father got a job. Sure, it wasn't quite what he was cut out for, but it would do for a start. Caretaker at the dairy Kate passed on her way to the park. And it was within walking distance. So, said Samuel, being crude for once, they knew what they could do with their means test, and he grinned at Monica like a cheeky schoolboy.

Her mother's comment was: 'What a comedown! I'm just glad none of our old friends are here to see it.' She fixed Kate with a warning eye. 'And, young lady, no mentioning it to your Aunt Norma when you write. Considering the mess she's made of her own life, she's still got enough gall to give *me* advice.'

Now that Samuel had a regular job, he was entitled to register with a doctor. The Bluebell Dairy had to provide a standard benefit fee to the doctor he chose, so that the insured person then became a panel patient, as distinct from a private, fee-paying patient. Samuel liked Dr Shearer as soon as he laid eyes on him. A tall, thin, grey-haired man, he had kindly eyes and a sympathetic manner and spoke with a soft Scottish accent. He soon became a supportive friend of the family and Monica often consulted him on what she called her 'nervous disorders'.

If Kate imagined that now, with her father's wages coming in regularly, it would be the end of Mr Patrick, she was mistaken. Her mother made it very clear that she enjoyed his company. 'Your father's so gloomy these days,' she'd tell Kate, in one of their rare mother-daughter talks. 'So different from the man I married.' She sighed. 'If anyone should be feeling distressed it should be me.'

So Gerry Patrick knew when he was well off and stayed securely lodged in the spare back bedroom of number 138.

One bright Sunday afternoon, when her father was busy in the back garden, Kate set off with her pad and pencils to the quiet spot she'd discovered in the playing fields of the club. An old railway carriage, once used for teas but abandoned years ago when the new pavilion was built, rested under the sheltering branches of an ancient oak. The wheels had been removed, wooden sleepers supporting the carriage instead.

The grass had been allowed to grow long here. Kate could hear it whispering as she strode through it. The buddleias and willow herbs and marguerite daisies were thronged with bees, a white butterfly pursued its waving, fluttering flight and a tabby cat jumped from a tree and skittered away in front of her.

Despite the spider webs and dust, the old coach was a perfect place for the privacy she craved. The seats were threadbare, stuffing showing in places through the torn covering. She'd brought a blanket and, folding it lengthways, tucked it across a seat, choosing a window overlooking the tennis courts. The wooden table between the seats, for this had once been a carriage from the dining car, was ugly, scarred with cigarette burns. Long ago, hearts had been carved into the once polished surface with initials denoting the undying love of young sweethearts.

Spreading her open pad across the table, Kate's gaze rested on the sunny day outside, the green of the English countryside, the white-clad figures on the tennis court. Head bent, hair hanging forward, almost concealing her face, she was unaware of the intruder until a voice, making her jump, said, 'Ah, I see you've found it too.'

She turned and saw Paul Konig standing in the narrow doorway of the carriage. He carried a canvas satchel under one arm. She smiled as he came forward, halting next to her seat. 'My own secret hideaway,' he said. 'I wondered how long before someone else discovered it.'

'It's perfect, isn't it?' she said, gazing about with gratification. 'I've been coming here for weeks now. Nobody else seems to bother.'

He slid into the seat opposite her, resting his forearms on the table between them. 'It's my one spot of peace and quiet,' he said. 'Although it's not always easy to find time to come here. I've been pretty busy these last few weeks.' He folded his arms across his chest, settling back comfortably. 'The members of the club haven't bothered you, then?'

She shook her head. 'No.' She'd taken care to avoid any members on her way through the sports grounds. There was silence now, broken only by the shouts of the tennis players: male voices, teasing, girls' shrill answers of protest.

Paul's eyes rested on the moving figures. 'Do you play tennis?' he asked.

'We played a little at the convent. Although the nuns considered it not very ladylike for growing girls to jump around in a short skirt or shorts.' She remembered her tennis classes with Julie. Everyone said Julie could play at Wimbledon if given the chance. Kate's own game was far less worthy. 'Do you?'

'I have, in the past.' The past again, his voice changing whenever he spoke of it. It was, she thought, clearly something to avoid.

His gaze settled on the sketch before them. She turned the pad for his inspection and he studied it, head on one side.

'Nice,' he said. 'You've captured those moving figures perfectly. You've got a wonderful eye for line and colour. Are you planning on going to art college next year, then?'

'I would love to go, but my parents think not. My mother doesn't believe there's any future in scribbling, as she calls it.' She could hardly tell him the real reason; that there was no money for such luxuries. Not any more.

'Pity. I'd hate to be ungallant enough to contradict your mother, but that . . .' and he dipped his chin towards the sketching pad, 'is a far cry from scribbling.' He looked out at the playing fields. 'My father's hobby was painting. At weekends he'd take his materials out to a lake near where we lived and happily paint all day. It would get dark and my mother would worry about him.' He smiled, reminiscing about those early days of his childhood. Before the bad times started, before those monsters took over his country, creating havoc and bitter memories. He recalled how he would sit while his father painted, skimming stones across the clear waters of the lake.

Again detecting the undertones of sadness in his voice, Kate said, 'Your father sounds like a very nice man. You said he was a teacher?'

'He was.'

Dark eyes belonging to a youth much older and wiser than his years gazed steadily at her. 'Sometimes,' she prodded gently, 'it helps to talk.'

He was silent for a moment and then nodded his head as though agreeing with her, remembering that January. The day that had started out like all the others of his happy life but had ended with such disastrous results. The world was on the verge of erupting. Things would never be the same again . . .

The wireless had broadcast Hitler's speech into every home in the country. The high-pitched voice full of fanatical fervour, becoming shriller and more exultant with every word. The Third Reich had begun. Hitler held the Chancellery. He and his collaborators had the future of the country in their hands; nothing could stop them now.

Frederick Konig sat before the fire in their comfortable sitting room in a Berlin suburb that evening and spoke of the air of excitement that enveloped the school where he taught. He'd arrived at his usual time to see a huge swastika flag waving from the flagpole above the building.

Pupils and teachers were swarming around the playground, talking and gesticulating in great agitation. Frederick Konig stood and stared, a feeling of horror overtaking him. Then someone, one of the more elderly teachers, shouted, 'Get that thing down from there. It's a disgrace. Who in his right mind . . .'

The rest of the exclamation was lost in the babble of voices coming from all around him.

The janitor, grinning insolently, replied that he didn't know where to find the key to the tool shed which housed the ladder. 'Then someone climb on to the roof and take it down,' yelled the white-haired teacher. 'I refuse to teach my pupils with that monstrosity hanging over us.'

'A sentiment with which I wholeheartedly agree,' said Frederick Konig. Without another word he disappeared into the school. The pupils, glad of the diversion from their studies, watched, discussing what might be the outcome.

A short while later Frederick was seen scrambling out of a dormer window. The crowd craned their necks, a few cheered. Most, however, muttered angrily under their breath. The opinion was that now Hitler was Chancellor the flag should stay up.

Frederick groped his way over the roof to the flagpole, rose to his full height and tugged at the flag until it came away from its moorings. With a gesture of contempt he threw it from him. Pupils and teachers watched as it fluttered to the ground, landing in a muddy puddle left by the previous night's rain.

Wide-eyed, Kate listened to the account of the beginning of Paul's father's downfall.

'For goodness' sake!' she breathed. 'What happened then?'

'Nothing. At least, not straight away. Although things in the country changed day by day. We had to submit to dozens of events staged by the Nazi party. Wherever you went there were columns of SS troops, shouting slogans, marching, singing. Friends of ours, Jewish friends, began to disappear. My mother was frightened. Both my parents were Catholics and were known to oppose Nazism. Father, especially, was a well-known union activist. When my mother begged him to leave the country, for the safety of all of us, he spoke of loyalty to Germany, asking if everyone felt like that, what would become of it? I don't think he had the slightest idea what the Nazis would do.' He gave a gruff laugh. 'No one could guess what the Nazis really had in mind.'

'What happened to the flag? Did they leave it after that?'

'You must be joking! Another was put up the very next day. The headmaster sent for my father and told him it was to stay there.'

'That's terrible,' Kate said, the scenes he described like a film unrolling before her eyes.

'I remember the night we were caught up in a rally in the middle of town. I was with a friend, a girl who lived near me, and we'd been visiting my cousin and were coming home later than usual. My friend's mother liked her in before dark. But that particular winter's day dark came early. The streets were crowded, people everywhere, crowds of them, all watching the brown columns of the SA, the thousands of blazing torches streaming up the Wilhelmstrasse. They had marched through the Brandenburg Gate, a glorious, inspiring sight for those who believed. Not us. We pushed our way through and ran the rest of the way home.' How could this young and naïve girl understand the terror that had possessed Hilda Steinberg and himself as they fled, hand in hand, through those noisy, crowded streets?

'Why didn't you want to stop and watch them?' Kate asked, artlessly. 'You could have explained to your mother where you'd been.'

Paul didn't answer. Instead he reached for the canvas satchel he'd laid on the seat next to him. Opening its flap, he reached inside and produced a blue picnic flask with a silver top. He poured a pale-golden liquid into the silver cup and handed it to her. 'Milk and sugar already in it,' he explained. 'I hope you like your tea sweet. My mother seems to think all young people need plenty of sugar for energy.'

Kate tasted the scalding brew. It really was too sweet for her but she said nothing, smiling and taking another sip. Paul sat back and watched the players in their white tennis outfits. She wondered what was going through his mind. Did he think back on the life his family had led, regretting their new one? A bit like her at times. Although she'd come to accept that life didn't always go the way you would like it to go.

They had so much in common, she and Paul Konig. She liked him, feeling a deep understanding as he told his story.

'So,' he said, 'now you know all about my dim dark secrets, how about telling me a bit about yourself.'

The memories were instantly with her, the hot sunshine and Ayah and the fun-loving little dog. The words tripped from her tongue and Paul sat back and listened, his gaze never once leaving her face. 'That must have been hard to give up,' he said at last. 'How did you view your return to England after all that?'

'I was only twelve, young enough to adapt. My mother's finding it harder, I'm afraid.' With this boy it was easy to talk. She watched his dark-eyed, sensitive face and thought how good she felt with him. Not at all self-conscious.

She finished the cup and handed it back to him. He poured out the remainder of the tea and, grinning when she quipped: 'Watch out for foot and mouth disease!' he turned the cup and drank carefully from the opposite side. Not in a nasty way as some might have done, but rather as if it was a huge joke.

One of the tennis players caught his attention and he said, 'That's Guy Ferris. I didn't know he was back this way.'

Kate followed his gaze to where a tall youth clad in grey flannels and a white open-necked shirt leapt agilely after a ball played by a girl with fashionably short dark hair.

'Never 'eard of 'im,' she joked. 'Who is he when he's at home?'

'Don't you know? He's only the son and heir of the oldest family hereabouts. He lives in that house at the bottom of your road . . .'

Kate viewed the youth with fresh interest. 'That old red-brick one? I didn't think anybody lived there. It always looks so deserted. Although I did see, once, a curtain move in an upstairs window and a face peer out. The face of an elderly woman. Would it be his mother?'

'His grandmother.'

'He *lives* with her?'

He shook his head. 'He spends most of his time at some boarding school in Scotland. Every so often he creeps out from under his stone and comes home. In the meantime, the old lady lives there alone with a bunch of ancient servants.'

She grinned. 'You sound as though you don't like him very much.'

He shrugged. 'He would have made a good storm trooper in Hitler's Germany. But I can well see why you thought the house was deserted. It's a dismal place. It'd give *me* the creeps if I had to live there.'

Mindful of the unkempt garden, she said, 'But it's so neglected. If they have money' – and you didn't refer to someone as a 'son and heir' if they didn't have money – 'why should it be left to – to *decay* like that?'

Paul packed the empty flask back into the satchel. 'There's a story that returning from the church after the baby's christening, the parents' car was involved in an accident and both were killed. Somehow, miraculously, the baby survived. His grandmother lost her own husband shortly after that and they say the shock of it all was too much for her. Although she took the baby in she became a recluse, seeing no one, seldom leaving the house.'

'How terrible!' Kate's sympathetic heart was touched. Here she was, getting all upset because her mother felt the need to take a lodger into their house; bemoaning the fact that she couldn't go to art college, while dreadful things like that were happening. It seemed as though Paul had had enough of answering her questions. He took a book from the satchel and, opening it, settled with his back to the window, his feet drawn up on the seat. He began to read. She remembered him saying: 'It's my one spot of peace and quiet.' He hadn't shown it, but he probably resented her being there, encroaching on what little privacy he had.

For a while longer she watched the white-clad figures enjoying themselves in the summer-afternoon sun. Quietly she sketched, lifting her gaze to regard Paul from time to time. When he finally closed the book – she saw by the cover that it was a volume of folk stories in German – he grinned as he saw his own likeness staring up at him.

'My goodness,' he said, turning the pad to face him, 'you are clever! You've even made me look prepossessing, if not downright handsome.' He smiled up at her. 'Do you really see me like that?'

She nodded and added a few sweeping additions: giving him a loose shirt-like blouse with full sleeves, a kerchief tied about his forehead, a balalaika held across his lap. She had got the proportions of the musical instrument wrong, but still it was easily recognizable. She looked at him. 'That's how I really see you.'

'A vagabond?'

'A gypsy.'

'My mother doesn't like anyone to know it, but she has gypsy blood in her veins. From long ago.' He regarded the portrait, head to one side. 'You're very discerning, young Kate. How can your parents not let you go to art college with talent like that?'

She looked away to where the players were collecting stray balls, going off in twos and threes to the clubhouse. The sound of their voices was clear in the still afternoon.

Seeing her discomfort, he said quietly, 'If you can't go to college, why don't you try night school? I'm sure there must be classes that would benefit you.'

'I'd thought of that. But it doesn't start until the winter.'

64

'Something to look forward to.' His voice was teasing and she blushed.
'My parents don't like me going out in the dark.'

'Don't look for excuses. I could always come over and walk with you.'

She could find no answer to that. He packed his book away with the
flask, buckled the leather straps on the satchel and slid out from behind
the table. Slinging the satchel over one shoulder, he looked at her. 'The
offer stays open if you're interested. Now, I'd better be going. I've still
got things to do for my mother. Are you coming?'

'I think I'll stay for a little while.' She was in no hurry to get back to the
house to listen to the inane comments from Gerry Patrick about the way
Daddy was laying out the back garden. It was a very warm afternoon and
drops of sweat had beaded her father's brow. In contrast, their lodger
reclined comfortably in a canvas chair on the small slabbed area,
watching Samuel with a critical eye.

She'd seen the way her father's lips had tightened, felt sure he would be
goaded into saying something rude. But the moment had passed when
her mother agreed with their lodger's comments, gazing at Daddy
disdainfully.

Kate had collected her pad and pencils and hurried away, not wanting
to hear the outcome of the difference of opinion.

She could see where the groups of young people emerged from the
clubhouse, carrying drinks, searching for a cool spot in which to sit. Most
of the shady places were already taken. Kate saw the dark-haired girl and
her escort making for the abandoned railway carriage; heard him exclaim
in answer to her objections that there were spiders and goodness knows
what else in the old carriage, 'With me around, you shouldn't be afraid of
spiders.'

She heard the girl giggle. 'No, only of you.'

'Now, is that a nice way to talk to your one and only! I thought you liked
being alone with me.'

'I do.' Kate heard the swish of their feet in the long grass. 'Come on,
then. But behave yourself, Guy Ferris. I don't want any of that – well, you
know.'

'I *don't* know. You'll have to explain it to me. Or better still, *show* me.'
Another giggle.

They were only yards away and obviously seeking privacy in the old
carriage. Suddenly flustered, Kate rose to her feet. She gathered her
things about her, then looked around for a means of escape. There was
only one entrance: the doorway which they were approaching. She'd feel
a right idiot if they came upon her now. She had no right to be here in the
first place, even though she wasn't doing any harm. Would Guy Ferris
see it like that or report her to the authorities? She didn't particularly
want to find out.

She scrambled along to the other end of the carriage, remembering the tiny kitchen-like compartment obviously meant for the dining-car attendant. There was a small sink, yellowed with age, things that scurried underfoot as she entered. The space was so limited she couldn't bear to close the door, feeling claustrophobic already.

Standing there, holding her breath, she listened to the couple's voices, their movements as they settled down on one of the seats. The girl said, 'I told you, *no!*'

The youth's voice was a low murmur. 'You didn't say that the other night in your daddy's car.'

'No, and I was immediately sorry I hadn't.'

'I can't believe that. You seemed to enjoy it enough at the time. You know you liked this . . . and this . . .'

There was silence. Kate could hear their breathing, the girl's protests becoming weaker, her cries of 'No!' carrying less weight.

Kate risked a peek. The nuns had skimmed over the facts of life, as they coyly put it, but the girls talked in the dormitories. Crudely put as they had been, her schoolfriends' descriptions had disgusted her.

What she saw now brought bright-red flushes to her cheeks. Hastily she stepped back, felt something crawl up her leg. Panicking completely, she screamed.

The next moment the door was wrenched fully open. Guy Ferris stood there, his mouth tightened in a straight, angry line.

'What on earth do you think you're doing? Who are you? What are you doing here, hiding like this?'

He looked about Paul's age, although where Paul was so dark, Guy was fair. Pale-blue eyes blazed at her as she tried to think up answers to his questions. Her pad and pencils had fallen to the floor and she bent to retrieve them, never once taking her eyes off him.

'Well, come on, I'm waiting.' There was all the arrogance of a public school and money in his voice. Behind him the girl had been busy readjusting her short skirt. Now, brushing her hair behind her ears, she came forward to join him. Peering over his shoulder, her gaze examined Kate critically. 'Who is she?'

'How the hell do I know, Lottie. You do ask the silliest questions. Someone, I would say, who has positively no right to be here. Come on, you,' and he prodded Kate in the chest with one forefinger, 'what's your game?' Then, raspingly, 'What's the matter, cat got your tongue?'

'She doesn't look like a member,' said the girl. 'Can't say I've ever seen her before.'

Kate drew a deep breath. 'I'm not a member. I sometimes come here to sketch. I'm not doing any harm, nobody uses this place any more . . .'

Rudely, the youth grasped her shoulder and pulled her out into the narrow corridor. 'Let's have a look at you,' he said. His gaze fell to the pad. 'Sketching, you say?' His lips twisted. 'Sure you weren't sketching *us*, my friend and me? I'd really have to do something about that if you were.'

Kate shook her head. 'No, no. Of course not . . .'

'Let's have a look, then.' He tugged at the sketch pad and she allowed it to slip out from under her arm. Turning the pages, he came across the drawing she'd done of Paul. The girl craned her head, standing on tiptoe to see. 'I know him,' she exclaimed. 'That's the boy whose mother has a shop in the High Street. Paul something or other. They're foreign.'

Guy Ferris went on turning the pages, glancing at each sketch. 'Well, as long as it wasn't us,' he said. 'The fat *would* have been in the fire.'

Kate's flush deepened. She tilted her chin, staring at him defiantly. 'I wouldn't waste my time drawing the sort of things you were up to.'

'Oh, oh, saucy little kid we've got here, wouldn't you say?' He turned his head to grin at the girl. 'What do you reckon we ought to do with her?'

The girl giggled and said, 'Oh, I'm sure you'll think of something.'

'Wait for me outside,' he ordered. 'I'll handle this.'

Lottie scowled but went. Alone with Kate Guy stood grinning, clearly enjoying the whole little scene.

'Now, what *are* we going to do with you, eh? How about me putting you over my knee and giving you a good spanking? Judging from the rest of you, I bet you've got a delectable little bottom.'

Kate's cheeks flamed even redder, if that was possible. Tugging the pad back from him, she held it to her chest, as though it was a shield. 'You and whose army?' she said tightly. 'You lay one finger on me and there'll be trouble.'

Pushing past him, she fled from the carriage, hearing his mocking laughter behind her. It was a damn shame. She'd really enjoyed going there to do her sketching. It had seemed like a secluded little world, away from the nagging worries of her life.

She hurried from the fields, through the grove of trees and into Wesley Avenue. Back at number 138, Daddy was sitting where Mr Patrick had been, on the canvas chair. His face was washed out. Her heart ached for him. The good-looking man who had once been so jovial now appeared far older than his forty-odd years. There was no sign of her mother or their lodger. As Kate latched the side gate after her, in her haste catching her ankle on one pedal of the bike she'd recently acquired – twenty-five bob, second-hand and a bargain at the price – Samuel looked up and said, 'Ah, Katie. Had a nice afternoon, then?'

'Not bad.' She would never mention the incident in the deserted railway carriage to her father. Piling one worry on to another, that was all it would do. But she'd tell Paul the next time she saw him. She pitied the poor old lady who lived in the red-brick house, having a grandson like that.

She sank down on the sun-warmed paving near her father's feet, her drawing pad on her lap. 'All alone? Where's Mummy?'

'Mr Patrick's gone off in his car. Said he felt like a drive. Your mother went with him.' Seeing Kate frown, he went on, in tones of vindication, 'She gets restless, you know, here in the house all day. She's used to going out, meeting people. He said they could drive out into the country, stop somewhere for tea.'

'Why didn't you go with them?'

'I didn't feel like it. Besides, I wanted to be here when you came home.' He smiled, one hand moving gently over her golden-bright hair, letting the silken strands slide through his fingers.

Kate sighed. 'Well, I'd better see about making us a pot of tea, hadn't I?' She rose to her feet. At the open French doors, she looked back. 'What about a bit of that fruit cake Mummy bought the other day? I know there's a couple of slices left in the tin.'

Her father smiled, settling back in his chair, legs stretched out to the sun. 'Sounds just the ticket,' he said.

Chapter Eight

'You mean he actually threatened to smack you?'

Paul sounded outraged. It was a Saturday morning and people were out doing their weekly shopping. He had caught up with her at the top of Wesley Avenue, before she turned into the High Street. Impulsively, Kate had told him about the incident in the old carriage. She nodded. 'He did. I wished I'd gone back with you then, believe me.'

'Bloody cheek!' Paul's expression was sympathetic. 'But don't let him upset you, Kate.'

'Don't worry, he won't. God, he's such a pompous ass.'

Paul couldn't have agreed more. 'As I said, ignore him. He seems obsessed with being disagreeable.'

Kate grinned. 'Maybe he's jealous.'

'What?'

'Perhaps he resents your good looks.'

'I wouldn't call myself good looking.'

'Yes, you could. You're a nice person for a start, friendly and generous. You help your mother as much as you can. And you have a very strong personality.'

Paul frowned. 'Now you *are* pulling my leg.'

'Possibly.'

They laughed.

Reverting to Kate's complaint, Paul said, 'All the same, I think you should tell your father. He does have a right to know. And the old lady should be informed just what her darling grandson is up to.'

Kate shook her head. 'No. Daddy's got enough on his plate without having to fight my battles.'

'I suppose I should feel honoured that you decided to tell *me*, then. Although I still say he can't be allowed to get away with talking to young girls like that.'

Kate's lips pursed, and she looked thoughtful. 'Pity, though. He's quite the most good-looking boy I've ever met.' Not that she'd seen many, she reminded herself, but that blond hair, almost as pale as her own, and his blue eyes were very attractive.

'Shame his manners don't match his appearance then,' Paul

69

murmured. 'Looks are only skin deep, Kate. He's a thoroughly nasty piece of work, believe me. Oh, he can be charming when it pleases him but don't let yourself be fooled by that. Again, it's only skin deep.'

Lips still pursed, she turned her head to look at him. 'You sound as if you've had a run-in with him at some time. Have you?'

'I should say so. He came into my mother's shop one day demanding to buy the bracelet which the model in the window was wearing. When my mother explained that it was fake jewellery, for display purposes only, he became quite abusive.

'It's just as well I was in the shop at the time and heard it all, otherwise I think he could have got really nasty. As it was, I came out and repeated what my mother had said, that it was fake and kept in the shop merely to complement the dress on the model. I don't think anyone had ever denied him anything before.'

Kate laughed. 'Maybe his granny!'

'Possibly. But he looked like thunder.'

'What on earth did he want it for? A fake thing like that?'

Paul shrugged. 'Would you believe, a gift for his grandmother on her birthday. Although the bracelet was quite pretty – fake emeralds, cut-glass, really, set in a metal that looked like gold, my mother has a drawerful of things such as that in her storeroom – I don't think his grandmother would have relished having her wrist go green after wearing it a few times.'

'You should have let him have it just out of spite.'

'I thought of that, but my mother murmured something about the old lady being a potential customer and that it wouldn't have made sense to place the shop in a bad light. As my mother explained to me afterwards – a wise businesswoman is my mama – the old lady wasn't short of a bob or two and she had to buy her clothes from somewhere.' He grinned. 'My mother is ever hopeful that one day she will achieve great things. Keeping at it as she does, I can't see anything stopping her. She really is tireless, Kate, working at it all day and for most of the night.'

Kate nodded. 'Of course. But you said, that time in the carriage, that the old lady never went out. Would she ever need new clothes?'

'Oh, once the little turd is home from his grand school, she comes out of her shell and goes gallivanting about with him. I've never seen them, I don't frequent the sort of places they visit, but I hear she dresses to kill.' He grimaced. 'Even if the dresses *are* twenty years out of fashion.'

Kate thought of the modest suburb in which they lived, the lack, except for the cinemas and pubs, of entertainment. Where would a young man take his grandmother on an evening out? As though reading her mind, Paul said, 'There's an ancient Rolls Royce they keep parked in a garage behind the house. Only brought out when *he's* at home. Otherwise there's the tube. Handy for London and the West End.'

She recalled standing looking up at the detached house, and remembered the wide tarred driveway that led, presumably, to the back and the garage. 'Did your mother ever manage to meet the old lady?' she asked, stepping to one side on the busy High Street to avoid a young woman pushing a pram with a whining toddler trailing a few steps behind.

He shook his head. 'No, we've still to have that honour. And if she's anything like her grandson I'm not sure that I want to. Even if it does mean extra business for my mother.'

Primly, Kate said, 'You shouldn't hold grudges in life. The nuns always taught us to forgive our enemies . . .'

'Love thy neighbour!' he grinned. 'Would you have forgiven *him* if he'd actually carried out his threat and smacked your – ahem, bottom?'

She flushed scarlet, hoping nobody in the passing crowds had heard him. Nose in the air, she said, 'He wouldn't have dared.'

Paul laughed. 'Don't count on it. You're still a child – still a little girl who has a lot to learn about the male sex. None of us can be trusted.' He turned his head to leer at her, playfully. 'Didn't your nuns ever warn you about that?'

She didn't like it when he referred to her as a little girl. 'The nuns warned us about a lot of things. Among the top ten was how devious the male sex can be, especially when they want something they can't have. Anyway, I don't want to talk about it any more.' She looked up at him. 'Where were you going, anyway?'

'I've got to call in at Mr Shipton's for a few things for my mother, and then the shop. Where were you off to?'

Kate had intended to take a leisurely stroll around Woolworths. It was her favourite occupation, next to her sketching. A shilling burned a hole in her pocket. Daddy had bought a second-hand gramophone for five shillings and sixpence out of his first week's wages. She wondered now if she should buy that new Bing Crosby record she'd heard on the wireless, or the latest issue of *Moviegoer*. Her mother had said that the magazine, filled with film stars and Hollywood gossip, was a waste of time. Rubbish. But how else was she to keep up with which film star was dating who if she didn't read it?

The nuns would never have permitted such a magazine on the convent premises. The fact that she could now purchase and read it quite openly, even if Mummy did turn up her nose fastidiously over its contents, made her little excursions to the High Street an adventure.

'Oh, nowhere special.' She could always pop into Woolworths on the way home. 'Why don't I come and see your mother? I'd love to meet her.'

They had reached the grocer's shop where she'd first set eyes on him. He stopped outside the front door and looked down at her. 'All right. I won't be a minute in here.'

The bell jangled as he pushed the door open and went inside, followed by Kate. Mr Shipton was busy serving an elderly woman. He stood behind the glassed-in dairy products counter, using a strand of wire to cut a huge lump of pale-yellow cheese from a slab. Placing it upon the piece of greaseproof paper spread across his palm, he offered it for inspection to the woman.

'That all right, ducks?'

The woman nodded. 'And some butter while you're at it, Mr Shipton. Half a pound will do.'

The grocer paused for a moment in his handling of the cheese and smiled across at Kate. 'Be with you in a moment, my love.' Paul he ignored completely.

From the side of her mouth she hissed, 'Don't you wish there was another grocer's shop in the street so you wouldn't have to come here?'

'Another grocer's shop wouldn't give us discount.' He spoke softly, so that only she could hear, and grinned down into her eyes. 'Don't let it worry you. It doesn't me. It's like water off a chicken's back to me.'

'Duck's back,' she giggled. 'I love it when you get your words wrong. You're so funny.'

'Actually, I'm very proud of my English,' he said complacently. 'Not often do I get it wrong. But if it amuses the children then I will continue to do so.'

There he went again, making another dig at her youth.

Kate wondered if he had any girlfriends. She'd never seen him with one or heard him speak of any. And yet a boy with his dark, brooding good looks, well, surely there must be someone?

Girls *must* be interested in him. Julie would undoubtedly have said, in her fake American accent, that with those smouldering eyes and jet-black hair, he sure was one handsome hunk of male. Julie considered herself an authority on boys.

Mr Shipton finished with his customer and turned to her. Still ignoring Paul, he said, 'Well, love, what's it to be today? A nice piece of cheese for your ma? Or we've got a batch of fresh raisin bread in. Lovely with butter and damson jam.'

Paul pushed her gently to one side. 'I require some tea, Mr Shipton. I think half a pound will do. And a bag of sugar and maybe a loaf of that raisin bread you recommend so highly.'

'If you think you can barge in, acting like a bloody earl, you've got another think coming,' said Mr Shipton sourly. 'I 'appened to be speaking to the young lady, not you.'

'Ah, but the young lady does not require anything today, Mr Shipton.' Paul smiled. 'Surely you have not got such a chip on your shoulder that you would refuse to serve me?'

Clearly provoked by the undisguised sarcasm in Paul's voice, the grocer opened his mouth and shouted, 'Ruthie!' The curtain covering a door behind the counter was pushed aside and the girl, like a timid little mouse, appeared. She was immediately sent scurrying for the required items.

Clearly nervous about something, she spilt the sugar on the floor, earning a hail of abuse from Mr Shipton, and fumbled so with the change that the grocer snatched the coins from her and dealt with it himself. As they left the shop, they could hear his voice lecturing the girl about keeping her mind on her work.

Kate grimaced. 'I'd hate to work for *him*. It must be sheer hell. I wonder what he did to make her so nervous in the first place.'

'Knowing Ruthie, it was probably more something *she* did. She's not – how shall I put it – not exactly a prize specimen, is she? Shall I amuse you again by trotting out one of my famous adages and saying, tuppence short of sixpence.'

Kate laughed, knowing full well he was teasing her. 'Tuppence short of a shilling,' she smiled. 'I should think working for Mr Shipton would reduce anyone to a gibbering wreck. It seems to me that all she needs is a little gentle encouragement. I'm sure she does her best.'

'She has to. Her father would beat the living daylights out of her if she came home sacked.'

They had commenced their walk towards his mother's shop and Kate turned her head to look at him. 'You seem to know an awful lot about the people hereabouts. Do you go around asking questions of everyone, besides me?'

'I am interested in people, if that's what you mean. If they want to tell me about themselves, I listen. If they don't, I don't force it.' He stopped walking, hefting the brown paper bag containing the groceries from his right arm to his left. His right hand on the shop door knob, he said, 'Are you coming in? You said you wanted to meet my mother. I'll amaze you by making the best cup of tea you've ever tasted and we'll have some of Mr Shipton's famous raisin bread. Although I'm afraid there won't be any butter or jam.'

Kate smiled and followed him in.

Ever since she'd first stood outside that shop window, fascinated by what she saw, she had wanted to meet Rosa Konig. Now, peering about her, she saw that the shop was empty, although she could hear voices coming from the open door of the back room. 'Mother will be with a customer,' Paul explained. 'That is where she does the fitting. If you'll excuse me, I shall go into the cupboard we call a kitchen and prepare the tea. You will be all right?'

'Of course.'

'My mother should not be long.'

Kate nodded and said again: 'Of course.'

Left by herself, the first thing she did was to inspect the window display from the inside. A curtain concealed it from the shop interior. Drawing this to one side, she peeped round the edge.

This week the model was dressed in a heavy silken gown in an exotic colour combination of crimson, purple and saffron. Strings of beads adorned her neck, hanging to the waist. Instead of the white-painted wheelbarrow, this time there was a large wickerwork birdcage with an exotic-looking parrot in it. Not a real parrot, Kate saw to her relief, but a very artistically stuffed bird. She caught her breath at the colours of the silk. Who would have thought that combining colours so dissimilar would have been so effective? She must try it herself sometime in one of her sketches. Perhaps she would draw Mummy lounging on a chair on the patio, wearing a dress of the same colours. Not that she had a dress of those colours, but Kate knew they would remain in her mind, clear and joyous. She would have no problem duplicating them from memory.

Behind her, she heard a voice call, 'Paul! Was that you, Paul? Come in for a moment, will you?'

The tiny kitchen was obviously out of earshot. Kate hesitated, then, letting the curtain drop back into place, went to the open door of the back room. Hesitating on the threshold of the room she could see Rosa Konig kneeling before a stout woman who stood with a bored expression on her face.

Suddenly aware of Kate's presence, Rosa looked up and frowned. She had been pinning the hem of the frock the woman had on. Her mouth full of pins, she removed them, sticking each one into the velvet pad strapped to her wrist by a band of black ribbon. 'And who might you be, young lady? Where is Paul? I thought I heard him come in.'

Kate hardly heard her question. Fascinated, she was staring at the work surface under the window which was covered with cuttings of fabric, bits of chalk and a pattern weighted down by large scissors. Beside it was a desk with a sketch pad and a vase full of crayons. Sketches were pinned around the wall and two tailor's dummies stood to one side. Kate longed to step closer and examine them all.

Slightly flustered, realizing that Rosa was looking at her, she said, 'I'm Kate, Paul's friend. He's making the tea. Do you want me to call him for you?'

The kneeling woman smiled. 'I don't think we need to disturb him then. And I daresay we could all do with a cup of tea.'

Timidly, Kate said, 'Maybe I could help, Mrs Konig? What did you want Paul to do?'

Dark eyes twinkled, regarding her shrewdly. 'Yes, maybe you can. I require another pair of hands to hold the dress up from the shoulders while I alter the waistline.' Playfully, she shook her finger at her customer. 'We've put on weight, haven't we, Mrs Portman?'

The woman simpered. 'A mite. A few ounces only. It's difficult not to when one is invited to so many functions.'

The waistline altered to Rosa's satisfaction, and still no sign of Paul, she handed Kate a notepad and pencil. 'Perhaps, my dear, you would be good enough to take down Mrs Portman's new measurements as I call them out?'

'I'd be glad to,' answered Kate, smiling. She felt entirely at ease in the atmosphere of the dress shop. Although at first Rosa Konig had seemed dark and forbidding, already Kate could feel an attachment forming between them.

She couldn't wait to get home and begin surrendering to paper the ideas that jostled in her brain.

The tape measure that hung around Rosa's neck was put into service and figures were called out. Kate wrote busily, lifting her gaze once to see Paul standing in the doorway. Leaning negligently against the door jamb, he grinned widely. Catching her eye, he gave an approving nod, as if to say: 'That's my girl!' A warm glow went through her.

Divested of her unfinished frock, promises ringing in her ears that it would be ready on time, Mrs Portman went happily on her way. Hanging the garment on its hanger, Rosa Konig looked over her shoulder to where her son and Kate were enjoying a cup of tea.

Joining them, she sat down on the chair Paul nobly vacated. He handed her a cup and saucer and she smiled, looking first at him and then at Kate.

'Now perhaps you will introduce us properly, no? I am afraid, my dear, Pauli can be very careless at times. So soon he is forgetting the rules laid down by his father.'

'I'm sorry, Mother.' Paul hurried into the introductions. 'You were busy with Mrs Portman and I didn't want to interrupt. This is Kate Linley. She and her family have not long come to live in the neighbourhood.'

Rosa inclined her head. 'How do you do, my dear! I am pleased to meet you. You made an ideal substitute for my forgetful son.' She finished her cup of tea and then rose, placing the empty cup and saucer on the counter. 'Now, I have work to do. And I'm afraid, my dear, Paul has too.' She smiled at Kate as though begging her forgiveness.

Kate felt herself flush. The nuns had been firm about a person never outstaying their welcome. 'I'm sorry,' she said. 'I'll have to be going anyway. My mother doesn't like me to be away for too long.'

'Prudent woman. But then, what harm can come to you, here in this very free country? Unlike my own poor land where the devil rules and everyone is so afraid.'

At the door, Kate turned once more to say, 'Goodbye, Mrs Konig. Thank you for the cup of tea. It was so nice meeting you.'

'You must make Pauli bring you again.'

Paul stood watching until she'd crossed the road and turned into Woolworths. Behind him, his mother called, 'Pauli? Don't go off again. There are deliveries I want you to make.'

Kate had vanished in the crowds. Paul sighed and rejoined his mother.

Kate's mind was made up for her because the latest copy of *Moviegoer* magazine wasn't in yet. She spent sixpence of her precious shilling on Bing crooning 'It's June in January', then wandered about the busy store, gazing longingly at the cosmetic counter; the lipsticks, eye make-up, rouges, boxes of powder. She lifted a tiny blue glass bottle of perfume – 'Midnight in Paris' – and sniffed it appreciatively. She couldn't wait to grow up. To be seventeen. To be able to use these implements of beauty, boast of a boy like Paul for a real sweetheart, not just a friend.

Summer was going so quickly. Once she had found a job, the process of growing up would come as quickly as summer had fled. As she emerged from the large store into the sunlight and turned down Wesley Avenue, she tried to imagine what it would be like to be loved. And to her mortification she found she had cast Guy Ferris in the role . . .

Chapter Nine

Kate was delighted to receive a letter from Julie saying that her parents had given their permission for her to visit Kate for a week. 'A whole week!' Julie enthused. 'What fun! I've got so much to tell you. I've been saving it up for weeks. Sister Hosea and that new young priest were caught together in the old summerhouse at the end of the garden and you never heard such a ballyhoo in your life . . .'

Kate smiled at Julie's enthusiastic way of relating bits of gossip about other people. Not in a spiteful way, though; she really thought Kate would be interested.

She met the early-afternoon train, buying a platform ticket and peering anxiously along the platform for the first sign of Julie. After squeals of greeting, the two girls gazed at each other intently, noting the changes. Of the two, Julie seemed to have grown up more than Kate. Her breasts pushed the front of her summer frock out in the most enviable fashion. Kate gazed down at her own chest. Still as flat as a pancake! Reading her expression, Julie said, 'If you wore a bra you'd be better.'

Kate flushed. 'Mummy would never permit that.' She glanced about at the people pushing past on the crowded platform. 'And don't go using words like that in public.'

The irrepressible Julie hooted with laughter. 'You mean bra? I can see I'm really going to have my work cut out this week, Kate Linley. You've grown into a positive prude these last two months.'

'No I haven't – well, my mother's always lecturing me on how to behave.' Kate laughed. 'I think she thinks I'll fall into bad ways.'

Julie grinned. 'Sounds interesting. You didn't let on in your letters that there were places around here where you could fall into bad ways.'

'There aren't. Not that I've discovered, anyway.'

'Well, there's still time.'

They had climbed the station steps and were walking along the High Street. 'Tell me,' Julie went on, 'what plans have you got for me for the week?'

'There's the pictures, and I've got a bicycle – I daresay we could borrow one for you. The countryside is quite nice and not too far away. Not a patch on Kent, of course, but not bad.'

77

As they walked they came abreast of Rosa's dress shop. Kate stopped, as usual interested to see the window display presented to the public.

This week the model was dressed in a simple knee-length dress of a delicate shade of green. A long chiffon scarf of pale tangerine was draped loosely about the neckline. White sandals with Cuban heels and four narrow straps across the instep completed the picture. A flimsy silk sunshade in the same colour as the dress rested over the model's shoulder. She looked the picture of elegance, ready for afternoon tea in the setting of some magnificent garden.

Julie regarded the display with interest. 'Hmmm, pricey,' she commented. 'Don't tell me you can afford to shop here?'

'Dream on,' said Kate wryly. 'I just wanted to show you Rosa's. The mother of a boy I know runs it. She makes all her own gowns – don't ask me how, she must work day and night. She is a Paris-trained couturière. Sometimes,' she couldn't help adding, nonchalantly, 'she lets me help her.' A small fib, one she needn't admit to Father O'Hanlan when she went to confession on Friday evening. She hadn't been in the shop since that first time with Paul.

Julie looked impressed. 'Fab! Is she French?'

'No, German. I'll take you in sometime and introduce you.'

Julie looked even more impressed. 'What's the son like? How did you meet him?'

They rejoined the throng of shoppers moving purposefully along the street. As they walked Kate explained about Paul and how they sometimes met in the fields of the Railway Club. She told of the disturbing encounter with Guy Ferris and the girl.

'Well, for someone who is supposed to have been miserable ever since she came here, you don't seem to be doing so badly,' observed Julie. 'What's he like, your charming neighbour?'

'He's not really a neighbour. The house where he lives is a little way down from us. As to what he's like, well . . .' Mentally she conjured up the fair hair, the pale-blue eyes that had gazed at her with such disdain. 'He probably could be quite charming – the girl he was with seemed to think so – but it didn't show that afternoon when he caught me hiding in that cubbyhole.' Her mouth twisted. 'I tell you, Julie, I was never so scared in all my life.'

Julie laughed. 'You, scared?'

'Well, maybe more humiliated. Anyway, Paul doesn't like him. He had some trouble with him once in the shop. I'll tell you about it later. He describes his coming home for the holidays as "creeping out from under his stone". I'm afraid Paul's got a very poor opinion of him.'

Julie looked thoughtful. 'I think I'll have to cast my eye over this Guy Ferris and see if I can't change his opinion of *you*, young Kate.'

'I'm not interested in his opinion. In fact, it wouldn't bother me if I never set eyes on him again.'

Another fib that should – but wouldn't – be admitted at confession. She very much wanted to see him again.

The two girls reached number 138 and Kate pushed the gate wide, allowing Julie to go before her. She closed it securely after her – dogs allowed to wander came into the garden if it wasn't shut, fouling Dad's new lawn. She let fall the polished brass knocker, rubbed vigilantly every Saturday morning before she did the rest of the Indian brassware. Monica Linley opened the door.

She had met only briefly the girl who stood now with her daughter. She hadn't known what to expect but she had to admit that this girl didn't look as though she would be a bad influence on Kate. She knew about Julie's father and his responsible job and was impressed.

Later, upstairs in Kate's bedroom, Julie brought her up to date with all the news. 'What happened to Sister Hosea?' Kate demanded excitedly. 'Did they both relinquish their vows and go off together?'

Julie laughed. 'I hate to pour cold water on that romantic streak of yours, but no, they didn't go off together. Not long afterwards Father Damian was packed off to another place and little Sister Hosea stayed, pale and languishing, with us.'

Kate shook her head. 'I don't think I'd like to become a nun.'

'I don't suppose you need to worry too much about that, ducks. You're not one for taking orders, are you? Remember the time you . . .' The two girls fell to reminiscing over the various times each had fallen into bad grace with Mother Superior. Julie felt in her handbag and to Kate's surprise – and faint shock – produced a packet of cigarettes.

Airily lighting one with a match, Julie leaned back on the bed, supporting herself with her arms, and puffed smoke into the air. Tilting her head so that the small white cloud drifted ceilingwards, she nodded towards the packet. 'Go ahead, help yourself. Don't tell me you haven't been seduced by the noxious weed yet?'

Against her better judgement, Kate accepted one of the small white tubes and allowed Julie to light it. The resultant coughing had them in stitches, clutching their sides until there was a knock on the door; and before either girl could react, Monica Linley poked her head inside. Her nose twitched, sniffing the air. Caught red-handed, Kate returned her look with an equanimity she didn't feel.

Monica's face remained expressionless. She said, 'Kate, didn't you tell your friend we think you're too young to smoke? You know your father doesn't like it.'

'Sorry, Mummy.'

'I suggest you put it out then. I just popped in to tell you tea will be ready in five minutes. Wash your hands and come downstairs.'

As the door closed behind her, Julie said, 'Ooops! Sorry! I forgot that not all parents are as liberal as mine.'

Kate opened the window wide and tossed her cigarette out. 'She won't blame you, she'll blame me. I don't suppose she'll ever change.'

Julie joined her and threw away her own stub of cigarette. 'Then I'll tell her they were my cigarettes, that I persuaded you against your better judgement.'

'Better to leave it. She'll only show off in front of Mr Patrick, putting on the caring mother act.'

'Who is Mr Patrick?'

'Someone they met in the hotel in Victoria. He loaned Mummy his car to drive down to the convent.'

'And he *followed* you here?'

'He came visiting and persuaded my mother to let him have the spare bedroom, said he hated the bed-and-breakfast place where he was staying.' Kate pulled a face. 'I don't blame him. It *was* pretty grim.' But why did he have to choose *us*? she thought.

After washing their hands and faces and dabbing some of Julie's Devon Violets perfume on their wrists and behind their ears, they went down to tea. Mr Patrick sat by the fireplace, the early-evening paper spread out before him, and Kate seethed to see him seated in her father's chair. He lowered the pages as they came into the room, peering round the side, contemplating with unconcealed approval the youthful charms of the new female in the house.

Over tea, charm oozed from him like oil and Kate was shocked to see Julie flutter her eyelashes, reacting to his fawning in a way her friend would never have believed possible.

She said as much to Julie later, when they were in the garden picking some early peas for supper. 'I just can't believe you could be taken in by that man! All that gushing and simpering. I find him totally repulsive.'

Julie reached for a handful of pods high up on the wigwam of canes Kate's father had erected to support the plants – they had grown so fast and so tall it had delighted him to just look at them – and popped open a couple. Tossing the small sweet peas into her mouth, she said, 'Couldn't you tell I was practising?'

Kate blinked. 'Practising for what?'

'For when I leave school. Let's face it, Kate, we don't get all that many chances to pursue our womanly arts. When something new in trousers comes along you grab it with both hands.'

Kate giggled. 'Not literally, I hope.'

Monica looked out from the kitchen, smiling as the wave of laughter drifted on the warm summer air. She pushed the window open to its widest extent, hearing Julie say, 'I'm glad to see you haven't lost your sense of humour. For a moment there I was thinking you had.'

Leaning out, Monica called, 'Don't be long with the peas. I want to get them on soon. The rest is almost ready.' She watched with a kind of envy as the girls turned towards her. Their faces were flushed with laughter and summer heat, their youthful beauty more noticeable because it was duplicated. She hadn't missed the attention Gerry had paid to Kate's friend at tea, and was dismayed at the slight pang of jealousy that stirred in her.

Maybe the girl wasn't as innocent as she looked! After all, there was that cigarette. Who knew what other vices she might have?

On Sunday, Monica excused herself from mass and the two girls went alone. Kate and her mother had taken to using the short cut Paul had told her about. It really did cut off quite a bit of walking on hard pavements, besides being pretty. The narrow stream wandered through the trees while the grass on each side was lush with buttercups and columbine.

The stepping stones, half a dozen flat stones strategically placed, enabling one to cross from one side of the stream to the other, were Mum's only objection. With the high-heeled shoes she insisted on wearing to church she would cling on to Kate's hand for dear life and wobble her way across.

It had rained heavily during the night; one of those summer storms that are a blessing, cooling the air and refreshing the gardens, and the stream today gurgled along merrily.

Few people used the path. They had almost reached the place where they came out behind the rectory garden when they heard someone call: 'Here, girls, come and see this.'

They looked at each other, brows raised. Julie said, 'What do you suppose it could be?'

Kate groaned theatrically. 'Maybe a body, stabbed in the back and left lying all night in the rain.'

Inquisitively, they pushed their way through the trees to where a man stood, back towards them, head bent. Curious, they edged closer. He looked like a tramp in his shabby clothing. It didn't seem in the least unusual for him to be in the woods. And then he turned. His trousers gaped open and he was holding something in his hand which he waved at them. 'A beauty, ain't it?' he grinned. 'Want a feel? I shan't charge you anyfink.'

Even Julie was deprived of speech. For long moments they stared at the pink snakelike thing, then, releasing the breath that was making her feel dizzy, Julie said, scorn in her voice, 'Oh, put it away, do. I've seen bigger things than that in a piece of cheese.'

He flushed an angry red at the insult to his manhood. 'Oh, you have, have you? Maybe you'd like to see it closer up then? Real close . . .'

As he began to advance towards them, still exposed, Kate took her friend's arm and pulled her away. They ran, shrieking with laughter.

Ran until they reached the steps of the church. Then stopped to catch their breath. 'God,' said Julie, 'the phantom flasher! Who'd have believed it!'

She produced a small handkerchief and they wiped the film of sweat from their upper lips, patted their hair, then walked into the church with a quiet sedateness that would have done credit to the most severe nun.

The experience had shocked Kate and she told herself that in future she would have to keep a sharp lookout for the vagrant. She should tell her father, but she knew he would insist on informing the police.

It was over, done with, not worth worrying about. And with Julie's sassy parting remark, they had come out on top . . .

Mass over, Father O'Hanlan intoned the blessing and with the rest of the congregation the two girls wandered out into the summer air. As they stood on the front steps, waiting for a break in the crowd being greeted by the old priest, Kate saw Paul Konig approaching them.

Inclining her head towards Julie, she hissed from the side of her mouth, 'You know that boy I told you about, the one whose mother has the dress shop in the High Street? Well, that's him over there . . .'

Now Paul stopped before them and Kate smiled and said, 'Hello. It's unusual to see you at church.'

'My mother had so much work to catch up with that she couldn't manage it today. So, for my sins, she asked me to make an appearance in her place.'

His eyes lingered on Julie. Kate said, 'You haven't met Julie, have you? She was my best friend at the convent. She's staying with me for a few days.'

'Lucky Julie.' To Julie's vast amusement, he bent and lifted her hand, carrying it to his lips. 'Enchanted.' His lips pressed against the suntanned skin. 'And I'm Paul Konig. But I suppose Kate has already told you about me. '

Kate grinned. 'Cheek! No need to sound so conceited. I only told her the bad things.'

Following her friend's line of teasing, Julie said lightly, 'That's all I'm interested in. I can't stand goody-goody boys.'

Laughing together, they dipped their heads politely to Father O'Hanlan as they walked down the shallow steps. Paul judiciously contrived to have a girl on each side. Casually slipping his hands through their arms, he said, 'What do you two gorgeous creatures plan on doing for the rest of the morning?'

'Nothing much. Whatever our fancy suggests.'

'Then may I offer you morning coffee? And I do believe there is some apple strudel my mother made the other day. You haven't lived until you've tasted my mother's apple strudel.' He turned his head, smiling down into each sun-flushed face. 'Sounds tempting, no?'

'Sounds tempting, yes,' murmured Kate. 'As long as we leave enough space for Mummy's roast lamb.' She'd tried to imagine the place where Paul lived, wondering if it was as bad as he had described. But if he was confident enough to invite them home then it must be passable. 'But won't your mother be there? I mean, if as you said she's busy, she might not relish visitors . . .'

'My mother's at the shop. She keeps most of her trimmings there and today it seems she has set herself the task of sewing dozens of tiny black jet beads, bugles she calls them, on to the bodice of a gown she has promised by tomorrow. Unfortunately, I wasn't able to help her with this.' He held out his hands, large, the fingers square-tipped. 'There are many things I can help her with, but there she sketches the cable.'

Julie blinked and caught Kate's eye. Kate smiled. 'He's always doing that,' she said. 'Confusing sayings. You mean, I take it, there she draws the line.'

And from the way he grinned, she wondered if he hadn't done it on purpose, knowing that it would amuse her and Julie.

They walked back along the woodland path, across the stepping stones, and Kate was relieved to see there was no sign of the tramp. The distasteful experience would remain a secret between her and Julie. She wouldn't even tell Paul about it. She'd become used to telling him everything that happened these days. But she couldn't tell him that. Any more than she could her father. Describing it would be too embarrassing. Even thinking of it brought a brighter flush to her cheeks. Having no brothers, the male anatomy was a mystery to her. After what the vagrant had displayed, it all looked pretty disgusting . . .

As they skirted the club playing fields on their way towards the railway footbridge, they could see where people had begun to filter into the clubhouse. Tennis players; bowls players in their white panama hats; golfers who, in spite of the heat, still dressed in plus fours and bright Fair Isle pullovers.

The footbridge that crossed the railway tracks was an iron structure of unbelievable ugliness. Once painted a dark grey, now there was more rust than paint. They climbed the steep steps leading to the crossing, their footsteps echoing in the Sunday-morning stillness.

'There was a bridge such as this near the house where we lived in Berlin,' said Paul. 'As a small boy I would stand with my father, holding tightly to his hand, and wait for a train to pass beneath. The steam would rise, swirling about us, making everything around us unreal. I loved it. It was a special treat. And when the steam cleared, there was the blue sky again and the glorious view with the lake in the distance. And everything as it had always been.'

Julie remained silent, sensing an underlying sadness in his words.

And then the picture conjured up by Paul's words became reality. There was a rumbling of wheels on the iron track far below. Thick white smoke was discharged in a suffocating fog as the iron monster thundered beneath them on its way north.

Julie sneezed. 'Ugh! That smell really catches in my throat!'

Paul was remembering a dark-haired girl who had protested in almost the same words. He often wondered what had happened to Hilda Steinberg. They had lived next door to the Konigs and Hilda's father had been an analytical chemist working for one of the large Berlin pharmaceutical companies.

The place where Paul now lived was a four-storey block of flats erected years ago. Built for the workers, no attempt had been made to beautify it. Ugly then, it was hideous now. Dogs with their ribs showing nuzzled in dustbins. None had collars and most appeared to be strays.

Kate couldn't suppress a shudder. It would be fatal to catch Julie's eye. Paul guided them through a rounded archway where a flight of stone steps disappeared into the murky gloom. Kate thought it must look like this throughout the seasons, rain or shine. The walls were covered to waist height in beige-coloured tiles. Most of them were broken and some had been removed altogether by an enterprising tenant.

Climbing ahead of them, Paul turned to say, 'Welcome to Paradise Buildings. Whoever named it must have had a weird sense of humour.'

The soles of their shoes stuck to some sticky substance as they climbed and Kate could see where someone had dropped a jar of red jam. She tried not to let her face express the disgust she felt and knew Julie was doing the same. Further up on the staircase, children played, banging on the iron railing that served as a banister. The sound reverberated throughout the closed-in space like a throbbing headache.

Wryly, Paul said, 'There are good ideas, there are bad ideas and then there are some really awful ideas. And I think inviting you to my home was one of them.'

Julie murmured a half-hearted denial and Kate said, 'Nonsense! I've always wanted to see where you lived.'

His gaze was pitying. 'Well, now you have.' Taking a deep breath, he added, 'Come on, it's not much further. The next floor.'

Kate didn't know quite what she expected. She was surprised by the fastidiously neat room that Paul indicated was their 'parlour'. Cream linen covers hung protectively over the back of the settee and two armchairs. Beautifully embroidered, they were edged in strips of lace that appeared to be handmade. On the broad windowsill a green china pot held an aspidistra. The leaves had a gloss that told of tender loving care. In fact, the whole room expressed that sentiment.

Waving a hand towards two closed doors, Paul said, 'Besides this, we have two bedrooms and over there's the kitchen.' Kate had noticed what she presumed were toilets at the end of each landing. The smell emanating from them warned her not to ask.

Paul heaved at the bottom half of the window, pushing it up so that the warm breeze freshened the air. Rearranging the lace curtains, he turned to say, 'I'll put the kettle on. Make yourselves comfortable. Won't be a sec.'

Squeamishly, Julie examined the dark-red velvet settee before she sat down. She kept her views discreetly to herself, although Kate knew she was dying to say something. They sat together on the settee, on their best behaviour. Paul must never know how much the first sight of his home had shocked them. From below the open window, children screamed, dogs barked. Two women paused as they passed on the landing outside and discussed someone called Dora. Their voices were loud, their conversation sprinkled lavishly with obscenities.

Paul carried a tray in and placed it on the low table before them. 'Who's going to be aunty?' he remarked, looking from one to the other.

'Mother,' corrected Kate. She leaned forward. 'I'll pour.'

The coffee pot was silver, gracefully formed, and the cups and saucers, decorated with roses, were of the finest bone china. Obviously proud of them, Paul explained that the set was one of the few precious possessions they had been able to bring with them when they fled Germany. 'So be careful,' he warned, handing them each a plate on which rested a slice of apple-filled pastry. 'My mother would be heartbroken if anything should happen to them.'

Julie bit into the cake and groaned with pleasure. 'Delicious! Your mother must be an angel to be able to bake like this, and sew dresses too. Kate's told me of some of the things she's seen displayed in the shop window.' She tilted her head to one side coquettishly. 'You can't tell me you haven't inherited some tiny talent from her?'

'My talents, if any, are for the more mundane things. If I ever have the chance, I'd like to become a journalist.'

Kate sipped her coffee. 'And then you can go back and report on the things you saw in Germany?'

A shadow crossed darkly over his face. 'Yes. The world has still to hear the full story. Someone must do it.'

Julie broke in, 'My father says the camps they are building all over the country are a great idea. That they will do wonders for the people who are sent there.'

Paul's look was one of deep pity. 'If your father only knew, Julie.

Shall I tell you of a neighbour of ours, a Jewish father of a family of six? One night the Gestapo arrived and he was taken away. We heard later that he'd been sent to one of those camps. Shortly afterwards the rest of his family joined him. My mother, in her foolishness, watched for a letter or postcard every time the postman came. But there never was one.'

'Probably too busy to write,' said Julie. 'My father says they have them working in the fields and growing their own food. It must be a very healthy life.'

'Healthy?' Paul shook his head at her innocence. 'There was another time when I was coming home from school on the tram and I saw one of the lorries which the SA used to transport people they had taken into "protective custody".' He sketched two marks with his fingers. 'Suddenly, one of the prisoners, a young man only a few years older than myself whom I recognized as being a student at the school where my father taught, and bleeding from a deep wound in the head, jumped from the lorry on to the running board of our moving trolley. People were just coming home from work and the trolley was crowded, but the passengers helped the man and made a space for him. Nobody said anything and it was suddenly very still on the tram. The conductor acted as though he had noticed nothing. Only one old woman took out a handkerchief, wiped the blood from the young man's face and said in a loud voice, "It's a damned shame what these scoundrels think they can get away with."'

He drew a deep breath, gazing into his cup. 'No one contradicted her and no one prevented the young man from getting off at the next stop where he ducked into a dark doorway before the lorry, which was stuck in dense traffic, could catch up.'

'What happened to him?' Kate's eyes were wide, staring.

'We never knew. Such things were not reported in the newspapers. I told my father what I had seen and he made enquiries, made quite a bit of fuss, in fact. The boy's mother was a widow and he was her only son. She was desolate.'

There was a bleak silence, followed by Kate's soft whisper, 'And your father wasn't able to do anything?'

Paul stared at her. 'Just after supper a few nights later the doorbell rang. Four SS men stalked into the house and demanded that my father come with them at once. They offered no explanation. My father wasn't even allowed to say goodbye to my mother or me. After days of anguish, my mother went to see someone she knew in the police and was told that my father had been shot while attempting to escape. That was their version, anyway. I often wondered if they would have bothered to tell us if we hadn't asked. Sensing danger to herself and me, it was not long afterwards that my mother began to make plans for leaving our home.

We arrived in this country with very little money to our name, hence,' gesturing around the room, 'this dismal abode.'

The two girls exchanged looks and Kate gave a slight shake of her head. She'd guessed at the sadness in Paul's life, but it was beyond her imagination to comprehend such things.

For the rest of that week, the two girls enjoyed each other's company, cycling into the nearby countryside, and drinking copious cups of coffee in a snack bar favoured by other teenagers, where they put the world to rights and flirted mildly with boys at other tables. After Julie had gone, Kate fell back into her old routine. Autumn crept in with storms and bitterly cold winds. She missed the times spent in the old railway carriage with Paul, but the weather had turned too chilly for that, also she had no desire for another run-in with Guy Ferris. With the autumn came night school, and when her father supported her in her desire to attend, reluctantly Monica agreed.

Night school was a revelation to Kate. Classes were held once a week in the local school behind the church which Kate attended. For the first few weeks, Paul or her father walked with her, not liking her to be out alone.

Soon she made friends with girls who lived near her, and they were able to go in a group. For most of them it was a social event, a way to meet boys. The actual artwork was incidental. They thought Kate's enthusiasm slightly odd but admired her perseverance.

Soon it would be December, and the festive season would be upon them. The Linleys would be spending their first Christmas at Wesley Avenue, and the times when Kate was engulfed by nostalgia were becoming less and less frequent. She was still without a job but had been advised by some of her friends in the art class that the pre-Christmas rush offered temporary work in plenty.

Chapter Ten

Vacancies for sales girls for the Christmas rush were advertised at Woolworths. Without telling her mother, Kate applied and was accepted. She was told she would be shown how to work the till, give change and fetch stock from the storeroom when necessary. She knew that her mother would consider it inferior, but as she was constantly on about Kate sitting at home, doing nothing, surely she would be the last to complain.

When she did break the news her father beamed, delighted at his daughter's resoluteness. Monica had the grace to say, 'Well, I suppose it's better than nothing.' Kate ignored the implied criticism and went off that Monday morning feeling as though she was facing Everest, aglow with that same pioneering spirit.

The work was fascinating though tiring, entailing a lot of standing. Kate loved the huge storeroom with its multitude of goods. Being Christmas, the display of toys was top priority. They were packed in alluringly marked boxes: tin drums; dolls in their fancy lace-edged dresses; coloured rubber balls and boxes of crackers. After a busy day in the crowded store her feet ached, she had never felt so tired in her life, but the feeling of satisfaction made it all worthwhile. The salary was poor, though – twenty-five shillings a week, of which she gave her mother a pound.

To her disappointment she was initially assigned to the hardware department, selling such dull things as watering cans, tin baths and cooking pots. After a while, however, her pleasant disposition, the way she handled customers, was recognized, and she was moved to the toy counter.

Now that she was working, the arguments about her continuing night school raged fiercely, until finally Monica, frowning at the stubbornness of her young daughter, said fretfully, 'Oh, for goodness' sake, have it your own way. You usually do.'

Kate felt as though she had won another victory. She would come home from work, have a quick meal and then, wrapped warmly in a woollen scarf and her new winter coat, go out again into the dark and foggy night.

Aunt Norma came up to stay with them for Christmas, and any ill

89

feelings there may have been between Monica and her sister were carefully concealed. Kate escorted her aunt on a conducted tour of the new house, leaving out Mr Patrick's room, and Norma conceded it all seemed very comfortable.

'Bit different, though, from what you're used to,' she remarked, coming back down the stairs to join Monica and Samuel in the sitting room. Monica confessed that it was but that given time, she supposed, anyone could get used to it.

To Kate's relief and, she suspected, her father's, Mr Patrick had announced that he would be spending the festive season with friends. Catching Kate's eye, careful not to let his wife hear, Samuel muttered, 'Didn't know he had any!'

Kate laughed, turning it into a cough when her mother glanced round sharply. The family went in a group to midnight mass, the night cold and peaceful; the voices of a group of carol singers floating to them on the chill night.

'Silent Night, Holy Night. All is calm, all is bright . . .'

Kate thought of Paul and his mother, spending Christmas so far from home and old friends. She wondered what an old-fashioned German Christmas would be like. Perhaps not so very different from their own. After all, wasn't it Prince Albert who had first introduced the old German custom of the Christmas tree to England?

Then she thought of the Christmases of her childhood in India, when it was hot and sultry and they sat on the lawn beneath the shade tree with its flame-coloured blossoms. Soon Cook would appear to tell them dinner was ready. Despite the heat, Monica insisted on roast turkey and all the trimmings.

On Christmas morning, Kate sat before the fire in their small sitting room and gazed out on the bleak landscape of an English winter. It had seemed so different at the convent. Especially when it snowed, when the trees in the grounds were covered in white and icicles hung like glittering Christmas decorations from the branches. On the pavements of London, snow quickly turned to slush, grey and disgusting, and the buses smelled of bodies and wet clothing.

With Kate working, Aunt Norma had said what a pity it was that they wouldn't be able to visit Selfridges. 'We could have gone to see Father Christmas,' she said, smiling at Kate. 'Or do you consider yourself too old for that nonsense these days?'

Monica answered for her. 'Of course she is. Much too old.'

Not to be outdone, Aunt Norma said, 'Well, what about a pantomime? We could go one evening. Remember the times we went to the Palladium, Monica? Father used to love it, I think it was the high spot of Christmas for him.'

'Money wasn't a problem in those days,' Monica reminded her sharply. 'It is now. Samuel has yet to start earning a decent wage. Although I'm grateful for Kate's meagre contribution it doesn't go far.'

The words were spoken with a sharpness that made Kate flush. She turned her face away, gazing into the leaping flames. One hand twisted the bracelet that had arrived through the post from Julie. It was a narrow band of silver made in the image of a snake, its tail pressed into its mouth, the eyes tiny ruby-red stones. Her present to Julie had been a book, *Tess of the d'Urbervilles*, bought with saved pocket money.

She dug her hands into the sagging pockets of her cardigan, shivering as smoke puffed outwards from the coal fire as someone opened the back door and a blast of cold air blew in.

After Christmas she returned to Woolworths for a week, helping to clear up the chaos left by the festive rush. Thus the temporary job came to an end and once more she was left floundering with time heavy on her hands. Praying that 1935 would be better.

But the new year brought news of more trouble in Germany. Following Hindenburg's death, Adolf Hitler had taken over the country and was now Germany's President. Kate listened to Paul's tirade over this perfidious act, not really understanding the reason for his angry words, but sympathizing with him anyway. Her own thoughts were occupied elsewhere.

Finally, sensing her mood, he said, looking at her closely, 'So, what exactly are *you* planning to do?' They were sitting in the old railway carriage. The air was crisp, breath misting before them when they exhaled. Spring was in the offing and here and there the green shoots of daffodils were showing, promising that winter would soon loosen its icy grip and the growing cycle would once again burst upon a dormant world.

Paul's flask was on the table before them, the book he was currently reading lying open, face down, beside it.

In answer to his question, she said, 'Work, I guess. Daddy says there's a vacancy for a junior clerk in the office of the dairy where he works. But I don't know if that's what I want to do.'

'They would train you.'

'That's what my mother says.' She gazed down at the sketch pad she was never without. 'I had hoped to . . .'

Reading her thoughts, Paul conceded, 'It seems a shame not to put those months of night school to good use. Isn't there somewhere where you could serve an apprenticeship in some form of art?' He frowned. 'Like drawing comics or something?'

'Miss Archer, who was our teacher at night school, gave the class some leaflets, suggesting we see if there was anything that interested us. Most of the class threw them away.'

'Bet you didn't!'

'No, I've still got mine.'

'So, what sort of opportunities did they offer?'

'There's something called a fabric designer that sounds interesting. Of course, it's years until you qualify and get a decent wage. My mother expects me to contribute to the household expenses again, and the pittance they would give me would be worse than Woolworths.'

Paul felt pity for the girl stir in him. She was still too young and immature to stand up to her mother. But the time would come and when it did he thought he knew who would have the last word.

He smiled. 'We're a right pair, aren't we, each of us following our conscience instead of our inclinations. You worrying about earning enough to help your mother, me longing to reveal the truth behind stories that plague our poor old world.'

'You still want to be a journalist?'

'I do. Oh, don't think I'm moaning about having to help my mother, spending precious time helping in the shop, delivering pretty dresses to clients all over the place. Until she gets on her feet, as you English say, I shall continue to help. Then one day perhaps when she has found a partner who can assist her in these things, I will follow my dream and you will see my name alongside reports in the most prestigious newspapers.'

'Oh, I do hope so, Paul. You've got the kind of – of sensitivity that would make a great reporter.'

Playfully, he brushed a clenched fist against her chin. 'What do you know about sensitivity or reporters, a little girl like you?'

Seeing the look that crossed her face, he added, 'You're going to have to toughen up, you know, and not read criticism in everything anyone says to you. You *are* still a little girl and pretending you're not won't make you grow up any quicker.'

Rising to her feet, she gathered her belongings together, stuffing them into the old satchel she used. She would be seventeen in another month or two. These constant references to her being a little girl, even though it *was* said tongue in cheek, continued to annoy her.

Soon, one day very soon, she'd show them how wrong they were. She'd make something of her life. She'd persuade her father to give his permission for her to enlist in the fabric designing place. It would act as a stepping stone to the things she really wanted to do . . .

Paul followed her from the old carriage, carrying his own satchel. As they walked, they spied a figure coming towards them. She heard Paul's grunt, his: '*Mein Gott*, look what the cat's dragged in!'

Squinting against the sunlight, she said, 'Oh, who?'

'That bloody Ferris boy. He'd better not say anything about us using the carriage. It's got nothing to do with him.'

Guy Ferris made a beeline for them, stopping and saying, 'Oh, oh, trespassing again, are we?' Boldly, his gaze examined a flushed Kate. 'Some people just can't take a hint.'

Paul pushed past him. 'Get out of the way, Ferris. If we are trespassing it's got nothing to do with you. You don't own the club, the Railways do that.'

'My family owns all the land hereabouts. Has done for donkey's years. We lease it to the club.' His lips curled in a sneer. 'Not like some, who don't even have a *country* to call their own.'

Paul flushed and made as though to step forward. Kate pulled him back. 'Leave it,' she said. 'It's not worth getting into a fight over.'

'Two poor little lambs who have gone astray,' derided Guy Ferris, his eyes on Kate. 'I hear you're in the same boat, running back to your bolt hole when things got tough.'

Kate went cold. The flush faded, leaving her white. Surely he didn't know about her father? No one knew about Daddy's bit of trouble. Did they? She'd die if she thought anyone had found out.

She felt Paul's arm take hers, pulling her almost roughly across the grass. 'Come on, before I lose my temper and take a poke at him.'

Behind them, Guy Ferris yelled, 'Go on, run away. There'll come a time when you won't be able to and you'll have to face facts.'

Frowning, Kate gazed up at the tight-lipped Paul. 'What did he mean by that?'

'Oh, he's an idiot. I don't suppose he knows himself what he means. It's just bravado. Empty talk.'

He refused to discuss it further and left Kate at her gate. She stood and watched him stride away, shoulders hunched angrily.

For Kate's seventeenth birthday, Paul, with an air of great self-importance, took her into his mother's shop and told her to select anything she liked from the bolts of material stacked neatly on a shelf in the back room.

Seeing the way her eyes widened, always a sign of shock, he'd discovered, with Kate, he laughed. 'Go on, my mother suggested it. She intends to make you a frock but would like you to choose your own material and colour. For your birthday.'

Kate could hardly speak. There were footsteps behind them and Rosa Konig entered the room. Kate swivelled round to look at her. 'Are you sure, Mrs Konig? I mean, all that lovely stuff! I couldn't possibly . . .'

Coming closer, Rosa patted her hand, her smile warm. 'Of course you can, Kate. I shall make you the dress of your dreams. Choose something pretty, you'll be the belle of the ball.'

Kate caught Paul's eye and saw him wink. 'Well, it's awfully kind of you, Mrs Konig. Kind and generous. But I'm afraid I don't go to any balls so it would be a waste . . .'

'Better give in,' Paul advised, grinning. 'It's much easier in the end. Mama wins every time.'

Kate nodded. 'All right. I don't know what my parents will say, but it's so very kind of you, Mrs Konig . . .'

Rosa held up her hand. 'Not another word on the subject.' Waving one hand over the array of silks and cottons, like a fairy godmother brandishing her magic wand, she said, 'Now I shall leave you to choose. Something pretty, yes?'

Watched by a grinning Paul, Kate finally choose a fine cotton voile in a delicate peasant print of various shades of mauve. Already she knew how she wanted it. Full-skirted, tight-bodiced, accentuating what little bosom she did have, perhaps not the height of fashion, perhaps a trifle ingénue, but hers.

Rosa said she had the perfect pattern and took her measurements, Paul being banished to the tiny kitchen to make coffee while all this was going on.

'But we will make the bodice not so tight, eh? For you are a growing girl and it is not good to have a dress too tight,' Rosa pronounced.

Seeing Kate's frown, she went on, 'You are thinking if we leave it too loose it will sag, no?' She shook her head. 'There are ways of overcoming such things. Handkerchiefs stuffed into one's bra are usually very effective.' She gazed down at her own generous figure. 'Would you believe that once I had to resort to such practices?' She sighed. 'Alas, no longer.'

The last measurement taken, Rosa stood back and looked at her. Somehow sensing the air of uncertainty that hung over the girl, she murmured, 'Something is worrying you, no?'

What was worrying Kate was what her mother would say when she saw the dress. She was so touchy these days. Would she accept it with delight or look upon it as charity, not realizing the kindness that lay behind the gift?

Kate sighed. 'I was just wondering what my mother would say.'

Rosa laughed. 'Your mama will be delighted. You'll see. One look at the girl in that dress and she will know she has a phenomenally beautiful daughter who one day will be the envy of every other girl in the room.'

Kate felt herself blushing. She bent her head over the material she had chosen, feeling its softness beneath her fingertips. Suddenly, the absurdity of the whole thing struck her and she began to giggle. 'Oh, I don't think anyone's going to feel threatened.'

'Then you have much to learn, my dear.'

Kate knew she would have to choose the right moment to tell her parents about Mrs Konig's kind gesture. She guessed that her father would be delighted. But Mummy . . . Mummy was a different kettle of fish altogether.

When Kate arrived home, Monica, who by some miracle was in this afternoon, came down the stairs, followed shortly afterwards by Mr Patrick. Her mother looked flushed, although the day was chilly. The fine weather had taken a nose dive and reverted back to damp misty mornings and dull afternoons. The daffodils Daddy had planted in the front garden were still not fully in bloom.

While her mother fiddled with her hair in front of the sitting room mirror, Kate went into the kitchen to put the kettle on. Mr Patrick followed. He came to stand behind her, closer than was necessary, as she touched a match to the gas. He said, in the tones of a jovial uncle, 'So I hear it's your birthday soon. Sweet seventeen and never been kissed, eh? Am I invited to the party?'

Fat chance! thought Kate. It was on the tip of her tongue to say, 'There's not going to be any party, and even if there was I wouldn't invite a creep like you,' but instead she gave him a withering look and pushed past him to join her mother in the sitting room.

Monica was outlining her lips with the scarlet lipstick she kept on the mantelpiece. Gazing at her daughter in the decorative mirror, she said, 'I thought I'd go to the first house pictures tonight. There's a good film on and it finishes today. There's some mince cooked in a pan on the stove. All you have to do is warm it up and boil some potatoes. There's a tin of peas in the cupboard.'

Kate wondered why her mother hadn't gone as she usually did to the matinée, but all she said was, 'What about you? Shall we keep some warm?'

'Oh, don't worry about me. I'll get something when I come in. You know I'm not very keen on mince.'

'What about Mr Patrick?'

The man said, 'I'm meeting some mates in a pub. We'll probably go out for a meal later on.'

Why did warning bells ring in Kate's ears when she turned to look at him and then back to look at her mother?

Monica continued to gaze into the mirror. 'Your father's arranged an interview for you tomorrow morning at the dairy. You'd better have an early night so you'll be fresh and alert.'

Kate felt resentment stir in her. 'Mum . . .'

'Speak to your father about it. Now, I'd better go or I'll never get in. It's Clark Gable and Carole Lombard and you know how people pack the cinema when they're on.'

Kate had the meal ready to lay on the table in front of her father when he came in from work. Rearranging the knives and forks on the starched white cloth, she explained about her mother going to the pictures. It irritated her that he should take it so calmly, without a word of reproach.

The tip of his nose was red from the wind and he stood before the fire, warming his hands gratefully. 'I hope she wrapped up warmly. My, but it's nippy for April.' He smiled at Kate. 'What price our first English winter for many years, eh? I'd forgotten how long and dark the days can be. Although you're probably used to it by now.'

'It didn't seem so bad at the convent. Although it did get pretty cold. Some of the girls had chilblains from November to March.'

'Hmmm, nasty things, chilblains. I remember as a boy . . .'

Busy with dishing up the warmed mince and mashed potatoes, Kate was too preoccupied with her own thoughts to listen to his monologue about childhood winters.

'Kate! Is everything all right?'

She banged the two plates down on the table and turned to face him. 'No, Daddy, everything is not all right. Mum tells me you've arranged an interview for me tomorrow at the Bluebell Dairy. Don't you think that was a bit hasty?'

Her father looked surprised. 'Katie, darling, I had no idea you felt so strongly about it. It's a nice clean job and you would be learning a good trade. Office clerks are always in demand . . .'

'No doubt they are, but what about *my* wishes? What *I* want?'

Samuel looked uncomfortable. 'It would be nice if we could all have what we want, love, but life doesn't work that way. Most of us have to settle for something else.'

Rising from her place at the table, Kate went to the sideboard. She pulled open a drawer and lifted out a leaflet that lay there. Handing it to her father, she said, 'Look, Daddy, that's what I want to do. I've underlined the item in red ink. Please say you'll at least think about it.'

Samuel perused the leaflet. Why hadn't Kate shown this to him before? Was she so dominated by her mother these days that she was afraid to share her thoughts with him? They had always been close, father and daughter. He should be more authoritative in his own home. Kick that bloody Patrick out for a start. But, no denying it, the extra money came in handy. 'Did you show this to your mother?' he asked.

Kate nodded, remembering the scene when she'd come home with the leaflet and handed it to Monica. The scorn with which her mother had read it. 'Yes, and she said I was to put all thoughts of it out of my mind.' With a rush, she went on, 'Oh, Daddy, I know I would probably have to leave home, probably have to go up to the Midlands somewhere and it might be ages before I could afford to travel down at weekends. But it would be worth it in the long run.'

Doubtfully, he asked, 'What exactly does a fabric designer mean? What do they do?'

Kate had asked questions of her teacher and knew all about it. 'They do designs for curtain material and settees and chair covers. If I can get into a big firm like Courtaulds I'd be made.'

Reading the thoughts behind his worried expression, Kate bent her head over her plate. If anyone had asked her what she was eating she couldn't have said. The food tasted like cardboard. She saw her father push his own plate away, the food barely touched.

'You know, my love, although I hate to shatter your dreams, I don't think your mother would approve of you travelling all that way on your own, and living in some boarding house miles away from home. It's hardly proper for a girl as young as you. You've had such a sheltered upbringing. You hear of such stories . . .'

Unable to contain herself, Kate rose to her feet, hands clenched into fists. She felt like pounding the table but thought that might be a little melodramatic. What she did say was: 'Oh, for God's sake, Daddy! I'm not a child, not your own little baby you used to carry around the garden, pointing out all the different kinds of flowers to. I'm seventeen years old.'

'Seventeen's no age,' said her father. 'I know you're disappointed, love, but I really do think we shall have to talk about this with your mother.'

Kate sat down again at the table. Might as well talk to the man in the moon for all the good that would do.

Chapter Eleven

Kate's fears were proved right. Monica refused even to discuss the matter of her training in anything else but an office job.

'Your father's put you up to this, hasn't he? Doesn't he realize the scrimping and saving I have to do to feed us all, let alone meet the mortgage? I can't afford to have a daughter of mine gadding off up north, fooling around with paints. And what about your wages? Fat lot of those we'd see.' Monica shook the leaflet angrily, holding it between finger and thumb as though it might bite her. 'I told you when you first showed this to me how I viewed the whole silly idea.'

'Daddy doesn't think it's silly.' Kate's chin lifted obstinately. True, Daddy was against it – guessing her mother's objections, he would be – but he hadn't said it was silly.

Monica turned away from her suddenly insubordinate daughter and reached for the packet of cigarettes on the mantelpiece. Angrily puffing smoke into the air, she turned back to Kate, her own face equally rebellious.

'Oh, you and your father, good for a cuddle, good for a joke. You and he find plenty to laugh at behind my back, I'm sure, but you're not going to pressure me into giving my permission for this foolhardy venture. You will go for that interview tomorrow at the dairy and that will be the end of the matter.'

The interview seemed promising and although they said they had several other applicants to see, Kate got the impression the job would be hers. Samuel brought home the letter offering her the position a few days later and said she was to start the following Monday.

It brought Kate no joy. The idea of sitting in a stuffy office all day was anathema to her. Her depression was lightened somewhat the next day by bumping into Paul. She was closing the front gate when she saw him striding towards her. He carried a flat box under one arm; lime-green and pale-mauve stripes on a grey background.

'My dress!' Kate gave a squeal of delight. Her hands reached for the box and he held it high above his head, grinning broadly.

'Don't snatch! Haven't you been taught it's rude to snatch? And I can hardly show it to you here, in the middle of the street, can I?'

'Come in, then.'

He looked doubtful. 'Is that all right?'

'My mother's washing her hair. She won't bother us.'

Only after she'd spoken did she remember she'd left the front door key on the kitchen table. There was nothing for it but to ring the bell.

Monica wasn't too pleased to have to answer the door while her hair was still wet. One hand holding a towel securely to her head, she glared at Kate and the young man she recognized as the Konig boy.

'Kate! You're surely not bringing your friends home at this time of day?'

Paul gave her his best smile, and bowed from the waist. 'Please do not blame your daughter, Mrs Linley. She has the most excellent manners. You see, I have something to show her and we could hardly stand out in the street while we looked at it.'

Monica's gaze fell to the box he held out for her inspection. 'What is it? And why are you giving my daughter presents?'

'It is for Kate's birthday . . .'

'Her birthday was last week.' A note of belligerence entered Monica's voice.

'Alas, it has taken my mother longer than she anticipated to make it. She is kept busy these days.'

'I really cannot see . . .'

Kate reached out and took the box from him, edging past her mother into the sitting room. Paul followed and with a sigh Monica closed the front door and trailed behind.

Placing the box on the table, Kate said, 'Perhaps if I open it, Mummy, you can see what we're talking about.' Removing the lid, she rifled through the sheets of tissue paper and lifted out the frock.

Holding it against her she went to stand in front of the mirror above the fireplace. She executed a series of dance steps. 'Isn't it perfect? Wasn't Mrs Konig wonderful to suggest it? Especially when she *is* so busy.' She gave a breathy sigh, gazing at her image in the mirror. 'This is going to give me such pleasure.'

Monica looked as though the pleasure was going to be all Kate's. Piqued because this week she hadn't had enough money for a visit to the hairdresser, she'd washed her hair herself over the kitchen sink, intending to dry it before the sitting room fire. How could she lower herself to do that now, with that boy standing there, grinning like a Cheshire cat? She had achieved a creditable turban-like effect with the towel but she still felt ridiculous.

What on earth was she supposed to say to this presumptuous young man and his audacious offer?

She made an angry exclamation and reading her face, Paul said, 'I'm sorry if we have done the wrong thing. My mother merely wanted to give Kate a special treat for her birthday.'

'Mum!' Kate's voice sounded breathless in the sudden hush.

'Is it your custom to go around insulting people?' Monica demanded scathingly of Paul. 'Do you make a habit of it? It's insufferable.' She glared at Kate. 'Just what were you thinking of, agreeing to something like this? Or was it your idea?' Turning back to the embarrassed Paul, she went on, 'No matter what my daughter may have told you, young man, we haven't yet sunk to the level of having to accept charity.'

Paul flushed. 'Charity was the furthest thing from our thoughts, Mrs Linley. As I said, my mother merely wanted to give Kate a birthday treat. A very special one. I'm sorry if you see it as anything else.'

Turning from him, Monica said, 'I suggest you show the young man out, Kate. And let him take his gift with him.'

Kate gathered the dress in her arms, holding it to her. Her cheeks scarlet, she glared at her mother. 'I will not! Mrs Konig made it for me, it would be no use to anyone else. You can't make me give it back, Mummy.'

Paul looked uncomfortable. 'Look, I'd better go. I'm sorry if I've upset you, Mrs Linley.' He looked at the defiant Kate. 'Perhaps it might be better if you gave it back, if your mother is so adamant.'

Kate's grip on the dress tightened. '*No!* It's mine and I'm keeping it.'

Monica looked like thunder. 'We'll just see what your father has to say about that, my girl.'

Kate knew it was an empty threat. Daddy would remain, as always, neutral. Silently, Kate followed Paul to the front door. Before he left she whispered, 'I'm so sorry, Paul. I don't know what to say. It's all been so horrible . . .'

'I have been through worse, Kate. Do not let it worry you.'

Keeping her voice low, she said, 'But it has. I don't know what's got into Mummy these days. She seems to fly off the handle at everything me or Daddy do.'

'Kate!' Monica's voice came from behind her in the hallway. 'Come in and close that door. It's damned cold with it wide open.'

A sudden urge had Kate standing on tiptoe, kissing Paul briefly on the cheek. 'I'd better do as she says. Thank your mother for me. I'll see you.'

'Yes, see you.'

Rejoining her mother in the sitting room, Kate began to pack the tissue paper back around the dress, folding it carefully, not looking at her mother.

Monica breathed through her nose, her lips tight. 'So you intend to keep it?'

Still Kate didn't look up. 'Didn't I say I was?'

'Don't get smart with me, young lady. You may think it's funny, I think it's serious.'

This time Kate did look up, gazing steadily at her mother's angry face. 'Why are you so against me receiving a birthday gift from the Konigs? Rosa – Mrs Konig – was merely being kind. And it *was* kind. She has enough work of her own without making things for a girl she hardly knows.'

'A girl who sees far too much of her son. A girl who is still only seventeen. He might be a very nice boy for all I know, but you can't get away from the fact . . .'

When she hesitated, Kate prompted, 'What fact?'

'Well, he's not like us, is he?'

'You mean because he's German? Oh, Mummy, what century are you living in?'

'I didn't say that . . .'

'No, you didn't have to. Your look said everything.'

'So, I am not entitled to have an opinion now, is that it? Suddenly you're too old to have to listen to your mother. Don't forget that not so many years ago we were fighting the Germans. They were our enemy.' Her lips pursed in a tight bud of obstinacy, her face arranging itself in her subject-closed expression.

With a sigh, Kate finished packing the dress. Fitting the lid carefully in place, she carried the box up to her room. What a fuss about nothing! Mummy had really gone over the top on this one. If Daddy backed her up about handing the dress back – she couldn't see it happening, but considering the mood her mother was in, he just might, if only for a bit of peace – if he did, Kate decided, drastic as the action might be, she'd rather burn the dress than hurt Mrs Konig's feelings by refusing her gift.

Her father didn't insist and Kate kept the dress, wearing it to the Bluebell Dairy's tenth anniversary party in the summer. The manager of the dairy and numerous other people complimented her on how much the dress suited her. It did more to enhance the rapid growing-up of Kate Linley than anything else.

The sun was hot overhead, the sky a cloudless blue, and the park, with its neat beds of summer roses seeming to shimmer in the heat, stretched before her. Kate breathed deeply of the crystalline air, fanning her face with her hand. Next to the railway carriage, the park was her favourite place. Here she could relax, could try to summarize the direction in which her life was leading her.

If she wasn't ecstatically happy in her job, at least, she consoled herself, she did have a job. The depression was slowly lifting but there were still a lot of people without work.

She saved every penny she could, aware that money meant

independence. She persuaded Paul to ask his mother if she could work in Rosa's, helping out on a Saturday morning. 'I could at least sew on beads and sequins,' she pointed out practically.

She was strolling past Rosa's shop one Saturday morning when the woman appeared at the door. 'Ah, Kate, I've been watching out for you. Have you time to come in for a little talk?'

'Of course, Mrs Konig.' Kate smiled and followed Rosa into the shop.

Luckily, it was a quiet moment when no customers were around. Rosa escorted Kate into the back room, brushed off scraps of material from a chair and indicated that she should sit down. 'I'll put the kettle on.'

'Oh, please don't bother for me . . .'

'Nonsense. I am always ready for a cup of coffee.'

Kate rose from her chair. 'Then let me do it. You sit down and take a breather.'

Rosa smiled. 'Take a breather! How quaint the English language is! But, alas, I have no time for "breathers".'

'You've time for a five-minute break, I'm sure,' Kate insisted. 'Besides, you did say you wanted to talk to me. Now please sit down and I'll make the coffee.'

'If you insist. I must confess my legs are painful today. Arthritis, you know.'

'I'm sorry. I didn't know that.'

'Sometimes it is a great effort to get up after I've been kneeling, pinning up the hems of dresses. But I should not grumble. We all have our crosses to bear.'

Kate nodded, thinking of her father and, in a way, herself. 'I'll make that coffee.'

Returning with two steaming cups, she handed one to Rosa and then, perched on the edge of the large cutting-out table, sipped her own.

'My son tells me you are interested in working on a Saturday morning for me.'

Kate nodded. 'Yes. I hope you didn't think I was being pushy, but I just love the idea of being surrounded by all those lovely materials and designs of yours.' Her eyes gleamed. 'It would be like living in a different world to the one in which I spend my weekdays.'

'And that is . . . ?'

Kate grimaced. 'Typing out letters and dreary statements for the dairy in which I work.'

Rosa waved a dismissive hand. 'I could not pay you much, but the training you receive will compensate for that. I do not wish to boast, Kate, but you could not receive a better apprenticeship anywhere in London.' She smiled. 'If you are really interested in fashion designing, of course.'

'Just you try me!'

'Shall we do that, then? Try you?'

Kate's face radiated her happiness and relief at having found this way to follow her dreams. 'I promise I won't let you down, Mrs Konig. I'll work hard.'

Rosa was pleased at Kate's enthusiasm. 'You could start next Saturday then? I open the shop at nine o'clock.'

'I'll be there on the dot,' Kate promised.

It was just after that that Paul obtained a position on the local newspaper. Published twice-weekly, the *Observer* printed stories of local interest, occasionally spicing up its columns with a robbery or fire. There was a 'Hatches, matches and dispatches' section, and the occasional report of a charity bazaar. The honour of reporting these fell to Paul.

'The pay's lousy,' he told Kate, walking with her one morning back from the High Street, 'but it will lead to better things.'

She turned her head, looking at him thoughtfully. 'You're still determined to be a journalist?'

'I am.'

She smiled. 'Righting the wrongs of the world?'

His mouth tightened. 'I know I can never bring my father back or get our Jewish neighbours released from whatever hell they are in. There is a saying: "Evil men prosper when good men do nothing." Or something to that effect. Anything, however small, is better than doing nothing.'

Kate had a sudden premonition, a sort of dark omen, of terrible events not too far in the future. An icy chill touched her spine and Paul, gazing down at her, saw her cheeks pale.

His first assignments included Beautiful Baby contests as well as the Births and Deaths columns. On one memorable occasion he was sent to report on a soirée at the Town Hall hosted by the Mayor. Walking with Kate a few days later, he told her, 'The only thing that made it worthwhile was recognizing at least two of my mother's dresses. The Lady Mayoress wore one, although how she ever got it to look so elegant on that figure of hers I'll never know.'

'Did they really look elegant? Did people remark on them?' queried Kate with an air of excitement. 'I hope you told them they were designed exclusively by Rosa?'

Paul grinned. 'Yes, to all your questions. Particularly the wine-coloured one worn by the Mayor's wife. You worked on that, didn't you?'

Kate nodded eagerly. 'I sewed the beads on the bodice. And,' proudly, 'your mother allowed me a free hand in the design. I'm glad it worked so well. She was taking an awful chance. It could have turned out quite ghastly.'

Paul looked smug. 'My mother has sound judgement. She would never have allowed it if she wasn't a hundred per cent sure.' He turned to grin at Kate. They had reached her gate and he put one hand on the top, pushing it open for her to go in. She slipped past him and closed it after her. 'She admitted to me afterwards that in her opinion she thought she had a new young Coco Chanel on her hands.'

Kate sighed. 'If only!'

Over the months, their relationship had continued on the cheerful boy-girl level it had always been. She'd seen Paul out with girls at the pictures and at the dances Father O'Hanlan sometimes permitted in the church hall. The knowledge that he knew other girls hadn't made her jealous. Paul Konig was nice, but it wasn't him she had set her sights on.

During that summer, Kate lived for the days when Guy Ferris came home. Knowing his habits, his fondness for a game of tennis at the club, Kate would sit in the old carriage, waiting for the game to finish. Then, elaborately casual, she emerged to begin the walk home. It seemed natural that their paths should cross. Insolent as he was, she still couldn't deny that he was the most handsome boy she had ever seen, with his height and lovely blue eyes, and the fair hair glinting in the sunlight.

'I do believe I've been smitten,' she wrote to Julie on a jocular note. 'Just talking to him makes me go weak at the knees. *Do* fall in love soon, *please*, and then we can compare notes.'

Whenever he saw her his steps would slow and he'd wait until she drew abreast.

'I'm sorry I was so rude to you that first time,' he'd said. 'I'm not usually that disagreeable.'

Diffidently, she murmured, 'It's all right.'

'No, it isn't. It was unforgivable.'

'I'm sure you didn't mean to be rude.'

'I meant it all right. But not especially to you. Anyone would have done.'

'Had someone upset you?'

He nodded and bent to pluck a blade of grass, thrusting it between his teeth. 'My grandmother. She insists on treating me like a child. She hates to think of me growing up.'

'My mother's the same.' Kate sighed. 'Parents can be a nuisance at times, can't they?'

'I wouldn't know. I never knew mine.'

Kate was covered in confusion. 'Oh, I'm sorry, I didn't think . . . Your grandmother must be a wonderful woman, taking the responsibility of both parents in your life.'

'But very strict. I don't really see all that much of her. I'm away at school most of the time.'

'Perhaps that's why she's so strict.'

'You could be right.'

'Where do you go to school?'

'Oh, a place in some godforsaken spot in Scotland. On the west coast of Scotland to be precise. Very bleak and windswept.' He grinned at her. 'It's supposed to make men of us.'

Mischief twinkled in Kate's eyes. 'And has it?'

'Has it what?'

'Made a man of you?'

He slowly lifted one eyebrow. 'That is something that still has to be put to the test.' Then, casually, as though he was discussing the weather, he said, 'Are you a virgin?'

Kate was shocked to the core. 'What?' Surely her ears were deceiving her? Could he actually have said that? Aloud?

'I said, are you a virgin?'

Her face flamed. 'I really don't think you have any right to ask a question like that.'

'No need to bite my head off.'

She resumed walking, her stride lengthening in order to ease her discomfort.

He hurried beside her. 'My, but you are touchy. And very pretty with your cheeks scarlet with indignation. So pretty you actually make my poor old heart flutter.'

How silky and practised his words were. And how confident he seemed. She thought of the dark-haired girl in the carriage with him, and for the first time knew jealousy. She glanced at him. He was still smiling, well aware of how confused she was. He found her exciting.

They had nearly reached his gate. Her own was only a few doors away. 'Excuse me,' she said, 'but I've got to go.'

'Why?' he challenged. 'What's your hurry? Look, I'm sorry. I started out by apologizing and here I am doing it again. Forgive?' And he looked so appealing she had to smile.

'Don't be silly,' she said. 'But I really do have to go.'

He caught at her hand, holding her prisoner. 'There's a good flick on at the Dream Palace this week. That new musical with Alice Faye. Would you like to go?'

Her heart cried yes but her instinct told her no. He was too polished by half; she just wasn't in his league. Yet. Maybe one day . . .

'I've seen it,' she lied, and escaped through her gate.

When next she saw him he was with the dark-haired girl. They were walking on the other side of the street and he waved his hand casually. The girl walking beside him gazed loftily across at Kate and smirked.

The Linleys' second Christmas in Wesley Avenue passed. Aunt Norma came again to stay with them. This time she talked endlessly of the two cats she had acquired and Kate had the feeling that when the time came for her to go home she was pleased. A neighbour had been looking after the cats but as Norma explained, cats were home-loving bodies and hated upsets.

'She talks as though they were children,' observed Monica scathingly.

'They probably are to her,' said Samuel.

'I'm going for a walk. Would you like to come?' Kate asked Samuel. It was a Sunday morning and she and Monica had not been long back from church.

Samuel considered the proposal, then shook his head. 'I won't, if you don't mind. I've got things to do in the garden.'

It was the end of February, one of Kate's most hated months. The ground was soft and muddy, with hardly a green shoot to be seen. They had had more than their fair share of rain, far too much to allow Samuel to get out and work on the garden. Consequently, he had neglected it of late and now, with this first fine Sunday for weeks, with patches of blue in the sky, he wanted to get out and begin preparing for the coming spring.

Walking down towards the sports ground, Kate looked up at the sky and wondered if, despite the promising start to the day, it was again going to rain. She had hardly left Wesley Avenue behind her when she spotted someone sitting on a rustic wooden bench near the clubhouse. Otherwise, the grounds were deserted. She was quite close to him and there was no turning back; he'd turned his head and recognized her. A thrill tingled through her. She'd wondered about his absence. Had he finished school yet? Was he home for good or was this just a holiday?

'Hello,' she said, halting beside the bench.

Guy Ferris frowned quizzically at her.

'How are you doing? How's school? And how is your grandmother?'

'We are both well and school's now a thing of the past. Thank God for small mercies. How's yourself? In a better mood than last time, I trust.'

She didn't answer.

A lock of hair had fallen over his forehead which she wanted to reach out and brush back for him. She thought not for the first time how lovely his eyes were, the sort a girl could drown in.

'Well,' he said, 'if you won't talk, you'd better get on your way, hadn't you?'

'I was going for a walk, why don't we walk together?' she said boldly.

'Is that what you want to do?'

She didn't have to think. 'Yes.'

He rose from the bench. 'Let's go, then. Lead on, Macduff.'

'How's Lottie?' she asked after a few paces.

He glanced at her with raised brows. 'Didn't you know? She got married. Some poor sucker with more money than sense, years older than herself. I haven't seen her since.'

'Oh, I didn't know,' she said, casually. 'I bet that upset you.'

He laughed. 'Now why on earth should you think that?'

'I thought you two – well, liked each other.'

'No more than I like most women. But don't quote me, dearest Katie.' He glanced at her. 'I must confess to liking you better than a lot I could mention.'

His 'dearest Katie' sent her heart hammering, her pulses leaping.

'But what about you and that German boy? Are you courting yet?' he enquired.

'*No*.' Had she spoken the word too emphatically? 'Paul's just a friend. And please don't refer to him as that German boy. He's very nice, really.'

'I'm not sure that we should think of *any* German as nice. After the way old Hitler's been throwing his weight around all over Europe. Goodness knows what'll happen when they stage the Olympic Games this year in Berlin. They say Hitler's threatened all sorts of horrible punishments if his own boys don't win the most prestigious events.' He grinned. 'America has a black runner named Jesse Owens who is tipped to win. They say Hitler's foaming at the mouth just at the thought of a black even competing against white men.'

'I don't see that it matters, as long as the best man wins. And if he happens to be black, well, so what?'

'It must be fascinating to have such an open mind,' Guy said. 'But what about you? What are you doing with yourself these days?'

'I slave over a hot typewriter in the Bluebell Dairy during the week and work for Paul's mother on a Saturday. Doing part-time work.'

'Yes, I can see you in the midst of beautiful velvet gowns and silky lingerie.' And his look, accompanied by the way he said it, made her blush.

Perhaps it was just as well that the first raindrops started just after this, for she was beginning, as always with this boy, to feel out of her depth. And, as always, the subject of the Germans made her feel uneasy.

Guy glanced up at the sky. 'Better run, it's going to throw it down.' He took her arm, and they ran all the way back to Wesley Avenue, stopping, breathless and laughing, outside the gate of his grandmother's red-brick house.

'Here I am,' he said, and nodding towards her house a few doors away, 'and there are you. Practically neighbours. And you know what they say about neighbours loving each other, don't you?'

He left the question hanging in the air and as the rain started in earnest, Kate turned and ran the short distance to her own gate. Bloody hell! she thought. Why does it always have to end like this? Me getting cold feet and refusing a date, or him acting like Valentino and frightening the life out of me?

★ ★ ★

Samuel stared at the plate of bacon, eggs, fried bread, sausage and tomatoes that Kate had laid in front of him for his Sunday-morning treat. 'Thanks, love,' he said, 'but I don't think I could eat all this. Not today.'

From the other side of the table, already digging into hers, Monica said, 'Why not today? What's different about today?'

Samuel gave her a disgusted look. 'In case you've forgotten, the King died yesterday.'

Monica tut-tutted irritably. 'Oh, for goodness' sake! As if you refusing breakfast is going to make any difference to that.'

'Not to the nation's loss, it won't, but it will to me.'

Monica tut-tutted again and Kate picked up her father's plate, saying, 'I'll put it to keep warm in the oven. It'll save cooking another breakfast for Mr Patrick.'

'You'll do no such thing.' Monica breathed heavily through her nose. 'You will cook Mr Patrick a fresh breakfast.'

Samuel gave his wife a disgusted look and went out into the garden.

This year – 1936 – was already proving to be a year of events. A civil war raged in Spain and now there was the death of a beloved King. The news had sent the whole nation into mourning. Old George had been much loved. Samuel wondered how this new King, the young Prince of Wales who enjoyed being seen in nightclubs, would cope. Distinct from the gay life which he seemed to enjoy, the newspapers reported that he had a feeling for the ordinary man. Especially for the Welsh coal miners who were having a particularly bad time this year.

The newsreels in the cinemas showed Edward striding with great purpose across ground littered with coal dumps, the aides surrounding him outnumbered by miners whose faces were still streaked with coal dust. This was a man for the people, the newspapers said. Edward would understand what the people needed.

And if he liked dancing with all the prettiest débutantes of the season, well, what harm was there in that? Wasn't he entitled to enjoy himself before the onerous duties of being King intruded?

Enjoying oneself took on a whole new meaning to the British public. The King was seen setting off on safari in Africa, always with a pretty woman in attendance, swimming from the side of a yacht in the Mediterranean. The women who accompanied him were invariably married, and the people began to wonder about the woman he would select to share the throne.

There was an air of gaiety about the land. Wonderful after the dour, dark days of the depression. Musical films from Hollywood were very popular, especially the ones starring two young dancers called Fred Astaire and Ginger Rogers.

Kate would walk for miles to see those two if they weren't showing at the Dream Palace or the other local cinema. A boom in popular music, encouraged by the dance halls, by the musical films from Hollywood, and to a lesser degree by the BBC, made ballroom dancing all the rage.

Kate began taking lessons in the small dancing academy above Rosa's shop. She would slip along there of an evening, with another girl from the office, and they would dance to the accompaniment of an old gramophone. Kate was reminded of Julie and their lessons at the convent. She and Julie corresponded frequently. Julie was now at a posh finishing school in Switzerland, hating every minute of it but resigned to the fact that in another year she would be free.

'All this education's all right,' she wrote, 'but it's not much fun. I can't wait to get out and meet life face to face. Boy, and then will I kick my heels up! Then I'll show you all a thing or two!'

Chapter Twelve

Rosa Konig looked up from her sewing as Kate entered the shop, carrying a large bunch of flowers.

'Lovely!' murmured Rosa. 'So lovely.'

'I thought they would look nice on the glass counter,' said Kate.

'What a charming idea.'

Paul had given her flowers for her eighteenth birthday, just passed, and Rosa smiled quietly, remembering the gentle scolding that had followed. 'You shouldn't waste your money like that,' Kate had told him. 'My father has a garden full of flowers.'

'So I should have nipped in and pinched some during the night, should I?'

'No, but...'

He'd grinned, patted her head and gone on his way.

Rosa greatly admired the bouquet that Kate now brought in every week. There were deep-blue larkspur, tall and elegant, yellow and white Dutch iris and a blaze of orange marigolds that Samuel hadn't been able to resist planting. 'Remember those marigold summers?' he had said, gently raking soil over the seed bed. 'It won't be the same but at least we'll still get the feel of them.'

Rosa held up the piece of silk she was hem-stitching, examining it with a critical eye. The colour was the deep blue of the larkspur. It would end up gracing the over-ripe figure of one of her customers. Smiling at Kate as she came back into the shop from the back room, carrying a white vase, Rosa thought how much more refined the dress would look against the girl's fair beauty.

With a sigh she went back to her sewing. Kate began to arrange the flowers in the vase, hearing Rosa say behind her, 'How I miss my own garden, Kate. Other things, too, of course, but my garden more than anything else.'

'You must miss your lovely home and your husband,' said Kate sympathetically.

'But of course!'

Kate gave the flower arrangement a last pat then turned to face Rosa. 'Never mind, perhaps in the not too distant future you will be able to afford a nice house with a garden. Remember the three new customers

111

who expressed an interest in our gowns last week? They all wanted
something along the lines of the dresses Mrs Simpson wears. That could
be very exciting, designing for them.' And, she thought quietly, *they*
weren't old *or* fat but fairly young and, she got the impression, not
without money.

Rosa raised her eyebrows. 'Mrs Simpson?'

'You know, the lady who the King is seen escorting all over town.
Now, if we could tempt someone like *her* into becoming a patron,
Rosa's would be made.'

'How swiftly the imagination of the young goes to work!' Rosa said
indulgently. 'Somehow I cannot see a friend of the King's patronizing
our little shop.'

But Kate's imagination had taken flight. 'What if she was driving
through the High Street and suddenly spied our window? From all
accounts she adores clothes. What if she stopped the car and got out to
look in the window then came in to investigate?'

Rosa couldn't help the chuckle that escaped. She made the last
tiny stitch in the blue silk and examined it, head to one side.
'Well, that certainly would be a feather in our cap, my dear, but I
think we have as little chance of that as the lady in question does of
becoming Queen.'

Kate smiled and reached behind the door of the back room for the
pale-mauve overall she wore in the shop. 'Well, it costs nothing to
dream. And what use are dreams if they don't come true?'

'At eighteen, dreams are playthings that all too often fade with
time.'

'Oh my,' Paul exclaimed, coming into the shop. He had overheard
the last few sentences and stood grinning at his mother and Kate. 'Such
homespun philosophy so early in the morning!'

'We were discussing the likelihood of the King's Mrs Simpson
coming into our little shop,' said Rosa. 'A most *un*likely occurrence in
my opinion.'

Paul caught Kate's eye and winked. 'Well, following Kate's
thinking, Mother, it costs nothing to dream.'

Kate looked wistful. 'But wouldn't it be nice? She's such a beautiful
woman, so well-dressed. I'm sure one of your mother's designs would
look wonderful on her.'

'My dear mama's designs look wonderful on anyone,' said Paul
proudly.

'Do you think he *will* marry her?' asked Kate. 'Wallis Simpson, I
mean.'

'Well, he *is* the King. I should imagine he can do pretty much what he
likes.'

'Which is more than we can do,' said Rosa briskly. She rose to her feet and went to hang the piece of blue silk with the rest of the dress in the fitting room. 'It's Saturday and weather like this should make us busy.'

Taking the hint, Paul grimaced and Kate turned to pick up a yellow duster. Polishing the top of the glass counter was therapeutic; the vigorous rubbing calmed the seething exasperation that boiled in her. Picking the flowers in the garden had helped, but not enough to expel the scene she had sat through at breakfast.

Samuel was still lucky enough to be in work, and with Kate's end-of-year salary increase, plus the small amount she earned at Rosa's, the family were better off financially. At least Monica could meet the mortgage and her weekly visits to the hairdresser were no longer threatened. Not to mention her regular cinema outings.

That morning, sitting at breakfast in the sun-filled dining room, Samuel buttered his toast then looked up to where Monica stood, pouring tea for him and Kate, and said, 'You know, my dear, I was thinking that as things are looking up at last, we could dispense with our lodger. Have the house to ourselves again, just you and me and Katie...'

Kate held her breath, knowing how touchy her mother was on the subject of Mr Patrick. She wasn't a fool, and even to herself she could no longer deny that their lodger's relationship with her mother had become – well, she thought, with a shudder, at the very least, foolhardy. Did Daddy turn a blind eye to it or was he genuinely unaware of what was going on?

Monica's attention wavered and the cup overflowed, tea spilling from the brimming saucer on to the white tablecloth.

Kate rushed to get a tea towel from the kitchen, hearing her mother's voice, low and grating: 'Whatever made you think things were looking up? You don't have to worry about meeting the bills, the rates and coal and electricity. Perhaps if you took a little more interest in how I manage, you might be less eager to criticize.'

'My dear, the last thing I meant to do was criticize. It's just that, well, you must admit our lives are a lot less restrictive now we are able to afford a few little luxuries. I really don't see why we should have to share our home as we do with a stranger.'

'You still think of him as a stranger after all this time? After he's done so much for us?'

About to ask what exactly their lodger had done for them, Samuel broke off as Kate came back into the room. Dabbing at the stain on the cloth, she tried to look as though she hadn't heard the discussion that had brought an angry flush to her mother's cheeks.

Kate heard Mr Patrick coming down the stairs – on Saturdays he tended to have a lie-in, seldom putting in an appearance till Samuel had started work on the garden. Gardening and Daddy had taken to each other like bees to honey. It was heart-warming to see the tenderness he lavished on the neat flower and vegetable beds and the square of lawn.

Today, however, Mr Patrick was putting in an unusually early appearance. As though he guessed that the discussion regarding his future was taking place. Most likely, thought Kate sourly, he'd been eavesdropping at the top of the stairs. She wouldn't put it past him.

Silence fell on the room as he took his place across the table from Monica. Kate wondered if her father, like her, had noticed the look exchanged between them. She bent her head over her boiled egg, slicing the top carefully, and heard Mr Patrick say, 'Do I hear family dissidence so early in the morning? On such a fine sunny day, too?'

'Wonderful how the ear picks up things that are not meant for it,' said Samuel.

Calmly, with an arrogance that had the muscles at the side of Samuel's jaw clenching in anger, their lodger went on, 'Oh, I wouldn't say I wasn't meant to hear. Surely that was the whole object of your discussion, in such loud voices, too?' He eyed Samuel across the table. 'Wouldn't it have been more gentlemanly to have told me to my face instead of speaking behind my back?'

Samuel's face flamed. 'Well, I can't say that I've noticed any gentleman around here, but seeing that you *have* heard saves me the job of telling you. You can stay until the end of the month, Patrick, but after that I want you out of here. Understand?'

Nonchalantly, Mr Patrick held out his cup and saucer for Monica to pour his tea. 'Perfectly.' He leaned across the table and reached for a slice of toast while Monica scuttled into the kitchen for his breakfast, kept warm in the oven. As she placed the loaded plate in front of him, he smiled up at her. 'Ah, thank you, my dear. A breakfast fit for a king.'

Samuel avoided anything disagreeable. It was to this negative aim that he devoted all his energies. Walking to work each morning, working at a job he knew was far beneath him, he did not object to any of that. Providing for his family meant everything to him. What he did object to was having a man – a man he didn't particularly like – poking fun at him at his own table.

Kate wished she was older, old enough to add her own twopenny-worth, to acquaint this man with a few home truths. Instead, all she could do was gaze helplessly at her father. She hated any kind of unpleasantness, too.

She stood up, pushing her chair back with such force that she had to grab at the back to stop it tumbling over. Feeling the eyes of the three grown-ups on her, she had mumbled a distracted, 'Excuse me,' and escaped into the garden . . .

Absorbed in her thoughts, she heard Rosa's voice behind her, gently teasing: 'If you polish that glass much longer, dear, you are going to rub a hole in it.'

Kate drew a deep breath, turning to face her. 'I'm sorry, Mrs Konig. I just feel so – well, confused.' She broke off, twisting the yellow duster between her hands.

Rosa said, gently, 'You have had a disagreement with your mother, no?'

'Not with my mother.' She smiled. 'It's nothing. It'll pass.' She turned and gave the glass a last wipe then tossed the duster on to its shelf beneath the counter. 'Now, what do you want me to do? Shall I begin on that bead work for Doctor Brooke's wife?'

Mrs Brooke was a new customer whose husband held an important position on the council. Kate was proud that Rosa considered her capable of executing the design the woman had chosen. Kate had proved expert at sewing on the tiny glass beads and produced many of the designs herself. Not for the first time would she bless the nuns for their skilful tutoring in fine sewing.

The customer would describe more or less what she wanted and Kate took it a step further. Illustrating with swift strokes, her pencil would fly over the paper, intricate patterns leaping out of the page.

This gown was a drift of sun-yellow georgette, skimming the figure, and the beads Kate was presently engaged upon were silver. The gown would look stunning. Kate was sure it would do justice to whatever event Mrs Brooke was planning to wear it at. And, hopefully, trigger off queries as to where it was purchased.

Rosa had begun suggesting that Kate offer her sketches to favourite customers. Shy at first, Kate soon gained in confidence, spending most of her spare time sketching ideas that came to her when she sat at her typewriter at work. She made sure her work didn't suffer, though, dragging her thoughts back when she became aware that others in the office were looking her way.

In place of the movie magazines she had spent her money on in Woolworths, she now bought fashion magazines. And she never failed to go to see a film where she knew the star was an elegant dresser. It was all food for her imagination; she thrived on it. She was still young but her ambition was to become partners with Rosa Konig, buying her own share of the business.

The customers loved her ideas and many of the gowns displayed in Rosa's window were products of Kate's inspiration. Even Julie had purchased a dress on one of her visits. Her letters told how friends at home had praised it; 'green with envy' was how she phrased it. Of course, it hadn't been one with the bugles and beads that were Rosa's trademark, but a simple cotton in pale yellow with a small bolero edged with white daisies of guipure lace. Julie's mother had been delighted, and had said she could buy more when she visited Kate again. So all in all, things were going well for Rosa's. Rosa went so far as to admit that they might employ another young girl to carry out the tasks Paul used to do.

'You know, dear,' she'd smiled at Kate, 'the cleaning and delivering of orders.' Hand-delivery was one of Rosa's specialities. 'Pauli is much too busy to help me these days.'

Paul's hours were varied and he often worked into the night. The editor of his newspaper expected him to cover a newsworthy event whatever time of the day it happened.

Kate just wished the atmosphere at home was as congenial as it was at Rosa's. The shop stayed open until eight on a Saturday evening but Rosa insisted that Kate leave just after the lunch hour.

'After all,' she pointed out, 'you were only supposed to come in for the morning. I don't want your mama accusing me of slave labour.' There was a twinkle in her eye as she said it.

'I don't mind. I like being here.'

'You are a young girl, you deserve to go out and enjoy yourself. In my young days, Saturday night was the most important night of the week. I'm sure times cannot have changed so much to make it different.'

A rainbow of coloured ribbons was spread out across the glass counter, Rosa's white hands busy untangling them.

'Don't you have a boyfriend, Kate? A pretty girl like you?'

Kate thought of Guy Ferris. Although he was home, he must be busy; she hadn't seen him since their encounter on her walk. She thought often of his grandmother. She'd seen cars draw up in front of the old house, people going in. It seemed the old lady didn't want for company. Once – only once – she'd seen her crossing the pavement to the parked car where a uniformed chauffeur held open the door. She was straight-backed and dignified, walking with a stick, and Kate had caught a glimpse of snowy-white hair and a pale face. Kate had watched for Guy but it seemed tonight his grandmother was alone.

Guy's fair good looks fresh in her mind, she pulled a scarlet satin ribbon free from the tangle and began to wind it slowly around her hand. 'Not exactly a boyfriend. Although there *is* someone I'm pretty keen on.'

Rosa smiled, a secret little smile. The girl had ambition, a promising career ahead of her. Her own beloved Pauli could do a lot worse . . .

The time passed quickly as it always did in the shop. With the sun bathing the High Street, customers who came in were agreeable, their thoughts clearly on summer holidays beside the sea. Rosa was for the first time experimenting with something she called 'Beach Pyjamas'. Made of the finest silk, in the brightest colours, they consisted of wide-legged trousers and a loose jacket-like top reaching to the hips.

116

Very daring, exclaimed the suitably impressed customers. But they really didn't know what their husbands would say if they appeared in something like that: I mean, *trousers*! No lady wore trousers. Only actresses like Joan Crawford in the pictures . . .

Rosa smiled at their shocked expressions. 'Well, start a trend, then. Be the first among your friends to wear them. I guarantee your husbands will be captivated.'

The women looked doubtful. On someone else, perhaps; not on their own wives . . .

Rosa held one of the outfits – a bright scarlet silk – below Kate's chin and watched the customers' uncertain expressions turn to ones of reflection.

One of the women stepped forward and fingered the silky material with an almost sensuous gesture. She was the youngest of the group and had the same delicate colouring as Kate. 'It really is lovely,' she agreed. 'Very tempting.'

'On madam it would indeed be tempting,' murmured Rosa smoothly. 'Your husband would deny you nothing in such a garment.'

There was a titter among the women and they nudged each other. It was clear that the husband of the young woman in question denied her little to start with.

As though making up her mind, the woman said, 'I'm going to! I'll take it, Rosa. Have you one in my size?'

'If this is the colour madam would like, this is your size,' said Rosa. She looked over her shoulder at the watching women. 'We have others, ladies, all colours and sizes, and what we cannot supply today we can soon have made up.'

Her smile was beguiling and the women eyed each other warily. 'Oh, come on,' urged their more decisive friend. 'Don't be such a lot of old fogies. I bet Mrs Simpson wears something like these on those Mediterranean cruises she shares with the King.' Catching Kate's eye she added in a whisper behind a raised hand, 'I bet *they* still wear 1900s-style bathing suits and woollen vests, even in summer.'

Kate managed to suppress a giggle.

Besides the scarlet creation, they sold two others, with promises to make two more for women who requested less vibrant colours. 'It will be bad enough appearing in public in *trousers* without adding insult to injury and parading like a scarlet woman,' they commented.

Closing the shop door after bowing the group of women out, Rosa accepted the cup of coffee Kate had ready and said, 'Well, our dear Lord will have to excuse me again from Mass tomorrow morning. That's me for the sewing machine all weekend, I'm afraid.' She gave Kate a conspiratorial smile. 'I hate to think what all this is doing to my soul.'

117

'I do wish you'd let me come in and help,' said Kate, with heart-felt earnestness. 'I don't mind, really I don't . . .'

'*Liebling!*' There was a wealth of affection in Mrs Konig's voice. 'I wouldn't dream of asking you to give up your Sunday. Don't you think you do enough – working all week in an office and spending part of your Saturdays in here – without coming in on your one day off? I *would* have your mama on my neck, as sure as God made little apples.'

Although hers was an argumentative nature, Kate left it at that.

Dodging the crowds in the busy High Street, turning into Wesley Avenue, Kate hoped that the heated feelings of this morning had been resolved. She found Monica reclining in her usual position in the garden, sunning herself and reading a book. In the kitchen the breakfast dishes were still in the sink, and there was a smell of cold fat from the frying pan left lying on the top of the stove.

Rebellion stirred in Kate. Resolutely she turned her back on the unappetizing sight, closing the kitchen door firmly after her. As she emerged through the open French doors leading to the garden, Monica looked up from her novel.

'Ah, just in time to make me a cup of tea, Kate.' She stretched, arms thrown wide in the warm sunlight. 'The sun always makes me so sleepy. But isn't it lovely, dear. If this weather keeps up I should be all nice and brown again in no time . . .'

'Where's Daddy?'

The abrupt question halted the flow of words. 'He went out, dear. Didn't say where he was going. You know your father . . .'

'I know, always good for a joke and a cuddle,' repeating the words Monica so often quoted about her husband. 'And where's Mr Patrick? What happened after I left for the shop this morning? Is that man going to move out at the end of the week?'

Monica's lips pursed, a sure sign of disapproval. 'Very crass of your father, Kate, to put it like that. But I really don't think it's any business of yours. Grown-ups do not usually discuss their affairs with their children. Not in polite society, anyway.'

'I think I have a right to know. He's my father and it's my home too.'

'Oh, dear, don't tell me we're going to have all that again? Really, Kate, for a girl your age you're very presumptuous.'

'An innocent question as to where my father is – that's presumptuous?'

When her mother showed no sign of answering but with a weary gesture picked up her book and began to read, Kate drew a deep breath and went back indoors. Almost out of habit she lit the gas under the kettle and began on the sinkful of dirty dishes.

Giving the top of the stove a hasty wipe, she made a pot of tea and carried a cup out to the garden. She plonked it down without a word beside her mother's chair, then retreated to the sitting room.

She was drinking her own tea, listening to a programme of dance music on the wireless when Samuel came home. In her hurry to rise from her chair, to speak to him, she almost upset her cup, managing just in time to save it from spilling on to the carpet.

'Daddy! Are you all right? I was so worried about you . . .'

Completely out of character, Samuel had spent the lunch hour in the Green Man, a popular watering-hole for the males of the town. And quite a number of the females, too. He'd lost all track of time and the landlord had had to resort to bodily force, pointing out that it was well after closing time.

His usually neatly brushed hair was untidy, hanging over his forehead, the knot in his tie was somewhere under his left ear and a pearl button was missing from his white shirt.

In the dimness of the hall he peered at Kate, grinning fatuously when he saw it was her. 'Ah, Katie! You're home!'

'Yes, and by the look of it, it seems you should have been home long ago.' She went to him and took his arm, guiding him through the door of the sitting room. 'A good strong cup of tea is what you need. Sit down and I'll get you one.'

His eyes vague, Samuel gazed about him. 'Where's your mother, Katie? Has she gone out? That Patrick fella went out just after you did this morning.' His mouth turned down at the corners. 'Your mother wasn't too pleased, I'm afraid. Not at all pleased, in fact.'

'She's in the garden, reading.'

Leaving her father sitting in the big armchair, she went into the kitchen and reached for another cup and saucer. Just as she was taking it to him, there was the scratch of a key in the front door, which was pushed open, admitting a flood of bright sunlight – and their lodger's voice: 'What a pleasant sight, being greeted with a cup of tea as I walk in!'

Kate didn't even bother to reply. She could see he was in a jovial mood – like her father, he looked as though he had spent the morning in the convivial company of other men escaping the sometimes traumatic problems of home. There was a graze on his cheek and a spot or two of blood on the collar of his shirt.

She continued on her way to the sitting room and placed Samuel's cup beside him on the small lamp table. He looked up at her. 'Did I hear that man's voice? Has he just come in?'

As he spoke, their lodger appeared in the doorway. Samuel was on his feet in an instant. Gerry Patrick stood gazing at him, then, with an air of contempt, said, 'If you don't mind me saying, old man, you look as though you've been in an accident.'

Samuel eyed him sourly. 'You don't look so good yourself.'

One hand was raised to the raw-looking graze. 'A slight disagreement over who should pay for the next round. It's not much.'

'Well, it will be this time.'

Monica, hearing voices, had risen from her chair in the garden and was about to step through the open French doors when Samuel hit their lodger. The punch caught Patrick on the jaw, knocking him sideways. He clutched at the embroidered cloth that covered the lamp table, and Monica gave a little scream as the glass reading lamp, followed by the cup and saucer, crashed to the floor.

Kate was to remember the scene that followed for the rest of her life. Her mother rushed to Gerry Patrick's side, kneeling and cradling his head in her arms. The look she directed at both her husband and her daughter was poisonous. Their lodger, although shaken by the unexpected blow, looked as though he was enjoying the fuss Monica bestowed on him.

'That was a cowardly thing to do,' she accused her husband, her voice grating. 'Despicable. You're just jealous because he's successful and you're not.'

Samuel gave a harsh laugh. 'That'll be the day, when I'm jealous of him!'

Kate wanted to cover her ears with her hands in order to block out the contempt in her mother's voice. Contempt for her husband . . .

Mr Patrick was struggling to his feet. Monica assisted him, giving him her shoulder to lean on. One arm about his waist, she led him to the door. 'Come on, let's get you upstairs.'

Samuel dropped into the armchair and sat with his arms dangling limply over the sides. A deep sigh shuddered through him. 'I've done it now, haven't I, Katie?' Then a sudden, completely unexpected smile lit up his face. 'But, by God, it felt good. I should have done it long ago. I always had the feeling your mother was falling completely under that blackguard's spell. Yes, I should have done it long ago. After he's gone she will settle down again, become her old self.'

Kneeling on the carpet, busy picking up the pieces of broken glass and china, Kate thought how easy it was to deceive oneself. Her mother would never return to her old self. She would always blame her husband for the change in their lives, harping constantly on the loss of the lifestyle they had once enjoyed. Never once trying to fit into her new circumstances.

Kate was lying in bed, trying to concentrate on a new Monica Dickens book, when she heard them quarrelling. She slipped from her bed and tiptoed to her partly open door with the intention of closing it. But something seemed to force her to stay there, cringing as she listened to the low, bruising words.

'It's just not right, you and me. It's never been right since we had to come home.'

'But it was.' Her father's voice rose on a piteous note. 'It can be again. We've got so much, each other, Katie . . .'

'That's not the point. It's not fair on me . . .'

'Monica, darling, we can work it out. We've always worked out our differences in the past . . .'

Kate heard something fall, as though her mother had brushed an angry hand across her dressing table.

'*No*, never, never, never! How much longer do I have to put up with this boring dump? A year? Ten years? I want more than this shabby life, Sam, much more.'

'So do I.'

Monica had worked herself up into an exaggerated state where she hardly knew what she was saying. Kate heard her sob, 'I wish I were dead.'

'I know the feeling.'

Kate heard the bedsprings creak, imagined her father crossing the room to where her mother sat before her dressing table, putting his arms about her.

Samuel's voice had changed, become more assertive. 'Look, all I really wanted was to make you and Kate happy, to keep you safe. You know, Monica, I do love you . . .'

Guiltily, Kate closed her door. Sleep was a long time coming that night.

In her dreams, everything was as it had once been, with sunshine and shadows falling across beds of bright flowers, and her parents laughing and happy, loving each other. But when she awoke, her pillow was wet with tears.

Chapter Thirteen

During the quiet few minutes the following Saturday, when Rosa and Kate were sitting enjoying a cup of tea, Paul joined them. He was on his way, he said, to report on a wedding reception at St John's, the local C of E church. 'It's the Mayor's daughter,' he said. 'She's marrying one of the partners of that imposing law firm in Park Avenue. These people certainly relish seeing their names in the paper.'

Rosa looked up at him. 'Where did she buy her wedding dress?'

Paul grinned. 'Gosh, Mother, I don't know, but from all accounts it's a real eye-opener. I expect I'll have to ask someone about that. It will all be in my report, don't worry.'

Rosa gave a barely suppressed snort and rose to her feet. Clearly disgruntled by the fact that the bride-to-be hadn't commissioned her gown from Rosa's, she went into the shop. The two young people could hear her moving about and Kate, catching Paul's eye, murmured, 'Oh dear, now you've hurt her feelings. Perhaps it might have been wiser not to have said anything about the dress.'

Paul shrugged. 'She's got enough to cope with already. Why does she think she can handle more? She's going to make herself ill if she's not careful.' He paused. 'Do you know, I sounded just like my father then. But my mama's always been a glutton for work. He was forever pointing it out to her. Her hands were never idle. Even when she was sitting with us of an evening she'd have a piece of knitting or needlework in her lap.'

Looking up, Kate saw the darkness of remembrance cloud his eyes, and knew he was back in that cosy room in the suburbs of Berlin, before the trouble came . . .

'Have some more tea,' she said, her voice brisk. 'There's plenty in the pot.' She moved to pick up his cup but he stayed her by laying one hand over hers. 'Tea,' he said lightly, 'the panacea for everything that ails you!'

There came the sound of the shop door opening, then voices and Rosa calling: 'Kate!'

Kate rose. 'I'd better go. Sounds as though the rush has started again.'

'Me too.' Paul glanced at his wristwatch. 'The wedding's at two

123

o'clock and I'm supposed to meet the photographer outside the church in – gosh, just ten minutes.' Looking at her, his mouth turned down at the corners. 'How time flies when you're enjoying yourself!'

Kate laughed. She preceded him back into the shop, watched as he went out into the sunlight, then turned her attention to the bevy of ladies who clustered about the selection of new summer frocks Rosa held on hangers for display.

The silken beach pyjamas were selling well. One or two of the ladies said that their husbands, as suspected, *had* frowned, but most had agreed they would look grand on the beach. There were sniggers; remarks whispered behind raised hands, 'And who knows what it might do for your love life!'

Kate pretended she hadn't heard. Ignoring Rosa's asides that it was time she went home, Kate stayed for the rest of the afternoon. Never before had she felt such reluctance to return to that silently hostile house.

Finally, just as the lamps were coming on in the High Street, she gave in to Rosa's urging and set out for home. The pubs were busy – the Green Man in particular. It offered a garden where rustic wooden tables and benches were positioned on a lawn. On this summer evening, there were families with children running around, and music from a large radiogram escaping from the wide open doors leading to the bar.

The music of one of the popular big bands floated in the deep purple of the early summer evening and Kate hummed the tune as she walked. Most of the shops in the High Street were either closed or on the point of closing. The front door of Mr Shipton's grocery store was shut tight although a light still shone from within. Through the window Kate could make out the bulky shape of the proprietor himself, obviously counting the day's takings. Beside him was the slumped figure of his assistant, Ruthie.

Seeing the girl look up, Kate lifted a hand in a wave. Ruthie's face in the cold hard light of the unshaded bulb stood out stark and white. Kate saw how she flinched as Mr Shipton turned to say something to her.

Kate sighed. No one, it seemed, was without troubles. Everyone had their own cross to bear. Just the other day, when she'd been to confession, she'd poured out to Father O'Hanlan the bitterness and hate she felt for Gerry Patrick and the way he'd upset their bright new life. She thought again about the words of the old priest: 'I shall call on your home, my child, the next time I find myself your way.'

Alarmed at the things she'd blurted out in the sanctuary of the confessional, she said, 'Oh, no, there's really no need. It's not your concern, Father.'

Sternly, he'd corrected her. 'It is my concern to be a member of each family and yet not a part of it.'

124

Whether he had called Kate was never to know. It would have been during the day, while she was at work. If he had, and Monica had guessed at the source of the accusation, then she had said nothing.

Kate was halfway down Wesley Avenue when she heard footsteps behind her. Running footsteps that seemed to stumble in their haste. In the deepening twilight she stopped, turning to see the dishevelled figure of Ruthie, the grocer's girl, hastening towards her.

The light from a nearby streetlamp illuminated the white face and wide, frightened eyes, the thin trickle of blood that ran from her mouth . . .

Kate caught her breath in distress. 'Ruthie! Whatever happened? Have you been attacked?'

Who could have done such a thing? Anyone knowing Ruthie would know she would have little or no money on her. What beast loose in their quiet little community would have stooped so low? Kate had seen her only minutes ago, safe in the shop with her employer.

The girl seemed too upset to answer. Sensing the uselessness of trying to question her now, Kate put one arm round her, murmuring reassuringly, 'Come on, let's get you home . . .'

Ruthie gave a little scream. 'Home! I can't go home in this state, miss.' Kate felt the shudder that ran though the thin body. 'Me dad'd kill me if he finds out, which he will, mark my words . . .'

'I didn't mean your home,' Kate assured her soothingly. 'You can come home with me, tell us what happened and I'll get my father to go for the doctor.'

A second scream followed. 'God, the fat would be in the fire then. And I can't afford no doctor.' She frowned. 'Look, just lend me your handkerchief and I'll wipe off some of this blood and try to slip into the flat without my mum or dad seeing.' She gave a grimace that caused her to wince, fingers going up to touch the split lip.

'Where do you live, Ruthie?' Kate gazed about her in the semi-dusk. 'In one of these houses?'

'Fat chance! We live in a place called Paradise Buildings, on the other side of the railway tracks.'

Kate nodded. 'I know it. Paul Konig lives there with his mother.'

'Yes, I've seen him about. That boy Mr Shipton ignores when he's in the shop. Mr Shipton don't like foreigners, German foreigners especially.'

'His prejudices don't stop him from taking rent from Mrs Konig,' said Kate scornfully.

'Oh, well, that's different, in't it? That's money.'

'Anyway, you look dreadful. I still think you ought to see a doctor. That lip . . .'

Ruthie drew a deep breath, then lifting both hands, raked the spread fingers through her tangled hair. Creating a semblance of order, she looked at Kate. 'Thanks, miss, but I really do feel a bit more settled now. On second thoughts it's better if I get on home. I can tidy meself up and be tucked up in bed before me mum and dad get home.'

'If you won't see a doctor, we ought at least to inform the police. You can't let whoever did this get away with it. You were *attacked*, girl. Don't you understand? That's classed as a crime.'

'I weren't attacked, miss. It was just Mr Shipton trying his old tricks.' She attempted another smile, wincing again at the cut lip. 'Tonight he just got a bit too carried away, that's all.'

Kate was horrified. 'Mr Shipton did this?' And from all accounts, he'd done it before, if not so violently. Kate had surmised that there was something unpleasant under the outward bonhomie of the grocer. No wonder the girl had looked so intimidated in his company. 'You can't let him get away with this, Ruthie. You *must* tell someone . . .'

'And lose me job, miss?'

'Would your mother and father prefer to have you suffer this kind of treatment than to lose your job? Wake up, Ruthie, this is the nineteen-thirties, not the Victorian age when women and children worked in the coal mines. You have *rights* now. We all do.'

The girl shook her head. 'Me mum and dad don't know how Mr Shipton is.' She drew another deep breath. 'Jobs aren't easy to get, miss. A girl like me, with 'ardly any education, well, we can't be fussy, can we?'

'But what will you tell them? I mean, they can't help but notice something is amiss.'

Ruthie shrugged. 'I'll think of something. Mum don't usually take any notice of how I look, and me dad'll be too muddled with drink to care.'

And she fancied *she* had problems, Kate thought grimly.

She made up her mind with her usual celerity.

'Look, Ruthie, what if I got you a job in Rosa's? Mrs Konig's always saying we could do with an extra pair of hands.'

Ruthie blinked. 'Doing what, miss? I don't know nothing about serving ladies with clothes.' Her mouth twitched. 'Mr Shipton's forever telling me how I couldn't even serve a customer with a dozen eggs without breaking half of 'em.'

A young couple wandered by, arms about each other. They glanced briefly at the two girls as they passed, continuing on their way.

Kate took the other girl's arm, urging her slowly along the road, their shadows thrown by the lamplight far-reaching before and then behind them. 'How are you at sewing? Have you ever done any?'

'Make all my own frocks, so I do, miss.' There was an air of pride in

Ruthie's voice. 'And the frocks for my little sisters.'

'So you know how to use a treadle sewing machine all right?'

'Mum's got an old hand machine, bought it from a stall in the market, she did. Never tried a treadle, miss.'

'Well . . .' Kate smiled. 'I expect you'll soon learn. In the meantime, we could do with someone to deliver orders to our customers and tidy up in general.' She hesitated for a moment, wondering if she was being too hasty. And yet Rosa had said, more than once, that the business was getting too busy for just the two of them. And with Paul working all hours – well, Ruthie would be an asset.

'I don't know what Mrs Konig would pay,' she said, 'but I'm sure it would be comparable to what Mr Shipton gives you.'

'As long as I'm bringing something into the house, miss, me mum won't mind where I work.'

The girl seemed to have made a miraculous recovery. There was no trace of the servility that had been so evident before. Away from the sharp eye of the supercilious grocer, she even sounded different.

It was wonderful what a little fresh hope could do for a person, thought Kate. If only it was that easy in her own situation.

Pausing beside her gate, the light left on in the hallway shining golden through the glass panels, throwing a warm glow over the small garden, Kate again felt pity stir in her. She remembered the cold iron spookiness of the railway bridge over which the girl must cross on her way home.

Looking towards the light, she said, 'My father's in. Won't you come in and have a cup of hot chocolate or something? You could use our bathroom to tidy yourself up . . .'

Ruthie was shaking her head. 'Thank you for the offer, miss, but I'd better not.' Once more she touched the split lip with gentle fingers. 'I don't especially want to explain all this, for I know I look a sight. It's best if I hurry over the footbridge to the flats. Goodnight and thank you for everything.'

She half turned, then looked back, hesitant as a kitten about to enter a strange room. 'Will you be in touch about the job, miss, or shall I call in and see Mrs Konig myself?'

'I'll speak to her, Ruthie. And please, my name is Kate. All right?'

If Ruthie had been able to smile, her grin would have been wide with pure delight.

Kate stood watching until the girl was out of sight, then paused a few moments longer, leaning over the gate, her gaze fixed on the light that had just come on in the side window of the house belonging to Guy Ferris's grandmother.

One day, she told herself, and it was almost like a promise, one day he would arrive in the doorway just as she reached the house. He would stop, his eyes crinkling at the corners as though amused at something she had said.

She stood and wished with all her might that he would appear, if only for a second. But of course he didn't. She imagined him idling away his summer vacation somewhere in the sun, perhaps the South of France. Girls flocking around him . . .

She sighed. Idiot! Allowing herself to be carried away by her foolishness. By the dreams she had wound about him. He probably wouldn't even remember her when he did come home.

She turned and fitted her key in the front door. The house was very quiet. Strangely quiet, for Daddy liked to listen to the Saturday-night play on the radio, which should be on now.

'Daddy?' Her voice seemed to echo in the stillness.

'In here, love.'

She pushed open the sitting room door, seeing her father lying supine in his big chair before the empty grate. Alarm quickened in her. 'What's wrong? Aren't you feeling well?' She watched as his hand fell and dangled over the arm of his chair. 'Daddy? What's the matter?'

Her father looked up at her, and then around the room distractedly, as if struggling to trace a sound or a memory or a fragrance. His eyes returned to Kate and he rubbed one hand across his forehead, as though trying to rid himself of an intense pain.

'Your mother's gone.'

Kate felt herself tense. She walked slowly to the side of his chair and stood looking down at him. 'Gone? What do you mean, gone? You mean she hasn't returned yet from the pictures?'

'I mean gone. Left us, Kate.' The words came out with an effort, and however feasible it seemed in view of Monica's past behaviour, it had to be a lie.

'Left us? How could she have left us? Where would she go?'

Almost casually, he held out a crumpled piece of paper. 'She even left us a going-away present. Go on, read it. It certainly made my day, I can tell you.'

Kate's eyes scanned the short note.

That scene last Saturday at breakfast was the last straw. For a whole week I've thought about it and I've decided I can't take it any more. Gerry feels the same, so we've decided to go away together. Really, Sam, it's for the best and it's better we recognize the fact before it causes any more unpleasantness.

Kate drew a deep breath and then said, 'I shouldn't worry too much, Daddy. You know Mum, how hasty she is.' She bent to drop a kiss on the top of his head. 'She'll be back in a day or two. You'll see.'

The question of Monica hung suspended between them. It delayed itself until after supper when she heard him go upstairs, heard his footsteps on the floor above her in the bedroom he had once shared with his wife. When he reappeared at the door, he looked ashen and so drawn her heart went out to him.

'Daddy . . . ?'

'She's taken all her clothes. There's nothing left. We've got to stop fooling ourselves, Kate. Your mother's gone, she won't be back.'

Chapter Fourteen

The wounds left by his wife's desertion were deep and traumatic to Samuel, and in spite of the reassuring things she said to her father, Kate often felt helpless. Lost, as if all the security had been knocked from under her feet, leaving her floating towards cheerless days and sleepless nights.

She revealed her feelings to Paul, blessing him for always being there to listen. Nothing she had ever told him had been repeated and she appreciated his sound judgement.

They were sitting in a local milk bar frequented by the young of the town, sharing a leather-covered seat. Feeling the need to talk to someone, she had arranged to meet him in her lunch hour for a sandwich. Only one other young couple sat in the far corner, and they were so engrossed in each other the ceiling could have fallen in and they wouldn't have noticed.

Paul put his arm around her shoulders and squeezed her protectively. 'Your poor papa has drained his cup of misery to the dregs,' he said, in a theatrically sombre way, making her laugh. 'But something good will come of it. Something always does. What is your saying? Every cloud has a golden lining?'

She knew he was trying to lighten the mood left by her story and gladly went along with it.

'Silver,' she said. 'A silver lining.'

He gestured airily. 'Whatever! There will be silver linings for everyone by and by, just you wait and see.'

'You should have been a song writer,' she said, 'instead of a junior reporter on our local rag.'

'One has to have been in love to become a song writer. Being in love is something I have yet to experience.'

He bit into his sandwich, made a face and then held it out to Kate distastefully. 'What *do* they use for tomatoes around here? These taste like rubber balls.'

Dad's tomatoes were a credit to his hard work, sweet and juicy. Kate wondered how anyone could go wrong in growing tomatoes.

'You should have ordered the egg and cress like I did,' she said. 'Having experienced their tomato sandwiches before, I steer well clear of them.'

131

He wrinkled his nose. 'Now she tells me!' Nevertheless, he took another bite. 'Have you heard that new jingle about Mrs Simpson?' he asked, washing the mouthful down with a swig of Coke.

'I don't know that I want to.'

There had been so many rhymes, most of them of a coarse nature, about the American woman who was the King's friend, and Kate was thoroughly sick of hearing them.

'It's quite clean. Based on that song, "That's My Weakness Now".'

Stubbornly, Kate shook her head. She reached for her handbag wedged between them on the seat. 'You sit and finish your sandwich. I've got to get back. The end of the month is always our busiest time at the office.'

He pushed his plate with the half-consumed sandwich on it out of the way and rose to his feet. 'Oh, all right, little Miss Prim, be like that. I'll walk with you. I've got to go that way.'

Later, she felt sorry for showing such little patience with him. He'd only been trying to cheer her up. Would she have treated Guy Ferris so brusquely?

She sighed and resumed her typing.

Guy Ferris wasn't here and it was a waste of time sighing and wishing he was. In times like this, when her spirits were at their lowest, all her suppositions about wishes coming true seemed banal. How could something come true just because you wished it? If she wished for her mother to get fed up with Gerry Patrick, would *that* come true, would Monica return, making their little family complete again?

Kate watched her father brood and become ill. The summer had passed into an early autumn, with grey skies and days of rain that made the garden impossible to work in. Samuel fretted that he couldn't get out to see to his dahlias and the few vegetables that were left. One day she came home to find him shivering in front of the fire. He looked weary almost to the point of exhaustion, with purple sagging pouches underneath his eyes, and a too hectic flush to his cheeks.

After a night spent coughing, keeping Kate as well as himself awake, he'd asked her to explain at work that he wouldn't be in that day. 'Get to the doctor,' she'd advised, using the tone of voice a wife uses to a recalcitrant husband, although it was a long time since Monica had shown concern for either his happiness or his health. 'Get him to give you some cough medicine.'

'I will, Katie, I will,' he assured her. 'You got your bus fare?'

Kate nodded. 'If the rain keeps up ask Mrs Bennett if she would phone the doctor for you. He couldn't expect you to go out in this.'

Kate had worried about her father whilst at work, wondering if he had taken her advice about the doctor. She made mistakes in her typing and was reprimanded by the chief clerk. Wisely, she'd tried to take her mind off her father and pay attention to her work.

And now here she was, breathless after running almost the whole way from the High Street bus stop, to find her father in damp clothing, shivering to beat the band.

'Dear God, Daddy!' she scolded. 'Why on earth didn't you change into dry clothing? And don't tell me, in spite of everything, that you actually *walked*, in *this* weather, to the doctor's?'

A fit of coughing shook him from head to toe. When at last he could speak, he gasped, 'I didn't go to the doctor's. After you'd gone, Katie, I sat awhile and felt better. The rain stopped for a bit and I thought some fresh air would do me good.'

She eyed him grimly. 'And?'

'Well, you know how I've been worried about the garden. There was still so much tidying to do before winter comes. I thought just a gentle half-hour wouldn't hurt me. But then, before I'd hardly started, the rain came again.'

'And you stood and got soaked!'

It was more an accusation than a question. Samuel actually blushed. Making a great show of bending to poke the fire, he said, 'We're going to have to order some more coal, Katie. The coal shed's just about empty.'

'I'll watch out for the coalman when he comes on Saturday,' she said. 'But never mind that now. Let's get you out of those wet things and into some dry clothing.'

'Tch, tch.' He shook his head. 'Katie, I never thought I'd hear you say that to your own father.'

She smiled. 'Well, let's put it this way. I'll help you upstairs and leave you in your bedroom. Put that new jersey on, the one Mum bought you last Christmas . . .' She bit her lip, seeing the sadness come into his eyes. 'Let's face it, Dad, we've got to talk about her sometime. We can't keep it bottled up like this.'

'I know, dear.' He sounded so dejected that tears came to her eyes. 'But not yet, eh? Not when I'm feeling so rotten.'

While he was upstairs changing, Kate slipped into Mrs Bennett's, apologizing for disturbing her when she was just getting supper. 'But my father's not at all well, Mrs Bennett,' she explained. 'I'm really worried about him. I didn't want him to walk to the evening surgery and I'm sure Doctor Shearer won't mind.'

'Oh, I'm sure he won't, dear.' She waved a hand in the direction of the telephone standing on its small table in the hall. 'Help yourself.'

133

'Thanks.'

Dr Shearer's housekeeper clarified what Kate already knew; that the doctor was at his surgery at this time of the evening, and after a long day it had better be important to bring him out once he'd returned home.

Kate assured her that it was.

'Very well, I'll inform him when he returns.'

'This evening, please!' prompted Kate. If they caught whatever it was in time maybe a day or two in bed – and off work, which was more worrying – could be averted.

'Yes, yes.' The housekeeper sounded irritable and banged the phone down before Kate could explain further.

Kate stood by, frowning worriedly, as the doctor examined her father. The examination finished, he rebuttoned Samuel's pyjama jacket then stood, winding his stethoscope around his hand before placing it back in the black leather bag.

'Will he . . .' Kate bit her lip. 'Will he have to go to the hospital, Doctor?'

At her words, Samuel looked worried. There was no national hospital service: instead hospitals charged patients fees in accordance with their means.

To his relief, Dr Shearer smiled and patted his shoulder. 'Oh, I don't think so, Samuel.' To Kate, he said, 'I'm afraid your father's got a touch of pleurisy. He will have to have plenty of hot drinks and bed. You'll have to keep a fire going in the bedroom, and keep him warm. He needs to put everything out of his mind but getting well.'

He looked around the room and asked, 'Is your mother about? Your father will need a lot of looking after.' Clearly, he couldn't see a girl of Kate's age doing this. He looked more closely at her, his eyes sharp. 'Your mother's all right, isn't she?' He could sense a mystery here, the way the girl's eyes avoided his.

'Yes, she's all right, Doctor. She's . . .' Kate worried a nail, searching for an excuse for her mother's absence. 'She's visiting my aunt in Buckinghamshire.'

The doctor snapped shut his black leather bag and glanced around the room to make sure he'd forgotten nothing. 'Well, my dear, I would suggest you get in touch with her. Someone will have to be on hand to attend your father at all times. And that's including the night.'

Kate nodded. She escorted the man down the stairs and saw him out. 'Thank you, Doctor.'

He settled his hat firmly on his head, glanced down at the prescription she held in her hand. 'Get that filled as soon as you can. And remember, keep him warm. I'll call again tomorrow. Get in touch with your mother, Kate. He'll need her now.'

After he'd gone, driving away in his black Ford, Kate shouted up the stairs that she was going to make a cup of tea and would bring Samuel's up.

A querulous 'Yes' drifted down the stairs.

She stood in the window of the sitting room, waiting for the kettle to boil, and thought of all that the doctor had said. She really ought to follow his advice and contact her mother. But even if she knew where her mother was, would Monica be remotely interested?

She watched the russet leaves drop from the trees and float slowly down on to the wet pavement. They clung there, lifeless and limp, and she thought how very like that she felt herself.

When the kettle had boiled, she made the tea and carried a cup up to her father. He looked woefully at her. 'Pleurisy?' Samuel said, and from the way he spoke it could have been the plague.

Kate telephoned in to the dairy the following day, explaining about her father's illness, adding that she would have to take time off too. She was put through to the manager and noted the exasperation in his voice when he said she *would* have to pick just now, when they were so busy. As though it was her father's fault; as though he had fallen ill deliberately, just to spite the manager.

'How long will you be away?' he asked, his voice brusque.

'I have no idea, Mr Morgan. But I'll be in touch and will keep you informed.' Surprising herself at the competent way she was handling the whole sorry business.

Obtaining permission from Mrs Bennett to make yet another phone call, she rang the hotel in Victoria where they had stayed. The receptionist said that a Mr Patrick had once stayed there but moved out a couple of years ago. No, they had no idea of his present whereabouts.

Thanking Mrs Bennett, handing her a shilling to pay for the two calls – more than enough money, but there might be other times when she might have to phone someone – Kate hurried back to her father.

Dr Shearer called regularly, making a great show of unwinding his stethoscope and sounding Samuel's chest. Kate would watch his face as he bent over the bed, trying to decipher his expression. But it remained carefully bland and his parting words, that she was doing a fine job in taking care of her father and that he'd call in again tomorrow, had to suffice.

He had been forthcoming enough to explain just what her father was suffering from, that it was an inflammation of the pleura, the membrane lining the chest and covering the lungs.

Thinking of the fever Daddy sometimes suffered, recurring even in England, Kate asked, 'But how long is he likely to be bedridden?'

Dr Shearer had asked again about her mother and Kate had blushed as she mumbled something about how her mother had the 'flu but would travel home just as soon as she was feeling up to it.

'Hmmm . . .' He eyed her shrewdly. 'Did you explain just how ill your father is?'

Kate nodded. 'Yes, Doctor.' Another lie, but she was beginning to find that going through life without telling a few white lies was virtually impossible.

Her blush had been noted, however; Dr Shearer's profession meant that he knew a lie when he saw one. 'Well, let's hope it will be soon. There is no quick way to cure your father of what ails him.' He felt sorry for the girl, trying so hard to be responsible and grown-up. In his book she was doing a grand job. That Monica's nervous disorders had been a ploy for sympathy had become all too clear. She was an attractive and vivacious woman and he'd felt she could have made much more of herself if she hadn't been so full of self-pity.

Kate hoped the doctor didn't think she was being unkind, or callous, but she knew that the meagre sick pay the dairy paid them would not go on indefinitely. Benefits for being off work due to sickness remained at a low fifteen shillings a week, without any dependents' allowances. Kate had no idea how many weeks' money her father would be entitled to, but common sense told her it couldn't be for much longer.

She'd had to give up helping Mrs Konig in the shop on Saturdays. Her days and nights were fully occupied. In her dreams she ran in a never-ending marathon up and down the stairs, hefting buckets of coal and bowls of hot soup. Tinned soup; she didn't have time – or the knowledge – to make the broth Daddy remembered from his childhood, thick with lentils and barley.

He was a patient sufferer, complaining only when the fire in the small bedroom grate died down or the coal refused to ignite and blew out smoke.

'You'll have to watch out for what that coalman gives you,' he told Kate, following a coughing fit after smoke had billowed out when wind invaded the chimney. 'He's taking advantage of you, love, giving you inferior coal, thinking you don't know any better.'

And he's a hundred per cent right, thought Kate. Her upbringing had hardly been one that included bargaining with a coalman on an icy-cold morning while his horse stamped impatiently and she shivered at the gate in her flannel dressing gown. The woman from three doors away would be out, similarly attired, handling the dust pan and brush with proficiency, scooping up knobs of manure deposited by the horse. A highly prized asset, it was every man – or woman – for himself when it came to this booty for the garden.

Monica had viewed the whole thing, like much in their new life, with loathing. 'As long as your father doesn't expect me to do it,' she'd told Kate. 'Why, I think even your ayah would draw the line at *that*.'

'I'll speak to the coalman,' said Kate, tucking Samuel's blankets in tidily. She straightened, viewing the bedridden man with a worried frown. 'But we owe him for the last two weeks, Dad. It's not easy arguing with somebody when you owe them money.'

She had reached her wits' end. When Paul arrived on one of his periodic visits, Kate had been crying. She opened the door to his knock, her eyes red, sniffing into a handkerchief. Before letting him in she'd peered round the side of the sitting room curtains. She wouldn't have opened the door to anyone but Paul or Dr Shearer.

Looking at her, he said, 'Hey, hey, what's all this then? Tears?' A shadow of alarm shifted in his eyes. 'Has your father taken a turn for the worse?'

'No, it isn't anything like that. Although he's no better. Oh, Paul . . .' She turned to face him, her eyes wide, alarmed. 'What am I going to do? We owe money to everyone we deal with, and some of them are getting – well, impatient would be putting it too mildly. Mr Shipton was so churlish with me the other day that I swore to myself I'd never go in his shop again. You know he blames me for taking Ruthie away from him. I dread going there. If there was another grocer's within easy walking distance I – and, I imagine, a lot of other people – would gladly shun him.'

Paul snorted. 'Mr Shipton is a philistine. His comments to me have long since become meaningless. Did you know, after that unpleasant episode with Ruthie, he threatened to cancel the lease on the shop my mother rents?'

Rosa had said nothing to Kate about it. But then why should she? Kate turned away. 'But you don't want to listen to my problems . . .'

'If I hadn't wanted to listen to your problems I wouldn't have come,' Paul said. 'I am pleased that you think you can confide in me, Kate.'

'Did he – Mr Shipton – go ahead and cancel the lease?' she asked. Although she hadn't been able to join Mrs Konig since her father became ill, without that glamorous atmosphere to think about she would be desolate.

Paul shook his head. 'Times being what they are, even that lout knows that rent in the hand is worth two in the bush.' Seeing her grin, he shrugged. 'You know what I mean.'

Already she was feeling better. Paul always had that effect on her. 'I'll make some tea – or coffee if you'd prefer. Stay awhile and talk to my father. He'll be pleased to see you.'

Samuel had met Paul before and liked him and he had had to admit that the young man was pleasant enough. But then, Daddy took everyone as he found them. His relations with the Indians with whom he had worked, and with those who worked in the house, were always excellent.

If only it had been the same with him and her mother, thought Kate wistfully.

Paul spent half an hour seated in the white basket chair by the side of the bed, talking agreeably to Samuel about football. Standing on tiptoe, as later she saw him to the door, Kate kissed him on the cheek.

'Thanks for coming, Paul. I'm sure you cheered Daddy up no end. Give my love to your mother and tell her I'll come in just as soon as I see my way clear.'

Paul thought of the hectic preparations taking place in the shop as Christmas approached. Ruthie was proving an asset. But she couldn't do the delicately fine needlework that Kate excelled in. Nor could she design outfits, and without Kate's drawing skills, something was lacking.

The following day, shopping in the High Street, Kate popped in to see Mrs Konig and Ruthie. 'Kate!' Mrs Konig's voice rose in a preliminary shriek, then she added, 'You have come back to us!'

How Kate wished she could answer yes to this. Paper patterns spread across the cutting-out tables in the back room, the scraps of material – silks, chiffon, fine English wool – all brought tears to her eyes. On the row of tailor's dummies standing at one side of the room, dresses in various stages of completion showed how busy they had been. Ruthie was sitting, head bent over a skirt the hem of which she was sewing with fine slip stitches.

'I'd love nothing better than to come back, Mrs Konig,' Kate said, accepting the inevitable cup of tea which seemed to appear from nowhere. Then she saw the young woman, dressed in the type of overall she herself had worn, follow Rosa from the tiny kitchen.

Her heart did a funny sort of tumble. Had they replaced her with someone else? You couldn't blame Mrs Konig if she had. Goodness knows how much longer she would be absent from work, risking her office job as well as this one.

Rosa smiled and said, 'This young lady has joined our staff, Kate.' She introduced the two girls: Kate Linley; Sarah Wells.

The name sounded familiar to Kate. And then she remembered her first visit to Mr Shipton's shop, and the fat woman resting on the chair talking about her daughter and pigs flying past. Kate had deduced that Sarah Wells was a lazy little madam; certainly not one to be proud of as a daughter.

Plumper than fashion decreed – wasn't it Mrs Simpson who had been quoted as saying that a woman could never be too rich or too thin? – Sarah Wells eyed Kate's slim figure and pale-silver gilt hair, and jealousy sparked in her eyes. Her own hair was a dull mousy brown. Although she'd tried to brighten it with an application of Egyptian henna the attempt had failed miserably, and reddish strands streaked through the brown.

'We had to find someone else,' said Rosa. 'We were getting so busy.' She took a delicate sip of the tea which she still hadn't got used to. Coffee was much more to her taste, but good coffee was expensive and the cheaper Camp coffee that came in a bottle an abomination. 'What I really need is someone to come in full time. Maybe, Kate, when everything is settled, you would consider it? I would pay whatever you earn at your present place of employment, maybe more.'

The girl was a favourite with the customers. She had a pleasant, mannerly way about her and her advice was eagerly sought in spite of her youth. Her eye for colour and texture was unique. For women who thought clothing was there only to keep them warm, Kate was a godsend.

While Kate was getting used to the idea, Rosa went on, 'But your poor papa? Tell me how he is, Kate. I have been heartbroken, thinking of you surrounded by all that worry.'

She didn't say: and all by yourself, too, but Kate heard it in her voice. Kate had had to explain to Rosa about her mother going away, thinking it best to be perfectly honest. Rosa had placed a lot of trust in her and so it hadn't seemed fair to keep her in the dark.

'It's taking a long time,' said Kate, looking down into her cup. 'The doctor says it's a matter of letting nature take its course. He gives Daddy medicine, bottle after bottle, and harps on about keeping him warm and giving him nourishing food. Beef tea and calves'-foot jelly . . .' She wrinkled her nose. 'Can you imagine anyone wanting to take calves'-foot jelly to make them better?'

Rosa smiled, shaking her head. She didn't even know what calves'-foot jelly was; some eccentric concoction that the mad English forced on their patients. Whatever it was, she thought she'd prefer to remain sick . . .

She lifted her cup to her lips once more, gazing at Kate over the rim. 'And there has been no word of your mother?'

'None. I've tried to get in touch but it's come to a dead end. I don't know what to do now.'

The desperation in her voice conjured up a sudden vision.

Mrs Konig saw again the cosy sitting room of her home in Berlin, saw the door burst open and the arrogant men in their grey uniforms lift her husband bodily from his chair. Without so much as an explanation they had taken him. She never saw him again . . .

Of course, there was no comparison between that and what this girl was going through. But her understanding was deep. She put out a hand and, taking one of Kate's, squeezed gently.

Chapter Fifteen

Samuel lay in bed, unable to eat. The food was the kind Kate thought good for him, but he pushed at his tray, staring disconsolately around him.

It was twenty years since he had slept without Monica by his side. He felt angry, ill-used. Monica should be here now, taking care of him, leaving Kate free to get on with her own life. Although it hadn't been Kate's choice to start work at the dairy, sitting behind a typewriter all day instead of following her dream, she had not complained but put all her energies into the training they gave her.

When the opportunity had come for her to take the part-time job at Rosa's, he'd been pleased. Even though it was only a few hours on a Saturday, at least it was something nearer her own heart.

And now even that, plus the jobs at the dairy, hers as well as his own, threatened to go down the drain. He picked up the book he'd been reading and tried to concentrate, to take his mind from his worries. It was a novel by Edgar Wallace, a writer he much admired, that Kate had got for him from the library. He could not read it. The print danced, the sense of the words registered hardly at all, the interest was gone.

That day's newspaper lay to one side of the bed, but even the excitement of the report of Amy Johnson arriving in Cape Town, after a flight of three days and six hours, held no interest.

'You're not eating, Daddy!' Kate scolded, coming into the room. 'You're never going to get better if you don't eat.' She bent to put a couple of knobs of coal on the fire. Since her little talk with the coalman, trying to hide her nervousness, the stuff he'd delivered had been better. Another battle won! she'd thought.

Wiping her hands, she turned to her father. 'If you don't fancy that, how about a bit of that sponge cake Mrs Bennett sent in and a cup of tea?'

Mrs Bennett had taken to bringing products of her baking to the back door once or twice a week. Apple pies, scones, Victoria sponges that melted in the mouth.

Samuel shook his head. He was losing weight and he had never had much flesh on him to start with. He felt as though he would never enjoy

141

his food again. He was miserable; the day was miserable, and by the look of the sky glimpsed through the bedroom window it would soon be raining again.

Kate lifted the tray from the bed and set it on top of the dresser. Her mother's portrait in a silver frame stared down at it, as though in disapproval. Kate settled on the place where the tray had been and looked at Samuel. 'You know, Daddy, I've been thinking. What if we ask Aunty Norma to come up for a while? I'm sure she wouldn't mind.'

He stared at her. There were dark circles beneath her eyes due to lack of sleep, and her whole demeanour was one of weariness. Dear God, he thought, she's so young. This really has been too much for her. In his selfishness he'd ignored her welfare, placed burdens on shoulders that were far too narrow to bear them.

'Would you like that, dear?' he asked. 'Shall we write and invite her?'

'Let's. I'll get on to it right away.' She rose, then hesitated before going through the door. 'Do *you* think she'll mind?'

'Well, she's got nobody but herself to worry about, and you know how much she likes visiting us.' He paused. 'Of course, this is a slightly different matter than coming to spend Christmas.' Catching Kate's frown, he smiled. 'Knowing the circumstances *and* Norma, I'm sure she will be offended if we don't ask her!' The sisters had never seen eye to eye about anything and Samuel would be pretty certain that in Norma's eyes Monica was the culprit.

The date was 13 December and by the time Aunt Norma arrived the King had broadcast the speech in which he said he could not rule without the woman he loved by his side. The newsreels in the cinema had shown the sad pictures of him walking from his car, carrying his small dog, boarding the ship that was to take him to isolation from his own country.

Aunt Norma shook her head. 'I don't know, things'll never be the same again.'

'Nobody twisted his arm,' said Samuel gruffly. 'He knew what he was doing.'

'Still, it seems such a shame. I mean, he was so well liked. Look how he cheered the coal miners and the other unemployed. You could swear he understood exactly what their feelings were.'

'I doubt it,' Samuel grinned. Reared in the splendour of royal palaces, surrounded by luxury, how could Edward know the feelings of the men whose gaunt faces stared into the lenses of the newspaper cameras?

Norma sighed and bent to rearrange Samuel's pillows, fluffing them with the expertise she gave to everything. Her coming had been a godsend, both to him and to Kate. Kate had been able to resume work at the dairy, thus ensuring that money was coming in regularly. Samuel's own job was being held for him, although he wondered for how long. He'd been off for a good number of weeks and although he was feeling better, Dr Shearer insisted he stay in bed so as not to risk getting another chill.

Christmas that year was, of necessity, a quiet one. Cards with their traditional pictures of robins, snow scenes and holly lined the mantelpiece. Samuel said he hadn't realized they knew so many people.

There wasn't one from Monica.

The doctor had allowed him to come down to a well-warmed sitting room. Kate made him a bed up on the sofa and stood, holding back the blankets, while supported by Aunt Norma, he swayed his way across the room.

Kate tucked the blankets securely about him, then stood back, smiling. 'There! All right?'

Norma had vanished into the kitchen. The kettle was singing its head off and she had some mince pies warming in the oven. Nothing to do with Mrs Bennett this time. Norma prided herself on her own pastry. They had decided not to bother with the traditional cake, thinking it might be too rich for Samuel to digest. Mince pies were all right, though. Norma had even made the mincemeat herself and so knew that only pure, fresh ingredients had gone into it.

It was four in the afternoon, not quite dark yet, but on the point of twilight. The sky and air seemed dark blue, lamps coming on everywhere and the pavements glistening with yellow light that gleamed in the half-melted snow. It had snowed overnight; light, wet flakes that drifted down and clung to everything.

Even though the room was warm, the stairs and narrow hallway had been icy. Samuel drew the green-and-black plaid blanket closer about his chest, grateful for the heat radiating from the roaring fire.

'Remember those other Christmases, Katie? The sunshine so bright and hot, the beds of marigolds old Ahmed always planted around the lawn? What wouldn't I give to be back there now.'

Kate turned from where she had been twiddling with the knobs of the wireless set. The station she'd selected was broadcasting carols, the pure voices of young boys filling the room.

'Would you really, Daddy?' He'd spoken this way before, but never with the intense yearning he manifested now.

Samuel decided that the time had come for him to confess. Kate was a young woman. It was only fair to tell her the truth. His voice trembled as he related the events that led up to his disgrace. 'You'd have thought, wouldn't you, that at my time of life I'd have been more discerning? That's always been one of my weaknesses, trusting people. Now I know I was nothing but a fool, throwing all that away because I *was* too trusting.

When it all came to light, the missing cash and fiddling of books, it was my duty to speak up. But I didn't, and so . . .'

He sighed, staring into the flames of the fire. 'If only . . .'

Kate's heart went out to him and she put her arms about his shoulders, saying quietly, 'It's all over now, Daddy, all gone. We've still got each other and that really is all that counts.'

Norma came back into the room bearing a tea tray on which was the plate of mince pies and three cups and saucers. She'd heard her brother-in-law's remark and Kate's reply as she came out of the kitchen. Never one for feeling sorry for herself, she expected this same discipline in others. If Samuel had been mobile she would have insisted on them taking the tube up to town and going round the shops. Followed by tea in a Lyon's Corner House and a show.

As it was, all she could do was try to make Kate's load easier to bear. She blamed her sister for everything that had happened. Monica could be a right little bitch when it suited her.

Norma had never forgiven Monica for instigating that affair with her own husband. Frightened and vulnerable and just back from the war, the horror of the trenches, of Ypres and its constant shelling, poor Douglas had been a soft touch for the scheming Monica.

After a spell in a military hospital, he had returned home, dispirited and filled with anxiety. The slightest sound made him jump; a car backfiring in the lane outside had him hiding under the bed, arms clasped about his head, crying like a baby.

Monica, then a precocious eighteen-year-old, came to visit. Her presence seemed to cheer him up. For a while he seemed better. Holding hands like a couple of children, they would take long walks in the quiet lanes and woods surrounding the little cottage. The village was very small: a post office, a couple of shops that sold everything, and a church. Beaton, in those days, didn't even possess a public house.

One day, coming back from a tiring journey into town, a journey that entailed two buses and much walking, Norma surprised the two of them on the settee in the sitting room. She dropped the shopping that had been the purpose of her trip, spilling the contents of the brown paper bags out on to the carpet.

For long moments she stood there, for once lost for words. Flat on her back, skirts raised to her waist, the slim form of her sister was shamelessly covered by that of her husband. For a moment they were too engrossed in what they were doing to notice her. Then, pushing at Douglas with both hands, Monica screamed.

Norma held herself perfectly still, her eyes on the brick-red face of her husband. It was all she could see, everything else blotted out of the picture. Her throat was constricted and dry. She felt nothing but horrified disbelief.

The next day Monica left, returning to their mother's house without even an apology. Norma had stood with her at the bus stop, both women grimly silent. Norma hadn't waited for the bus to depart, but had turned and made her way back to the cottage without even a farewell wave.

If Douglas had shown remorse it might have been different. But he hadn't. Soon it became obvious that Monica's sudden departure had brought about a relapse. The ghosts of dead comrades returned to haunt him. It seemed he had more affinity with the dead than with his own wife. He would walk by himself in the woods, staying away all day, returning only when the sun went down. Once he became violent and attacked Norma. She dabbed pancake make-up on the black eye left by a clenched fist.

A complete breakdown followed and shortly afterwards he was sent to what the local paper described as a 'place of restraint'. Norma visited him once a year, on his birthday. Sometimes he was talkative; other times he would just sit, staring out of the window, seemingly unaware of her presence.

Biting into the pastry she remembered so well from the school holidays spent at Norma's cottage, Kate mumbled, 'Umm, your baking really is the cat's whiskers, Aunt Norma.' The words: 'Pity the talent never rubbed off on my mother' hung on the tip of her tongue but she stopped herself in time.

'Don't forget to make a wish, Kate! It's your first bite, remember?'

'As if I would forget such an important custom,' grinned Kate. Briefly, she closed her eyes and made her wish.

Disturbed by her sudden, recent thoughts of Douglas, Norma jumped to her feet. 'I'll top up the pot, shall I? I see from the *Radio Times* that Mantovani is going to play after this choral concert. I love Mantovani. Don't you, Sam?'

The diminutive brought tears to Samuel's eyes. Monica would sometimes call him Sam . . .

'Better than those so-called swing bands any old time,' he said, grinning at Kate.

Kate made a face at him.

When Norma had disappeared into the kitchen, he said, 'What did you wish for?'

Kate pretended indignation. 'Now, now, Daddy, I would have thought you knew better than that. You know you're not supposed to tell. A wish made like that is a secret.'

He stared into the cherry-red heart of the coal fire and said, 'My wish was that we could all be together again, just like in the old days.'

'Oh, Daddy!' Kate's tender heart went out to him. After all that had happened, he still wished that! She went to kneel by the sofa, taking his hands in hers. In spite of the warmth of the room they were cold and clammy. 'My wish was to make lots of money and be able to give you everything you want.'

'You've already given me all that I could expect and a whole lot more.'

'Daddy, I just want you to be happy.'

'As long as I can be with you, my love, I'm happy.'

Samuel's recovery was slow, but finally Dr Shearer gave him permission to get dressed and sit in the garden. 'As long as he's well wrapped up,' he told Kate, with a warning frown. 'Another chill and we could start the whole thing over again.'

Kate assured him that she would follow his instructions to the letter. Spring promised to be early that year, with the days mild and sunny. Knowing his patient's fondness for his garden, Dr Shearer cautioned, this time looking at Samuel, 'And no picking up a fork or spade, hear? Not even a trowel.'

'I've bulbs to plant,' said Samuel. 'They're late going in as it is. If I leave it much longer they'll come to nothing this year.'

'Hard cheese,' said Dr Shearer bluntly, making Kate smile. 'Ask your daughter there, what's more important, late-flowering bulbs or your health?'

His voice gruff, Samuel said, 'You're mollycoddling me, the two of you. My Monica would never have mollycoddled me the way you are.'

'Yes, well . . .' said the doctor. 'Your Monica's not here to see, so let's just bear in mind what I've said, shall we?'

Kate had confessed to Dr Shearer one day the truth of her mother's absence. He'd been shocked, although he hadn't shown it. He liked the Linleys, had come to feel that he was a friend rather than just their local GP. He said to an apprehensive Kate, 'I know how you must be feeling, my dear, and my heart goes out to you and your father. But I'm sure everything will turn out well and your mother will see how foolish she's been and return to her family.'

Kate's lips twisted. Then he has more faith in human nature than I do, she thought.

Norma had returned to her cottage and her two cats which were being looked after by the good-natured neighbour. Before leaving she obtained a promise from Samuel that he would come down and stay a couple of weeks in the country with her.

'Do you the world of good,' she insisted. 'Eggs and farm butter and lots of milk. As well as all the fresh air you can stomach.'

Samuel promised faithfully that he would. Dr Shearer agreed that it was an excellent idea. Give it a couple of weeks, he said, just to make sure. Samuel opened his mouth to ask another question, but Dr Shearer stalled him. 'As for work, that will take a little longer, I'm afraid. Pleurisy takes its toll of a body, you know, you have to give it time.'

Throughout the long weeks of her father's illness, Kate went reluctantly to the dairy. At the end of the day, she would hurry home, stopping to buy the evening meal on the way. Always something quick and, of necessity, cheap.

The blow came one Friday, when, going into the accountant's office to collect her wages, Kate was also handed an envelope addressed to Samuel.

The elderly accountant suddenly spied an ink mark on his desk and, avoiding her eye, rubbed at it assiduously with the corner of his handkerchief. The ink spot proved difficult to remove and still avoiding her gaze, Mr Burke said, in a gruff voice, 'I'm sorry, Miss Linley, but I've had my instructions. Believe me, I'm very sorry but with times as they are . . .'

Kate didn't have to have a science degree to guess the contents of the envelope. Forcing a tight smile to her lips, she said, 'I understand, Mr Burke. Following the doctor's instructions, it may be some time before my father is able to work again anyway.'

Although she tried to sound calm and dauntless, Mr Burke detected the tremble in her voice. He felt as though he'd just kicked a beloved puppy or struck a child. 'Perhaps, when your father is feeling better, he will call and see us,' he suggested.

'Yes, perhaps he will.'

This time he smiled. 'In the meantime, we felt it was about time you were earning more. You will be, let me see, nineteen this year?'

'That's right.'

'Well then, you will no doubt be pleased to see we have included a little extra something in your pay packet.'

In the sitting room, with a background of raucous laughter from a variety show being broadcast on the wireless, Samuel tore open the cheap buff-coloured envelope. Kate watched him read the single folded sheet of paper. Afterwards he pocketed the few pound notes they had bestowed on him, screwed the letter into a ball and threw it with the envelope on to the fire.

'So . . .' he said, turning to Kate, trying to hide the cold trembling inside him, 'so that's how it ends, is it? Thrown out on to the scrapheap again. It seems nobody wants me.'

Kate sighed. Feeling sorry for himself would help no one. 'Daddy . . .'

'Your mother was probably more far-seeing than we gave her credit

147

for. She guessed what was coming, and got out in time.'

Kate tried again. 'Daddy, don't be daft! You hadn't even become ill when Mum left. How could she have seen this coming?'

Samuel reached for his pipe, hidden behind the clock on the mantelpiece and forbidden since his illness. He'd been good about not smoking but guessing his feelings, the indignity he must be suffering, for once Kate couldn't blame him.

Nineteen thirty-seven saw the coronation of the new King, George, and his Queen, Elizabeth. Parties were held in the streets, long tables placed end to end and covered in snowy white sheets, wooden benches along each side. Flags and bunting fluttered in the breeze, decorating anything and everything. Old wind-up gramophones were brought out and stood on tables. Anyone who had records to spare came running out, adding them to the pile that was already there.

The inhabitants of Wesley Avenue held a neighbourhood meeting to discuss if they should follow the trend. Only a tiny majority of the new owners were in agreement, the rest mumbling about noise and the litter that would be left afterwards.

'Mean lot of beggars,' said Paul, discussing this with Kate. 'How often do you have coronations in this country? What's a bit of noise and litter once in a blue moon?'

'I know,' Kate nodded in agreement, 'I was disappointed too. Still,' looking on the bright side, 'there'll be streets where partying'll go on all day. Easy enough to track one down.'

'Paradise Buildings is planning one. I wasn't going to bother but I'll go if you want to go.'

'Try and keep me away,' Kate laughed. 'It will be the high spot in my life.'

'What a very dull life you must lead then,' teased Paul gently.

As though mindful of the happy event, the weather remained warm and balmy. And Kate celebrated her nineteenth birthday. In spite of Samuel's fears his bulbs showed their green tender shoots in plenty of time to flower before the summer became too warm. He was even well enough to go with her and Paul to the party held in front of the grim Paradise Buildings.

It was the first time he had been this way, and he had never guessed that such streets could be within walking distance of the lower-middle-class snobbery of Wesley Avenue. England was really an eye-opener, he thought. He gazed at the shabbily dressed women and children who ran, shouting and singing amongst the laden tables. Poverty cheek by jowl with those who considered themselves more affluent.

Not that it seemed to bother the residents of Paradise Buildings. Enjoying themselves wholeheartedly, they sang all the popular songs of the day and of days gone by: 'Knees Up Mother Brown' and 'Tipperary' and, as the purple twilight fell over the scene, 'Pennies From Heaven' and 'The Music Goes Round and Around'. There was no shortage of food. Everyone provided something and what the people didn't eat the scavenging dogs and cheeky sparrows did.

'Having a good time?' Paul asked, sitting beside Kate on one of the benches.

'A wonderful time.'

Paul glanced across to where her father stood talking with a couple of men. All held pint pots in their hands and Samuel seemed to be enjoying the male company. The local breweries had supplied the kegs of beer that balanced on stands behind each table. Despite the eager participation by most of the men present, there was no sign of drunkenness or disorderly behaviour.

'Your father seems to be enjoying it.'

'Yes. I'm glad. It'll buck him up, being with other people. Now he's not working, he sees nobody but me. He seems, sometimes, to withdraw into a world of his own.' Kate's gaze rested on her father. 'It worries me.'

'Sad. I thought he had become reconciled to things.'

'He'll never do that. He blames himself for all that happened. He says if he'd been a better provider my mother would still be here.' Tears filled her eyes and she blinked rapidly, hoping that the dusk would hide them from Paul.

It didn't. He rose to his feet, pulling her with him. Someone had just put on a record of 'Deep Purple' and couples were beginning to dance. 'Come on,' he said, 'don't let's get morbid. This is supposed to be a happy event, remember?'

'I'm sorry. Of course it is.'

She let him lead her to the part of the road that had been left clear for dancing. The smooth, almost sensuous music helped her to relax, to ease the tight feeling of sadness that suddenly overwhelmed her.

Everyone was enjoying themselves. Why should she be any different?

Paul was a good dancer, his grip firm about her waist, guiding her among the crowd, some of whom, although quiet, were by now decidedly unsteady on their feet. She saw Ruthie dancing with a young man with glasses and slickly brushed-back hair. Ruthie was laughing, her cheeks flushed.

Following Kate's gaze, Paul said, 'It's nice to see Ruthie enjoying herself.'

'I forgot she lived here.'

'A well-known family in Paradise Buildings are the Smiths. Her father's exploits on a Saturday night are legendary.'

Kate looked puzzled, and Paul explained, 'His imbibing exploits in the public house, I mean.' He smiled down at her. 'But then, who are we to condemn? Perhaps Ruthie will have better luck than her mother in choosing a partner. I know the lad she's dancing with and he seems a steady sort.'

When the record came to an end it was turned over and the jerky rhythm of a conga filled the night.

Paul laughed. 'Not me.'

'Me neither.'

When they came off the 'floor' he was still holding her hand and only reluctantly let it go.

'I'll go and see if there's any lemonade or something, shall I?' he asked, noting the warm flush to her cheeks, the thin film of perspiration on her upper lip.

Over by the beer barrels someone broke into an impromptu version of 'God Save the King' and filled glasses and voices were raised in toasts to the new sovereign and his family. 'Here's to the little princesses,' Kate heard someone shout. 'God bless 'em.'

Poor Edward and the elegant but disliked Mrs Simpson were things of the past, already history.

Kate saw her father making his way towards her and moved up on the bench to accommodate him.

'Hi!' she smiled. 'Enjoying yourself?'

He glanced around him, looking vague, as though wondering what he was doing there. 'It's all right. I just can't help wishing your mother was here with us, though.'

'Oh, Dad!' She patted his hand. 'I doubt very much if Mum would have wanted to attend something like this. A bit beneath her, wouldn't you say?'

He looked even vaguer. 'Perhaps you're right.'

Kate felt a tingle of anxiety. 'You *are* all right, though, aren't you? Say if you feel tired. We can go home.'

He shook his head. 'No, Katie love, not tired. No more than usual, anyway. Just...' He frowned, trying to put his feelings into words. 'Just wearied, I guess. As though everything is too much trouble.'

'You'll be all right after a couple of weeks spent with Aunty Norma.' It had been arranged that Samuel would travel down to his sister-in-law the following week.

'Your Aunt Norma is pleasant enough, but she fusses too much.'

Kate grimaced. 'A little fussing never hurt anybody.'

'Oi, Sam!' The shout came from the group of men with whom he had been talking. He looked towards them. 'This keg's nearly finished. If you want another beer you'd better come and get it now.'

Kate gave his arm a little push. 'Go on, Dad. Enjoy what's left of the evening.'

Paul returned, carrying two glasses of fizzy lemonade. He handed one to Kate then sipped his, glancing at Kate.

'All right?'

'A bit warm, but refreshing.'

'I saw you talking to your father. How is he?'

'He wouldn't admit it but he's a little tired, I think.'

Paul took another sip. 'So, what's going to happen now?'

Kate raised her eyebrows. 'Oh, this will probably go on till the early hours.' She grinned. 'Or as long as the beer holds out, anyway.'

'I wasn't referring to the party but to you and your father. What's going to happen to you two?'

'Daddy is going off to spend some time with my aunt and I'll try and keep the home fires burning.'

He glanced at her in the semi-darkness. 'My mother mentioned that she'd asked you to come and work full time at Rosa's.'

Kate hesitated, taking another sip of her drink. 'I wondered about that, whether it was a firm offer or if she was just feeling sorry for me.'

He frowned. 'We all feel sorry for you, Kate, but not in the way you mean. There's nothing patronizing about it, we just want to help you.' He took hold of her hand again, squeezing it. 'Don't you know you're an asset to the shop? So many of her regular customers have asked when you're coming back.'

'Nice to know you're missed,' smiled Kate.

She took another sip. She missed the muddle of the back room, the ideas tossed at her by customers who had become her friends. Ideas which she had sketched and turned into reality; fashionable flowing gowns or slim-fitting woollen costumes. And the dream of one day owning her own place was constantly in the back of her mind. Lately, she had felt too debilitated and insecure to allow such figments of her imagination to excite her.

Even her dreams of Guy Ferris had had to take a back seat to more pressing matters. Like putting food on the table, taking care of her father.

Paul said, teasingly, 'I've never known a girl take so long to make up her mind. Is the prospect so disagreeable that you have to think about it?'

'No, no, it's wonderful, Paul. Truly wonderful. Of course I'll do it.'

'Will you tell Mama or shall I?' Paul queried. 'She'll be over the sun.'

'Moon,' Kate corrected, absent-mindedly. 'Over the moon. And I'll tell her.'

He gave that shrug that she knew so well. 'Whatever!'

By the time they started for home, Samuel had imbibed a little too well if not wisely. Unsteady on his feet, it took Kate and Paul, who insisted on staying to help, all their strength to get him up the steps and over the railway bridge.

Puffing, panting, alarming Kate more than a little, Samuel gasped, 'God, why do we have to come this way?' He stood gazing up at the flight of iron-runged steps that seemed to rise forever before him. 'I'll never make it.'

'Yes, you will,' muttered Kate firmly. 'Paul will help. Besides, to go by road is miles and I doubt whether we'd get a bus at this time of night.'

Finally over the bridge, Samuel swore he would never use it again.

'Well, there's not much likelihood of you having to,' said Kate drily. 'Not unless you've met some unattached lady who lives in Paradise Buildings and who has proffered an invitation for you to visit her. In which case you'll have to grow wings and take to the air.'

'Now that would be something,' said Samuel. 'I suppose I could always do an Amy Johnson for you.'

Kate laughed, and Paul knew that the memory of her laughter, like church bells calling one to mass, would always warm him.

Chapter Sixteen

A small gathering of women crowded round the window of Rosa's, admiring the window display to which Kate was just putting the finishing touches.

Carefully she hung the rows of flame and amber beads round the neck of the model, adjusted the bandeau of yellow silk on the dark wig and stood back, the better to view the whole effect.

The eye-catching display brought gasps of admiration from the small crowd; the combination of the multicoloured chequered silk shirt and Chinese-yellow wide legged sateen pants was daring enough to bring blushes to the cheeks of some of the more delicately reared women.

Kate nodded politely to the people she recognized, old clients of Rosa's, and slipped back into the shop behind the curtain.

Rosa stood sorting out a gay profusion of coloured beads on top of the glass counter. Beside her the tall white vase holding flowers from Samuel's garden augmented the appeal of the small shop.

Kate had resumed her habit of bringing a bunch in every Saturday. They were much admired by the ladies who shopped there, one or two enquiring if Mr Linley sold the products of his garden. Kate had to admit that he didn't.

'He ought to take up market gardening,' said one woman. 'I for one would gladly patronize him.'

The now established garden practically took care of itself. Samuel had returned from Aunt Norma's with a more healthy look and admitted he was sleeping better. But as time passed Kate couldn't help but notice the air of introspection that surrounded him. Since his return from Aunt Norma's, even his garden seemed to have lost its allure.

Sadly he was still out of work. It seemed, sometimes, to Kate, that he always would be . . .

'Are you sure the colours you have used are really appropriate?' queried Mrs Konig, lifting her head from her task. 'Do you think flame and amber blend well with the bright colours in that shirt?'

The six months Kate had been working full time with Rosa had given her a feeling of self-reliance, the confidence she had lacked before. Now she smiled. 'You have only to look out of that window to see their effect on passers-by,' she exclaimed. 'Bright colours are *in*; nobody wants to look at grey and beige and sluggish browns any more.'

'Still, they all have their place in fashion, my dear. Our customers, as you well know, range from the very young – girls whose mothers have brought them along to be fitted out – to the very elderly. Pearl greys and pale coffee shades are more to *their* liking.'

Although Kate adored working with Rosa, sometimes the longing for a shop of her own, where she could mix scarlet with purple or black with orange if she so wished, was almost unbearable.

Rosa was wonderful; Kate would never be able to express her gratitude for the experience she had gained working for her. But Rosa's penchant for sticking to the well-established methods she had learned in her youth stirred the beginnings of rebellion in the younger woman.

As always when it seemed that controversy might spring up between them, Kate said, 'I'll make us a cup of tea, shall I? Before the crowd come breaking down our door.'

Rosa smiled. 'One can always dream, *liebling*.'

Sarah was in the back room, sweeping up material discarded after cutting the patterns and Ruthie was out delivering orders on foot. To put it bluntly, Ruthie had not lived up to their expectations of her. The times Kate had come across her, standing lost in a daydream, gazing from the window of the small back room, were innumerable.

'She is young,' said Mrs Konig. 'At that age one dreams of many things.' She felt sorry for the girl, knowing something of her family background.

More likely she was dreaming of the boy with the slicked-back hair and glasses with whom she had been dancing at the coronation party, thought Kate. A wonderful woman was Rosa but too tolerant for her own good.

Kate went into the kitchen to put the kettle on. The caddy was empty and she went back into the shop, saying she would have to go out and get a packet of tea.

Rosa left her task of untangling the strings of beads and opened the cash till. Her gasp of shock made Kate hurry to her side.

'What is it?'

'The money. The four five-pound notes Mrs Portman gave me to settle her account. They're gone.'

Kate frowned, moving closer. 'They can't be!'

But they were. The drawer, divided into sections to take coins and notes, was empty of all but a handful of silver coins.

Rosa stood as though turned to stone, staring into the drawer.

A perplexed Kate repeated, 'It can't be! Nobody's used the till this morning.'

It was early, the shop had not long been open, and Mrs Portman had been their only customer. And Rosa herself had deposited the cash in the till.

Which left Ruthie or Sarah. And Ruthie had departed on her round of deliveries before Mrs Portman had come in.

'Has Sarah been alone in the shop since we opened?'

Kate nodded. 'I was doing the window and asked her to fetch me the window cleaner.'

Rosa drew a deep breath. 'And I was in the back room checking that we had enough black bugles to finish Mrs Burke's dress.' Trying to be fair, she added, 'She would only have been alone in the shop for a couple of moments . . .'

'Time enough.'

Rosa nodded and called, 'Sarah!'

The girl took her time in answering, finally appearing in the doorway of the back room, broom in hand, a sulky expression on her face.

'Wot's wrong? Wot is it?' She leaned on the broom, one hip jutting out, her hair taken back in a ponytail, long strands of it hanging over her cheeks.

Looking at her, Kate thought: she really is no asset to the shop. Rosa had been patience itself, trying to get her to tidy herself up. To no avail. Sarah would appear each morning looking as though she had got out of bed and without benefit of brush or comb come straight to the shop. As most of her work consisted of cleaning in the back room or kitchen, where no customers caught sight of her, it didn't matter. But this was too much . . .

Quietly, Rosa began: 'Sarah, did you have occasion to go into the till this morning for anything?'

The bold eyes flickered towards Kate then back to Mrs Konig. 'No. Why should I 'ave?'

Rosa seemed reluctant to voice her suspicions, so Kate uttered the words for her.

'Because there's some money missing. Four five-pound notes to be exact.'

Sarah gave her a look of pure hatred. 'Wot, you sayin' I took them?' The tone was insolent, challenging.

'I'm not saying anything of the sort, Sarah.' Kate darted a look at Rosa. The woman was looking uncomfortable and most uneasy. Taking her silence as permission, Kate went on, 'It's just that – well, there isn't anyone else . . .'

Sarah lifted her chin in a show of defiance. 'There's Ruthie. What's so wonderful about little Miss Ruthie that you're accusing me instead of 'er?'

'How about turning your pockets out and proving it, then?' Kate suggested tightly.

'I don't 'ave to do no such thing.' Sarah let fall the broom. Stepping over it, she went into the back room and emerged a moment later with her coat. 'I'm off. I'm not staying where people accuse me of stealing . . .'

Surprising Kate, Rosa stepped forward. With a forbidding look, she said, 'Right, you can go. But before you do I advise you to turn your pockets out. Then we shall see what we shall see.'

The girl clutched her coat to her, glaring at her employer. 'I won't. You're not in your own country now, where they can make you do anything they want. *You* can't make me . . .' Her tone was sneering and unpleasant.

'Then perhaps a call to the police will settle matters,' said Rosa, reaching for the telephone on its stand to one side of the cash till.

The girl swaggered a few steps towards the shop door and stood staring at her. 'You won't get away with this, you know. I'll 'ave me father come and sort you out. 'E's good at dealing with the likes of you.'

'I should be delighted to see your father,' smiled Rosa. 'Perhaps acquaint him with the more nauseating characteristics of his daughter's nature.'

''E wouldn't believe a word *you* said. Why should 'e?' the girl jibed.

This had gone far enough, Kate decided. Her voice cold, she said, 'Either you turn your pockets out or we phone the police. The choice is yours.'

From Sarah's expression it was obvious that she didn't want the police involved.

'Oh, orlright.' Sulkily she thrust her hands into the pockets of her coat, first one then the other. A moment later four large black-and-white notes fluttered to the floor. 'There,' she smirked. ''Appy now?'

'Entirely happy, thank you.' Rosa bent to pick them up. 'Happier still when you depart my premises.'

Without a word, Kate picked up the discarded broom and vanished into the back room to finish the sweeping. After that she popped out and bought the packet of tea. A good strong cup helped. For once both women were glad that no customers arrived to disturb them.

Nothing further was said about the affair and when Ruthie returned and asked about Sarah Mrs Konig had a plausible answer ready. Sarah had given notice, she said blithely, having found another job. She knew that if the two girls should meet, Sarah wouldn't be keen on blabbing about the circumstances surrounding her hasty departure.

There was time now for Rosa to cast an eye over the window. Although she hadn't changed her mind about the colour combination Kate had used, she had to concede that it was extremely effective.

'It still lacks something, though,' she murmured, head on one side. Kate had placed the model to one side of the window and it left an empty space that needed – what? Nothing bright or gaudy; there was enough of that in the display already. No, something subdued but eye-catching.

'A dog,' said Rosa. 'A large red setter type of dog. It would be perfect.'

Kate wrinkled her nose. 'Yes, it would. The only trouble is we haven't got a model of a dog . . .'

Rosa clicked her fingers, turning to her. 'But we have! In that shed at the back. Don't you remember, Kate, the display of the little girl in a red-and-white spotted dress throwing a ball for a . . .'

Joyfully, Kate breathed: 'A poodle! A small black poodle!'

How could she have forgotten? The display dated from before she had come to work for Rosa. But the times she'd stood on the pavement, memories flooding back at the sight of the little dog, were countless. The model dog was depicted crouching on its tummy, head lifted in a cheeky stance. Kate could almost believe it was real.

She was already on her way to the back door and the small walled yard at the rear, when Rosa warned, 'It might be in poor condition, Kate. Remember, it's a while since I used it.'

'We'll soon spruce it up. Don't worry. A good brushing will work wonders.'

Rosa smiled at her enthusiasm. 'If you say so.'

Passing through the tiny kitchen, Kate took the shed key from its hook near the door and crossed the yard. Throwing wide the door of the shed, she pulled the string just inside, lighting up a cobweb-covered bulb that hung from the ceiling. The place was a treasure trove! If Ali Baba had opened his cave to her she couldn't have been more thrilled.

Stacked neatly on shelves were boxes in which she presumed was packed the fake jewellery Rosa used for the window. On the oilcloth-covered floor was the colourful parrot in its wicker cage; the white-painted wheelbarrow with its cargo of imitation flowers; the plywood backdrop that depicted a stone sundial set against beds of bright flowers.

Other things, too, that she hadn't seen before. Tennis racquets propped against the wall, side by side with folded sunshades wrapped in cheesecloth to keep them clean.

Then her eye fell on the dog.

Poor thing, it was covered in dust and cobwebs. She lifted it gingerly, hoping the spider who had made its abode there wasn't at home. The black glass eyes gazed blankly at her and she felt tears come to her own. So like poor little Paloma's; only the cheeky glint of mischief was missing.

Behind her she heard Ruthie exclaim, 'You're never goin' to use that thing, are you, Kate?' There was a shudder in her voice. 'Why, you'll get your hands all mucky and there might be spiders . . .'

Kate smoothed the palm of one hand over the curly black fur. 'It's only dust, Ruthie. It will brush off. And the cobwebs are ancient. The spiders must have taken themselves off to better premises.'

She heard Ruthie laugh and turned her back on the array of goodies, making sure the door was locked securely behind her.

Back in the shop, under the amused gaze of Mrs Konig, she used a stiff brush to untangle the thick black wool. Lovingly she created the bushy, curly look of the poodle and when she had finished even Ruthie had to admit it looked 'real cute'.

It was the middle of the week and thankfully the shop wasn't busy. Kate climbed back into the window and stood the dummy dog to one side of the model. As an afterthought, she placed a bright orange ball between its paws, to make it look as though it was begging for a game.

Rosa and Ruthie stepped outside and nodded their approval. Grudgingly, Rosa had to concede that it was delightful. 'So lifelike, it could be real.' She smiled at Kate. 'But then you are so clever, my little Kate. So very clever.'

Kate was still in the window, fussing with the wide-brimmed straw hat she had decided the model should wear. It was supposed to be a bright sunny day; she was taking her dog for a walk and the breeze was strong. Kate twisted one wax arm so that the hand was raised as though holding the hat in place.

Even Paul had to admit it was 'something' when he came to visit them later that afternoon.

'The dog is just like the one I had,' said Kate, wistfully. 'It brings back such memories.'

Paul's gaze was thoughtful. 'You miss your little poodle very much, don't you, Kate?'

In their talks in the railway carriage, Kate had babbled on about her life in India, about Ayah and Paloma. Paul had seen it unfolding before him: the hot sunlight, the dust and the graceful white bungalow. And, in the foreground, the little black dog, nose to the ground, snuffling out fresh scents.

Paul could not help but compare it to his own life in Germany. Just as happy, just as contented – until the troubles began . . .

'I do. Even after all this time I can still imagine her scampering across the lawn, chasing butterflies. She could never catch them, of course, but it wasn't for lack of trying.' Her face revealed so clearly the joyful yet sad memories. 'She used to love to roll in the flowerbeds where old Ahmed planted the marigolds. When you cuddled her she smelt of marigolds. I'll remember that smell as long as I live.'

'I, too, had a dog,' said Rosa, sadness in her voice. 'Remember old Bruno, Pauli?'

Paul nodded. 'One of my fondest childhood memories.'

'And you've never considered getting another one?' queried Kate.

'No animals allowed in Paradise Buildings, I'm afraid.'

Kate grimaced. 'I should have thought, with all those dogs running around, that few people take any notice of *that* rule.'

'When we moved there,' said Rosa, 'we could hardly afford to feed ourselves, never mind a dog. Now we don't have time to look after one, with Pauli so busy and me here all day.'

Ruthie piped up, 'But there's nothing to stop you getting one, Kate. Your father's at home. He could look after it.'

It was an idea, thought Kate. An idea worth examining. Also, it might wake Samuel out of the torpor into which he had lapsed. A master of inactivity, as Paul once referred to him. Although it had hurt Kate at the time, she had come to accept that the description fitted. Maybe a dog would be the answer . . .

Before Paul left, she asked, 'What happened to Bruno?'

'Not long after my father was taken, Bruno went missing. We thought it was his usual lady friend, one he had visited over the years.' His gaze fixed on the opposite side of the street, Paul gave a long, shuddering sigh. 'One morning, opening the door to bring in the milk, my mother found him on the front step. His throat had been cut . . .'

Rosa gave a groan and put her hands to her eyes, as though trying to block out a sight too harrowing to bear. She hurried away into the cutting room as Kate said, 'Paul, I'm so sorry. I should never have asked . . .'

'Yes, you should.' Paul's voice was rough. 'Citizens of the world should ask about these people, should know that on their doorstep is the biggest danger the world has ever known. That if they continue to do nothing it will be too late.'

He looked down at her, his eyes dark and full of anguish. 'That is why I have applied for a position on a daily newspaper where, if I am lucky enough to be offered the job, I can write about the things that people should know.'

Rosa hadn't returned and Kate felt she could ask. 'Does your mother know? About the job, I mean?'

He shook his head. 'Not yet. I'll tell her when I hear for certain whether I have got it or not.'

'Will you have to go away?'

'I hope so. It's what I've wanted to do – dreamt of doing – for years. To go back to my own country and report the misery there.'

'Walk over the bridge again and look at the lake?' she murmured. 'And look up that girl you knew?'

'Amongst other things.'

'If you *do* have to go away, how long will it be for?'

He shook his head. 'I've no idea. But we're jumping the gun now. They may not want me.'

'They'll be crazy if they don't.'

He grinned. 'Nice to have your confidence.'

Quietly, she said, 'I'll miss you, Paul,' thinking what an understatement that was.

He gave a gruff laugh and gently brushed with his closed fist across her jawline. 'No, you won't. You'll have other things to keep you busy. You won't have time to think of me.'

Chapter Seventeen

It was hot in the shop and Kate pushed a strand of hair back from her eyes. They had had an extremely rewarding month with the order books filling rapidly. Sarah had been replaced by a young woman who seemed bright and keen to learn. A godsend, Rosa called her, thinking of the untidy Sarah.

Sylvia Foster was a tall, thin girl a year or two older than Kate. She wore her dark hair in a pageboy bob, with a fringe almost covering her eyebrows. She told Rosa she'd worked her apprenticeship in a large fashion store in Oxford Street but had had to leave and try for a job nearer home when her mother became ill.

According to her references she showed particular promise. Kate, who liked most people, didn't like her. Sylvia was *too* keen, too pushy. The way she smarmed over Mrs Konig was sickening. The wide, innocent eyes hung on every word spoken by Mrs Konig. As though, thought Kate, she was listening to the word of God. Nobody could be that ingenuous.

But Mrs Konig was pleased with her new employee and that was all that mattered. 'My dear husband always declared that one door opens when another one closes,' she confided to Kate at the end of Sylvia's first week. 'I believe we have found something of value in Miss Foster.'

The bell behind the shop door jangled and Kate looked up to see Guy Ferris enter. Her eyes widened in surprise.

She hadn't seen him since the time they had walked together across the sports field. What on earth could have brought him into Rosa's? She hoped he wasn't after another piece of fake jewellery for his grandmother's birthday or some such nonsense. How embarrassing to have to refuse.

Through the open door she could see the large imposing car parked at the kerb. A uniformed driver waited by the passenger door, one hand on the silver handle. On the back seat sat Mrs Ferris, straight and regal, her sharp beaky nose and pale face outlined through the glass.

Guy smiled when he saw Kate. 'Good morning.' His gaze swept round the small interior of the shop. 'The last time I was in here I was nearly thrown out on my ear.'

'Good morning, Mr Ferris.' Kate lowered her eyes to the *Vogue*

161

magazine which she had been studying. 'If you just want to talk then I'm sorry, I'm busy.'

'I'm relieved to see you have no customers present. My grandmother prefers to have the entire attention of the assistant to herself.'

Kate didn't know if she cared for his attitude. This was no large and exclusive emporium in the West End but a small dress shop – although lately Rosa had changed the name to Rosa's Boutique – in a quiet London suburb.

'Your grandmother, Mr Ferris?'

'My grandmother, Miss Linley.'

The patronage of someone as influential as Mrs Ferris would give their business a real boost. Kate straightened from the glossy pages covered in pictures of glamorous models.

'Wouldn't your grandmother care to come in? Mrs Konig won't be long, she's just popped out to bank yesterday's takings.'

After the incident with Sarah, Rosa was careful not to keep too much cash in the shop. Instead of banking once a week she now banked every day.

'Why so formal? The name is Guy,' he corrected quietly. 'And I rather think my grandmother wanted to consult you in preference to the German woman.'

Kate flushed at the trace of the old arrogance she remembered from their first meetings. Also at the way he referred to Rosa. But before she could reply, he stepped out of the shop and beckoned to the uniformed driver. Ever alert, the man swung open the passenger door and stood to attention as the elderly lady climbed out.

Leaning on a gold-topped cane, she walked across the pavement as though she was entering the throne room at Buckingham Palace. Kate's knowledgeable eye studied the pale-grey gown overlaid with a lace skirt of the same colour. Four strands of pearls encircled her throat, in the fashion of the late Queen Alexandra who, it was said, wore them to hide a nasty scar on her neck.

Passers-by stopped in their tracks, trying not to stare but unable to help themselves. One didn't see an apparition like Mrs Ferris every day. Elderly men who know who she was tipped their hats but youths made snide remarks from the sides of their mouths and girls giggled.

Mrs Ferris ignored them all. She swept into the shop and stood gazing about her. Kate stood, frozen to the spot, completely at a loss. Please God, she thought, let Rosa come back soon. She would never live it down if she lost such an important customer.

Sylvia was in the back room, engaged in some fine hand-stitching on a gown of black chiffon for one of their younger customers. But in any case, Kate didn't want Sylvia's ingratiating presence tainting the atmosphere. The new girl could be a little overpowering at times, although Kate had to admit she was a good worker.

Resisting an impulse to curtsey, Kate nodded politely to Mrs Ferris and murmured a good morning.

The woman gestured with her stick towards a small gilt chair placed in front of the counter. 'The chair, girl, the chair. Am I supposed to stand while discussing business?'

Kate's flush deepened. 'I'm sorry. Of course . . .'

Hastily she stepped forward and moved the chair to where the woman waited. Guy leaned against the counter, one elbow resting on the polished glass. Inclining his head towards the vase of freshly cut flowers, he sniffed appreciatively then smiled at the flustered Kate.

'Lovely,' he said, and Kate got the impression he wasn't just referring to the flowers.

Avoiding his gaze, she saw Mrs Ferris settled on the chair then stood back, smiling, guessing that it would be better if she allowed the old lady to speak first.

Mrs Ferris sat, back stiff, chin up, one liver-spotted hand resting on the top of the walking stick while allowing her gaze to wander round the shop.

'I was attracted to your window display,' she eventually said. 'You have a pleasing manner of getting it exactly right. And I have heard some good things about your German dressmaker. Tell me, girl, do you design and make all your garments? I refuse to patronize anything shoddy.'

Kate lifted her chin. 'We don't – that is, Rosa doesn't – tolerate shoddy work, Mrs Ferris. Rosa takes a pride in what she does. You won't find anything better in any of the couture houses in the West End. And Rosa is not just a dressmaker but a trained couturière.'

'Tut tut!' The woman frowned. 'An impertinent attitude is not auspicious for business. And you know my name, I see! I don't recall ever having been introduced.' Her whole manner seemed to indicate that people who worked in dress shops would not be numbered amongst her acquaintances.

Kate's chin lifted higher. Resentment began to simmer inside her. 'Your grandson and I have on occasion met walking in the Railway Club grounds. And I know you live in that big house a few doors down from ours. I've seen you walking to your car and once at an upstairs window.'

Mrs Ferris turned her head to glare at Guy. 'You never told me you knew the young lady.'

Guy grinned. 'There are lots of things I don't tell you, dearest Grandmother.' He walked over and bent to plant a kiss on the expertly coiffured white hair. 'But I thought we'd come here to discuss a new gown for that charity event we're going to next month?' he pointed out smoothly.

Mrs Ferris tapped her stick impatiently on the carpet. 'We did, after I'd allowed you to persuade me to patronize the local traders.' She pursed her lips. 'I usually go up to Town to purchase my dresses. But after my grandson had spoken so highly of Rosa's I made up my mind to give you a try, if only to keep him happy.'

It sounded to Kate as though keeping her grandson happy was the most important thing in her life.

Suddenly businesslike, Kate said, 'We design exclusively for our customers, Mrs Ferris. If you could give me some idea of the event your grandson mentioned and the kind of gown you want, I would be happy to show you some sketches.'

'It is a charity dinner at the Savoy, so it will be an evening affair. I wear only greys or varying shades of brown. Nothing in black; I abhor black. Black is for old ladies.'

Kate had to hide a smile at this as Mrs Ferris went on, 'So although I admire the colourful display in the window, I want nothing flamboyant.'

The stick tapped again, authoritatively.

Kate turned to go into the back room where the folios of sketches were kept. 'If you'll excuse me, Mrs Ferris. I won't be a moment.'

Sylvia looked up from her sewing. 'Need any help? I thought I heard voices . . .'

Kate shook her head. 'No, thank you. You'd better get on with what you're doing. Mrs Konig likes to deliver on time and that dress was promised for tomorrow.'

Sylvia held the sewing needle up to the light, squinting as she threaded another length of black Silko. 'Well, if you need any help, just call.'

Busy sorting through the pile of designs, most of which had been produced by herself, Kate didn't reply. Sylvia gave a huffy sniff and bent her head over her work. The black chiffon played the very devil with your eyes, she thought. Despite the good light shining through the window behind her.

She heard Kate breathe a thankful 'Ahh!' and watched her return to the showroom. A right little madam *she* was, that Kate Linley, Sylvia thought. Airs and graces wasn't in it! A disagreeable smile quirked her lips. Well, time would tell. Mrs Konig would soon discover what a treasure she had in Sylvia Foster.

And then Miss High-and-Mighty would be out on her ear.

Kneeling at Mrs Ferris's feet, Kate spread out the sketches on her lap. She had no idea of the woman's likes or dislikes, apart from the colours she had stipulated, and so could only judge by the comments Mrs Ferris made.

Guy approached to lean over his grandmother's shoulder, every so often putting in his twopennyworth. Catching Kate's eye, he would wink, making Kate fumble, dropping the sketches to the carpet.

Between them they came up with two designs that both Mrs Ferris and Kate thought appropriate.

'In pale grey, do you think?' the woman queried, holding the sketch at arm's length, head on one side. 'Or perhaps a pale coffee?'

The sketch she finally chose, with a little prompting from Kate, was of a floor-length gown with a flatteringly draped shawl neckline and cape-like sleeves. Kate had designed it to be made in satin with an overlay of fine silk lace, but as she explained it could be created in any material Mrs Ferris chose.

Daringly, Kate added, 'But not in either of the two colours you mentioned.'

The woman stared at her. No doubt it was all right for Mrs Ferris to give people unwanted advice but not for them to give it to her. 'Kindly explain yourself, young lady.'

Suddenly, Kate realized she was no longer frightened of this autocratic old woman. Mrs Ferris seemed to recognize this and a glint of respect showed in her eyes.

'I think a pale shade of pink would compliment you so much more. You have a lovely skin, so delicate, and pink would look wonderful with your hair.'

Mrs Ferris sniffed. 'Don't be silly, child. I haven't worn pink since I was a girl. No, it shall be a pale-coffee colour and the material velvet.'

Surprisingly, Guy spoke up for Kate's idea. 'I think a pale pink would be enchanting, Granny.' He caught Kate's eye, grinning. 'You'd have all the old codgers after you.'

'Don't be ridiculous, Guy. It's bad enough listening to the young lady's frivolous ideas without you encouraging them.'

'The palest shade of rose in satin with a silk lace overskirt, just like the design,' said Kate, coaxingly. She could see the vacillation in Mrs Ferris's eyes. 'You really would be the belle of the ball.'

Just at that moment the shop door opened and Rosa came in. She looked flustered, breathing hard. 'I'm sorry I was so long, Kate. *Mein Gott*, you would never believe the queues in that bank. And the staff – so slow . . .'

She paused in her explanations, seeing the old lady seated in the gilt chair, with Kate at her feet, sketches strewn everywhere.

Hastily, Kate rose. 'Mrs Konig, this is Mrs Ferris and her grandson.'

Guy gave a wide grin but didn't tip his hat, which he hadn't removed since entering the shop. A bad breach of etiquette as far as Rosa was concerned. Her own Pauli would never have acted in such a manner.

'Mrs Ferris is thinking of using our services for a gown for a society event in Town,' Kate explained. 'We've decided – at least, I think we've decided – on this.' She held out the sketch for Rosa's inspection. 'We just can't decide on the colour or material.'

Rosa held out her hand, which Mrs Ferris took limply in her own. Guy she completely ignored. 'Good morning, Mrs Ferris.' She looked down at the sketch. 'No doubt about it, it can be made in no other way than the way Kate has designed it.'

Mrs Ferris sat up even straighter, her lips firming. No one – but *no one*, argued with her. And she was blessed if this German woman was going to do it now.

Before she could speak, Rosa said, 'My first step when I meet new clients is to "eye them up" – I think that is your English expression – looking at their figure, their age and trying to sum up their lifestyle.' She could sense the tension in the air and added, smoothly, 'You have difficulty in accepting Kate's suggestions, do you?'

'If I give you the commission for my dress, can I be sure that it will be made to my specifications, colour- and material--wise?'

'Pale coffee in velvet?' said Kate enquiringly.

Mrs Ferris hesitated, then rose to her feet. 'Perhaps not. Perhaps, just for a change, we will try the pink.'

'And the satin and overlay of lace?'

Mrs Ferris glared at her suspiciously. Was the young girl being sarcastic?

Guy came forward and took her by the arm. 'Come on, Granny. Face it, Kate's made up your mind for you. Leave it to the experts.'

Claiming the last word, Mrs Ferris turned at the door and said, on a cautionary note, 'The palest of pinks, remember.'

Then directing her gaze towards Rosa, who had deliberately kept in the background, she said, 'Your young assistant tells me you are a trained couturière. If that is so, I am surprised you choose to work in a place like this rather than one of the fashionable houses in Town.'

'I prefer working on my own, with the help of a few trusted assistants.'

Mrs Ferris sniffed. 'Hoity-toity! I suppose you find it a challenge.'

'I do, and there is nothing I love more than a challenge. I have had some pretty weird and wonderful requests, from an amazing quilted wedding dress to a funeral outfit with a thick black lace veil hanging from a hat like a tent. I can make anything from a simple shift dress to a ball gown grand enough to greet your King and Queen in.'

'Well, considering that I won't need anything quite so ambitious, how long will this take? I shall need it by the end of next month.'

'Most outfits usually require an initial consultation, which I gather you've already had with Kate, and then there will be fittings. Three or four is the norm. And, of course, your selection of the material we are to use.'

'Humph!'

Mrs Ferris tapped her stick again. Leaning on her grandson's arm she walked back to the car. Rosa followed, a respectful step or two behind.

Guy settled his grandmother inside and Rosa heard her mutter something to him. Before climbing in beside her, he turned and smiling at Rosa, said, 'My grandmother asks me to tell you she will be here tomorrow at noon.'

Rosa's mind went into overdrive. Would she be able to order and have delivered by then the satin and lace required? It didn't give her much time . . .

She would dispatch Kate personally to Town to fetch it after placing the order by telephone.

'That will be quite satisfactory.'

Politely, Kate had waited at the open door of the shop until they had gone. Then she let out a whoop that had passers-by looking at her, and hugged Mrs Konig.

'We've cracked it! Our first really important customer.'

Rosa smiled. 'And our first really difficult one.'

Kate laughed. 'Oh, I don't think so. I bet the old girl's a pussy cat under that tough exterior.'

Missing out on the fun, hearing Kate's laughter, Sylvia Foster appeared from the back room. 'What old girl?'

'Mrs Ferris.' Kate's answer was terse.

Sylvia directed a look towards Rosa, frowning. 'Should one of your assistants be allowed to speak of a customer in such derogatory terms?'

Kate grimaced. 'Oh, grow up, Sylvia! As if I'd say it to her face.'

'Even I alluded to her as being difficult,' said Rosa soothingly. 'I have met her kind before – servants who make her life easy, and too much money. In Germany we were surrounded by such people. Now the shoe is on the other foot and other people have the money and the power.'

Ingratiatingly, Sylvia said, 'Let me make you a cup of tea, Mrs Konig. We can't have you down in the dumps now, can we?'

Rosa nodded and picked up the phone. 'And I'll get on to the wholesalers to order the material. You, Kate, can go up to Town to fetch it.'

Chapter Eighteen

The tube train roared through the tunnel and emerged into the white-tiled station. Passengers surged through the doors. Everyone hurried towards the lighted sign that spelled 'Way Out'. They stared directly ahead, oblivious of those hurrying beside them. Kate could feel the rush of warm air as the train gathered speed and vanished into the dark mouth of the far tunnel.

She showed her ticket at the barrier then climbed the stairs leading to daylight and the crowds of people that thronged Oxford Circus. Red London buses edged their way through the traffic, the ever-patient drivers taking the day-to-day annoyances in their stride.

Who'd be a bus driver in London? she thought, standing on the kerb of a narrow side street, waiting with a crowd of other people to cross. Taxis swished by, affording glimpses of pampered passengers driven in comfort to their destinations. Instead of which Kate was forced to join the bus queue with the rest of the common herd, trying to peer above people's heads in order to see if her own bus was anywhere in sight.

It was murder! One would have thought, in the middle of the afternoon, that the streets would be quiet. But was the centre of London ever quiet? she wondered. Maybe it was just as well that she hadn't taken a job in the city. Could she really have endured this crush every day? It would seem like a life sentence, strap-hanging on the tube, being pushed and shoved by other equally irritated workers.

Her bus came and she jumped on, finding a seat near the window. She paid her twopence and the conductor clipped her ticket then returned to his vantage point on the platform of the vehicle. She knew the way now by heart, having been sent numerous times by Mrs Konig to fetch parcels of material.

At first, this had been Ruthie's job. But she confessed that the underground system terrified her, and the crowds of hurrying people had her confused. After going missing for most of one day, Mrs Konig had decided that in future Kate would take over this task herself, Ruthie concentrating on local deliveries.

Kate alighted from her bus and turned up a narrow alley. This district was renowned for its history. Sometimes Kate wished she had taken more notice of the nuns' teaching of past events. The buildings

169

looked so old, as though they had been there for hundreds of years – and they probably had.

Later, carrying the brown paper parcel containing the precious satin and lace – a lovely shell pink she was sure Mrs Ferris would love – she made her way back to where she would catch her bus. To her surprise she saw Paul Konig come out of a nearby building and walk towards the same bus stop. She hadn't seen Paul since he'd told her about his hoped-for new job. He spotted her at exactly the same time, and a look of delight lit up his face.

'Kate! What are you doing in the big bad city? Playing hooky, eh?'

'Not at all. Shopping for your mother.' She held up the parcel. 'Material for a gown for Mrs Ferris.'

Paul's eyebrows rose. 'Mrs Ferris?'

'Guy Ferris's grandmother.'

'I know who Mrs Ferris is. You were lucky to get that, weren't you?'

She smiled. 'Luck had nothing to do with it. We sweet-talked our way into a lucrative little deal. I only hope there's more to come after this.'

'What's she like?'

'Oh, your usual dignified old lady. Although perhaps not so usual. She has an air about her that could be intimidating if you let it.'

'And you didn't let it?'

She shook her head. 'No. I was a teeny bit nervous at first, but after a while I got the feeling that we could have got on quite well together. Like they say – her bark was worse than her bite.'

Paul looked pleased. 'I'm glad. Mother could do with that kind of boost.'

They had reached their bus stop, and joined the end of the small queue.

'But what about you?' enquired Kate. 'I thought most of your assignments were local ones, not in Town.'

He grinned. 'The assignment I've just been on has paid off handsomely. I've got that job. Remember I told you about it? The one on the *London Post*.'

Kate looked pleased. 'Well, good for you. Maybe things are looking up for both of us at last.' Now, she thought, if Daddy could just get another job, everything would be fine.

Her father had been in such poor spirits lately it distressed her to see him. He rarely left the house, going only as far as the nearest corner shop for the daily newspaper and the ounce of pipe tobacco he'd taken to using again. Kate hadn't the heart to scold him, although she guessed Dr Shearer would object.

The red bus appeared in the distance and the queue moved forward with sighs of relief. Kate climbed aboard with Paul close behind her.

They went upstairs, for she knew Paul sometimes liked to smoke. Choosing a seat at the front, they settled down.

'So it'll be goodbye to covering weddings and Beautiful Baby contests and dreary Town Hall events?' Kate said teasingly. 'It will be the real thing now.'

Paul nodded. 'Eventually. Although not at first. I still have to find my feet. It will all be experience. My idea later is to try freelancing.'

Kate looked at him. 'Freelancing? You mean, working for yourself?'

'That's right. As an unattached journalist, independent of any newspaper.'

'Sounds a bit chancy. You wouldn't have a regular wage or anything. Would you be able to manage?'

''Course.' Paul's look was scornful. 'You know my plans, I've spoken of them often enough. I can't wait to get back to Germany and write about what's happening. The truth, not the rubbish Joseph Goebbels manipulates with such cynical disregard for the truth.'

The fear which descended like a dark shadow every time he spoke of his homeland made Kate shiver. What was it about that prospect that was so dreadful? It was as if she could see into a future that was macabre, that ended in blackness and flames reaching towards the sky . . .

She gave herself a mental shake. She knew how ambitious he was, was sure nothing would stop him once he made up his mind.

'But . . .' She hesitated. 'Wouldn't you rather stay here? I mean, there must be plenty of things to report going on here in England. And – couldn't it be dangerous if you went back?'

He knew she was right. It could be dangerous. He couldn't deny he was frightened but knew it was important to go back – and keep on going back to enable the truth to be told.

He unfolded the newspaper he carried and spread it open on his lap. 'But talking about my new job I nearly forgot. There's an advert here in the pets section that might interest you. A black poodle for sale, six weeks old. "Friendly and frivolous" is how the advert describes it.' He looked up from the fine print, smiling at the sudden look of buoyancy on her face. 'Doesn't that sound like just what you're looking for?'

'Well, I wasn't exactly *looking* for one, but if I was it certainly sounds tempting,' admitted Kate.

'Then let yourself be tempted. For once in your life do something *you* want to do and don't think of your father.' Seeing the way she frowned, he added, 'Oh, I know that sounds heartless and whatever else you are you aren't heartless. I didn't mean it like that. Think of the pleasure you'd get, and it would be such company for your father while he's at home.'

They almost missed their stop talking about the poodle. The station platform was crowded and they waited in the crush of people for the train to come roaring through the tunnel. On the train it was too noisy to talk and so the question of the advertisement was dropped.

'But you take the paper,' urged Paul. 'You can think about it.'

Paul left her at the station, explaining he had to report back to the office. 'And give in my notice,' he grinned, obviously delighted at the idea. 'They won't like it but it's a tough old life and it's too bad if they don't.'

As they parted, he called after her, 'And tell dear Mama how pleased I am about her new client. Keep it up and you'll be able to move into larger premises.'

'A dog!' said Samuel. 'A new puppy! I don't know about that. It would be a lot of work.'

Kate felt irritation wash over her at his show of lassitude. 'Nonsense. It might be just what you need.' Something to worry about other than yourself, she thought. 'You could take it for walks. Do you good. You used to walk a lot in the park.'

Victoria Park was a joy of green acres and paths winding through flower beds. Kate remembered how her father had loved to walk there. But, sadly, not lately . . .

'I don't know,' Samuel repeated. 'I don't suppose it's house trained . . .'

'It's six weeks old,' said Kate. 'It would hardly be house trained at six weeks. But we've got a garden. It shouldn't be too difficult. And you remember how intelligent that breed of dog can be? I'm sure that wouldn't present a problem.'

Samuel slumped further into his chair, a perplexed look on his face. If he said 'I don't know' once more, Kate thought, she'd scream. Getting through to her father was becoming more difficult every day.

She opened the newspaper Paul had given her, showing Samuel the page on which the advertisement was printed.

'Anyway, it's there if you want to consider it.' She'd ringed the half-dozen lines in pencil.

Samuel peered at it doubtfully. 'How far away is it?'

'Not far. Only in Fairlee Avenue.' Fairlee Avenue was on the other side of the railway line, which meant Samuel crossing the dreaded bridge. Contemplating this, she added, 'Or why don't you wait and we could go together one evening?' That might be a better idea.

Samuel turned the pages to the cricket scores and began reading them.

'We'll see,' he said, and Kate was forced to leave it at that.

Mrs Ferris arrived promptly at noon the following day. Rosa saw her comfortably seated then draped the lovely pink satin over Kate's extended arm and covered it with the lace.

The two women waited for the exclamation of delight they were sure they would hear. But Mrs Ferris had too much sang-froid to disclose anything but the faintest glimmer of excitement in her pale-blue eyes.

Head on one side, she said grudgingly, 'Humph, the colour's all right, I suppose.'

'And the material?' queried Rosa. 'You like the material, no?'

Guy, who had accompanied her and who stood slightly to one side, as close to Kate as he could get, murmured encouragingly, 'Come on, Granny, admit it. You like it.'

'It's very attractive,' his grandmother conceded. She leaned forward in her chair and fingered the fine lace. 'I shall require it before the end of next month.' She looked up at Rosa. 'Would there be a problem there?'

'The end of next month would be fine,' Rosa replied confidently.

'*Before* the end of next month,' Mrs Ferris corrected her.

Kate heard Rosa's heavy sigh. 'Give me a date and I shall personally see that it is finished on time.'

Mrs Ferris rose majestically to her feet. 'Very well, you may take my measurements and begin whatever else is necessary.'

Rosa directed a triumphant look towards Kate and ushered the woman into the back room. Sylvia was banished from her place at the window where she sat putting the final touches to the black chiffon.

'Go and help Kate in the shop,' commanded Rosa, reaching for her tape measure.

Sylvia, with an awed look at Mrs Ferris, went. As she came out of the back room she gave Guy an arch smile and said to Kate, 'Rosa said I was to help you in the shop.'

'There's nothing to do in the shop,' Kate replied. 'Unless you want to help Ruthie tidy up the storeroom. Goodness knows, it needs it.'

Sylvia pouted. She didn't like being given orders in front of someone as prepossessing as Guy Ferris. She knew who he was, of course. Everyone knew the Ferrises. That bitch Kate Linley wanted him to herself, she thought. With his grandmother out of the way it would be the perfect opportunity for a little flirtation.

Sylvia hadn't failed to notice the way he'd eyed her as she came from the back room. A salacious look that had set her heart thudding. She wasn't to know it was an unconscious action on Guy's part. A look he directed at every girl he saw. As natural to him as breathing.

'Well, you had better get on with something,' Kate said, with a touch of asperity. She hated the way the girl stood, insolence in every line of her body. 'Mrs Konig won't be too pleased if she comes back and finds you just standing there.'

'You're just standing there!'

The pert answer made Kate's cheeks flush. Before she could speak, however, Guy said, 'Kate isn't just standing here, she's entertaining me.' He grinned at the two girls. 'After all, you can't leave a mere male all alone in a ladies' dress shop. Who knows what secrets he might stumble across?'

Guy hadn't seen anyone toss their head in quite the fashion Sylvia achieved as she left the room. 'I don't think she likes you,' he said softly, smiling at Kate.

'I think you could be right.' Kate returned his smile. 'She hasn't much going for her in the way of charm but she's a good worker, skilful with a needle and at cutting the patterns. Everything has to be cut on the bias these days,' she explained, 'and she's a whiz at that.'

Guy came closer, standing just in front of Kate. 'But *I* like you.' He bent his head until he was disturbingly close, gazing into her eyes. 'I'm just amazed it's taken me so long to ask you again for a date.'

'Well, we didn't exactly hit it off when we first met, did we?' smiled Kate. 'As I recall, you were quite rude. In fact, *very* rude.' She blushed. 'You threatened to smack my bottom.'

He tutted. 'As you say, we didn't exactly get off on the right foot.' He moved a step closer. Kate stood with her back pressed against the counter and so could go no further without pushing him aside. 'But I can be forgiven for one blunder, surely.'

'It wasn't just one time. You were rude to both Paul and me that day in the club grounds.' She remembered pulling Paul back as he went to hit Guy. 'You weren't my favourite person after that, I can tell you.'

'But that's all in the past. I was nice to you after that, wasn't I, the few times I walked you home?'

Kate had to concede that he was.

'And I promise I'll be on my very best behaviour if you come out with me.' He placed his hands flat on the top of the counter on either side of her. Now she really was captive. 'After all, I did persuade my grandmother to visit your establishment.'

'Look,' she said, turning her head to one side, for his breath was warm on her cheek, doing all sorts of things to her equilibrium, 'I really ought to be working. You've no idea how busy a small place like this can get.'

Please, please! she silently begged. Let somebody come in. Anybody, to break this situation that she felt was fast getting out of hand.

'Not until you say yes.' He leaned even closer, his mouth only inches from hers. 'I know all the best places, I can promise you a good time. There's not many girls in this place I would say that to.'

As though in answer to her prayer, Rosa called from the back room, 'Kate! Would you come in, please?'

'I've got to go.'

Guy drew back, giving a mocking little bow. 'Her mistress's voice. But you're not getting away that easily. How about that new picture at the Dream Palace? You can't have seen it for it only started last night.'

Kate hadn't seen it and had to admit as much.

'Tonight then?'

Rosa's voice sounded again. 'Kate?'

'All right, all right, but I must go.'

'Call for you at seven thirty then. We'll catch the second house.'

As Kate turned to hurry to do Rosa's bidding, the bell above the door jangled and someone came in. If it was a customer, she thought, she would have to call Sylvia . . .

Turning to look, she saw it was Paul. He waggled his fingers and said, 'Hi!'

'Hi! Excuse me, but duty calls.'

Paul had overheard Guy's last remark. As Kate slipped into the back room, he now stood regarding the other man with something akin to repugnance. It had sounded very much as if a date had been arranged. He would never have suspected Kate of being capable of such duplicity, surprised at the rush of pure jealousy that swept over him at the thought of her going out with this Ferris bloke.

Yet why should he be jealous? He was fond of Kate, true, but in a big-brotherly way. Ever since their first meeting, his one wish had been to protect her. To safeguard her against the likes of Ferris. He glared at the other man and said in a gruff voice, 'Hello! You seem to be getting on with my mother's shop assistant very nicely.'

'Oh, I was just waiting here for my grandmother when the young lady starts fluttering her eyelashes at me.' Guy grinned. 'What's a fellow to do in the circumstances?'

'Yes, I noticed she had to chase you all around the shop to catch up with you.' The sarcasm in Paul's voice could hardly be missed.

'Well, when she gives you a look like that, you can hardly walk away, can you?'

Paul drew a deep breath. 'Look, Ferris, overlooking your lying, conniving nature, I can laugh about some things. But when it comes to Kate Linley, I'm afraid I lose my sense of humour.'

'Oh, I wouldn't do that, Konig. I have a feeling you're going to need it.'

Paul's fists clenched and he took a threatening step forward, only getting a grip on himself when the sound of Kate's laughter echoed from the back room. 'I'm warning you, Ferris, I'm going to do all I can to stop her getting hurt.' The anger in Paul's voice couldn't be ignored.

'I'm trembling like a leaf,' Guy sneered. 'I couldn't give a purple shit what you think, you German bastard. In fact, knowing now how you feel about Kate I'm inclined to go all out to get her.'

It was just as well that at that moment Kate came back. She was followed by the regal Mrs Ferris. The old lady was looking like the cat who'd pinched the cream. The soft pink had done wonders for her complexion, just as Kate had promised. It was obvious, too, that Rosa was pleased. Further orders had been pledged and Rosa envisaged a whole new world opening its doors to Rosa's Boutique. For with Mrs Ferris's custom tucked safely under her belt, who could say that the old lady's wealthy friends wouldn't follow!

If Rosa had been a betting woman she would have put her last penny on that.

Paul stood by the window, his shoulders tense and an air about him that troubled Kate. He glared at her and rubbed his hand through his dark hair.

Guy was looking smug, as self-satisfied as his grandmother. Kate could feel the tension in the shop and wondered just what had transpired.

She thought about her promised date with Guy for that evening and a tingle of excitement ran through her. In a funny, perverse way she was looking forward to it.

She just wished that Paul wouldn't look at her like that.

Chapter Nineteen

Samuel threw down the book he'd been reading. It was too nice a day to sit indoors. He felt he should be outside, doing something energetic. But Dr Shearer had forbidden him to work in the garden and he knew Kate would be cross with him if he disobeyed the doctor's orders. He gazed about him at the sitting room. The brass ornaments on the mantelpiece could do with a rub-up. Monica had insisted they be polished every Saturday without fail. Kate had been too busy these days to worry about them. He shouldn't be so idle, he told himself; should help Kate more.

Going into the kitchen, he opened the cupboard door where the household cleaning agents were kept and took out the tin of Brasso. A clean duster and an old newspaper to spread across the kitchen table and he was ready for action. Diligently he began rubbing the cloth soaked in Brasso across the brass. It was hard work. Messy work. His hands were soon stained with the strong-smelling white liquid. Idly perusing the newspaper before him, he began to read the adverts. The circled one caught his eye and his hands stopped their assiduous rubbing as he read again the piece referring to the puppy.

As though commanded by some inner voice, he stood up and after washing his hands at the sink, drying them on a tea towel – something Monica had frowned upon – and leaving the cleaning implements on the spread-out newspaper, he put on his hat and coat and left the house.

Kate obtained Mrs Konig's permission to leave the shop a few minutes early that day. It was already ten minutes to six when she closed the shop door behind her and hurried down the street. There were things to buy for her and Samuel's supper.

The house was empty when she arrived home. She regarded the newspaper spread across the kitchen table, the tin of Brasso, standing with its top off, the used cloth and the brass vases. She grinned wryly, thinking: It's like something out of the *Marie Celeste*! Bored with doing nothing, Daddy must have decided to clean the brasses and then, equally bored, had left them and gone out into the sunshine. He was so absent-minded these days, he couldn't seem to concentrate his mind on anything for more than a few minutes.

177

She cleared away the Brasso and the cloth, replaced the half-cleaned vases on the mantelpiece and deposited the newspaper in the dustbin. Unloading the groceries on to the kitchen table she thought of her date with Guy and decided it might be soothing to have a good, long soak in the bath, using some of the fragrant bath salts Julie had insisted on leaving the last time she visited.

'Go on, take them,' Julie had urged, pushing the fancy bottle towards her. 'Fat lot of good they are going to do me, stuck in that place.'

Julie was now in her last year at the Swiss finishing school. On her last visit to Kate, she had acknowledged that she really didn't know what she wanted to do when that year was up – apart from having a good time!

Thinking of the way her own dreams had gone astray, Kate had said, 'But surely you have *some* idea? I mean, there's no question of having to accept the very first job that comes along because your mother needs the money.'

Then, seeing Julie's look: 'I'm sorry,' she mumbled.

Julie patted her hand. 'Don't feel bad about it, sweetie. My worst nightmare is that they'll organize one of those stuffy little jobs in some boring old art gallery and hide me there until I'm ready to marry.'

Kate had laughed. 'Doesn't sound too horrific!'

'It is when you have ideas that don't comply with theirs.'

'I thought you said you didn't know what you wanted to do?'

They were in the bathroom. Julie had just finished setting Kate's hair in a new style. Curled all over with a fluffy fringe, Kate didn't think she would maintain the new look after Julie had gone.

Julie had peered into the mirror above the handbasin, wet the tip of one forefinger and stroked it across her eyebrows. 'After being incarcerated among the nuns for so long, I think what I'd really like would be to become a high-class call girl. Now, that really *would* be something.'

Kate knew when her leg was being pulled. 'I'm sure you'd make a positively stunning one,' she had replied in a serious tone.

Julie stood back and regarded herself in the mirror. 'Or one of those models that stand starkers on the stage at the Windmill Theatre. If they move as much as a finger they've had it.'

Kate shivered. 'Sounds chilly. I hope they have good central heating.' It was easy to play along with Julie's little jokes, even if, at times, they had shocked her.

Now, soaking in the rose-perfumed bath, Kate mentally thanked her friend for her generosity.

She had just finished drying herself and was tying the sash of her candlewick dressing gown when there was a knocking on the front door. Uttering a 'Bloody hell!' under her breath, she ran downstairs to answer it.

The shape she could distinguish behind the coloured glass pane set into the door loomed large and dark, and for a moment she hesitated. It wasn't Daddy, he had his own key, and Paul's build was slimmer and not so tall. Glancing quickly through the open door of the sitting room as she passed, she saw that the mantel clock showed five minutes past seven. Too early for Guy; unless he was too impatient to wait until the agreed time. Well, he'd just *have* to wait until she was ready, that was all . . .

The knock came again, compelling, insistent. Something that couldn't be ignored. Clutching the collar of her gown closer about her throat, Kate opened the door.

A uniformed policeman stood on the path. Gravely he removed his helmet and tucked it under one arm.

In a voice that was completely devoid of emotion, he asked, 'Miss Linley? Miss Kate Linley?' And as he spoke a feeling of panic overcame Kate, making her tremble. She held the gown tighter about her neck, her knuckles whitening.

An instinct that was quite beyond her understanding had her saying, 'It's my father, isn't it? You've come about my father?'

'I'm afraid so, miss.' He looked so disconsolate that she felt sorry for him. The silly old fool's got himself into some sort of trouble, she told herself. Remembering the scene with Mr Patrick, when Samuel had lost his temper and lashed out at him she said, 'Have you got him tucked away in the station somewhere for his own safety?'

The policeman seemed to be having difficulty in finding the words to answer. Kate looked down at her dressing gown and said, 'I'll have to get dressed.'

She'd never had a policeman on her doorstep before. Should she leave him standing there, closing the door in his face, or ask him in?

She opened the door wider and indicated that he come in.

She dressed hurriedly, imagining Samuel in a cell with bars across, just as she'd seen in James Cagney films. Her mouth turned down at the corners. She knew that later she would laugh over it with Daddy but at the moment it wasn't funny.

On the other hand, it might be a good thing. Shake him out of his lethargy. Sometimes a shock did that for a person . . .

When she came back downstairs she picked up her coat from where she'd thrown it over the settee and slipped her arms into the sleeves. If Guy called for her while she was still out she wondered what he would think. Still, it couldn't be helped. She just hoped this wasn't going to take too long. Tucking her handbag under her arm, she turned to face the constable. 'All right, let's get him home.'

It was only then that he spoke. 'I'm sorry, Miss Linley, but they've taken your father to the General Hospital.'

Now thoroughly alarmed, one hand went to her mouth. 'He's been hurt?'

Ringing through her head, she heard his voice. 'I'm sorry to have to inform you that your father is dead . . .'

Wide-eyed she stared at him. Her brain had gone quite numb as the full meaning of his words sank in. 'I don't believe you. How can he be dead?'

The young constable put one hand on her shoulder, his expression one of profound regret. 'I'm sorry, but I'm afraid he is.'

His words were like arrows through her heart. Wildly she shook her head, blonde hair flying across her cheeks. 'You're wrong,' she protested.

'Your father, Samuel Linley,' he stressed. 'We found a letter on him with this address on it. For some reason that we haven't yet ascertained he seemed to be taking a short cut across the railway line. There are gaps all along the fence, as you probably know; kids use it all the time, we just can't keep up with the little devils . . .' He coughed. 'Can you think of any reason why he would have been doing this?'

Her voice barely a whisper, she said, 'He found it difficult to climb the steps of the bridge . . .'

The policeman nodded. 'The train must have been on him before he even saw it.' Through the pain and grief, Kate visualised the scene and felt icy terror. The policeman was taking her by the arm, urging her to sit down.

She heard his measured steps as he went into the kitchen to put the kettle on. She sat huddled in her chair, her lips ashen, her cheeks hollow. The puppy, he must have gone to get the puppy . . .

From the direction of the kitchen she heard the plop of the gas being lit, then the policeman reappeared in the doorway. 'Won't be a sec boiling,' he said soothingly. 'Have a cup of tea and then I'll take you along to see the b – I mean, your father . . .'

'Oh my God!' Kate sat motionless, rigid with shock, her normally flawless skin greyish white and mottled. 'Dead!' she repeated, and as she did so, something inside her snapped. As though an elastic band had fractured, leaving her broken and helpless.

The inquest was something she would remember for the rest of her life. The verdict was accidental death. No one was to blame, said the coroner. The driver of the train that had killed her father was a grey-haired, elderly man. He stood in the courtroom, so clearly distressed that Kate couldn't find it in her heart to hate him. His voice a bare whisper, he said, 'The train had just left the station, gathering speed, and I saw a man appear from a gap in the fence and begin to walk across the rails. I couldn't do anything,' he kept repeating, as though trying to convince himself. 'I tried but it was no good. We were going too fast, it was impossible to stop in time.'

The coroner asked if he had any idea why the deceased should want to cross the railway line when there was a footbridge close by. The driver hesitated, glanced at Kate then just as quickly looked away. 'I couldn't swear to it, sir, but I'm almost sure I saw a small black dog – a puppy, really – dash across in front of Mr Linley. He bent to pick it up and . . .' His face contorted; he was still apparently so upset that the coroner excused him.

Aunt Norma came down for the funeral, as did Julie. Paul and his mother attended and Kate saw Guy Ferris come in late, choosing am empty pew at the back of the church.

Father O'Hanlan, with Norma's help, organized everything. Turning a blind eye to the fact that Samuel hadn't been a religious man, Father O'Hanlan didn't see why he shouldn't be buried amongst good Catholics in the pretty churchyard.

During the mass, Kate kept glancing over her shoulder, sure that her mother would appear. She thought of that Sunday at the convent when Monica had arrived late; conjuring up the memory of the pretty woman walking down the aisle, slim and chic.

Julie was sitting behind her, next to Paul and Mrs Konig. She caught Kate's eye and reading her thoughts, shook her head. Samuel's tragic death had been given a dignified write-up by Paul in the local paper. Surely if Monica was anywhere close she would have seen it, forgetting their past differences at such a time?

A couple looking like man and wife sat towards the back. Kate wondered who they could be. She was sure they weren't immediate neighbours for she knew most of those by sight. Mrs Bennett was present and a few others who had known her mother.

After Guy Ferris had arrived, when the service had already begun, Kate knew that her mother wasn't going to appear.

She turned back to look at the casket resting before the altar. She stared at it, tearless now, seemingly unaware of the singing, the prayers, the eulogy. Norma had to put a hand under her elbow to remind her to stand or kneel.

At the end of the mass, as Father O'Hanlan blessed the coffin, Kate whispered, 'Daddy, please forgive me. It was my fault. I should have gone myself.'

'Kate,' Norma whispered.

Kate looked at her with unseeing eyes then turned to gaze once more to the back of the church. Even now she was sure her mother would come. But Norma, who knew her sister better than Kate ever would, would have been surprised if Monica had turned up.

The organist began to play the recessional hymn. The pallbearers, preceded by Father O'Hanlan, began to move slowly down the aisle.

The congregation followed. At the grave, Julie edged her way forward to stand beside Kate. Paul came and stood on her other side. He reached out and took her hand, holding it tightly. Kate could feel the strength there, the compassion. Her gaze lifted from the black hole where they were burying her father and met Guy Ferris's eyes. He gave her an encouraging smile, making the thumbs-up sign.

She had not seen Guy since the day of her father's death. A wreath of yellow gladioli and creamy white stephanotis had arrived. With it was a handwritten note from Mrs Ferris extending her own and her grandson's condolences.

Aunt Norma dropped red roses down on to the coffin. Through a haze of tears, Kate followed her example: bright orange marigolds, causing eyebrows to rise. Kate didn't care. Daddy would know what it meant.

Early that morning, before the dew had had time to evaporate, she had crept into the garden and gathered as many of the marigolds as were in flower. If people thought it rather odd, that was their privilege. It was her last goodbye to her father.

Suddenly, tears blurring her vision, she turned and began to run, away from that terrible place, away from the solemn bunch of people who stood there like black crows. Away from the dull thud-thud of the earth being shovelled on to the casket.

She heard footsteps behind her, catching up. Arms went round her from behind, halting her mad rush.

'Kate, stop this.'

It was Paul. His own face looked ashen under the thick black hair, the eyes darker than ever.

She turned and buried her face in his coat. 'It was my fault. My fault, Paul. I should have remembered how difficult he found the steps of that bridge, how puffed-out they made him. I should have gone myself.'

'If anything, it was my fault for drawing your attention to that advert in the first place. If I hadn't done that . . .' He nuzzled his mouth against her hair, feeling it soft and silky beneath his lips. 'Well, we can probably go on blaming ourselves for the rest of our lives, but it won't do any good. We have to get on with things.'

She pushed him away, sniffed and accepted the folded white handkerchief he drew from his top pocket. She snuffled into it then handed it back. 'I know. Mother Superior would have frowned at me for carrying on like this.'

'I'm sure Mother Superior would have done no such thing. On the contrary, she would have been proud of you for carrying everything off so well.'

'I couldn't have done it but for Aunt Norma and Julie. And, of course, you and your mother.'

She looked back at the crowd that was slowly breaking up. Norma and Julie were huddled close together, looking towards the trees under which she and Paul stood.

'At one point I thought of that poor little puppy and almost broke down,' Kate murmured. 'To have such a short life . . .'

As tears started again in her eyes, Paul grasped her shoulders and gave her a little shake. 'There will be another puppy, somewhere, sometime. You can always think about it once you've sorted yourself out.'

He felt Kate shiver. She drew a deep breath. 'Never! Never again. I've said this before. If I'd stuck to my covenant then, Daddy would still be here. It really is all my fault.'

Now wasn't the time to argue with her, Paul decided. He'd heard people say things like this before. Hadn't he and his mother said it when they left Germany, swearing never to return?

Now he looked forward eagerly to starting his new job on the *London Post*. Enough time had gone by; now he was ready to return . . .

With his arm about her, guiding her over the rough ground, they walked back to join the small gathering at the grave. The couple she had noticed in the church came over and introduced themselves as Mr and Mrs Brett.

'We're so very sorry, dear,' the woman said, taking Kate's hand in both of hers. 'We met your father only briefly, when he came to enquire about the puppy. He seemed such a nice man. We had no qualms at all about handing the poor little thing over. We were sure it would be going to a good home.'

Her husband said, weightily, 'Your father told us a little about your other dog, the way they couldn't bring it to England. We are both so very sorry. We are sure our little one would have given you the greatest of pleasure.'

Kate thought of the little dog and tears started afresh.

'We're going to have to sit down and talk about this,' said Norma firmly. 'I really think you'd be better coming to live with me, Kate. You can't stay here on your own.'

They were in the sitting room, the sun streaming in through the leaded windows. It was two days after the funeral. Julie had returned to her school. Such a short visit but her presence had been comforting.

Aunt Norma had decided to stay on a little while longer. Although Kate protested that she would be quite all right, Norma had made up her mind. No young girl should be left alone and unchaperoned in a wicked city like London. Or, in this case, a suburb of London.

Kate tutted. 'Oh, Aunty Norma, of course I'll be all right. I'm a big girl now, remember.'

'Not that big. And I've seen the way that Paul looks at you, not forgetting the other one.'

Knowing Norma was referring to Guy, Kate said innocently, 'I can't think who you mean. I didn't realize there were so many young men hanging around, all looking at me.'

'You might not have noticed, my girl, but I certainly have.'

Too late Norma realized she was sounding like Monica. Altering her approach, she went on, 'How would you cope, dear? There's the expenses of the house, the mortgage. Be reasonable, now. How could you possibly hope to pay all that?'

Kate pursed her lips, looking thoughtful. 'I shall have to take an evening job as well as my day one. They are always wanting ticket-sellers for the booth in the Dream Palace, as well as that other place.'

Norma looked horrified. 'And walk home at that time of night all by yourself?' Her mouth firmed. 'I don't think so.' There had been a spate of attacks on women in the vicinity of the High Street which Paul had reported on. Some particularly nasty. Norma knew her brother-in-law would never rest in his grave if he thought his young daughter was putting herself in danger. She shook her head, repeating stubbornly, 'I don't think so.'

'Then I'll let this place go and get a room somewhere. A one-bedroomed flat shouldn't be too expensive to run.'

Norma wasn't convinced.

Neither, for all her brave talk, was Kate.

She worried a nail, looking about her at the reminders of their life in India; the brass peacocks on the mantelpiece, the small round mahogany table set with ivory, the wall where hung the curved scimitar which was supposed to have belonged to some Indian prince.

The idea of a one-bedroom flat wasn't all that appealing. Yet what could she do? Aunt Norma was offering her a kind of sanctuary, away from the worries of making ends meet. Living with Aunt Norma she probably wouldn't even have to go out to work. It was cheaper living in the country, her aunt grew most of her own vegetables and in season there were apples and other fruit in abundance.

Kate thought of the pretty cottage with its thatched roof, the quaint old-fashioned village in which it had rested for hundreds of years. The cottage didn't have an inside toilet, not even a water supply. You had to go into the back garden to the well with its moss-grown stone wall and pulley system and lower a bucket on a rope in order to obtain water for everything. Preparing for a bath was a nightmare.

Once there, Kate knew it would be goodbye to all her dreams of eventually owning her own shop, designing her own clothes. Goodbye to Paul and Guy and the supporting enthusiasm of Rosa. Although, she had to remind herself, Paul wouldn't be with them for much longer anyway but away on assignments that beckoned with a skeletal finger . . .

She shivered. Why was she allowing herself such morbid reflections? Why, whenever she envisaged the future, did she see Paul, helpless and in pain, in a space so confined he couldn't move?

Aunt Norma patted her arm. 'Well, we won't talk about it now. There's plenty of time to make up our minds. I've told my neighbour that she can have the cats until the end of the month.' She laughed. 'She loves old Timmy.' She looked at Kate. 'He's the tabby, remember?'

Kate nodded. Old Timmy was getting on for fourteen now, incontinent and smelly.

Aunt Norma continued, unabated, 'I'm consoled by the fact that if anything happened to me they would both have a good home.' She lowered her head and peered closely into Kate's eyes. 'And before I go, I'm determined to see that you are settled in a good home too.'

Although Aunt Norma insisted that Kate wasn't ready to go back to work yet, staying at home was too claustrophobic. A few days after the funeral she appeared one morning at the shop doorway. Sylvia and Ruthie both looked up as Kate entered. The delight on Ruthie's face cancelled out the sudden hostility on Sylvia's. While Kate had been away, Sylvia had been top dog, with Ruthie at her beck and call and Rosa consulting her for advice on ideas she usually sought from Kate.

Ruthie ran forward and impulsively threw her arms about Kate, giving her a hug. 'Oh, you can't know how pleased I am to see you, Kate. But are you all right?' Frowning, she stood back to gaze at Kate, noting the paleness of the skin, the faint purple shadows under the eyes. 'You don't look well.'

'Perhaps you should have stayed home a bit longer,' said Sylvia, cattily. Her voice said: You're not going to be much good to us if you're going to be gloomy all the time.

'I'm perfectly all right,' murmured Kate. 'But thank you for your concern.'

From the back room she could hear the sound of the sewing machine. She pushed open the door and went in. Rosa was seated at the old-fashioned Singer, head bent industriously, foot rocking in an easy rhythm on the treadle. She looked up as the door opened.

'Kate! My little Kate!' She rose from the machine, hurrying forward to hug the girl, so fiercely that Kate pleaded to be allowed to breathe.

Rosa stood back, regarding her with a frown of concern. 'Ah, but you are so pale! It has been a terrible ordeal for one so young. You have come for a visit, no? I will get Ruthie to make us some coffee . . .'

'Well, you know I never say no to a cup of your coffee. But this isn't just a visit. I thought, if you needed me, I'd come back to work . . .'

Rosa was delighted. 'If we need you? Just listen to the child!' She gazed at the ceiling as though appealing to the good Lord for guidance. Rosa's arthritis had been playing her up more than usual and Kate's return would be a godsend.

'How did the fittings for Mrs Ferris's dress go?' Kate enquired.

Rosa gave a negligent wave. 'Oh, that is all completed now.' She laughed. 'Although she treated all of us with a grandiloquence that at times became irritating, we finally came to the finishing touches. She seemed satisfied with the dress and I was relieved to see Ruthie set off to deliver it.'

They fell to talking about the many customers who had enquired about Kate's health. All expressed compassion at her sad loss.

The bell above the shop door jangled and before they had even had time to enjoy the coffee Ruthie had made, the shop was full. Mind you, it didn't take many customers to pack the small boutique to overflowing, and Rosa later confided that she was actively seeking new premises. The idea excited Kate.

'Still around here?' she queried.

'But of course. I must keep a home for Pauli to come back to. And many of my clients have been faithful to me. If I moved to another district I'm afraid I might lose them.'

'Has Paul started his new job then?'

'He started last Monday.' Rosa shook her head, a fond smile lifting her lips. 'He has to go into the city by underground every morning and so must rise from his bed earlier than he is used to. And sometimes he works weekends and at night. I seldom see him, but' – using one of the English expressions she had picked up – 'mustn't grumble. He seems to enjoy it.'

The customers were delighted to see Kate back. Not that they hadn't been served well by Rosa, they explained hastily, but Kate had a touch all her own.

She forced a smile to her lips. She had to put her sadness behind her and concentrate on the future. She would have given anything to have her father back again. As he used to be, jolly and laughing. But unfortunately that could never be. No amount of wishful thinking or remorse would bring back the dead.

They spent a breathless morning with customers discussing styles and colours and it was lunchtime before there was a break. Sylvia went off to the corner caff, as she called it, and Ruthie made a fresh pot of coffee before she, too, vanished to whatever hidey-hole she frequented during her lunch break.

Rosa closed the door on the last customer then joined Kate in the back room. She lifted the silver jug, looking at Kate enquiringly.

Kate nodded and held out her cup. Norma had insisted on making sandwiches, egg and watercress, before Kate left the house that morning. Now she pressed Rosa to share them with her.

Although Rosa had spoken casually about Paul's new job, Kate detected that underneath the glibness an air of unrest prevailed. 'Has he ever spoken to you about his idea of freelancing?' she asked, as though there had been no break in their conversation.

One of Rosa's hands went to her bosom. '*Mein Gott*, such ideas that boy has! Even as a child he had beliefs about his future that took my breath away. I must confess, Kate, that his father helped him. If he is planning on something else he has said nothing to me. The trouble brewing back in Germany is not something I would want my son caught up in.'

She sipped her coffee, her eyes suddenly vacant. 'We came over here to escape all that. Pauli would be putting his head in a noose if he went back.'

Kate wondered how much Paul had told his mother of his visionary ideas about reporting the truth to the free peoples of the world. She thought of the newspaper stories of riots in the Sudeten areas of Czechoslovakia, the whispered tales of concentration camps, although few people believed they were as bad as had been reported. The never-ending stream of goose-stepping men carrying banners marching before the arrogant leaders of Germany.

Ominous happenings.

Where was it all going to end?

Chapter Twenty

Kate heard the postman as she came down the stairs a few mornings later. One long buff-coloured envelope lay on the mat. She bent to pick it up, turning it over in her hand, and read on the back the name of the firm of solicitors who were dealing with the mortgage.

She carried it into the kitchen where Aunt Norma was pottering about getting breakfast. She looked up as Kate entered.

'Post, dear? Anything nice?'

Kate pulled a face. 'I have a feeling it's something *not* nice.'

Her aunt lifted the cosy from the teapot and poured Kate a cup, then added milk and sugar. She knew what Kate meant. It was something Norma had been dreading for weeks. Acting on Kate's behalf, she had tried to negotiate, to no avail. To her consternation she had discovered that Samuel hadn't made any mortgage payments for some time before his death.

The solicitors acting for the bank had been patient but, as they had explained in their last letter, they were answerable to a higher authority and as much as they felt sympathy for Miss Linley, they could not allow this dereliction of duty to continue for much longer.

Seated opposite Kate at the table, Norma guessed the girl's reluctance to read the letter. She said gently, 'Want me to open it?'

Kate shook her head. Hurriedly, tearing the flap in her haste, Kate opened the envelope and drew out the folded sheets of paper.

Norma watched her expression change from hope to utter despair. Hastily she pushed back her chair and came round the table to Kate's side. Without a word Kate handed her the letter. The closely typed lines blurred for a moment before Norma's eyes and then she was reading the words that had shaken her niece to the core.

They were sorry, etc, etc, but in view of the fact that Miss Linley seemed either unable or unwilling to keep up the payments they were afraid they would have to repossess the property.

There was more, legal jargon that Norma didn't bother to read. She refolded the sheets of paper and thrust them back into their envelope. She would much rather have held them to the lighted gas ring, dropping the ashes in the sink. But that wasn't the way to go about things. She had to be sensible, do whatever was best for Kate.

Norma knew in her own heart what was best for Kate.

'So,' she said, 'that's that. We know where we stand now.' She glanced at the girl's pale face. 'A cooked breakfast or toast?'

'Nothing. I couldn't eat a thing.'

'You're not leaving this house without something inside you. A piece of toast at least.'

Kate acquiesced. She smiled, reaching for the jar of marmalade. 'Has anyone ever told you you're nothing but a big bully? Why don't you pick on someone your own size?'

Norma breathed a sigh of relief. 'That's better. Life's a bugger, isn't it? But we can't allow it to get us down.'

While Kate clung to the sassiness that was one of her charms, the Fates might just pick on someone else on whom to vent further fury . . .

Paul came into the shop just before midday and despite his mother's protests that they were busy, dragged Kate off to a proper lunch.

'Really, I'm not hungry,' Kate said as they took their seats at their favourite place in the High Street. The café was filled with the lunch-hour crowd and somewhere a wireless was playing music: Cole Porter's 'Night and Day'.

'A growing girl like you should always be hungry,' Paul said. He signalled to the girl who was serving. She came over to them, leaning one hip against the table as she took their orders. Remembering the tomatoes, Paul ordered a mushroom omelette for himself while Kate said she'd have a slice of Bovril toast.

He viewed the plate the girl set in front of Kate with frustration. 'Aren't you going to have something else? Something a little more substantial?'

Kate reached for her knife and cut the toast in half. 'No, this is fine. I told you, I'm not hungry.'

'When you lose your appetite, then something's the matter. Come on, tell Uncle Paul all about it.'

There was a moment's silence while Kate collected her thoughts. The music in the background was very soothing. Music always had a calming effect on Kate and suddenly she found herself blurting it all out. The almost certain knowledge that she would be losing her home . . .

'Unless they can find my mother and she agrees to continue with the mortgage, and somehow I can't see that happening, then I'm out on the street,' she finished with a grimace. 'Aunt Norma has been twisting my arm suggesting I go to live with her. She's been wonderful, so kind, I don't know how I'd have managed without her. But as for going to live with her . . .'

Kate had spoken often of the tiny village where Aunt Norma lived.

To Paul it sounded just the spot to recuperate from all the sadness that Kate had inherited. She'd told him of the walks through the woodlands, of the narrow dusty lanes where horses stood in fields, gazing placidly over the fence while in the background cows grazed on bright-yellow buttercups and thick masses of clover.

Paul seemed to be deliberating. Frowning, he cut into his omelette with the side of his fork. Kate bit into her toast and watched couples at other tables. They were laughing and talking, seeming to have not a care in the world.

'You could always come and live with us.'

Paul's words made her pause. She placed the toast back on the plate and looked at him, remembering the time she'd visited the flat with Julie. 'How could I do that? You've only got the two bedrooms.'

'You could have my bedroom and I could sleep on the couch. I'm not home all that much lately. My mother would love to have you.'

Living in Paradise Buildings! Kate's lips twisted. 'I couldn't deprive you of your bed. It's a kind offer, Paul, but I really can't accept.'

She recalled climbing the staircase to Paul's flat, the dirt and noise, not to mention the smell. She castigated herself: now she was thinking like a snob. Paul didn't deserve this. But no one could deny the place was pretty awful . . .

Reading her thoughts in her face, Paul said, 'I know. I've been trying to persuade Mama to move for the last year, but she won't hear of it. She says every penny she can spare must go into the business.'

'I can understand that. She was talking not long ago about looking for new premises.'

'And knowing my mother, she will find them.'

'Wouldn't it be lovely to thumb our nose at Mr Shipton and give him notice that we're going to quit?'

He grinned. 'Nothing would please me more than thumbing my nose at Mr God-Almighty Shipton. But we're getting away from the subject. Always remember, my offer still stands. But maybe it won't come to that. Your father worked so hard on the gardens, both front and back, it would be a damn shame to hand them over to somebody else to enjoy.'

Kate's eyes were suddenly bright, tears shimmering on the lashes. 'I know. I think that upsets me more than anything, the thought of strangers living in our house, sitting in our garden. And it *will* come to that, I'm afraid. There's just no way round it. Apparently Daddy had been skipping mortgage payments for months.'

Paul reached for her hand over the table, squeezing it tightly, then glanced at his wristwatch. 'Better get you back. Mama will be thinking we've run away together.'

Kate gave a shaky laugh. 'Now *that* would solve everything, running away together.'

'Gretna Green being our destination!' he grinned. Yet something in his voice told her he wasn't joking, that the words he spoke came from the heart.

She bit her lip, groping for her handbag and gloves. 'Yes, well . . . You might have all the time in the world but I'm afraid I haven't.'

Despite his usual objections Kate paid for her share of the meal. There was an everlasting argument over this but Kate always won.

Outside the skies were grey and it had begun to rain. Everyone rushed by under open umbrellas. The rain was cold against her face and Kate shivered as they dodged the hurrying people. Outside Mr Shipton's grocery store, Paul stopped. 'I've got to get another jar of that coffee Mother likes. It's a damned nuisance but only he sells it. You go on . . .'

'No, I'll come in with you. Aunt Norma mentioned she needed some macaroni. It seems we're having that with cheese tonight.' Taking Paul's arm, she walked into the shop. 'It will save me buying it on my way home.'

Mr Shipton stood talking to Mrs Wells. Every time Kate saw the woman she seemed to have gained a few more pounds. As she turned to observe them enter, the chair she was seated upon creaked under her weight.

As usual Mr Shipton ignored Paul and served Kate first. The girl who had replaced Ruthie was a peroxide blonde, as hard as nails. Kate didn't think she'd object to any of the grocer's 'little tricks' as Ruthie had. As the girl wrapped her box of macaroni up, Kate was aware that Mrs Wells was examining Paul with a jaundiced eye.

As though unable to contain the observation a moment longer, the woman blurted out, 'Yeh, look at 'im, standing there as bold as brass.'

Paul ignored her.

'Cheeky sod! Sacked my Sarah, so they did, on the spot, suddenly decided they didn't need 'er. No references nor nothin'.'

Unable to control the seething anger that swelled in her, Kate turned to glare at the woman. 'Did your precious Sarah not tell you the reason she was sacked?' Seeing the sudden uncertainty in Mrs Wells's eyes, Kate went on, 'Just a little matter of helping herself to the takings, that's all. She was lucky we didn't call the police.'

'Oh, aye, that's just the sort of thing you'd do, isn't it?' The woman wiped her nose with the back of her hand, sniffing loudly. 'Anyroad, Miss High and Mighty, you've no room to talk. Yer mum going orf with the lodger, deserting you and yer dad. Fine goings on, I must say.'

Kate felt sick. How on earth could Mrs Wells know this? Or did everybody know? Gossip spread like wildfire in suburbs as small as this. She sought frantically for something scathing to say, but her mind was too shocked.

Mrs Wells transferred her gaze back to Paul: now that she'd started, there was going to be no stopping her. 'As for the likes of you, the quicker you go back to Germany the better for all of us.'

Her laugh rang out, strident and jeering. Turning to look at Mr Shipton, who had been listening to her harangue with a look of enjoyment, she added, 'Just see 'im strutting down the street with that 'Itler and 'is cronies, can't you? Ought never to be in England, that sort. Ought never to 'ave bin allowed in in the first place.'

She turned her attention back to Paul. 'Why don't you go off to Whitechapel and join that Oswald Mosley? I 'ear 'e's looking for your sort.'

Paul knew she was referring to Sir Oswald Ernald Mosley who had established the British Union of Fascists. He had been in the news lately, leading marches in the East End, inciting anti-Semitic violence. Some of the locals had marched with him, others had attacked them. The newsreels in the cinemas had shown scenes of violence, of police trying vainly to restore order. As one MP commented in Parliament: it was 'one of the nastier aspects of British politics'.

Paul strode over to the counter, grabbed a jar of the coffee his mother liked and feeling in his pocket flung down the correct change. Some of the pennies rolled away beneath the counter and with a gesture of utter disgust Paul pushed them further under with the toe of his shoe.

Mr Shipton's nostrils flared in anger. ''Old on there, don't do that! I'll never get 'em back.'

Paul's lip curled. 'Tough,' he muttered. 'If you ever find them you'll see there's enough to pay for the macaroni as well as the coffee.'

The grocer rounded on Paul and for a moment Kate thought he was going to hit him. 'Don't you talk to me like that, you young toad. You should count yerself lucky that you're still being served in this shop.'

'That can easily be remedied,' replied Paul.

'And what are *you* smiling at, madam?' asked Mrs Wells, glaring at Kate. 'Think it's funny, do yer, speaking back to yer elders and betters?'

'Oh, I wouldn't say that,' countered Kate. 'Especially the bit about betters. And I wasn't aware that I *was* smiling, although you're both so pathetic a body couldn't be blamed for it.'

Mrs Wells sniffed. 'Only idiots smile at nothing.'

Paul slipped the jar of coffee into his pocket and grabbed Kate by the arm. 'Come on, let's get out of here. I find myself suddenly squeamish in the presence of these two objectionable people.'

'Objectionable *and* prejudiced,' said Kate. At the door, she turned to view the overweight woman with distaste. 'Goodbye, Mrs Wells. Be sure to remember me to your daughter. I hear she's still out of work. Can't say that surprises me one little bit.'

Mrs Wells glared. 'Well, the cheeky little madam! My Sarah'd make mincemeat of 'er if I told 'er wot she said.'

Walking back to the shop, their coat collars turned up against the rain, Kate could feel how disturbed Paul was, his anger almost tangible.

Slipping her arm through his, she said quietly, 'You said once that you didn't let that man's rudeness bother you any more. Don't let yourself down now.'

'I don't mind for myself, but when someone starts on you I see red. I wanted to lash out and knock his bloody block off.'

Kate smiled. 'Now that's a sight I'd dearly love to see, Mr Shipton with his block knocked off.' She squeezed his arm. 'Fighting talk, Paul. Better keep it for those articles you are going to write about all those nasty types in Germany.'

She knew he didn't like her joking about Hitler and his cronies and so she squeezed his arm again. 'Sorry, forget I said that. Let's talk about something else.'

They were talking about something else when they arrived back at Rosa's. Still seething with indignation at the scene they had just left, thinking of Kate having to face the irate grocer every day for her shopping, Paul had reverted to the subject of her search for new accommodation.

Mrs Konig listened to the discussion from her place at the sewing machine – seldom did she bother with a lunch hour, preferring to stay open and, if she wasn't busy with customers, get on with her sewing. Her foot on the treadle slowed then stopped. She pushed the frock on which she had been working – a crisp cotton lawn in a red-and-white Paisley design for a client's young daughter – to one side and stood up.

Rarely had she heard Paul speak in so angry a voice. The strong protective instinct that she felt for her son and which she knew she would never forfeit, whatever his age, came to the fore.

'Tsk, tsk!' she stood in the doorway, gazing at her son and a flushed Kate. 'Whatever you two are arguing about I'm sure it can be resolved in a mannerly way.'

'It's Kate.' Paul's voice was belligerent. 'She's being stubborn.'

Rosa pursed her lips and looked at Kate.

'Your son won't take no for an answer,' said Kate hotly, the flush mounting on her cheeks. 'He's insisting that I come and live at your place.'

Rosa was shocked. That Pauli should suggest such a thing! And to an innocent young girl like Kate! 'I don't think that's at all funny,' she said, stiffly.

Paul grunted. 'You won't think it's funny when she's been thrown out on to the street, either.'

Rosa frowned, and Kate hastened to explain. She was in the middle of expounding on the letter received that morning from the solicitors when Ruthie and Sylvia returned from their lunch break.

Rosa gave Kate a warning look and pushed her son towards the door. 'Off you go. I'm sure you've got better things to do than stand here laying down the law to Kate.'

There was a flurry of customers but as soon as they were quiet again Rosa asked Ruthie to make some tea and bring it to her in the back room. She beckoned to Kate to follow her.

Aware of Sylvia's inquisitive stare, she closed the door then turned to Kate.

'I understand perfectly your dilemma, dear, and you must realize Pauli is only trying to help. I know he worries about you.'

'I know, Mrs Konig, and don't think I'm not grateful. But I really can't see myself living like that, sleeping in Paul's bed while he sleeps on the couch.'

'He's away a lot and will in all probability be away for longer periods. I'm sure, in the interim, until you find something to your liking, you would be comfortable enough in Paradise Buildings.' She smiled. 'And it would all be perfectly respectable and above board, as you English say. I would see to that.'

Kate had to laugh at the implication that Paul could be anything but respectable and above board.

'We'll see.'

She reminded herself that she still had to face Aunt Norma. There had been no time for lengthy discussions this morning. Her aunt had had all day to brood over the letter. What sort of conclusion would she have arrived at? wondered Kate.

For all that, what conclusion *could* she arrive at?

Kate stood in the kitchen, stirring the cheese sauce with a wooden spoon while Aunt Norma drained the macaroni over the sink.

Norma had said little since Kate had arrived home which meant she was saving it up for later. The sauce began to thicken and Kate removed it from the gas ring. She placed it to one side and looked at her aunt.

'It's ready.'

'Good, so's this. Get the plates out of the oven.'

It was much easier to eat in the kitchen. There was no Monica looking down her nose in her superior way. The small gate-legged table was just big enough for the two of them.

The discussion Kate had been dreading came as they ate.

'I've been thinking.'

Kate looked up as her aunt spoke. 'I've been thinking, too.'

'And what sort of a solution have you come up with?'

'Well, I've already been offered a place – but I can't go there. There isn't enough space.' She toyed with her food, moving it about on the plate, frowning. 'I suppose I could always look for a room or a flat in the local paper.'

'And live alone, in a strange place?' Norma looked incensed. 'Why, you've never been alone in your life. There's always been someone there for you, your father and then the nuns. And me in the school holidays.' Norma thought of her own existence, lonely even with her beloved cats. 'You wouldn't know what to do with yourself, child.'

'I've never minded being by myself. And I'm not a child. In fact, I rather like my own company. Those times in the railway carriage, when there was nobody there but me, were so peaceful it was lovely.'

'That's different. You chose to be alone then. How would you like it, day after day, and the nights as well? What if you became ill, with no one to look after you?'

'I'd be working for most of the day and there's always work to bring home at night.'

Rosa's business was flourishing, there was no doubt about that, the colourful gowns and beachwear much in demand, and if the small sideline in accessories and costume jewellery hadn't really taken off yet, that didn't matter. Rosa's Boutique was an established business, comparable to any but the most exclusive names in Town.

Kate knew that Rosa had been keeping an eye open for larger premises and thought of how excited the woman had been when just the other day she had confessed that she thought she'd found them.

'That place opposite the Dream Palace,' she'd said. 'You know, it used to be a sports shop. It's been empty for months and I went with the estate agent after I'd closed the shop last night and had a look around. It's perfect, Kate. It's far larger than you would think from outside and it's got a huge storeroom at the back which could be divided into small rooms for fitting and the actual sewing. I'd get more machines, hire extra staff.' She sighed, shaking her head.

'And when I think of how I first started, I have to pinch myself to prove I'm not dreaming. Did I ever tell you about the time I couldn't even afford to buy new patterns?'

Kate shook her head. 'No.'

'Well, the whole thing was to be run on a shoestring. I think that is the proper expression, no?'

At Kate's affirmative nod she went on, 'As I said, there was no money for paper patterns so I carefully unpicked a couple of dresses I had, both very elegant, both with a designer label sewn into the back. The sum total of the wardrobe I was able to bring from Germany. I cut patterns from them on to an old newspaper and used those patterns for many a frock, altering them slightly to give them a new look.' She smiled at Kate. 'I have come far since those early days, no?'

If Kate had been a more demonstrative person she would have hugged her. 'You've done splendidly,' she said, warmly.

Aunt Norma was saying, 'There you go, off into one of your daydreams again. How can you talk of looking after yourself when you're always in a fantasy world all of your own?'

She bent over the table to reach the teapot, lifting it and pouring herself and Kate a cup. 'You'd soon get fed up sewing all evening as well as during the day. No, the best thing for you is to come and stay with me. The town's within easy reach on the bus, although they're not all that frequent, and there are picture houses there and a dance hall.'

She took a sip of her tea, meeting Kate's eyes over the rim of her cup. 'At least you wouldn't be lonely.'

Kate drew a breath of warm air, redolent of the rich cheese sauce. 'It's what is known as being adaptable, Aunt Norma. I'll be all right.'

Norma rose and began gathering the used dishes, putting them in the sink and turning the hot water tap. 'You girls these days! I don't know! I just wonder what your poor father would say, could he hear you now.'

'He would probably be proud of me,' said Kate with more confidence than she felt.

Norma sniffed her vexation. 'Well, seeing that you've made up your mind, and you always were a stubborn little baggage, Kate Linley, then I suppose we'd better make an appointment with those solicitors with regard to the disposal of the house.'

Chapter Twenty-One

Rosa Konig packed the carefully folded gown in between layers of white tissue paper and laid it in the flat purple-and-green-striped box. She was alone in the shop. She made a point of arriving before eight so that she would have a quiet hour to herself before the girls arrived and the shop opened for business.

She liked to make herself a cup of her favourite coffee and read the paper, turning first to the society column. The goings-on of the English nobility never failed to amaze her. All that swapping of partners, making it sound respectable by referring to it as broken engagements and divorce!

It had been bad enough last year with that Simpson woman and poor Edward. At least he had acted in an honourable fashion and married her, even though he'd had to give up his throne to do it.

She wondered if she would ever get the chance to make gowns for one of the Fashionable People. She always thought of them in capital letters. Or would Mrs Ferris, not the most fashionable but the most wealthy, be the best that she could ever hope for?

Smiling, she turned the pages. Towards the back she came across the accommodation to let columns. In times like these, with jobs scarce and money short, empty rooms could not be allowed to remain empty. Children were expected to share a room, sometimes even a single bed, and the resulting empty bedroom would be let to a lodger.

Thinking of Kate's plight, Rosa's eye ran down the columns. There was an abundant choice: bedsitting rooms in houses all over London, inexpensive enough for even the most lowly paid shop girl; one-bedroomed flats costing a little more.

Kate should have no trouble in finding somewhere nice. Casting her eye down the list again, Rosa noted that most of the locations given were in East London or across the river. Considering the price of public transport today, unthinkable.

She considered her son's suggestion that Kate should come and live in Paradise Buildings. The germ of an idea flourished in her mind.

There was the sound of knuckles tapping on the glass door and looking up Rosa saw Kate standing there. She closed the paper and thrust it under the counter next to the yellow duster.

Offering Kate a cup of the coffee she had already made, Rosa said, 'I was just looking through the paper to see if there was anything suitable for you, Kate. However, they were all miles away and it would mean catching buses and the underground. And I presume you would prefer a place around here, wouldn't you?'

Thinking of the crowded tubes, the endless time waiting for buses, Kate grimaced. 'You can say that again! I'd hate having to catch a bus or train every day.' She sipped at her coffee, looking at Mrs Konig. 'But if you're suggesting again that I take Paul's bed then the answer's no. Oh, I'm not being a prude or anything like that, it's just that Paul works so hard and such long hours that it wouldn't be fair to expect him to sleep on the couch.' She'd found it hard and lumpy the few times she had sat on it when visiting Paul. No, that proposal was quite out of the question.

Gazing into Rosa's dark eyes, realizing that the woman was only considering her best interests, Kate's tone softened. 'But thank you for thinking about me. Don't worry, I'm sure to find something suitable.' She grimaced again. 'If not, then like hundreds of other people, I'm just going to have to endure a lifetime of buses and trains!'

She reached out to take Rosa's cup. 'It's no big deal. How about some more coffee before the rush starts?'

Rosa accepted the cup and said reflectively, 'I discussed with Paul last night about that place I'd been to see.'

'And?'

'He thinks it's a good idea. Providing we can keep the business expanding like it has been. We would have to redecorate the entire place, though. It could be expensive.'

'The very reason why you have been living like a church mouse all this time,' said Kate. 'Salting away every penny for the silver lining that will follow all those rainy days.'

Rosa looked puzzled, and Kate laughed. 'Never mind. I'm sure you get the drift.'

'But it would be marvellous, wouldn't it?' enthused Rosa. 'You must come with me to see it, Kate. We could work wonders in such a setting.'

The door bell jangled and Ruthie and Sylvia appeared. Ruthie was immediately sent off to deliver the prettily wrapped box while Sylvia carried the used coffee cups into the kitchen.

From then on it was one succession of women after another. Arriving in groups of twos and threes, they chattered like a cageful of sparrows, beseeching Kate to design something special, just for them. It seemed there was to be a big social event to which most of them had been invited. The idea now was to outdo each other in style and glamour.

Kate drew low necklines and narrow shoulder straps, skirts cut with the fullness fanning out from the hips. Of thin silk or chiffon, a shoulder cape trimmed with dark fur tied loosely about the neck and allowed over one shoulder.

One that proved to be a favourite was a gown of light-blue silk crêpe with vertical bands of openwork embroidery across the bodice. The split skirt revealed a matching silk slip.

Designs selected and orders given, the women went on to day attire. They murmured excitedly over mid-calf-length winter frocks showing the prevailing long, narrow line. Some had high, curved necklines and padded shoulders, others draped cowl necks. The popularity of fox-fur trimmings was something Kate abhorred but she bowed to her customers' wishes, at the same time maintaining the effect of neat and uncluttered lines.

She drew attention to Rosa's new range of costume jewellery, matching earrings and brooches, many of which were designed in the popular sun-ray motif.

'Expensive?' murmured one client doubtfully.

Since the emergence of Rosa's Boutique husbands had frowned at their wives' increasing demands for larger monthly clothes allowances. Where once they had been satisfied with a frock made by the 'little woman down the road', they now refused to patronize anyone but Rosa.

The client turned the sun-ray brooch over in her hand. It was made of clear dark-blue stones. 'Pretty, though.'

'And not in the least expensive,' pointed out Rosa.

Other women eyed the brooch acquisitively, making up the woman's mind. 'I'll take it. And the earrings.'

Before leaving for work the next day, Kate told her aunt she might be home a little later than usual. 'Mrs Konig's taking me to see the new premises she's got her eye on. It will be wonderful if we can afford them.'

'All right, dear, I'll keep your supper warm.' Aunt Norma worried that Kate hadn't yet come up with somewhere nice to live. She would be leaving in a few weeks – her neighbour, although good-hearted, couldn't be expected to look after her cats forever. Besides which, they wouldn't know her when she did go home if she left it much longer.

That the shop had been so successful Mrs Konig could afford to think of moving into new, larger premises was great. Now, if only Kate could find somewhere nice and homely to live, Norma could return with an easy mind to her quiet little village and her cats.

It was a few days later that Rosa broke the news. Waiting until just after closing, when Ruthie and Sylvia had gone home, she said, 'I've got something to tell you, Kate. I hope you won't think me an interfering old woman, but I heard of a one-bedroomed flat going in our buildings and last night Pauli and I went to see it. It's on the top floor so you wouldn't be bothered as we are with people walking past you on their way up to higher floors. I admit *I* would find the climb too arduous but a young girl like you . . .' She laughed. 'Good for the figure, no?'

Kate thought of Paradise Buildings and inwardly cringed. Still, she mustn't let this kind woman see how she felt. And it would be cheap. Well within her means.

'What was the flat like?'

'Pauli says it needs redecorating but that would be no problem. He has offered to do it. If,' she explained hastily, 'you decide you would like to live there. It is an easy walk to work and what is more important, after a busy day and in wintertime an easy walk home.'

'And you think it's all right, do you?'

Kate had never realized how much faith she put in Mrs Konig's advice.

Rosa made a gesture that was pure Continental. 'With new wallpaper and carpets covering the rather scuffed floorboards, your own things about you, it should be very nice.'

Kate's mind was working overtime. She could keep her own bed and the carpets from her room and the sitting room. She already had a stove and kitchen fittings and the three-piece suite from the sitting room. Besides all the curtains and a bathroom cabinet.

Reading Kate's deliberations in her face, Rosa said, 'Why don't you come home with me now and have a look at it? It won't remain empty for long, dear. You would have to make up your mind fairly quickly.'

Kate grinned and reached for her coat. 'You've talked me into it before I've even seen it,' she said.

Passing her own house, where she knew Aunt Norma would be waiting for her, Kate ran in to explain to her aunt what her plans were. 'It's just across the railway bridge, Paradise Buildings, so I won't be long. Don't wait for me but have your own supper.'

'I'll keep yours warm.' Norma smiled and nodded to Rosa who had insisted on waiting at the gate. 'Good evening, Mrs Konig.'

Rosa smiled and nodded back. 'Good evening. I'm sorry to kidnap your niece like this but I promise it won't be for long.'

Norma stood at the door and watched until they disappeared in the trees fringing the grounds of the Railway Club. Paradise Buildings! She shuddered. She had never been inside the place, never wanted to, but she'd heard about it. Common working-class folk of the worst kind lived there, kept their coal in their baths, so it was said, while the lavatories . . . She shuddered again. She didn't want to think about the lavatories.

As Kate repeatedly reminded her, she was a big girl now and able to take care of her own life. Poor little soul, thought the kind-hearted

Norma, with a mother like she had it was just as well the girl *was* so self-reliant. Confident enough to take up abode in a place like Paradise Buildings instead of coming to stay with Norma in the beautiful countryside around Aylesbury.

Facing every day that frightening iron structure bridging the spot where her father had been killed . . .

Norma couldn't help admiring her for putting a brave face on this truly awful situation.

The stairs were just as smelly as Kate remembered them. Groups of children clustered on the landings. Roller skating seemed the favourite pastime. Small boys and girls showed considerable skill in gliding backwards and forwards along the passages leading to the different flats. The echoes of iron wheels on stone floors rumbled distressingly loud in the enclosed space.

'Why they can't do it outside I'll never know,' grumbled Rosa, puffing her way up in front of Kate.

Rosa had obtained the key for the empty flat and with a flourish flung open the front door. Kate tried not to notice the garishly coloured wallpaper. It would defy anyone without the most vivid imagination to decipher the huge orange splodges that made up the pattern. To Kate they looked like the crazy outpouring of some demented mind.

Looking at her, Rosa said, 'I know. Distressing, isn't it? One wonders how *anyone* could have chosen such an outlandish wall covering. But the bedroom isn't so bad and the kitchen and bathroom are passable. And as I said, Pauli has promised to help you redecorate.'

After touring the flat, which took mere minutes, Kate said, 'I suppose it could be made to look nice.' She went to the sitting room window which was at the front. Being on the top floor the view was impressive: wide stretches of green countryside in the distance, the twin silver lines of the railway tracks and behind them the red roofs of the new houses in Wesley Avenue.

'And the view's not bad,' she added. She turned to Rosa. 'I'll start decorating this weekend.'

Rosa nodded. 'And I shall tell Pauli to keep the weekend free in order to help you.'

Going back down the stairs, they almost stumbled over two little girls who sat on the cold greasy steps nursing their dolls. Kate smiled at them and, placing a finger against her lips, said in a whisper, 'Shhh, mustn't wake them, must we?'

The two mites, looking barely four years old, gave her a malevolent glare then went back to nursing the scruffy, almost hairless dolls.

As they continued on their descent, Rosa said, 'I'm afraid you will find the children are highly suspicious of adults in Paradise Buildings.

It's better not to try and make friends, Kate, for you won't succeed.'

Rosa tracked the caretaker of the flats to his lair in the basement and handed back the key. 'Miss Linley will take the flat,' she told him in a voice that to him sounded imperious.

He nodded. 'All right. The sooner she moves in the better, before those bloody little demons that live here break in and begin their vandalizing.'

Kate was shocked. 'But they are only babies . . .'

The caretaker grunted and hung the key on a numbered hook behind his desk. He could have ignored her remark but seeing that she was young, and inexperienced in the ways of Paradise Buildings, he said, 'Babies are wot you wheel about in prams, miss. Once they're mobile, believe me, they're not babies any more but well on the way to an early set-to with the police.'

Aunt Norma wasn't at all happy about Kate going to live in such a place. She made no secret of the fact, repeating aloud her distrust of her niece's future surroundings. 'I do wish you'd come with me, dear,' she was saying even as they waited for the train that was to take her home.

The guard's whistle shrilled and she gave Kate a hasty kiss and climbed on to the train. 'Now promise you'll keep in touch! I shall expect a letter at least once a month. And Kate . . .'

'Yes, Aunt Norma?'

'If by chance you should hear from your mother, let me know immediately.'

Kate touched one forefinger to her tongue and traced a cross over her heart. 'I promise,' thinking even as she said it that that wasn't likely. Her mother had made her bed and was obviously enjoying lying on it. Probably in some sunny spot on the French coast. Whatever kind of life she was living, clearly it was better than the one she had had here.

A feeling of sadness came over Kate whenever she thought of her mother. Sadness for lost hopes and what might have been. But, she told herself briskly, she had no time for that. There was too much to do to think of the past. The future was what mattered now.

Before leaving the house for the last time, she went out into the back garden and with one of her father's trowels dug up a bunch of marigold seedlings. Every year they seeded themselves and there were three times as many now as when Daddy first planted them. She stood on the lawn, on that frosty spring morning, and gazed about her. A passer-by seeing her face would have thought she was in some beautiful old cathedral, gazing at the wonders of God.

Daddy had created all this from bare soil! She prayed that whoever bought the house would love and look after this small garden just as tenderly.

Careful to disturb the thread-like roots as little as possible, she planted the seedlings in a red clay pot she found in the shed. They would stand on the windowsill of her new kitchen which she'd noticed caught most of the sun.

That way there would be no forgetting that hot sunny country where she had known such happiness.

Meanwhile work on the new flat was going well. Paul was a brick. His Sundays for the following three weeks were given up to standing on a stepladder, whistling shrilly as his brush moved swiftly over the horrible orange wallpaper. He'd have to give it two coats, he explained. From where she knelt with a smaller brush painting the skirting board, Kate nodded.

At the end of the month, when Rosa saw the flat she could hardly believe her eyes. In the bedroom and sitting room, the doors and windows and the skirting board were pristine in a brilliant white glossy paint. The walls of both were painted a restful shade of green, while the kitchen was a bright sunny yellow.

The transformation was astounding.

Rosa stood with the two paint-stained young people and said with great satisfaction, 'I think you have both created a miracle. Kate, I'm sure, will be very happy here.'

Chapter Twenty-Two

Summer was suddenly upon them and the warm weather brought out the crowds. The High Street was thronged with people, mostly women looking for holiday wear in Rosa's Boutique.

Rosa stood in the doorway and welcomed her customers, smiling and nodding, addressing the regulars by name. Business was booming. In fact, since they had moved to the larger premises she could honestly say it had doubled.

There were two windows now, one either side of the door, both so large Rosa guessed it took all of Kate's ingenuity to do the displays. Still, with the treasure trove she had to choose from, most of it new, she never seemed to lack for ideas.

Kate had been living in Paradise Buildings for two months now and to all intents and purposes appeared to have settled in well. It was nice having the girl nearby, Rosa thought. Especially now that Pauli had gone. He had suddenly taken it into his head that he'd had enough of working for other people and shocked her by giving his notice to the paper.

'Don't be so hasty,' she had warned. 'Think carefully of what you are doing.'

'I've thought, Mama, and I'm sure. I've saved enough money to be able to pay my way for the time it will, hopefully, take me to become established.' He smiled and kissed her warmly. 'And just think, I can send you news of all your friends back in Germany and the people I knew as a child.'

If, some sixth sense warned him, there were any of them left . . .

Although his going had upset her, she told herself she ought to have been expecting it.

On that misty morning when she and Kate had accompanied him to the station, his excitement had been overwhelming. Not even trying to hide her misery, Rosa had repeated endlessly, 'Are you sure you've got your warm vests and those socks I bought for you?'

'Yes, Mother, I'm sure. And,' stalling her boundless questions with a raised hand, 'may I remind you that it is also summer in Germany and the sun will be shining.' He bent and gave her a hug. 'I won't be cold. And when winter comes, if I am still there I shall remember your warnings and wrap up well.'

He had turned to Kate. 'And my little Kate will look after my mama and write me all the news, no?'

Kate blinked the tears from her eyes. 'You bet!'

Goodbyes were horrible. Later Kate told Rosa that she hated them. They stood and watched the train steam out of the station. Rosa wished with all her heart that her son had remained in his nice safe job on the paper and not put his life in danger by returning to what was now unknown territory.

Pauli had promised to be discreet, to avoid situations that might involve danger. But he was so headstrong, so like his father. Rosa crossed herself and offered up a silent prayer that her only child would come back safely. It was, she thought, as though he was going off to war . . .

'Rosa!'

It was Kate calling. Rosa dragged her thoughts back to the present and went into the brightly lit shop. The place had been completely renovated. There were lots of full-length mirrors, tinted a pale pink, giving the viewer a rosy bloom that was somehow reverential; an abundance of gilt and velvet drapes; and an alcove where two deeply padded sofas provided a comfortable place for customers, weary with spending their husband's money, to sit and enjoy a cup of Rosa's coffee.

It was while Kate was taking a well-earned break later in the afternoon that she saw Guy Ferris coming into the shop. His grandmother had become an integral part of their business and Kate wondered if he had been sent to place another order.

It had become the practice for Kate to go round to the old lady's home, taking designs of the garments she thought Mrs Ferris would like. With autumn not too far away it was the warm dresses and skirts now that took Mrs Ferris's fancy.

She had confessed to Kate that she hadn't spent so much on clothes in years.

'Then it's time you spoiled yourself,' Kate told her daringly.

'Guy has been telling me that for years. But I must admit that the fashions in vogue did not excite me. Not as much as they have done since I met you and Rosa.'

Kate was treated like an honoured visitor, offered tea and jam sponge and tiny triangular sandwiches. Guy would laugh and tell her the old lady was fattening her up for Christmas.

Kate had looked at him questioningly, head tilted to one side. 'Why, what's happening at Christmas?'

Surprising her, he bent and dropped a kiss on her lips. It was the first time he'd attempted any kind of familiarity. Kate decided she liked it.

'Just make a wish and it's yours,' he told her.

She smiled at him now and, mindful of the customers, said formally, 'Good afternoon, Mr Ferris. Lovely day, isn't it?'

'Far too nice for you to be stuck in here missing all that sunshine.'

'What's a poor working girl to do? Who would pay my rent if I didn't work?'

Too late she realized that the words sounded like a come-on. The easy availability of girls drawn by his family's wealth must have made him accustomed to this. Although she found him attractive, she certainly didn't want to lead him on. When she committed herself to a relationship – and in her case it would have to be marriage – she would have to be very sure it was the real thing.

She thought back to the first time she had seen him, to the dark-haired girl with whom he had played tennis and then lured to the old railway carriage. Had that girl been one of a long line of old girlfriends, added and then crossed-off like a shopping list?

She was thankful that the shop was so full of people. When he gazed at her in the way he was doing now, strange things happened to her heart. She didn't know how to deal with it. The nuns hadn't said anything about feeling like this . . .

'Well, what does a poor working girl do on her days off?' he teased.

'Usually put my feet up after doing the housework.'

He moved closer until he was almost touching her. 'We never did go on that date, did we? Remember, the time I asked you to go to the pictures? We never did organize another one.'

That was the day her father died, she thought, and felt a lump come to her throat. Over the lump, she said, 'It wasn't a very happy time for me. I'm still getting over it. And then there was the house and moving into a new flat . . .'

Mindful of the curious looks customers were giving them, he said, 'Look, we can't talk here. What if I wait for you after work? We could go and have a drink or something.'

Sylvia was coming their way, smiling ingratiatingly at Guy. Hurriedly, Kate said, 'All right. I finish here about eight. By then most of our customers have gone. I could try and get out a few minutes earlier.'

'You do that.' He gave Sylvia a smile that had her squirming with rapture. Then, from the side of his mouth, gangster-fashion, he breathed to Kate, 'OK, doll, see ya.'

The disappointment on Sylvia's face as he turned and walked away was comical to see.

'Humph!' She greeted Kate with her usual bad grace. 'And what did *you* do to make Mr Ferris leave in such a huff?'

Airily, Kate replied, 'I don't think it was me, Sylvia, but the sight of you coming towards us. He was telling me he'd had a bad day,' she continued, fabricating her story as she went along, 'and thought your smarmy manner a mite too much for him.'

Sylvia looked outraged, and Kate thought that had there been a cat present, Sylvia would have kicked it.

At ten minutes to eight, when there were only a few customers left, Kate asked Rosa if she could go early.

Rosa nodded. 'You've worked hard today, dear. We all have. Off you go. See you on Monday.'

Guy was waiting on the pavement outside the shop. After greeting him, Kate told him about Sylvia, concluding, 'I really oughtn't to tease her, but it's so easy. She gets her back up faster than anyone I know.'

He reached for her hand and without ceremony tucked it under his arm. Placing his own hand over it as it lay on his sleeve, he said, 'Forget Sylvia. Forget work. What about that drink, then?'

'Anything you say.' A nice cold drink in a tall glass would be ideal after the warm summer afternoon.

The Green Man had its doors flung wide, and people were sitting, whole families of them, at the rustic wooden tables while small children ran and shrieked over the lawns. From the open doors came a cacophony of sound that even from this distance had Kate's ears ringing. She hoped he wouldn't suggest the Green Man . . .

He didn't. He said, turning his head to look down at her, 'You've not been in the club yet, have you?'

'No.'

'Right, we'll go there.'

Feeling a ridiculous panic overcome her, she looked down at her plain cotton summer dress. 'I'm hardly dressed for that, Guy . . .'

'There's nothing special on. Just a few people who gather of an evening to socialize and share a drink.' His eyes appraised her as though she was a luscious offering on a silver tray. 'Even dressed like that, you'll knock 'em dead.'

'Well, if you don't think anyone will mind . . .'

'When you're with me, nobody would dare say a word.'

They walked down Wesley Avenue on their way to the club. Passing number 138 Kate averted her eyes; the house had been taken by a family with small children. She had met them once before they moved in and that silly lump had come again to her throat as she noted the all too obvious happiness of the young wife, the pride of ownership in the husband's eyes.

She imagined the little ones in her old bedroom, lying in their beds listening to a bedtime story read by their mother. Perhaps there was a swing in the garden where they swooped over the marigolds, shrieking with laughter.

She prayed fervently that their father hadn't dug up the marigolds...

'Penny for them,' said Guy, glancing down at her as they walked.

'Worth far more than a penny, although you wouldn't think so,' she replied lightly.

Guy would never understand the wretchedness of losing your home. Thinking of her childhood, she amended that to second home. The Ferrises had lived in that old red-brick house for generations. Guy knew nothing else, if you didn't count the dour boarding school in Scotland to which he had been sent at an early age. But he'd always had this house to come back to. Nothing could take it away: it would always be there.

They walked past the old railway carriage where the grass was long and wild flowers hid demurely in its lushness. The rays of the setting sun glinted redly on the grimy windows, giving the impression of lights and people enjoying themselves where she and Paul had sat...

'This place always reminds me of when I first met you,' Guy said. 'I was pretty awful, wasn't I?'

She nodded.

'I know I've said it before but I'm really sorry. I apologize unreservedly.'

'Apology accepted,' smiled Kate.

'It wasn't that I didn't like you. In fact, I was enormously attracted to you, Kate. Far more than I have been to any other girl.'

'Go on,' she encouraged teasingly when he fell silent. 'I like it.'

'I'm spelling this out because I wouldn't want you to get the wrong impression. In other words, I want you to know that my motives are entirely honourable.'

'Sounds serious,' she smiled.

He turned his head to look down into her eyes. 'Would you consider us becoming serious?'

'Guy, this is ridiculous.'

'I don't think so. On the contrary, I think it could turn out rather nice.'

His expression, and the glint in his eyes, told her what he meant by that. She shivered at the prospect.

Now that he had got that off his chest he felt better, he told himself. The way had been laid, the snares set.

Holding lightly to her arm, they walked through the trees and across the grass to the white clubhouse. She had never been this close before. There was a wide veranda where on that warm evening people sat and talked, half-filled glasses before them. They greeted Guy in a jocular manner, at the same time appraising Kate with curious eyes.

Guy led her through the open double doors and into the softly shaded lights of the clubhouse. A number of men stood with their drinks, leaning on the bar. Small tables with red cloths were set about the sides of the large room, leaving the centre, Kate imagined, clear for dancing.

Guy guided her to one table and pulled a chair out for her. At nearby tables women on their own turned to scrutinize the newcomer. Kate wondered what they were thinking: another of Guy's conquests?

Tilting her chin, meeting their gazes serenely, she smiled and then turned her attention to Guy who was enquiring what she would like to drink.

'That is,' he said teasingly, 'if you're old enough to drink.'

'I'll have an orange juice, if you don't mind,' she told him.

His brows rose. 'Nothing in it? Gin, or vodka perhaps?'

'No. Just plain orange. Thank you.'

He shrugged and went over to the bar. She saw the men there make room for him as he joined them. One or two turned to examine Kate with bold eyes, then turned back to say something to Guy. He laughed and others joined in. Kate felt suddenly uncomfortable. Aware of the other women's gazes which had never left her, she opened her handbag and pretended to be searching for something inside its depths.

Guy took his time, seemingly caught up in one of those long-winded drawn-out jokes that men standing at bars love.

There was hearty laughter when it finally came to the punch line. One of the women from a nearby table rose and walked over to stand behind the man who had told the joke. He ignored her completely until she gave him a dig in the ribs and muttered something in a low voice.

Kate heard him call to the bartender for 'Another drink for the little woman.'

Carrying her drink, she retraced her steps, but this time to where Kate sat. Standing behind the empty chair, she said, 'Mind if I join you?'

Kate snapped her handbag shut and pushed it between the leg of the chair and her right foot. 'No, of course not. Please do.'

Although she looked older, Kate recognized her as the dark-haired girl who had been with Guy on their first meeting in the old carriage. Guy had called her Lottie. He'd since mentioned that she had married. Lottie pulled out the chair and sat down. 'It's just that it gets so boring, sitting by yourself while your husband spends the evening sharing rude jokes with his cronies.'

Lottie wore her hair differently now, more sophisticated; parted to one side and waved softly over the ears. The dress she was wearing wasn't one of Rosa's – Kate would have known immediately if it was, besides which she'd never known Lottie patronize the boutique. Kate guessed it cost plenty; a clinging plum-red silk that left her arms and most of her shoulders bare. Kate felt like the village maiden in her own simple cotton.

Kate heard herself saying: 'Why do you come then?'

Lottie considered her question then gave Kate a superior smile. 'Nothing else to do. It's become a tradition, the club on a Saturday night.' She took a sip of her drink, a bright-green syrupy liquid in a long-stemmed cocktail glass. Kate thought it looked horrible. The woman went on to say, 'I'm Lottie, by the way. Lottie Dixon. For what it's worth,' gesturing towards the bar, 'that's my husband, John. I remember you from somewhere. Can't think where it was.' She took another sip of her drink. 'Are you planning to join our little club? We could do with some new blood.'

'I'm here as Guy's guest.'

The glass was once more lifted to her lips. 'Does that mean,' she said, transparently curious, 'you're Guy's new blood?'

Irritated at the woman's rudeness – new blood indeed, it sounded terrible – Kate tried not to let her feelings show. She turned her head to look in Guy's direction. He was taking his time!

'I'm not Guy's new anything,' she said, forcing a calmness she didn't quite feel. After all, her visits to the club might become a way of life if she started to go out with Guy.

She stifled a laugh and Lottie glanced at her. 'What?'

'Oh, nothing. I was just thinking . . .' Just thinking all right, pre-empting the future.

'Are you and Guy . . .' Lottie waggled one hand in a sign that Kate supposed must indicate something unmentionable.

A flush spread to Kate's cheeks. Fortunately, Guy arrived back at that moment, saving her from further embarrassment.

A frown darkened his good looks as he noted the woman's presence. He didn't even greet her although she smiled and murmured a hello. Instead he said, looking at Kate, 'I see you've met Mrs Dixon.' He shifted his gaze to Lottie and his voice sharpened as he added, 'You'll find Mrs Dixon a great one for dishing the dirt. Anything you want to know about any member of the club, you just have to ask her.' A thin smile twisted his lips. 'Eh, Lottie? Isn't that right?'

Lottie Dixon jumped to her feet, knocking her own glass and the one Guy had brought Kate flying. Liquid spilled over the red cloth. Pure hatred blazed in her eyes. Flouncing to the bar, she informed her husband in a voice loud enough for the entire clubhouse to hear that she wanted to go home. *Now*, her tone demanded.

The group of men exchanged glances and shrugged. John Dixon downed the last of his lager and moved unsteadily away from the bar. Kate could hear him arguing with his wife as they walked across the veranda and down the steps.

Tight-lipped, Guy snatched Kate's glass up and returned to the bar for a refill. Kate felt gauche, imagining everyone's eyes on her. When he returned, Guy slammed the glass down in front of her, narrowly missing spilling that too, and took a deep gulp of his own drink.

Tentatively, Kate began. 'Guy . . .'

'What did that woman say? With what nastiness was she filling your mind?'

'She introduced herself, told me her husband was at the bar and then asked was I a new member.' She smiled, trying to lighten the situation. 'Nothing nasty, I assure you.'

'She didn't talk about me?'

'No. Why should she?' Kate leaned across the table and placed her hand over his. 'Why, what kind of nasty secrets are *you* trying to hide?'

To her surprise, he swallowed the last of his drink and said roughly, 'Come on, drink up.'

Kate wasn't going to allow herself to be bullied into anything before she was good and ready. 'Why? We've only just got here.'

'Because this place depresses me, that's why.'

Kate took in the pink shaded lights, the array of chairs set at the far end of the large room.

'I think it's rather nice, actually. Very comfortable.' She glanced down at her wristwatch. 'Besides, it's too early to go home yet. We're here, it was your idea. We can at least stay for another drink.'

She heard his sigh. 'Kate, don't be tedious. One of my pet hates in life is women who argue.'

Kate sat back in her chair, and crossed her legs. Her fingers curled about the stem of her glass, moving the base slowly in small circles on the red cloth. Her eyelashes fluttered and came down slowly over her eyes. It was a purely spontaneous gesture; the ancient womanly instinct for getting your own way. 'Aren't you being a little selfish?'

Her change of mood had him grinning. 'Yes. If I were a woman I wouldn't have anything to do with me. All right, one more drink and then we'll go.'

'Don't be there all night,' she called after him as he strode across the floor to the bar. She pursed her lips and glanced round at the remaining women. They had converged on one table and sat in a circle like Macbeth's witches, deep in conversation.

Coming back, carrying the drinks, Guy too looked over towards the women. 'Bunch of old crones,' he said. 'I don't know that it was a good idea bringing you here.'

'Can your reputation be that bad,' she said, teasingly, 'that you don't want me to hear the gossip?'

'There isn't any gossip. At least, not the sort of gossip you're implying. Anyway, let's talk about something else. For instance, what are you doing tomorrow?'

'Washing my hair and cleaning the windows.'

'Sounds like fun.'

'Why, what did you have in mind?'

'I've seen you on that old bike of yours. I haven't ridden a bicycle for years. If the weather is nice, how would you feel about a picnic? We could ride over to the reservoir. I know there's a bicycle somewhere in our garden shed. I'll get old Doby, the gardener, to rake it out and give it a good cleaning.'

Kate was uncertain of her feelings. This wasn't brotherly, gentle Paul Konig she was contemplating spending the day with, but Guy Ferris, about whom gossip almost certainly circulated in the club. In spite of his denial, his agitated response to Lottie Dixon's presence made her suspect that his exploits were fairly shocking.

She took a breath to say she really did have to wash her hair and there was so much to do in the flat that she couldn't possibly afford to spend the day cycling all over the country. Then she met Guy's eye and didn't say it after all.

'All right, Guy. If it's not raining.'

'It won't be raining. I guarantee it.'

Chapter Twenty-Three

They had arranged to meet outside Paradise Buildings at an early hour. The pearly, brilliant morning shimmered all about Kate as she wheeled her bicycle through the front door and out on to the road. It was one of the things she'd held on to when coming to live here. Its back wheel fastened with a chain and padlock, it leaned against the wall behind the stairs. So far, the youthful vandals of the flats had left it in peace.

Guy was already waiting. Mounted on a fast-looking racing bike – she wondered if her own ancient model would manage to keep up with it! – he looked fit and handsome in khaki shorts and a white open-neck shirt.

Kate had pulled a dark beret over her hair and wore shorts similar to his, with a short-sleeved blouse. Short socks and laced walking shoes completed the picture of a healthy young woman looking forward to an energetic day out.

Sports and outdoor activities were popular, and biking was particularly fashionable with young couples.

His eyes examined her as she approached him. 'You look fabulous,' he said.

She laughed. 'In these old things?' Looking down at her shorts and flat shoes.

'Fabulous in anything.'

'How do we get to this reservoir?' she queried, changing the subject. Somehow she never minded Paul's teasing remarks, but with Guy they were provoking, often containing a double meaning.

He pointed westwards. 'We follow the road in that direction. I'm not sure how far it is, about three miles, I reckon.' He grimaced. 'We should have used the car.'

Kate shook her head. 'Not the same. Besides, it was your idea. You're not going to get out of this one as easily as you escaped last night at the club.'

For a moment his expression darkened. 'And what's that supposed to mean?'

Kate sighed. Thinking back to the débâcle at the clubhouse, she didn't really want to go into all that again.

Perched on the saddle, the toe of one foot poised steadyingly on the tarmac, she said, 'Nothing. Come on, let's get started.'

Between neat rows of houses built of red brick, they cycled along avenues planted with young trees. The streets were long, the house numbers going into the hundreds. But Guy insisted they were heading in the right direction.

'Although I'd forgotten what a bloody long way it was,' he admitted. 'We could have put the bikes in the boot of the car and travelled in comfort.' His face was flushed, beads of sweat standing out on his forehead.

'No!' Kate was adamant. 'We need the exercise.' She didn't want to remind him again that it had been his idea.

But when the scene before them changed to acres of green, with the stretch of silver water dazzling with sun pennies, she gave a sigh of relief. For all her valiant words, she knew she was going to be sore tomorrow, her muscles long since unaccustomed to such exercise.

A thin wind flattened the long grasses at the side of the water. 'So peaceful,' said Kate thinking aloud. The sound of church bells drifting across the reservoir reminded her that there had been no time to attend mass that morning. In fact, on a lot of Sunday mornings lately there had been no time to attend mass. She'd have Father O'Hanlan paying her a visit if she wasn't careful . . .

The spot for their picnic, selected by Guy, was close to the water, on a smooth patch of grass that had recently known the blades of some council mower. Leaning his bike against an adjacent tree, he looked back at her. 'All right?'

Kate nodded. 'Perfect.' Thankfully she leaned her cycle next to his, then lifting her arms high as though in prayer, she stretched luxuriously.

Startling her, arms came from behind, circling her waist, pulling her backwards. 'At last, my darling.' Warm breath blew into her ear. 'Do you have any idea what your presence beside me has been doing to my senses?'

She turned in the circle of his arms. 'Guy . . .'

His sensual mouth sought and covered hers, gently at first, then with increasing pressure. The tip of his tongue forced her lips apart, hovered tantalizingly against hers, and then entered her mouth with a suddenness that sent a shaft of desire coursing through her. She felt dizzy and the only way she could stand upright was to wind her arms about his neck and cling to him.

'Kate, you darling girl,' Guy groaned as the kiss ended. 'Have pity on me.'

Her eyes, blue as sapphires, shining with the feelings he was arousing in her, gazed at him uncomprehendingly. 'It's me who needs pitying,' she said, 'I feel smothered, suffocated . . .'

'Have you no idea at all of the effect you have on me, Kate? I've been more patient with you than I have with any woman.' He pulled her closer to him, his mouth wandering over her cheek and temples. Snatching the beret from her head he tossed it aside on to the grass. The fingers of both hands tangled in her shining hair, pressing against her scalp.

'I am torn between my longing for you and my fear that you will turn away from me in disgust if I should allow myself to get carried away by my natural feelings,' he murmured against her lips.

Sense came creeping back, overwhelming Kate's bewilderment. She pushed at his shoulders, feeling the warm flesh and muscle against her palms under the thin white shirt. 'Guy, stop that! Behave yourself. If you're going to continue like this then I'm going home.'

He caught her hands in his, and lifted them to his lips, kissing each finger with infinite slowness and sensuality. He was amazed at his own restraint, considering that he had come here with only one thought in mind.

For several moments neither of them spoke, simply looking at one another in silence, then he said, 'You're too great a prize to lose now, my love. I suppose I'd better give way. I don't want you riding off on your own, leaving me all frustrated and lonely.'

Kate moved back a couple of steps and stood, hands on hips, looking at him. 'Well, that's exactly what you *will* be if you try that again.'

He raised one hand, palm outwards, in a gesture of surrender. 'Pax? No hard feelings? But you can't pretend you didn't enjoy it. I could tell.'

She shook her head, smiling. Her forgiving nature coming to the fore, she said, 'No hard feelings. Now, let's eat. I deliberately didn't bother with breakfast, so I'm starving.'

On a red-and-white checked cloth they spread the sandwiches and fizzy drinks which both had brought in their saddle bags. The stone-coloured bottles of ginger beer were warm and Guy immersed them in the water at the edge of the reservoir.

'If it was a lake or a river we could swim,' he said, coming back to throw himself down on the spread blanket he had thoughtfully provided.

Hellbent on seduction, it had been a blow to his self-esteem when Kate had acted so retiringly. It had been a tough fight to stifle his burning need to possess her. For the rest of the time they spent there he acted the perfect gentleman, offering a hand to help Kate to her feet but releasing it immediately afterwards.

Even so, Kate was glad when clouds appeared to block the sunlight, throwing a sudden chill over the countryside. Looking up, she said, 'I think we ought to get back. It looks as though it might rain.'

For a moment it seemed that Guy was about to argue. He thought of her firm rejection earlier, then told himself he would be a fool to spoil everything now. All the same, as he mounted his own bicycle, watching her long gold-tanned legs poised on the pedals, he was unable to resist a muttered oath of frustration.

In bed that night, listening to the sounds of the various wireless sets of her neighbours echoing through the shoddy walls, all tuned to a different station, Kate thought about her day with Guy. He was such a confusing person. Would she ever understand his rapid changes of mood?

She thumped her pillow and turned over in bed. She remembered the sudden moment of alarm when he'd caught her from behind. And the burning need that had arisen and how his kiss had had her trembling with excited bewilderment.

Although she wasn't sure that she liked that tongue bit.

Had he thought her a silly little ninny, reacting as she had? Julie would have dealt with it in a sophisticated manner, she was sure. Had Julie ever been kissed like that?

She smiled, thinking of her best friend, and tired by the exercise and fresh air, at last fell asleep.

Letters came from Paul, telling her about the family with whom he was boarding. 'It's more comfortable than an hotel,' he wrote, 'and a lot cheaper. The food's better, too. Grandpapa Jenson, who prospers in the dignified name of Naldo, knew my grandmother. I strongly suspect that there was a romantic liaison between them in the dim, idyllic past. He speaks of her as though she were still here. I never realized she was such a flirt. He has a yellowing photograph of her which he carries next to his heart. "The pretty English one", he calls her. One of many such photographs, he assures me, carried by other men who loved her.

'The work is progressing well: I am able to send copy back most days to the daily which deals with me. I hope you read it, Kate. Censored as it is, anyone with a discerning eye will see the truth buried beneath the stories that do get through . . .'

Rosa sat on one of the small gilt chairs and read the letter Kate had handed her that morning. Paul wrote regularly to his mother, of course, but those he sent to Kate were more relaxed, not so conventional.

Rosa folded the letter neatly and handed it back to Kate.

'His grandmother? My mother, a flirt, indeed!' For all her huffiness, a twinkle showed in Rosa's eyes. 'I know the Jenson family about whom he writes. The old man especially. For all his age a right roué. It would appear that age has not altered him. I remember, one time . . .'

Her eyes took on a faraway look, as though she was gazing into some hazy mirror of the past. Catching Kate's eye, she smiled and shook her head. 'He was a middle-aged man and I a young and impressionable girl.'

Kate smiled. 'I bet you were a flirt, too.'

Rosa pretended shock. 'Me? The very idea!'

Kate made a point every morning of buying the paper that printed Paul's communiqués. Sometimes there would be word from him, sometimes not.

When he did write it was of the people he saw on the streets, how they gave the impression of being happy, healthy, friendly, all united under Hitler – a far different picture to the one related in private by the Jensons.

His eyes had been opened, he wrote, to all manner of new things. Underneath the surface, hidden from the tourists during those splendid, late-summer days in Berlin, and indeed overlooked by most Germans or accepted by them with startling passivity, there seemed to Paul to be a degrading transformation of social life.

No secret was made about the laws which Hitler passed against the Jews or about the government-sponsored persecution of these luckless people. They had been deprived of their German citizenship, confining them to the status of 'subjects', excluded from private or public employment to the extent that more than half of them were without means of support.

They were denied not only most of the luxuries of life but also the necessities. They found it difficult, if not impossible, to purchase food. Over the doors of the groceries, of bakeries and butchers' shops, were signs, 'Jews Not Admitted'. They could not buy milk even for their youngest children. Chemists' shops refused to sell them medicines or drugs, hotels would not give them a night's lodging.

Eminent physicians and lawyers were kicked out on to the street, and left to find whatever shelter they could for their families.

And always, wherever one went, one saw the distressing signs: 'Jews Strictly Forbidden'.

Word-of-mouth news filtered through of names that for decades to come would send a shiver down the spine of peoples all over the world: Dachau; Buchenwald; Ravensbrück; and the dreaded women's camp in Mecklenburg.

Kate read and felt fearful for Paul's safety. People in England had got it all wrong. The camps were not, as her father had supposed, a sort of cheap holiday centre for the workers, but something infinitely more sinister.

Kate tied the sash of her dressing gown, slipped her feet into slippers

221

and went into the kitchen to put the kettle on. It was early, the kitchen filled with morning sunshine.

The pot of marigolds had done well. If a little lanky, they had faithfully produced the glorious luminescent blooms of bright orange loved so well by herself and her father. She leaned forward and breathed in the aromatic scent. 'Good morning!' she greeted them. 'You've got another lovely day of sunshine ahead of you by the looks of it.'

The kettle was singing and she scooped tea leaves into the brown glazed pot, just big enough for two cups, poured on the boiling water and carried her tea tray into the sitting room. She had made the flat comfortable; her own little nest, as Rosa referred to it. The stairs and the noise were, she told herself, something she would overcome in time. The children had accepted her and even some of the more presentable dogs wagged their tails whenever they saw her coming.

She was happy; Guy was taking her to the new picture at the Dream Palace and afterwards had promised her a late supper in one of the new roadside inns that were springing up all about the countryside.

Lately she had found herself watching him, thinking how totally different he was to the Guy she'd met in the old railway carriage. Even to the Guy of that first outing on their bikes.

Oh yes, she very much approved of the new Guy. And he was such fun to be with! When he chose he could have her in stitches.

She realized she was seeing him in a completely new light.

And not once had he attempted to replay the scene when he'd kissed her at the reservoir. Although if he did try again, she thought she might not be quite so uncooperative.

She heard the letter box in the front door rattle, the soft thud of mail dropping on the mat. She switched on the wireless that stood beside the fireplace. Lovely! Bing Crosby singing. She adored Bing Crosby. Then carrying her cup she went to investigate.

It was a letter from Aunt Norma.

She seated herself beside the window so that the sun could warm her shoulders, and read her aunt's letter. The opening lines had her putting her cup down on the table with a trembling hand. Aunt Norma wrote that Monica had been in touch.

That bugger's deserted her, in Liverpool of all places! She sounds in a bad way and is threatened with eviction. He hadn't been paying the rent for weeks it seems before he left. She says she doesn't want me 'interfering'. I'm to stay away. What do you think, Kate? I have a feeling I should catch the train and insist that she comes back with me. She can have my spare bedroom, as she's done many times in the past.

Kate placed the cup and saucer in the sink, and left it to wash later. Hadn't Daddy said that something like this would happen eventually? Gerry Patrick was a no-good philanderer. She'd never known how her mother could be taken in by him.

At work that morning Rosa could tell that something was worrying Kate. She seemed preoccupied and irritable, not in the least like her normal sunny self.

Ruthie eyed her warily and stayed clear. She had enough troubles of her own with the young man with the slicked-back hair. He wanted her to go on holiday with him, a week in Brighton. Just the two of them, camping at a site he said he'd stayed at before.

'You'd love it,' he'd said, cajolingly. 'It's so free and easy and we'd be alone, together.'

That was what Ruthie was worried about. Being alone together. Her mother would never allow it. Her mother seldom took an interest in what she did but as sure as God made little apples she would know something was up.

And Bill was pressing for an answer . . .

She'd discussed it with Sylvia and Sylvia had laughed. 'Don't tell her you're going with him, then. Tell her you're going with another girl.'

Ruthie pushed her hair back from her face, frowning over the delicate stitching she should have been concentrating on instead of thinking about him.

If she did go and her father found out, he'd kill her . . .

Kate came in to the back room and stood gazing down at her. 'You're not making much headway, are you?' she said. 'Mrs Konig wants that dress ready by tomorrow.'

Ruthie sniffed. 'I'm doin' me best. I got things that're worrying me.'

'We've all got things to worry us but we don't let them disrupt our work.'

Behind them, Sylvia, busy at the cutting table, looked up and said, 'My, we are crabby today, aren't we? Guy Ferris found someone else, has he?'

Kate gave her a scornful look. 'Pity you don't have something to think about other than Guy Ferris. As it is, you're such a sourpuss I can't see any boy ever fancying you.'

Sylvia looked murderous. Kate hadn't chosen a very good moment, not when her adversary was holding a pair of cutting shears in her hand.

Rosa heard a shriek and passed through the door of the back rooms as fast as her bulk would allow. Just in time she managed to stop Sylvia's headlong rush, shears held threateningly above her head. She wrenched them from Sylvia just as the bell on the shop door tinkled. Rosa glared at her staff as a voice called: 'Hallo? Anyone at home?'

Through her teeth Rosa hissed, 'That will be Mrs Marks coming for

223

her fitting. Now the lot of you behave yourselves else there will be some new faces around here. Understand?'

Ruthie lowered her head over her sewing and Sylvia returned to the winter skirt she had been cutting from its tissue paper pattern. Both girls said in unison, 'Sorry, Mrs Konig.'

Rosa nodded and glared at Kate. 'You, Kate, come with me.'

Later, after the customer had departed, Rosa suggested that Ruthie make them all a cup of coffee. Sylvia followed her into the room they used as a kitchen, leaving the other two women alone.

Rosa looked at Kate. 'Now, hadn't you better tell me what is troubling you? You've been like a – how does your English expression go? – like a cat on hot bricks, all day.' She leaned forward, patting the girl's slim hand. 'Come on, Kate, remember a trouble shared is a trouble halved.'

Kate thought about this. It made sense. She said, 'I received a letter from my Aunt Norma this morning. My mother has been in touch. It seems...' she lowered her voice, not wanting either of the other two girls to hear, 'the man she was with has gone off and left her. She doesn't want my aunt to interfere but I feel someone should.'

'Why did she write to your aunt if she didn't want her to interfere?' asked Rosa.

Sensible question, thought Kate. One she hadn't thought of.

Rosa went on, 'My guess is that she does want someone to interfere but doesn't want to admit it. She'll be short of money too, I take it?'

Kate nodded. 'Do you think she would thank me for going to her?'

'Were you my daughter, I would welcome it.' Were you my daughter I would never have done such a dastardly thing in the first place, thought Rosa.

Seeing Kate's indecision, she went on, 'Business is quieter now, most people are on their summer holidays. Take a few days off, Kate. Go to your mother. There must be some way you can help her.' She smiled. 'I know if I was in that position, one look into my Paul's face would make the world all right again.'

'I might,' said Kate, not committing herself. 'I just might do that. Now, where's that cup of coffee?'

That evening, in plenty of time to catch the first house at the pictures, Guy called for her in his grandmother's car. Kate had asked him not to, or at least to park way down the road. It caused such a stir, a car like that outside Paradise Buildings. But he always ignored her. She suspected he took a delight in the furore of excitement it created.

She put off telling him about her trip to Liverpool until the picture was over and they were walking to the car park at the back of the cinema.

'Why?' His question had a ring of sharpness. 'Who is in Liverpool that you want to see?'

'It's my mother,' she blurted out. 'I've just discovered that's where she is.' She bit her lip. 'She's in trouble, Guy. I've just got to go and see if there's anything I can do to help.'

To her surprise, he didn't argue. He didn't like it, she could tell, but he didn't argue.

'You'll need money,' he said, holding the car door open for her. 'The train fare and – well, you'll let me take care of that.'

'I wouldn't dream of it, Guy. I can manage.'

'Don't argue. What did I once tell you about women who argue?'

He pushed back his cuff, looked at his watch and said that in the light of events, he'd better forget dinner and take her home. 'If you're facing a long train journey tomorrow you had better have an early night. But we can afford time to have one little drink.'

'All right.'

They came to the roadhouse which had been built at the edge of woodland. There was an open space in front, on which were parked half a dozen cars. Lights shone from windows and the glass-fronted doors. Guy drew up between two equally impressive cars, pulled on the brake and turned off the engine.

'I feel a bit out of place,' Kate said. 'I've never been here before. It's supposed to be awfully grand.'

'It's all right,' he agreed. 'Come on, I'll buy you that drink.'

They left the car and crossed the gravel yard to the door. There was a porter standing inside. He gave Kate a disapproving look – she looked too young to be here – then he recognized Guy and immediately rearranged his expression.

'Good evening, sir.'

'Good evening,' said Guy and headed straight for the bar. The before-dinner crowd had got there first and it was a squeeze to get served.

'Blast!' muttered Guy, trying to elbow his way through. 'We should have gone to the club.'

Over his shoulder he said to Kate, 'I'm having a Scotch. What do you want?'

Kate opted for her usual orange juice. She looked about for an empty table, saw one in a corner and signalled to Guy that she was going to take it.

'All right, for God's sake go ahead and grab it before someone else does.'

She saw his face reflected in the mirror behind the bar, saw the angry expression. She was a little afraid of Guy's anger. Like his other emotions, it was so unpredictable. But although he was frowning she thought it might be the crowded bar that irritated him. She went to the table and after a while he joined her. It was too noisy to talk properly and Guy said, 'I can't think what possessed me to bring you here. I'd forgotten how busy the place gets. Drink up and I'll take you home.'

He put out his half-smoked cigarette, grinding the stub into the ashtray as though he had a grudge against it. He finished his drink and set down the empty glass, then, with a complete change of face, turned and smiled at her. Reaching for her handbag where it lay on the table, he opened the clasp, and despite her protests, shoved a handful of folded notes into its interior.

'That'll get you to Liverpool and bring you back. Promise you won't stay away too long, though.'

She opened the handbag and felt the crisp notes beneath her fingers. 'Guy, I told you, I can't . . .'

'Not now,' he said, 'people are looking.'

Parking again in front of Paradise Buildings, he got out and walked round to open her door for her.

'I'll pay you back,' she promised. 'I really will. And thank you.'

'Oh, you will.' And there was something in his voice that sent a shiver through her. She turned to go but before she could move he put his hand around the back of her neck, drew her face towards his and kissed her mouth. His lips were warm from the whisky and as they stood there she felt the pressure of his body against her own.

She made no effort to pull away, to walk to the lighted entrance of Paradise Buildings. The night was dark and quiet, and there was no one about to see them.

'Darling,' he whispered. His arms tightened about her and their lips met again. And because she didn't want that kiss to end she moved closer so that she could feel his warmth against hers. She lifted her arms and clasped them tightly about his neck.

'I want you so much, little Kate,' he breathed huskily. 'You'll never know just how much I hunger for you . . .'

When his hands slid down her thighs and pulled her still closer, the old warning bells sounded in her ears and she found strength to push him away, even though deep inside she trembled with anticipation.

'I'd better go,' she said. 'Thanks so much for the loan of the money.'

'You are not to stay away long,' he warned.

For a moment she stood in the overhead light of the buildings, seeing his outline against the darkness. Then she turned from him. She climbed the long staircase feeling drunk. Shadows were all about her, for most of the light bulbs illuminating the stairs had been broken by children throwing stones. Her footsteps echoed eerily, as in a dream.

Back in her flat, thoughts of her mother brought reality back with a bump.

Chapter Twenty-Four

All through the morning, as the train steamed northwards, Kate tried to keep an open mind, trying not to think of her mother and what might be waiting when she arrived at the address her aunt had sent her. According to Norma, her mother hadn't once mentioned Samuel. 'She can't know about him, dear, or she would have said,' she wrote. 'Do you feel like going alone or, in spite of what your mum said, would you like me to come with you? If you would, give the corner shop a ring on their telephone. They will always take a message.'

Kate remembered the little shop, grocery-cum-post office, and the affable couple who ran it. Aunt Norma had included their telephone number in her letter.

Although Kate dreaded the coming confrontation she knew it had to be faced. If only to acquaint her mother of her father's death. Surely Monica would be devastated, putting the blame on herself, saying if only she'd stayed . . .

The train journey was long, the carriage dreary with its prickly dark-blue seats and old-fashioned pictures of seaside resorts above them. An elderly woman travelling with a little girl offered Kate one of her sandwiches. 'Cheese, love,' she said, smiling. 'After paying the fare I don't have money to take a meal in the dining car, much as my little granddaughter would like to.'

Kate hadn't thought about food. She'd forced herself to have breakfast, a couple of slices of toast with marmalade, but that had been hours ago.

She smiled at the little girl, who lowered her head shyly over the doll she held in her lap. 'I know, I enjoy eating in the dining car too. But I'd love a sandwich, thank you.'

Arriving at Lime Street station she watched the pair hurry towards an elderly man standing behind the barrier. Probably the child's grandfather, Kate guessed. She watched them embrace and the old man lift the child high and kiss her soundly on the cheek. They looked so pleased to see each other. Kate sighed.

She stood looking about her, completely overawed by the huge, high-domed station. The vast place echoed with the roar of the train engines, the shouts of the porters, the clamour of the pushing, heaving tide of passengers coming and going.

Outside the streets were darkening and a light mizzle greased the pavements, chilling Kate's face and ankles as she walked. She stopped to ask a burly policeman in a cape, the rain gleaming silver on his shoulders, the way to Saxon Lane, the address Aunt Norma had sent. He directed her to a tram stop and told her that any tram that stopped there would take her to her destination.

The rain started in earnest, rolling along gutters, gurgling down drains. Streetlamps, not long since lighted, were blurred by the constantly falling rain.

Sheltering as best she could in the dark recess of a shop doorway, Kate waited. The tram came towards her like a ghost ship in the darkness. She climbed aboard. It was full to overflowing, people huddled together on the narrow seats. She asked the woman seated next to her if she would let her know when they came to the stop nearest to Saxon Lane.

The woman smiled. 'Glad to, my love. I'm goin' a couple of stops further on so I'll give you a nudge when we get there.'

Kate watched through the rapidly misting window as they trundled past lighted shops and hurrying homeward-bound people. Some time later she felt an elbow nudge her and a voice said, 'The next one, love. That's your stop.'

'Thanks.' She stood up and went to wait at the door for the tram to stop. When it came to a halt she jumped forward on to the pavement, thus avoiding the flowing gutter, then stood gazing about her. The light of the streetlamp was just strong enough to see the street names and the numbers on the doors.

Saxon Street. It began right where she was standing. The address she'd been given said number 37. Not too far to walk, then. Pulling her collar up about her ears, she set off. The weather had been so nice in London that she hadn't even considered she might need a raincoat or an umbrella.

She paused outside number 37. There was a tiny garden, dripping with sad-looking laurel. It was a three-storey house; once the home of a *nouveau riche* businessman, she guessed. Converted into flats, it looked down at heel and shabby now. Much like what she could see of the surrounding district.

Her loud and persistent knocking on the door brought a woman who scowled and asked what she wanted.

'Does a Mrs Linley live here? I want to see her.'

The woman frowned at her accent, so like the top floor back tenant who had been deserted by her man friend and who, if she didn't pay her rent arrears soon, would be out on the street before you could say Jack Robinson.

Putting her thoughts into words, she said. 'The one who owes rent?'

She stood back, opening the door fully. 'Arl right, ya better come in.'

Kate complied. The rain had made it cold out. It wasn't much warmer in the house. She stood shivering while the woman made sure the door was securely bolted. Satisfied that it was safe – Kate guessed that in this district you would not be casual about leaving front doors open – the woman pointed up the steep flight of uncarpeted stairs. 'Up there,' she said. 'The top floor, the room at the back.'

Kate thanked her and began to climb. The house was shabby beyond compare. Doors of rooms were scarred and hadn't seen a paintbrush in years. Carpets were either threadbare or nonexistent. If she'd thought the hotel in Victoria unendurable, how much worse must it be condemned to live here?

Breathlessly, she reached the small landing at the very top. There were two doors, facing each other across the landing. Remembering that the woman had said the room at the back, Kate knocked. Total silence greeted her. She knocked again, then pressing her cheek to the door panels, said in a low voice, 'Mummy! It's me, Kate.' She tried the handle and pushed but the door wouldn't budge. 'Are you there? Please let me in. I have to see you.'

Inside something stirred. There was a rattle of bolts being drawn and the door opened a few inches. A face peered out. Wild eyes gazed back at her. Kate couldn't believe it was her mother. She stepped back a few paces. 'I'm sorry, I must have the wrong door . . .'

'Kate!'

Kate stared. It *was* her mother. Placing the flat of her hand against the panels she pushed hard and the door flew open. The fine clothing was gone. The hair had been allowed to grow and hung untidily about the pale face. A woollen cardigan that long ago had seen better days was clutched about the thin figure with fingers whose nails were bitten to the quick.

All thoughts of taxing her mother with betrayal of her husband vanished. Kate's heart twisted inside her, seemed to hesitate in its beating then commenced a thudding that alarmed her.

She stepped into the room. 'Mum! Oh, Mum!'

'Kate! Little Katie! Is it really you?' Monica peered beyond the girl to the dim landing as though fully expecting to see someone else appear. 'Is your father with you? Or have you brought Norma?'

Grim-faced, Kate shook her head, slamming the door behind her with her foot. 'No, I came on my own. Aunt Norma thought you might not want to see her. After all, you did say in your letter you didn't want any of her interference.'

'So I did.' Monica turned to where a single gas ring stood on top of a kitchen table. The yellowing stone sink under the window was piled with used dishes and a chipped enamel pan. 'But I knew somehow you would come.'

229

Kate stood and watched her as lethargically she set about filling the kettle from the tap in the sink then stood waiting for it to boil. As though this was a social visit, she said to Kate, 'You'll take tea, won't you?'

Mindful of the clutter of unwashed dishes in the sink, Kate lied, 'I had a cup at the station buffet. What I really want to do is talk. There are – things you must know, Mummy. Things *I* must know.' She ignored her mother's invitation to sit down. There was only a kitchen chair and the bed and she didn't fancy sitting on either. What she did fancy was getting her mother away from this depressing place and into warm and decent clothing. And hearing Monica's version of what had happened to Gerry Patrick.

Her voice businesslike, she said, 'We're catching the next train back, Mum. I'm sure you don't want to stay one minute longer in this place than you have to.'

A shabby coat hung on a nail behind the door. There was no sight of a hat and no evidence of the fox fur which once Monica would have guarded with her life.

Kate lifted the coat down and guided her mother's arms into the sleeves. Like a baby, she thought. Pity washed over her. It stayed with her while she gathered the few belongings Monica said she needed: a flannel nightgown; incongruously a pair of high-heeled shoes of costly lizardskin that Monica had prized, her wedding and engagement rings, which her mother slyly removed from their hiding place in the wall where the plaster had crumpled with the damp, leaving a small hole. Holding out the grubby handkerchief in which the rings were screwed, she said proudly, 'I managed to hold on to these. He took just about everything else, my fur, my good suits and coats. What little money I had.' Her face crumpled. 'Oh, Kate, it was a nightmare. Your father will be so upset when he hears . . .'

This, thought Kate, must surely be the nadir of her entire life. Having to tell her mother about her father's death. How did you start? Was it better to blurt it out quickly, although that surely would be more of a shock, or wait for the right moment and gradually work your way up to it? *Was* there a right moment?

She took a deep breath. Better get it over with. The kettle had started to sing, a thin stream of steam curling from the spout. Perhaps, after all, a cup of tea might help. They could sit and talk and Kate could answer her mother's questions as compassionately as she knew how.

And there were other questions that needed answering. With whom was her mother going to stay? Kate had become used to her freedom and independence. Her new abode of one bedroom would soon become unbearable with the two of them sharing. And Kate already knew of her mother's opposition to staying with Norma.

Suddenly she thought irritably: I'm too young to be expected to make decisions like this! And yet her mother was in no fit state to do it.

Monica was sitting on the bed, staring at her with a confused frown. 'Katie . . .'

Kate strode across to the singing kettle and turned the gas off. 'We'll have that cup of tea after all, shall we? It's miserable outside and quite chilly. Where do you keep your tea, Mummy?'

'In the cupboard under the sink.'

A half-bottle of milk and a cup of sugar jostled for space on the crowded draining board. Kate carefully washed two cups under the cold tap. Scorning the filthy tea towel, she left them wet. The milk was on the turn but passable. Adding plenty of sugar to the dark brew, she handed a cup to her mother then seated herself opposite her on the old kitchen chair.

'The woman who opened the door to me said that you owed rent. We'll have to get that sorted out before you leave.'

'It isn't much,' said Monica wryly. 'You'd be surprised how little they charge for the privilege of living in such luxury.'

Kate looked at her. That was a good sign, wasn't it? The return of Monica's sense of humour? 'How much?' she persisted.

Monica named a sum. Although it was small it would use just about the last of the money Guy had insisted Kate take. After paying for her mother's single fare back to London, she had hoped to be able to hand some back to him, promising the rest at a later date. She wouldn't be able to do this now. But she *would* repay his kindness. Kate Linley would be beholden to no man.

Her mother was saying, 'Gerry left me, you know.' Her eyes held a faraway look, as though she was reliving exciting times. 'For a while we lived in Edinburgh, Gerry had business up there. There was plenty of money and he spoiled me, urging me to spend as much as I wanted. Then something happened, he didn't confide in me so I never knew exactly what it was, and we moved to Manchester. That was all right for a time until he came home one day and said we'd have to move again. I was getting fed up, Kate. I told him I wanted a stable home, somewhere I could settle. Goodness knows I'd had enough moving about recently with your father. If this was how it was going to be, I might just as well have stayed with him.'

She spoke so matter-of-factly, as though she was discussing some inferior job she'd left for one that offered better prospects. 'And yet Gerry was so full of life, so passionate in bed . . .'

She cast a quick glance at Kate's outraged face as she said this. 'Do I shock you?' she said. 'I shocked myself when I discovered I could feel like that. I think Gerry was surprised at my own ingenuousness. Your father was never very . . .'

She made a vague gesture with one hand. 'Anyway, to cut an increasingly sorry story short, we ended up in Liverpool, in this disgusting hole. Gerry went out one morning on what he said was a promising meeting with former business acquaintances and never returned. That was over a month ago. We'd been short of money before, that was when he pawned my fox fur and the decent clothes he'd bought me. The worst shock was when I opened my handbag to silence the woman's eternal moaning about overdue rent and discovered he'd taken all my money too. Not that there was much, a few pounds. But they would have tided me over until things became better.' She sighed. 'And if I waited here long enough, I thought, surely he would come back for me . . .'

Listening to the piteous story, Kate too wondered at her mother's naivety. After Gerry Patrick had left her penniless, pawning everything of value she owned, Monica could still think there was a rainbow round the next corner.

'Well,' Kate said in the sudden silence, 'if your things were only pawned we can always get them back.'

Her mother was shaking her head. 'Not without the pawn tickets and he held on to them.'

'And that's when you decided to write to Aunt Norma?'

Her mother nodded.

'Well, that seems to be that.' Kate sipped her tea while thoughts chased around in her mind like fallen leaves in a windstorm.

'How is your father? Is he still working?' There were no apologies, no excuses for having left her family in the lurch. Only a kind of petulance that it hadn't worked out. 'Stop daydreaming, Kate, and tell me.'

Hearing her mother's voice, suddenly demanding answers, Kate knew she could put the sombre task off no longer. Somehow, sitting in that small, dank room, with the dreadful clutter of an untidy woman about her, Kate dug deep into her reserves of strength and told her mother everything.

Chapter Twenty-Five

Monica's reaction on first setting eyes on Paradise Buildings had been predictable. Kate would never forget the look of horror on her mother's face when she led her up the stairs and opened the door of her small flat.

Monica had shuddered, and muttered something about hitting rock bottom. Kate had ignored her. She was proud of her little flat and certainly didn't consider it 'rock bottom'.

Certainly a step up from that place where she'd found her mother, thought Kate rebelliously. Nothing could have been as bad as that. She'd found the neighbours friendly enough, some of them, anyway. Not all. Some were antagonistic towards her, using up space in what they considered *their* flats. Mrs Konig was near enough to give advice and encouragement, although she didn't make a nuisance of herself, only going up to Kate's place if she was invited.

Occasional evenings they would spend sewing in either Kate's or Rosa's sitting room. Rosa was always loath to ask such a favour but Kate didn't mind. Over their sewing they would talk about their respective past lives; Rosa about Paul when he was a little boy, about her husband and his job. She'd sigh, 'Such a wonderful man, Kate. So gifted in handling his young students. Even after all this time it is difficult to believe that such a thing could happen.'

The conversation would shift to Kate's life and her eyes would become dreamy, her hands still in her lap. But with Monica living with her the visits from Rosa had stopped. When Kate had taxed her about this, Rosa replied that the last thing she wanted to do was intrude on her and her mother's privacy. Kate guessed that with Monica present she couldn't relax, sensing the waves of animosity coming her way. Kate never had been able to understand just why her mother should dislike Mrs Konig so much.

Kate had been looking forward to a long soak in a hot bath and a companiable chat with her mother over the happenings of the day.

Instead of which she had come home to an irritable woman who complained of the noise made by the children on the landing outside the front door and the incessant barking of a dog that seemed to have been left on its own in a nearby flat. Behind her, Kate heard her mother say, 'That awful man from next door came begging for another cup of sugar this morning. What with him *and* the dogs...' Monica shuddered. 'These people have absolutely no control over their children *or* their animals. You should complain to the caretaker, Kate. Really you should. He must be made to do something about it.'

'It doesn't often happen,' said Kate appeasingly. 'The children have to play somewhere – and you must admit it's a bit chilly to play outside – while most of the time the dogs are left running loose in the front.'

'I know. And that's another thing that should be stopped. It's a disgrace, all those dogs fouling the pavements and making a damn nuisance of themselves. Their owners should be made to get rid of them.'

'What about the children?' enquired Kate, trying to control her temper. 'Should the parents be made to get rid of them too?'

Monica sniffed. 'Trust you to have opinions that are in direct opposition to your mother's,' she said. 'It seems that your time with your father hasn't changed you one iota. You're still the same self-opinionated young madam you ever were.'

And you're just the same spoiled, inconsiderate woman you were, thought Kate. Then as guilt washed over her she said, consolingly, 'Why don't you go out for a while? You said you hadn't been out all day. Why don't you walk over to Mrs Bennett? You always enjoyed her company. I'll see to the supper.'

Monica shuddered. 'How can I possibly face Alice Bennett, or anyone else for that matter, knowing *they* know I'm living in this dump?'

Kate wanted to throw back her head and scream. She had counted on her mother having their meal ready, as she'd mentioned before leaving for work that morning that she was going out with Guy. He'd arranged to take her to a small social event at the club. Kate wasn't particularly looking forward to it. She had never quite taken to any of the women who were to be found there; too snobbish by half and such gossips! Guy had laughed and said she was imagining things. 'They can be quite nice when you get to know them,' he told her. 'Just give them a chance.'

During the autumn months that she had been going out with him, Kate had given them every chance. On the surface all was friendly banter. Underneath she could sense the hostility that Guy didn't see.

And there was another thing; Monica's aversion to being left alone in the evenings. Instantly jealous whenever Kate admitted to having a date with Guy, she would say, 'Oh, don't mind me, will you? Off *you* go and enjoy yourself. Don't give a thought to your poor mother sitting by herself all day and then all evening.' All right, she conceded, she had a comfortable chair and the wireless and, if nothing on either wavelength interested her, the latest Agatha Christie from the library.

It was easy for Monica's jealousy to spill over into ill-humour. 'You've always been one for thinking only of yourself,' she complained. 'You and that father of yours. I feel so vulnerable, living in these conditions. There's no one to protect us now and things can only get worse. I tell you, Kate, my nerves won't stand it.'

Patiently, Kate asked, 'Won't stand what, Mother?'

'Won't stand the noise and inconvenience of living in this place. Do you know a woman shouted at me this morning? Leaned out of her window and actually shouted at me. I didn't know where to look.'

'I thought you said you hadn't been out all day.'

Monica looked away. 'I needed cigarettes. I had to go to the corner shop. I'd much prefer it if you bought them for me, Kate. I hate going to that place. So grubby and the shopkeeper's so rude.'

Kate sighed. 'What did the woman shout at you? And why?'

'Does there have to be a reason?'

'There usually is,' said Kate mildly. 'Perhaps she wasn't shouting at you, perhaps she was shouting at one of her children. It's the way they communicate here, by shouting.'

She bent to turn down the gas. 'If you don't want to visit Mrs Bennett why don't you take a walk up to the High Street and have a look round Woolworths?' she suggested. 'They've got all their Christmas goodies out, and they are staying open late tonight. It's like an Aladdin's cave, all those packed counters and decorations and Christmas trees.'

She thought back to the happy weeks she had spent working behind the toy counter at the large store. Those weeks seemed to belong to another life. As of course they did, for then her father was still with them. She turned from the stove to look at her mother. 'Have you any money on you?'

Another sore point with Monica was the pitifully small amount of money Kate could give her. Monica still expected her cigarettes and to be able to replenish her make-up whenever she needed. Kate attended to everything else, the food and bus fares and the twice-weekly outings to a matinée at the pictures. And then there was the rent. Her salary now that Rosa's was doing so well had risen steadily but it was still a hard slog, trying to make ends meet.

Monica opened her handbag and admitted to having a mere half a crown on her, and Kate handed out her last ten-shilling note. Until the next pay day they would have to exist on whatever was already in the food cupboard.

Making a great show of reluctance, although Kate knew full well that with the affluence of a ten-shilling note, she couldn't wait to get away, Monica put her coat and hat on and left.

Kate started on the supper, peeling potatoes and carrots, shelling peas. She'd found a nice piece of steak at the butcher's; that, with fried onions and the vegetables and mashed potatoes, together with the soup she'd made from marrow bones and which had been simmering all day, would make an appetizing meal.

Through the kitchen window a panorama of lights from the new estates twinkled through the wintry darkness. And, coming at a fast pace, clearly visible under the streetlamps, the scarlet gleam of Guy's new MG.

Guy had been wonderful, so understanding about the money he'd lent her. Kate promised she would pay him back just as soon as she could. He'd pulled her to him in a tight hug. 'Forget it,' he'd said. 'There's no hurry. Just give me a little more of your delectable company and we'll call it quits.'

But Kate knew she could never do that. She reminded herself: beholden to no man! That had become her motto and she intended to stick to it.

Because of the steam from the pot of soup, the small window over the sink was open, and craning her neck she could see where Guy had parked his car. Kids ran forward, and he gave the biggest a handful of pennies, his protection against the vandalism of his precious new car, an early gift for his twenty-first birthday next month.

Kate smiled and gently touched the browning remains of the marigolds in their pot. They had done their duty, blooming well during the summer. Now, with winter upon them, they were dying. It would be sad if next spring nature declined to restore them to their former glory. She dwelt for a moment on this. What a pity people couldn't be the same as plants. Coming to life again when summer dawned!

There was the sound of footsteps on the stone stairway, a loud knocking on her door. Kate put down the ladle with which she had been stirring the soup and ran to open the door.

'Hi!' he said, smiling broadly. The pleasure Guy got each time he saw Kate never diminished. Sometimes it took his breath away. He'd never felt like that about a girl before. And his grandmother, albeit a little grudgingly, had had to admit she was very nice. 'A well-brought-up young lady,' she'd called her. Mrs Ferris's account with Rosa's was a cherished thing. It flattered her sense of superiority that she received the best of attention from Rosa and her young staff. The churlish Sylvia made quite an exhibition of herself, the way she fawned over her. And never again did Kate hear the elderly lady refer to Mrs Konig as 'the German woman' in the tone she had once used.

Kate smiled back. 'Hi!'

She stepped back as he came into the room. A quick glance about assured him that her mother wasn't present. Unless, he thought, his heart sinking, she's in the bedroom.

Seeing the glance, Kate grinned. 'It's all right, Mummy has gone for a walk.'

Guy smirked. 'How very obliging of her. I never seem to get you alone these days.'

'You do,' she argued. 'What about when we go to that ice-skating place together or for a drive in your new plaything?'

'That's not being alone. I mean,' and he leered in true profligate fashion, *'really* alone.'

Their relationship had moved on during the last few months and although Kate enjoyed his company, she still wished he wouldn't be so possessive. He'd made quite a scene the last time they'd gone skating, when a young man had pulled Kate on to the ice and twirled her into a waltz.

He moved closer now. Kate retreated playfully. 'I'm supposed to be cooking the supper, Guy. I'm sorry, but I really thought Mummy would have had it waiting and I would have been ready when you called.'

'Instead of which, you've been left to do the dirty work. I swear, Kate, one day they'll make you a saint. Saint Katherine. You deserve it, the way you put up with that woman's selfishness.'

Kate had to admit that at times her mother could be bothersome. 'But she's my mother. What else can I do?'

'Bothersome! That's putting it mildly. She takes everything and gives nothing in return. Look how she expected you to let her move in here with you, knowing there was only one bedroom.'

Kate picked up the ladle to stir the soup. 'I don't mind sleeping on the couch. It's not bad, really.'

'There you go, making excuses.'

She hated it when Guy began this type of discussion about her mother. But if only he could have seen her mother's distress when Kate broke the news of Samuel's death! Afterwards, drying her eyes, she'd said, 'He was a good man, Kate, your father. I didn't appreciate him. Oh, it was fine in the beginning, with a nice house and servants and a social life many people would envy. But later . . .'

Kate could have discussed it with Paul. Paul would have understood. She missed her times with him, the quiet teasing, the way he would gaze at her latest drawing, head on one side, and solemnly pronounce his verdict. Verdicts that varied from 'Hmmm, not bad!' to 'Brilliant!' Guy had never shown the slightest interest in her drawing . . . He came up behind her now and removed the ladle from her hand, placing it on the draining board. 'Leave that.' His voice was firm, commanding. 'Let your mother finish it herself when she comes back. You're coming out to dinner with me.'

He overcame any objections she might have had by turning her in his arms and placing his lips on hers, kissing her until she was breathless. 'I can't, Guy,' she gasped when at last she could speak. 'I'll have to wait at least until she comes back.'

He gave her a little push towards the bedroom door. 'No, you won't. Go and do whatever you have to do to get ready. Only be quick about it. You should know by now that I'm not a patient man.'

He took her to a small Italian restaurant quite recently opened on the outskirts of town. The proprietor made a fuss of them; Guy Ferris was a well-known name hereabouts and his custom was eagerly sought. Italian cuisine was something new to Kate. She viewed the piled-up plate of pasta covered with a delicious-smelling sauce with apprehension. She'd never eat all that! To be perfectly honest, she would have much preferred the steak and onion supper she'd been preparing when Guy called.

Still, with a bit of care, it might just do for another meal tomorrow evening. She thought fleetingly of her mother's expression when she returned from her walk, finding the flat deserted. Still, there *was* food there. All she had to do was finish cooking it.

Kate found the pasta surprisingly tasty. Guy ordered a bottle of wine, repeatedly tilting it over her glass. At last she covered her glass with one hand. 'I've had enough, Guy. I'm not used to drinking this stuff.'

When the attentive waiter placed before her a silver dish of ice cream covered with nuts and cherries all thoughts of her mother flew out of the window.

After the meal and the wine Kate would have been quite happy to have gone home. But Guy insisted they visit the club. Over the months she'd learned not to question his wishes. It was a losing battle, any kind of an altercation with Guy.

In the club, the overheated, overcrowded room had been rearranged for cards. Groups of small tables were occupied by people intent on their hands. All the ladies were dressed correctly in evening gowns. A number smoked cigarettes in long ivory holders.

As Guy and Kate entered the room, the women looked up from their cards with smiling mouths and eyes that did not miss a detail of Kate's simple dress, or the coat folded over her arm and which was seeing its second winter.

Guy told her it was a whist drive. Kate looked dismayed. 'I don't play whist. My mother used to play when we were in India but I never learned. I'm sorry, Guy, you should have said.'

She didn't play any card games. The nuns had frowned on such things. Julie had once remarked caustically that there was probably something in the Bible forbidding it.

Kate looked about her, feeling foolish. 'You said a social evening. I thought you meant dancing and a few drinks . . .'

The girl with the dark bobbed hair who had played tennis with Guy called from a twosome at an end table, 'Come and join us, Guy. I need a partner and so does my friend.'

'Don't blame me for your shortcomings,' Guy muttered below his breath. 'Increasingly I'm learning things about you that you can't, or won't, do.'

About to repeat the infantile 'I'm sorry' again, she changed her mind. Pulling her arm from where he held it by the elbow, she marched out of the clubhouse. It was too cold for people to be taking their drinks on the veranda and in the darkness, feeling alone and utterly foolish, she made her way towards the scarlet car.

How could she stay so attracted to Guy when he was so changeable? Or was it some quirk in her own nature that found the mercurial part of him so fascinating?

She opened the door of the car and climbed in. It was cold and she slipped her arms into her coat sleeves, pulling them down over her hands in an attempt to keep warm. Would he stay in there and have a drink – a couple of drinks – leaving her to cool her heels? Maybe she ought to go back, apologize . . .

It wasn't very pleasant, sitting here alone on a winter's night. In all probability considered by all a complete idiot, giving them something else to talk about.

'That silly girl Guy Ferris is going out with!' She could hear them now. 'Far too young and immature for his tastes. *And* she works in a shop . . .'

Across the years, she heard Mother Superior at her sternest say: Katherine, this is no way to carry on. One does not walk out on one's escort. Go back this minute and apologize . . .

She sighed and pushed open the car door. If Guy wanted to play cards then she could always sit and watch.

She heard the crunch of footsteps on the gravel surround of the clubhouse. Yellow light from the veranda shone on fair hair and Guy's figure materialized from out of the darkness.

Hastily, Kate moved back on to her seat. He approached the driver's side of the car and slid in beside her. He sat quietly with his hands on the wheel, gazing ahead into the dark night. Then he turned to look at her.

'Well?'

She recognized it as a question but didn't know what to answer. So she uttered again those childish words that she always seemed to be expressing to him. 'I'm sorry, Guy. I guess I made a fool of myself in there, didn't I?'

'You did.'

'If you want to go back in I don't mind. I'll sit and watch.'

'What makes you think I want to rejoin that bunch?' He turned again to look at her. 'Let's drive into the country. I'm forever saying that I'm never alone with you and then I take you to places where people eye you up and talk. That makes me a fool, too.'

Kate laughed. 'Poor Guy!'

'Poor *you*, having to put up with what my grandmother calls my funny moods.' In the closeness of the car he gave her waist an intimate squeeze. 'I'm just so glad that it was you I chose and not any of those scrawny girls I played tennis with.'

Kate thrilled at his words. With his looks and elegance, and the important people with whom he was acquainted in the community, Guy could surely have any girl he chose. Yet he wanted *her*, Kate Linley, and joy sang in her heart knowing this.

He switched on the engine and within minutes they were speeding along a road that led eventually to the countryside. The night wind sang in their faces, whipping up the colour in Kate's cheeks. Her hair streamed behind her like a bright silver banner. She had allowed it to grow long and now it reached her shoulders, smooth and shiny and well brushed.

They reached the open country and raced along a deserted lane. As though it had been arranged, the moon appeared from behind a bank of clouds, seeming to add a touch of magic to their already heightened feelings.

Guy knew he was playing with fire, but her very nearness inflamed his senses. He knew she was still innocent of a man's lust, even though he'd been trying his best to persuade her that nothing was wrong between two people who loved each other. It was a line he'd used with some success on many a girl.

Slowing his headlong speed, he brought the car to a halt at the edge of a track where in the distance the moonlight gleamed on a red-roofed farm house.

For a brief moment a small tremor of fear stirred in Kate. It lasted only as long as it took him to pull her to him, holding her tightly on the leather seat. Then it was gone. Dizzy sensations swept through her. Surely no human body could stand such intense delight?

And surely it was sinful to feel like this? She should have been warned. After that time on the picnic when he'd kissed her, she should have been warned . . .

But she could feel the heat in her cheeks, and more than that, the fire of his need and hers racing through her in a way she had never before experienced.

She heard his groan as he drew back his head, gazing down at her with wild eyes. 'I've got a blanket in the back of the car,' he said hoarsely. 'Lie with me, Kate. Let us pretend for a little while that you and I are in our own little nest, with no one to bother us. Let me show you how much I love you.'

And foolishly she went along with him, watching as he spread the blanket on the rough grass. He held out his hand to pull her down with him and she went willingly.

Her senses swam as his well-practised seduction aroused her. She felt his hands pushing her coat to one side, his fingers unbuttoning the large white buttons that went from throat to hemline on her dress. One hand slid through the opening. He could feel the warmth of her breast beneath the artificial silk petticoat and cotton bra

His lips left hers and moved lower, seeking that gentle swelling.

At once, she reacted. He felt the sudden movement of alarm in her and frowned at her struggle to free herself from the intimate embrace. She pushed at his hands and twisted her body away, gazing at him in mute appeal.

He sat back on his heels, unable to smother the muttered oath of defeat.

'Now what?' His voice was a low growl in the darkness.

She wasn't going to say it again, that stupid 'I'm sorry'. It had been wrong to allow him to get this far, her fault as much as his. But she knew she had acted in the only way possible if she was to remain true to her upbringing.

She listened to his angry voice. 'Don't tell me you get a kick out of leading men on and then giving them the proverbial kick in the teeth? I warn you, Kate, one of these days it's not going to work and you'll regret it.'

He was making her sound like a coquette. She wasn't that stupid, she knew about babies. She thought back to the talks in the dormitories after lights-out, the giggles and gasps of disgust as the girls who claimed to know all about these things enlightened the innocent.

She had read of girls who had become pregnant and been chased out of their homes by outraged parents. They usually ended up having their illegitimate babies in the workhouse, after which the so-called 'wrongdoers' spent the rest of their lives in a county asylum. The girls never knew the fate of their babies. If they asked, they were told they had been given away for adoption.

She had discussed this once with Julie who had called it rape, pointing out that the man involved got away scot-free.

All this flashed through Kate's mind as she buttoned her dress and pulled her coat tightly about her.

In spite of her resolutions, she heard herself say, 'I'm sorry, Guy. I should never have let you go so far. I regret it already.' She rose to her feet and walked slowly back to the car. Trying to lighten the situation, she gave a small giggle, adding, 'And, let's face it, it's hardly the time or the place, *or* the weather, if it comes to that, for our first . . .'

Not knowing how to phrase it, she bit her lip.

Guy swore again and lifting the blanket thrust it into the back of the car. 'Our first act of love together, is that what you mean? Those nuns taught you well. I didn't know there were set rules as to where or when that could happen.' He came closer and lifted her hands, as he had done once before, kissing each finger separately. 'I only know I would give my life if you would let me show how much I love you, Kate darling.'

Her cheeks dimpled. 'Then my love wouldn't be much use to you if you had to give your life for it, would it?'

'You're so quaint and old-fashioned, Kate. As a matter of curiosity, under what circumstances would you – shall we say, allow someone to make love to you?'

Kate raised her brows. Surely he must be joking? She climbed back into the car and waited until he'd taken his seat behind the steering wheel before she answered. 'As you said, the nuns taught me well. Also my father who, in spite of everything, was an honourable man.' He noted that she didn't mention her mother. 'I can't ever imagine doing anything like that outside marriage.'

There, he thought, the warning was plain and clear. A ring on her finger or nothing. He had never considered himself the marrying kind, although he knew his grandmother expected it of him sometime. So far he'd never met anyone he wanted to marry. Imagine waking up every morning with the same face on the pillow beside you. Not at all his scene.

And yet, looking at her profile, the silver moonlight frosting her hair, remembering the warm flesh that had lain so briefly beneath his hand, he knew he could very easily be tempted to change his mind.

It might be fun, teaching this girl the rudiments of sex.

Kate opened the door quietly, tiptoeing into the kitchen to put the kettle on and make herself a cup of tea before she went to bed. For the first time she realized how late it was. Mummy would be fast asleep. Better not to wake her . . .

But whatever faults Monica Linley possessed, deafness wasn't one of them. The plop of the gas as Kate touched a match to it alerted her. She slid out of her bed – Kate's bed – and went into the kitchen. Picking up the cheap alarm clock that stood on the windowsill, she said pointedly, 'Well, young lady, and what time do you call this?'

Kate had a headache; her eyes felt as though grit lined her eyelids. Any exhilaration she had felt with Guy had faded as she climbed the sticky, badly lit stairs. A row with her mother was the last thing she needed.

Aware of her mother's eyes glued to her back, she reached up for a cup and saucer and placed them on the table. 'Do you want a cup?' she asked, taking out a bottle of milk from the food cupboard.

Grudgingly, Monica conceded that she wouldn't mind. Watching Kate pour the boiling water into the pot, she said, 'You know I don't like you being out so late. I worry.' Hearing Kate's sniff, she went on, 'Well, I do. Is it so hard to believe, a mother worrying about her daughter? I mean, you read of such things . . .'

Kate added two spoonfuls of sugar to her mother's cup and stirred briskly. 'I was out with Guy, so there was no need for you to worry. I told you I was going out with him, Mummy. If only you'd listen to me once in a while.'

'No need for sarcasm. I forgot. I happen to have a lot of other things on my mind at the moment. You wait until you're in charge of a home and a young family. You'll know then the worry you've caused me.'

Kate sipped her tea, saying nothing but thinking plenty. Her mother, in charge of a home and family! It was too preposterous to warrant a reply. She picked up her tea and made for the door. 'I think I'll take this to bed with me,' she said. 'I've had it. Goodnight, Mummy.'

To her surprise, Monica followed her to the sitting room and kissed her on the cheek before saying, 'I like that Guy Ferris. You could do a lot worse than marry a man like that.'

And Kate, while she made up the hard settee with sheets and blankets for the night, wondered why she should feel so hesitant about grabbing such a prize.

Chapter Twenty-Six

Winter that year, for the Germans, came swiftly, hitting them hard. Paul Konig was invited, along with other correspondents, to the glittering New Year's Eve reception held in a splendid new hotel reputed to be Hitler's favourite. He stood in a corner, feeling itchy and uncomfortable in his hired evening clothes. All around him were the richest, most influential members of the Nazi party. Women in elegant billows of silk and satin, necks gleaming with gold or diamonds; men in dress uniform, smiling, drinking, joking with wealthy comrades.

The reporter from a famous Berlin newspaper appeared at Paul's side. 'Enjoying yourself, Konig? *They* certainly know how to enjoy themselves, don't they?' He raised his glass to his lips. 'Nice to be able to celebrate the perfect end to a perfect year.'

'Perfect for who?' asked Paul tersely. 'Far from perfect for some I've been in contact with.'

'You mean the Jews? Don't feel sorry for them, they've had it coming for years. Our beloved Führer knows how to deal with that scum.'

'It's always possible that he could be wrong. Have you ever considered that someone just might *do* something about it before long?'

The man gave a gruff laugh. 'Who? Who would have the guts to try and stop him?' His lips curled as he looked at Paul. 'The country you have deserted us for? Dear little old England? Don't get me wrong, I love England – the green countryside and the hills of Scotland and Ireland, I have fond memories of holidays spent there – but they wouldn't stand a chance against the might of our armies.'

Paul looked at him with scorn. 'You reckon?'

'Oh, I know what they say, push the English bulldog far enough and it will turn on you. But if they were at all interested in the poor little downtrodden Jews,' making a joke of it, 'they would have done something long ago. The Führer has been in power for almost five years. Each year shows him gaining in strength, our nation gaining in strength. If we have to we will fight for our *Lebensraum*, our right to breathing space for our expanding population. We would never allow anyone to push us back into the chaos we suffered after the last war.'

Paul had had enough of the man's bragging. He pretended to see a familiar face across the room. 'Excuse me,' he murmured, beginning to move away. 'There is someone with whom I must speak.'

There was, apart from his associates on the various newspapers, no one that he knew, not a single friendly face in the mass of people gathered to celebrate the New Year. A pang of homesickness for the land he had made his own suddenly overcame him. He wondered how his mother, and Kate, were celebrating. He could see Kate so vividly, that bright, open face, the pale-blonde hair falling straight and shining to her shoulders. He never could decide if he preferred it loose or done up in one of those elegant little chignons she sometimes wore. If she imagined they made her look older she was wasting her time. To Paul, she would always be the funny little girl he'd first met in Mr Shipton's grocery store, sticking her chin out and defending him against the man's rudeness.

He sighed and was making his way to the bar when a face from the past came into view.

'Hilda! Hilda Steinberg!'

The dark-haired girl turned to beam at him. The mop of hair looked more unruly than ever – he remembered her cursing it when she was a child living near him, her mother's vain efforts to tie it back with a ribbon. The face that once he had compared to that of a naughty angel looked far older than her years. There were shadows beneath the eyes, lines running from nose to mouth. She wore a dark wine-red gown that left her shoulders bare and he noticed how the bones stood out on shoulders that were once pigeon-plump.

He took her hands in his, gazing down at her. 'It's been so long!' To his dismay he heard his voice shake. 'I thought you were . . .'

'Dead?' Unbelievably she laughed. 'Not yet. They've got to catch me first.'

'But is it safe? I mean . . .' making a gesture to the couples whirling by, 'what if someone recognized you?' Hilda came from a Jewish family and the hunting season was always open on Jews.

'I am the respectable Mrs Jones now. It's hardly likely I would be recognized.' She laughed again. 'How's that for a transition?'

'Jones?' He thought back to the days of their youth. Even though she was a couple of years older than him, he'd had a crush on her. Had daringly kissed her a number of times on those summer picnics by the lake. Now only memories were left of a time that was a sweet but nebulous dream. 'You married into the English family who lived in the corner house?' His eyes darted about the room. 'Is your husband here with you? I should like to congratulate him on his excellent choice.'

A shadow descended over her face. She looked down at the toe of her dancing slipper. 'I would give ten years of my life for him to be with me, Paul. But there was an accident. He was killed in a car crash not long after we were married.'

'I'm sorry. So sorry, Hilda.' There was a short silence during which a group of men and their partners standing near burst into spontaneous laughter as some Aryan wit made a joke about Poland.

Paul gave them a distasteful glance, then said, 'What are you doing now? Are you still living in your old house?'

'Yes, we have been lucky in that respect. But the rest of the street was commandeered long ago by the Nazis. They take great delight in commandeering things.' She glanced up at him. 'Your house is now a community centre for the Hitler Youth.'

His mouth tightened as he imagined hordes of overbearing young boys in leather breeches stampeding through the large airy rooms. That hateful twisted cross and the face of their leader with his ridiculous Charlie Chaplin moustache decorating the walls. He could remember helping his father adorn those walls with new wallpaper, in his mind's eye could see the pattern: a faint silver stripe on a greyish background, their laughter ringing through the house as he managed to get, as his father put it, more paste on himself than on the paper.

Suddenly he felt sick.

Hilda reached out and touched his hand. 'Better not to think of it.' She forced a smile. 'Anyway, what are *you* doing here? Have you returned? This is the last place I would have expected to see you. I thought you hated our new masters. How is your mother? Is she here with you?'

'Such a lot of questions,' he grinned, 'but then you always were a great one for asking questions.' He glanced towards the bar, a row of white-covered tables across the width of the room. 'I was just about to get another drink. Would you like one? Then we can perhaps find somewhere quiet to sit and talk about the old days.' A thought struck him. 'Unless, that is, you are with someone . . .'

'I am, but he won't notice if I vanish for a few minutes.' And she indicated a group of uniformed men across the room. They stood with glasses in their hands, well fed, their faces red and shining. Paul could hear the sound of their voices loud and arrogant above the music, but not what they were saying.

He raised his brows, looking at Hilda. 'One of those?'

'I'm afraid so. Needs must, you know, and all that claptrap. He ensures that we live without fear. Fear plays a big part in the lives of most Jewish Berliners these days, Paul. My mother lives with me and it is not easy for her. But it would be far worse if we didn't have Hans's protection.'

Her gaze rested on the group of men. 'Hans is kind in his own way. He does not demand too much from me and what little he does is meaningless.'

Paul felt as though he'd been punched in the solar plexus. He thought of Kate, of Kate being in that position, exchanging favours for food and safety, and a terrible anger overtook him.

'If there's anything I can do,' he said softly. 'Anything at all . . .'

She shook her head, the dark curls swinging across her white shoulders with the movement. 'We manage, Paul, but thanks for the offer. It's the best one I've had all evening.' Then, seeing how his expression tightened, she reached for his hand, holding it loosely in hers. 'Forgive me, I sounded a right tart then, didn't I? It's the times we live in. You have to become hard as nails in order to survive. The words meant nothing.'

He turned his hand in hers, squeezing gently. 'I know.'

He ordered their drinks, surprised that she also drank whisky, and followed her to a glass-enclosed veranda where chairs were set about for those wishing to relax. Or, as they couldn't help but notice, couples seeking shadowed privacy for illicit flirtations.

He handed her a glass and waited for Hilda to settle herself in an overpadded chair before following her example.

She asked again about his mother and he told her of Rosa's struggle to make good. 'She opened this dress shop, making and selling exclusive gowns. It was hard work, but you know my mother, once she gets an idea into her head it doesn't hang around but has to be fulfilled. Just before I left she had moved into larger premises. *I* happen to think she's on to a winner.'

Hilda smiled. 'I remember her telling me once how she'd trained in Paris under some famous name. I'm so glad she was able to capitalize on this. I take it she would never come back?'

At Paul's negative movement of the head, she said, 'Anyone who has got out of this country would be a fool to return.' She sipped her drink, looking at him over the rim of her glass. 'You haven't said why you came back.'

'I became a journalist on the local paper, after a while moving on to a London daily. When I thought I'd gained enough experience I left to go freelance. That's what I'm doing now, reporting the glorious news of our Führer to lands overseas.'

She looked at him. 'And you've had no trouble?'

'If by trouble you mean have I had any interference in my work, the answer's yes. They censor everything that leaves the country but I have found a way to word my articles so that anyone with any knowledge of these people will understand.'

He sat forward in his chair, head inclined towards her. 'But you haven't told me the full story of what happened to you and your family.'

She turned her face away from him, staring through the large glass windows that surrounded them. 'As you know, it wasn't widely known that we were a Jewish family. So for a few years we were left in peace. I fell in love with William Jones and married him. Just after that my father was taken one night by the SS. I only knew about it the following morning when I went to visit my mother and found her almost incoherent with worry. I telephoned William from her house and he came home from his office. He was a tower of strength. He took over everything, even going to the SS headquarters to find out where my father was being held.'

Paul listened, remembering his own father, the circumstances that were so similar. Reading the expression on his face, Hilda said gently, 'I know. It's painful, isn't it, remembering?'

Through clenched teeth, knowing the answer before he voiced the question, he said, 'And?'

'William was treated courteously – he was, after all, a British subject and Germany had no quarrel with Britain. Even so, he got nowhere. It took all week, William going every day to the headquarters, telephoning, everything. My father had vanished. It was like he had never existed.' She gulped at her drink, as though trying to eliminate a nasty taste from her mouth. 'You must know better than anyone how it turned out, Paul . . .'

He nodded. There was no need for words. They both knew what had happened to her father.

'A few weeks later, someone came to give us a small bronze urn which they said contained my father's ashes.' He saw the shudder that went through her. 'After that, William was terrified that they would come for me and my mother. He sent us to someone he knew in the country. A friendly family who lived on a farm far away from anyone else. It was just after that that William himself was killed, driving home from work one evening. It had been raining heavily and the roads were slippery. They told me the car skidded. Poor William never had a chance.'

She turned her head again, this time to gaze into the crowded ballroom. Despite the fancy gowns of the women, the music and laughter, this was a scene of assurance, of power; it stated more forcibly than marching troops or rumbling gun carriages that here in this room were the conquerors who would rule for a thousand years and would defy anyone to prove otherwise.

'I've always thought that William's death wasn't entirely an accident. But of course I'll never know. My mother and I returned to our old house by the lake and waited for events to take their course. The consequence was a visit from the man who has partnered me here tonight. He offered me his friendship and protection against nosy busybodies. I knew what he would eventually demand but by then I couldn't have cared less. My one and only prayer was for Mama and I to be safe in a country run by tyrants.'

Paul lifted her hand to his lips, kissing it tenderly. 'I'm so very, very sorry, Hilda. You must have been through hell.'

She gave a wry smile. 'Hell was once the steam rising from beneath us on that railway bridge. Do you remember, Paul? You used to tease me into believing that the devil opened the doors of hell and the steam from the fires rose earthwards.' He nodded and she went on, 'Lately I have been close enough to hell to know it by heart. I came here tonight to say goodbye to the old year. These last few have brought me nothing but unhappiness.'

A flurry of snowflakes fell against the windows, hanging there like white feathers. Like the snowflakes, tears fell on her cheeks. She brushed them away angrily.

'Now that I have found you again, Paul, we must not lose touch. You must come and see us. Come and have tea tomorrow.'

'What about your friend?'

'Oh, Hans is kept busy for most of the day. He only appears around dinner time.' She grimaced. 'He enjoys his food – and other things.'

Paul couldn't stop the question on his lips. 'Why do you do it? After what they did to your father, how can you tolerate him near you?'

She lifted her chin and looked him straight in the eye. 'Only another woman would understand the answer to that question, Paul. We are still able to live in our old house, we have food and drink and even a couple of servants. As long as Hans is with us I know we are safe.'

'You wouldn't try to get to England?' he said. 'Perhaps when I go back we could arrange for you and your mother to come with me?'

She shook her head. 'A lovely dream but an impossible one, Paul. I shall stick it here until the end. Hans talks these days of a war with England. Your Mr Chamberlain is a weak man, no match for the Führer, I'm afraid. If there was a war, what would you do? Would you stay in England and fight against your own people, or come home and fight for the Fatherland?'

Paul could not answer that one. The answer he gave would place him firmly on the other side, and all he could do was pray that he would never have to choose.

Kate was also faced with a question she couldn't answer. It was quiet in the shop and Ruthie had waylaid her in the back room. Sylvia and Mrs Konig were out, Rosa to visit her lawyers in the High Street over some technicalities with the lease of the new shop, Sylvia to purchase new materials for the coming spring season.

'He first asked me last summer, Kate, but I dithered so long it was too late to book and now he's insisting I go with him this summer.' Ruthie looked worried, frowning, biting her nails fretfully. 'I don't know what to do. Part of me wants to go with him but another part says it's all wrong. Besides, me mum'd have me guts for garters if she ever found out.'

Kate knew exactly how she felt. Hadn't those fears encroached on her craving to surrender to Guy? So a fat lot of advice she could give. She said, 'You really need to seek the advice of someone older than me, Ruthie. Why don't you ask Mrs Konig when she comes back? I'm sure she . . .'

'Oh, I couldn't!' Ruthie looked alarmed. She lifted one hand to cover her mouth, gazing at Kate with wide eyes. 'I couldn't possibly discuss something like this with Mrs Konig. She wouldn't understand, she's much too old.'

Kate racked her brains for an answer. Finally she said, 'It's still a long time until summer. Maybe when it comes you'll have decided without help from anyone else.'

Ruthie nodded. 'Yes, maybe . . .' Her tone was doubtful.

Kate smiled. 'Maybe by then you'll be planning a wedding and then there'll be nothing to worry about.'

Their peaceful moment was disturbed by Sylvia returning from her buying expedition. She'd entered the shop quietly, sliding the door open with such stealth that the bell didn't jangle. For long moments she'd stood listening to the two girls' conversation. It was her favourite pastime, eavesdropping. Now she pushed the back room door wide and sauntered through.

'So, what are you two up to? Someone getting married?'

Kate looked at her with dislike. 'One day you're going to listen like that and hear something to your own detriment. Believe me, I'll be the first to applaud when that happens.'

Sylvia's thin lips twisted in a sneer. 'Oh, don't bet on it, Linley. None of us are indispensable and I'll probably still be here long after you're gone. Now that's something you *can* bet on.'

She directed her malicious gaze towards Ruthie. 'It sounds to me, young lady, as if you and that scrawny boyfriend of yours have been misbehaving yourselves. Which doesn't surprise me in the least, coming from the sort of family you do. Guttersnipes, the two of you.'

Ruthie's cheeks flamed. Tears flooded her eyes and she made a hasty dash for the small outside toilet, slamming the door behind her. They heard the bolt shoot home, an angry, rasping sound, duplicating Ruthie's distress.

Kate turned on the other girl. 'Does that make you happy, then? Driving poor Ruthie to tears? People like you ought to be strangled at birth.' Wearily she turned away from the hard dark gaze. 'Oh, for goodness' sake go away and let me get on with my work.'

'You can't get on with your work because you talk too much with Ruthie. As soon as Mrs Konig's back is turned the two of you get together and gossip. I wonder what Rosa would say if she knew just what was going on under her very nose!'

Kate longed to turn back and slap her. Instead she went into the shop, blessing the intervention of the jangling bell heralding the arrival of a customer.

Kate was finding her work more fascinating than ever. Fashions were changing. Hats were getting bigger, their brims wider, often turned back off the face in what was called the sailor style. Evening dresses were still long and not nearly so tight, their skirts flowing from the hips achieving a fluid line. The accessory side of Rosa's Boutique was clearly a hit with the clients, great care being taken with jewellery. Hats and gloves, belts, shoes and bags were chosen to complement the clothes.

Eastern European or peasant-style embroidery was fashionable, and the window model that week was romantically eye-catching in a full-skirted outfit with an off-the-shoulder blouse of fine white muslin heavily embroidered in glorious shades of red, blue and green.

Kate found great satisfaction in sketching designs for those blouses. Rosa now employed a team of women who worked at home, transferring Kate's ideas to the delicate fabric. There was never any shortage of pieceworkers, forced to stay home for one reason or another. Some had small children, others a disability, and the extra money always came in useful.

At the other end of the scale, tailored suits with padded shoulders and shorter skirts were becoming the rage, with the emphasis on a narrow waist. The rather severe look of the suits was lightened by decorative buttons.

Kate's relationship with her mother was becoming unbearable. In the confined space they were forced to share tempers were kept at simmering point, especially now that the weather was too wet and cold for Monica to go out much. She had developed a cough which Kate blamed on her smoking, heavier now than she ever remembered it. But Monica argued it had nothing to do with her smoking and everything to do with the conditions in which they lived.

'I mean, look at it,' her mother would say, waving a dismissive hand about the small sitting room. 'I might just as well have stayed in Liverpool and waited for Gerry as come with you to this dump. The fire throws out more smoke than heat and you're never here.'

She drew a lungful of smoke from what was her third cigarette in half an hour – Kate wasn't counting but you'd have to be a fool not to notice – and the coughing began again.

Kate rushed to get a glass of water which Monica accepted without even a thank you. The fit over, she handed the glass back to Kate and went on as though there had been no interruption. 'You don't know how lonely I get. And now with the days so short – I have to put the light on at half past three – it makes it all very dreary.' Peevishly she took another drag on the cigarette. 'I'm sure your father would never have wanted me to suffer as I am doing now.'

Kate stared about the room which her mother had dismissed as a dump. A small and very inadequate fireplace, a kitchen that was either too hot or too cold.

It broke Kate's tender heart to see how the marigold plants on the kitchen windowsill withered, cringing in the cold. When she rose from her hard couch the next morning to find that they were dead – really dead, not just hibernating for the winter – she thought of her father's loving handling of the seedlings and sat down on the crumpled bedclothes and wept.

'Kate, how's that cup of tea coming along? You're taking an age this morning.'

Kate's fingers clasped at the tiny gold crucifix on its chain about her neck and closing her eyes she prayed: 'Oh, dear God, please let something happen, something to enable me to make up my mind about our future, my mother's and mine.' For common sense told her that she could not continue like this for much longer.

Guessing Kate's dilemma, Rosa was the soul of tolerance in the shop, somehow keeping the peace between Sylvia and little Ruthie. Not so tolerant was Guy Ferris. He and Kate continued to see each other but with the weather so damp and bitter there were no more bicycle rides into the countryside or even rides in his open-top MG. On these evenings his grandmother's Rolls took over. One night they went to the pictures, sitting in the back row where nobody frowned if a couple showed affection and kissed throughout the film instead of watching it. Kate laughed, saying, 'You sure have got a one-track mind, Guy Ferris,' as she pushed at his hand, sliding up over her silk-stockinged knee. 'Come on. I want to see this picture, it's supposed to be excellent.'

He paused in his advances long enough to dart a look at the screen. Cary Grant at his impeccable best smiled at his leading lady while he poured a cocktail from a silver shaker. 'You surely don't prefer him to me, do you?' Guy said.

'Chance would be a fine thing,' she answered teasingly.

He growled deep in his throat and pretended to take a bite from her neck, earning a reproving look from a woman seated near them.

After the film he took her to a late-night café where he ordered coffee. Sliding up close beside her on the leather seat, he produced a small silver flask from his pocket, unscrewed the top and poured a liberal amount of something into her coffee. He did the same to his own. Kate stared suspiciously at the two cups. 'What was that?'

'My grandmother's very best brandy. It'll warm the cockles of your heart, make you relax.'

She sat up straighter. 'I'm very relaxed, thank you. What a thing to do to a perfectly good cup of coffee! And for your information I don't like brandy.'

'It seems to me you don't like a lot of things a normal girl should like.' He drew back, scowling, looking like a spoiled child.

'There, I've upset you.' She laid a hand over his. 'I didn't mean to. It's just that – well, when you get like that I *can't* relax. I get all tightened up inside. I honestly don't know how to handle it, Guy.'

'You don't have to give it a second thought, my darling. Just loosen up a little and I'll do the rest.'

Her lips twisted wryly. 'I'll bet!'

He lifted her cup and held it under her nose. 'Smell that! The best, most expensive brandy in the country. Go on, take a sip. I swear you'll love it.'

She sighed and took the cup from his hand. 'If it'll make you happy . . .' She sipped experimentally, decided she liked it after all and took a mouthful.

He grinned. 'There, easy when you know how, eh?' His own coffee finished he beckoned the waiter to bring two more. Another bountiful dose from the flask was added and Kate felt a pleasantly warm glow spreading through her, warming her to the tips of her fingers and toes.

She heard herself giggle. 'I suppose after this you'll be wanting to get your licentious way with me, will you?'

His hand reached for hers and turned it over on the table, and his thumb began a slow, sensuous rubbing on her palm. 'The thought *had* crossed my mind.' His eyes were hooded, gazing at her, and she felt the warm flush from the brandy, coupled with those eyes, turn her insides to jelly.

She closed her own eyes against that sorcery and the world began to spin. 'God, what do they make that brandy *from*? I feel as though I'm floating on air.'

She felt his arm slip about her waist, lifting her from her seat. 'Go ahead, float,' a soft voice said in her ear. 'You'll find it's the most wonderful feeling of them all.'

'I will?' She sounded surprised. Floating on air, unsteady on her feet – on second thoughts maybe it wasn't so wonderful after all. And what would her mother say if she went home in this condition?

Guy had no intention of allowing her to go home – at least, not yet. Holding her firmly by the elbow, he urged her back to where the stately Rolls was parked at the kerb. He helped her into the passenger seat and tucked a plaid car rug about her knees. She rather liked that, him acting so kind and fatherly. She leaned her head back against the seat and closed her eyes. The lovely car seemed to glide over the rain-slicked roads. It was true what they said about Rolls Royces, she thought. All you could hear was the soft ticking of the clock.

Imagine having the sort of money that provided such luxury! Behind her closed eyelids came visions of holidays in the South of France, of the exquisite white villa which Guy had bragged about so often. Perched on a hill overlooking the sea, his grandfather had purchased it long before Guy was born. She thought of the money Mrs Ferris spent on clothes from Rosa's. One evening gown would keep her, Kate, in dresses, coats *and* shoes for a whole year.

She screwed her eyelids tight in a bid to stop the dizzy feeling. She should never have touched that stuff. Strong drink, even diluted with coffee, was a new experience for her. She didn't think she wanted to repeat it in a hurry.

Momentarily, Guy turned his eyes from the road to gaze at her. 'What's wrong? You're not going to be sick, are you? Do you want me to pull in to the side of the road?'

She shook her head, causing the dizziness to return. 'No, I'll be all right.' She gave a little laugh. 'You must think me a right ninny, reacting like this over a little brandy. I suppose I'm just not used to it, that's all.'

'An adorable ninny,' he corrected. He steered the car towards a lay-by where a five-barred gate guarded a frost-hardened field. 'We'll stop for a bit, let you stretch your legs. You'll feel better after a breath of fresh air.'

He got out and came round to her side, opening the door and pulling the rug from her legs. Remembering the last time a rug, or rather a blanket, had been involved, Kate clutched at the woollen fringes, a stubborn look on her face.

She began, 'I don't want to . . .' and he cut in with: 'Don't be a little fool!' His tone reflective, he went on, 'Maybe the brandy wasn't such a good idea after all. Come on, get out. We'll walk up and down for a bit. Surely you don't have any objections to that?'

She shook her head. 'You're a sweety, Guy. I really don't know why you bother with me. I must be a real pain in the neck at times.'

'The pain is situated somewhat closer to my heart,' he said solemnly.

She turned to look at him, too quickly, and stumbled on the rough ground. He caught her and held her and she said, 'Guy, please don't start all that again . . .'

He brushed her words aside as though they were an insect on his sleeve. 'You can't go on saying no for ever, sweet Kate. You couldn't be that cruel.' His mouth was very close to hers now and his breath was warm on her skin. She was mesmerized by the night, by his nearness and the inevitability of what was to happen. The brandy had done its job, weakening her resistance. And now the languor she was

255

experiencing at his touch was subtly changing into a searing longing to be fulfilled. The feverish excitement at being held close to his body, his lips only a whisper away from hers, was suddenly almost more than she could bear. Instinctively she pressed herself against him, feeling the tension inside her relax, a most wonderful sensation of lethargy taking its place.

She felt his hand slip under her knees, the other about her waist and she was lifted and carried back to the car. And there in the darkness of the car, he was whispering, 'You knew it as well as I did, darling Kate, that one day you would belong to me. We will honeymoon in the sunshine in that white villa by the sea. It is isolated and tranquil. It will be the perfect start to our new life . . .'

Chapter Twenty-Seven

Kate woke the next morning and stared about her, surprised that she was in the familiar surroundings of her own sitting room. Guy must have brought her home. The last thing she could remember was the soft darkness in the back seat of the car, his voice murmuring in her ear, his hands . . .

With a gasp, she pushed back the blankets and swung her legs over the edge of the couch. The carpet felt icy to her bare feet. Looking down, she realized she was in her nightgown. Dear God, surely he hadn't delivered her to her mother in the state she remembered being in! She'd never hear the last of it if that were so. Her mother must have undressed her and made up the settee.

Kate shuddered. Try as she might, she had no recollection of events after he'd settled her on the leather seat of the Rolls. Only of darkness and harsh breathing and movement above her. She stood, reaching for the dressing gown draped over the back of the couch, and slipped her arms inside. She tied the sash so tightly that it cut into her waist; as though it was a suit of armour, protecting her from the outside world.

She stumbled to the mirror which she'd brought from the house and which now hung over the small fireplace. A paper-white face gazed back at her, the dark-ringed eyes wide and filled with apprehension. She was standing there, leaning with both hands on the mantelpiece when Monica emerged from the bedroom.

'Well, they say still waters run deep, but who'd have thought you could be so devious!' As Kate turned to look at her, the question clear on her face, Monica went on, 'Oh, don't worry, he left you to my tender care and I put you to bed. Can't say, though, that I relish being woken up at three in the morning.' Hands on hips, she faced the bewildered girl as though defying her to deny it. 'Well, aren't you going to say something? Like offering an explanation for instance?'

Kate turned wearily and went to bend over the settee with its rumpled bedding. Automatically her hands began to fold the sheets and blankets, placing them one atop the other to stow away in the deep cupboard in the fireplace recess. 'I don't want to talk about it,' she said.

'I don't suppose you do, young lady, but *I* do. Your poor father would be turning in his grave if he could see how you've been carrying on.'

The words 'You're a fine one to talk!' almost escaped Kate's lips but she swallowed them hastily. How could she explain to her mother when she didn't know herself what had happened? She made for her bedroom. 'I have to go to work. With the New Year approaching we're extra busy now. Everyone seems to want new evening gowns.'

'That's right, walk out on something you can't handle. Your father had that down to a fine art too.'

The sneering tone of Monica's voice caused a scarlet flush to stain Kate's cheeks. Her lips tight, she turned to face the older woman. 'And you were always good at jumping to conclusions. We'll talk tonight, when I come home. But now I have to get dressed.'

During the morning, choosing the time that was busiest, Mrs Ferris arrived in full regalia. Bowed from the car by the uniformed chauffeur she was then escorted across the pavement to the shop door by a middle-aged woman Kate knew as Miss Grimes. She'd giggled with Ruthie over this, describing her as Mrs Ferris's personal maid: 'A sort of lady-in-waiting.'

'Just like the Queen,' said Ruthie.

'Not quite, but not far out,' laughed Kate.

At her appearance, Ruthie melted into the back room; one look from those hooded eyes intimidated the girl and she wasn't afraid to admit it. Sylvia, on the other hand, stepped craftily forward and pulled out a chair. She stood hovering over it until Rosa waved a dismissive hand which had Sylvia, looking mutinous, banished to attend to a woman who stood undecidedly examining two frocks. 'See if you can help madam to make up her mind,' said Rosa.

Then she turned her full attention to the white-haired woman. 'I can only say how delighted we are to see you again, Mrs Ferris,' she said. 'You wish to commission something for the New Year's festivities, no?'

Mrs Ferris gazed about her, her expression inscrutable. 'I most certainly do, but that is not the main reason for my visit.'

Rosa frowned. 'Oh dear! I do hope there is nothing wrong.' Her thoughts were running to seams coming apart, to hems descending or even cascades of beads scattering from the last gown Mrs Ferris had purchased.

To her relief, Mrs Ferris smiled. 'Don't look so worried, Mrs Konig. If it's not too inconvenient, I would like to borrow your young assistant for a few minutes.' Her eyes rested on Kate, standing to one side, ready to hurry forward when she was needed. 'A private talk. I promise not to keep her too long.'

Rosa looked flabbergasted. 'Kate, you mean?'

Mrs Ferris nodded that elegantly coiffured head. 'Five minutes only. I promise.'

Burning with curiosity Rosa waved Kate towards the shop doorway. Not too sure whether she agreed with this or not, Kate went. The chauffeur saw them seated comfortably then the car moved smoothly from the kerb and along the road. There was an uneasy silence which ended with Kate saying, pointedly, 'We're really very busy, Mrs Ferris. I can't be away for long . . .'

'I do not intend to keep you. I made my promise to your employer and I mean to keep it. Just as I am fulfilling my role as guardian to my grandson.'

Kate drew a sharp breath. So this was all to do with Guy! With what happened last night! She might have known. The class to which he belonged didn't mind a little philandering by their sons or grandsons, just as long as it went no further.

Sentences formed in her head, ready to quickly reject anything Mrs Ferris might say. Even so, a deep sense of mortification overcame her at the thought that Guy didn't have the courage to face her himself. 'Look,' she began, 'my friendship with your grandson, if that's what all this is about, was enjoyable. If he wants to end it that's all right with me. But I really would prefer to discuss it with Guy himself . . .'

'My grandson drove down to Southampton early this morning to catch the next sailing of the *Queen Mary*. His presence is required in New York . . .' Hearing Kate's sharply drawn-in breath, she went on, 'Yes, we have business interests there. He will be away for some time.'

'But why so secretive?' demanded Kate. 'He said nothing to me.' She looked up, sudden suspicion in her eyes. 'Did he know he was going?'

'Indeed he knew, Kate. The trip had been arranged for some time.'

In the sudden silence the faint ticking of the clock on the dashboard seemed loudly persistent, sparking flashes of memory. Memories of the dark night, the smooth leather seat of the car, Guy's protestations of undying love . . .

She remembered the white moon shining on frozen fields, the silent struggle. She heard his words: 'All right, I'm sorry.'

And her own husky answer. 'I should jolly well think so too.'

'I'm sorry for coming on too strong, and for being bloody-minded with you when you objected. It's as well to know how we both feel before we embark on some deathless relationship.'

'Meaning?'

'Meaning that I've gone about this all the wrong way.'

She sighed. 'I thought you realized that I – well, that I feel differently about some things than other girls you've been out with.'

'It's engraved on my memory like words cut into stone.' Although his tone had been flippant she could tell he was hurt. And then he'd kissed her again and the memory faded, to be replaced by sensations that had left her sighing his name. And that was when he'd spoken of the white villa and how wonderful it would be to honeymoon there, knowing full well he was leaving the very next morning . . .

Brusquely Kate said, 'I think you had better take me back, Mrs Ferris. I don't believe there's anything else to say.' And anything *I* have to say about that grandson of yours would not be to your liking.

Mrs Ferris nodded. 'I know. I said I wouldn't keep you long, and all we've done is talk trivialities. The fact is, my dear, Guy asked me to see you, to put a proposition to you.'

Over breakfast that morning, Guy had hurriedly begged his grandmother to see Kate and explain things before she heard of his overseas trip from some other source. And then he'd instructed her to speak to Kate on another matter.

She was aware that Kate was looking at her, a question forming on her lips. 'What proposition? I don't understand.'

'My grandson wants me to set you up in a shop of your own. We both think you have potential and I seem to remember Mrs Konig once telling me that that, indeed, was your ambition . . .'

Kate was holding up one hand, as though warding off further words. 'Hold on. That *is* my ambition, I don't mind admitting it. But why should you want to do that? It could be years before I felt capable enough to start out on my own.'

'What if I offered to buy the business from Mrs Konig? She could remain a sort of sleeping partner, guiding you along the right path.'

Kate shook her head. 'I couldn't, *wouldn't* countenance such a thing. Mrs Konig has been good to me. I wouldn't dream of betraying her like that. Besides, what makes you think she would be agreeable to selling?'

'Who said anything about betrayal? It wouldn't be that, merely good management. It happens in business all the time.' Mrs Ferris smiled, the thin lips barely moving. 'As for not wanting to sell, well, everyone has their price and I do not suppose Mrs Konig is any different.'

'You can think what you like, Mrs Ferris, but I'd rather not participate in such a deal. When I get my own shop – *if* I get my own shop – then I'll know I've done it off my own bat and not in some underhanded way . . .'

She paused, seeing the look in the woman's eyes, reading the thoughts behind them. It was obviously many years since anyone had dared go against her wishes. Kate went on in a conciliatory tone, 'I don't mean to sound churlish and I thank you for the thought, but I really can't see myself running a business such as Rosa's. Not for a few years, anyway.'

Mrs Ferris looked blank, as though she couldn't believe that her offer had been refused. Stiffly, she said, 'You do know that my grandson's in love with you, don't you? That one day he intends to marry you? The

Ferrises do not usually agree to shop assistants marrying into the family, any more than they would a domestic servant.'

Kate felt shock at Mrs Ferris's blithe mention of marriage, but anger stirred in her too. 'Don't you think this conversation should be between me and your grandson, Mrs Ferris, and not a third party?'

The woman looked down her aristocratic nose. 'Hoity-toity!'

'You say Guy will be away for some time?' Kate queried. 'I still can't understand why he didn't tell me himself.'

'My grandson is a law unto himself, Kate,' and there was compassion in the woman's voice. 'He has been spoiled and now, I think, is the time to remedy it. Don't you?'

Without waiting for Kate's answer, the old lady leaned forward and with the end of her walking stick tapped on the glass partition that separated them from the chauffeur. When he slid back the panel she said in a commanding voice, 'All right, Simpson, you can take us back now.'

Monica grew more distant by the day, smoking more heavily than ever, lapsing into deep silences of an evening when Kate tried to talk about the happenings in the shop, or the exciting designs she had in mind. With the Christmas and New Year rush the shop had been really busy, with many late-opening nights and weekends spent helping Rosa. There had been no word from Guy; surely, with the advent of this new air mail, he could have got a letter to her by now?

And to heap one trouble on top of another, she'd heard not a thing from Paul.

Paul was enjoying his renewed friendship with Hilda. Had it not been for the brown-shirted ruffians who roamed the streets, constantly on the lookout for trouble, he could have imagined he was back in the days when Hilda and he were teenagers, with his father still alive and teaching at the large boys' school. Hilda told him of the plight of some of their friends who had broken off their studies and were planning to leave Germany while the going was good. Others were staying on, unable to believe as yet that the one country in Europe in which they felt at home was about to turn against them.

Then intruding upon his flights of fancy would appear the portly figure of Hans in his grey uniform. His small pig-like eyes would examine Paul as though he were a piece of meat on a butcher's slab, causing a shiver to run down his spine. He wondered again how Hilda could bear him near her, bear him touching her. But for all his dislike, Paul had to admit that the man was kind where Hilda and her mother were concerned. He saw they wanted for nothing.

At first Paul visited the house for afternoon tea. Only when Hans was away or on late duty did he begin accepting Hilda's dinner invitations. Hilda seemed glad of his company and they spent hours reminiscing, talking of picnics by the lake and fancy dress parties at Christmas.

Dutifully he sent his reports back to the newspaper in London. News came of the end of the Spanish Civil War, and Britain and France's recognition of Franco's government. Then came Germany's occupation of Bohemia, and Hitler's announcement of his non-aggression pact with Poland, followed by a naval agreement with England.

One evening Hilda suggested they go out to the theatre. There was something she badly wanted to see and the woman next door, a kindly soul who was fond of Hilda's mother, offered to stay with the old lady. It was later, sitting in a small café enjoying a drink before he took Hilda home, that the trouble began.

At a table near them, three young Jews were having a quiet drink. Overhearing their conversation, Paul gathered that they were celebrating one of the group's birthday. Other couples sat about, talking quietly, drinking. The mood was peaceful, the night, for January, surprisingly mild.

With the arrival of four of the rowdy storm troopers who roamed the flag-plastered streets of Berlin, making life miserable for many people, the peace was shattered. Catching sight of the young Jews, they stopped in their tracks, looked at each other and then began to advance on the table.

Quietly, the youths stood up, collected their belongings and made their way to the door. The storm troopers were there before them.

Paul heard one of them say, 'Leaving, are we? And just as we've met! Now I don't think that's at all polite, do you?' and he turned for confirmation from his cronies. They agreed that it wasn't. 'Stay and amuse us,' the bully went on. 'I hear you lot are good at dancing. Entertain us, then. Go on, dance.'

The young men looked at each other with terror on their faces. To refuse would mean real trouble, and that was something to avoid at all costs. The café owner hurried forward and put a record on the gramophone, winding the handle and smiling unctuously over his shoulder at the brown-shirts, who seated themselves at a nearby table and began to clap to the rhythm of the music.

Paul cringed as the youths began to dance, and he saw the way Hilda's face flushed scarlet. The dance wasn't to the bullies' liking and they rose and as one moved forward to knock the young men to the ground, kicking them as they lay there. The youths curled up into foetal positions, arms wrapped about their heads in an effort to shield their faces from the brutal kicks.

One by one the rest of the café's customers crept away and once again Paul witnessed the effect Nazi brutality had on the minds of ordinary

Germans. Not one would dare to lift a hand to help the young Jews. The storm troopers shouted for beer, and while the café owner was serving them, the Jews saw their chance of escape and took it, vanishing into the darkness on unsteady legs.

Now the only other customers left were Paul and Hilda. Paul knew that to be seen with a Jewish girl could start a bout of shouted insults that might end in a fight. He wasn't prepared for that to happen, but neither was he prepared to let the Nazis completely spoil the evening for himself and Hilda. He would leave when he was good and ready and not a minute before.

Lifting the bottle from which they had been drinking, he held it invitingly over Hilda's glass. 'One more and then we'll go?'

Hilda's eyes darted over to the men at the nearby table, but she nodded anyway. Taking his time, Paul finished his drink then went round to hold the back of Hilda's chair while she stood up. The movement seemed to galvanize the brown-shirts into action. 'Ah,' the talkative one said, 'you're not leaving too, are you? I don't think I could bear that.' His gaze rested on Hilda. The fleshy lips pursed. 'Jewish bitch! Stay a while and entertain us.'

Paul lifted Hilda's fur stole from the empty chair where she'd thrown it and placed it about her shoulders. He could feel the icy shudder that went through her at the insulting words. Quietly, he said, 'My friend and I have to go. I'm afraid you'll have to find your entertainment elsewhere.'

As one they barred his path. Paul moved forward in a purposeful way and Hilda clutched his arm, her eyes wide and terrified. 'Please, Paul, don't. For my sake!'

Her voice was so urgent, and the expression on her face so suddenly tragic, that he stopped in his tracks. He turned to her, his face flushed with fury. 'I'm not afraid of a bunch of drunken brown-shirted buffoons,' he said, making sure that they heard, then added, 'Silly bastards,' in his best English.

One stepped closer, saying in guttural English, 'Then you should be, my friend.' His gaze raked Hilda, cowering at Paul's side. 'Why do you accompany a Jewish bitch? Aren't there enough good German girls to satisfy your tastes?'

'My tastes have nothing whatsoever to do with a bunch of drunken idiots like you,' Paul replied roughly.

He heard Hilda's voice, low and urgent, beside him. 'Don't antagonize them, Paul. Please, let's go.'

He glanced down into her pale face. 'All right, if you say so . . .' His words were cut short by a blow across the back of the head which sent him reeling. He heard Hilda's scream as one of the men grabbed her in a bear-like hug. As Paul fell to the ground he heard the men's laughter, again Hilda's scream. Then heavy boots were kicking him in the side, in the back and stomach. They came from all sides and above his grunts of pain he could still hear Hilda screaming . . .

Chapter Twenty-Eight

It seemed only yesterday that Julie had been arriving at the station on that first visit. Difficult to believe that more than four years had passed. Now the young lady who stepped off the train had that elegant look imparted by posh finishing schools and a wealthy background.

There in the dimness of the station Kate had to blink twice in order to recognize her friend. Julie looked the picture of spring in her slim-skirted outfit of chocolate brown with a thin stripe of a lighter shade running through it. A tiny hat – a hat! thought Kate with amusement, Julie wearing a hat! – covered in fine veiling tipped bewitchingly over one eye. A blouse of a pale-peach colour frothed in crisply curling frills from the neckline of the jacket.

The friends embraced and Kate said, laughingly, 'You look a million dollars. And here's poor me in my last winter's coat.'

'It's all right,' said Julie soothingly. 'No one would know. Actually, black's very smart.'

Kate grimaced and looked down at the loose-fitting woollen coat she wore. Normally she didn't wear black; it reminded her too much of Sister Devota. The bright-scarlet silk scarf tucked in at the neck made it look less severe. 'Yes, well,' she said, 'we can't all have rich parents.' Adding, as an afterthought, 'Forget I said that. I didn't mean it to sound like sour grapes.'

Kate linked her arm in Julie's and bent to pick up Julie's one piece of luggage in her free hand. They walked along the platform towards the stairs. Men reading newspapers while they waited for trains cast admiring glances their way: two smart young women, one dressed in the height of fashion, the other perhaps a little more dowdy but nevertheless eye-catching as her silvery-blonde hair swung across the shoulders of her black coat.

They emerged into the bright April sunlight and Julie gazed about her at the crowded High Street. 'It never changes, does it? Always so busy and industrious.'

There was little sign of the war preparations that were happening all over London. Gas masks had been issued to civilians after the Munich Crisis and most people in London carried them, slung on a webbing strap over one shoulder. Julie said, 'Women and children are being evacuated from London. People are worried, but I can't say I see any signs of concern here.'

'Who would want to bomb poor little us?' said Kate jokingly. 'There's nothing here that could possibly interest the Luftwaffe.'

'Oh, don't let's talk of boring old war, anyway,' said Julie. 'Tell me what you've been doing. How's that nice Paul Konig getting on? Is he still in Germany?'

Kate nodded, a frown creasing her brow. 'We think he is, although neither his mother nor I have heard from him for so long. His last letter was before Christmas. Even his newspaper hasn't received any contributions for months now.'

'Oh dear!' Julie's mouth turned down at the corners. 'What do you think could have happened?'

'I wish I knew. The editor of the paper he was sending his articles to made enquiries but he didn't get very far. Then Mrs Konig wrote to the family Paul was staying with and all they could tell us was that Paul went out one evening and never returned. It's all very worrying.'

'I can imagine. You liked him, didn't you?'

'Liked, yes.'

Julie shot her a shrewd glance. 'Only liked? But of course, I forgot the volatile Mr Ferris.' Although Julie had never actually met Guy, Kate had written about him so much in her letters that Julie felt she knew him. On each of her visits to see her old school friend, Guy had been away, first at that dour school in the Highlands, then on business for the family firm. It seemed there were many branches to this business and they kept him busy.

Julie's own life had taken on a hectic pace since she had left the Swiss finishing school. Her parents had been living in Singapore where she'd had the time of her life, attending tennis and social parties, swimming in the warm sunshine. But now they were back in England life had become dull and boring. In fact, boring was her favourite word of the moment. And coming here was even more boring . . .

Looking about her as they walked down the familiar street, past the familiar shops where, as she'd observed to Kate, nothing ever changed, Julie wondered why she still bothered. Her interests had become poles apart from Kate's. The things they used to talk about – sometimes till late at night, lying in the twin beds in Kate's room in Wesley Avenue – held no attraction for her since her new life had begun. But one couldn't ignore the close bond that had always held them together. Julie's conscience pricked her.

Forcing a lighter tone, she asked, 'How's your mother keeping?'

'She's all right. She's decided to go and stay with my aunt in the country for a couple of weeks.'

Maybe, thought Kate, before Julie went back she would tell her of the sulkings and rows that, these days, made up her mother's life. Thankfully, the idea of staying for the period of Julie's visit at Aunt Norma's had appealed to Monica. Aunt Norma's husband had at last passed away and the mystery that had puzzled Kate since she first went to stay with her mother's sister was revealed. Aunt Norma's husband confined to a mental hospital all those years! Kate thought. How terrible for her poor aunt!

On hearing the news, Monica immediately said she thought she should be with her sister. Kate had been amazed but had agreed with alacrity, then felt guilty at how relieved she was.

Rosa had granted Kate a few days off for Julie's visit. Kate racked her brain for interesting things to do to fill the time, thinking ruefully that she couldn't hope to compete with Julie's hectic stay in Singapore. Still, it would be nice having a good old chatter. And perhaps Julie just might fancy a few days' quiet after her recent activities.

There was that new Emlyn Williams film, *The Corn Is Green*, showing at the Dream Palace. She thought Julie would enjoy that.

And this time she would make sure that Julie met Guy. He had not long returned from his visit to the States and Kate had had little time to see or talk to him. She knew she had to hear from his own lips the things he had told his grandmother; about buying the shop, and marriage. Somehow, the thought filled her with trepidation.

They popped in at the shop on their way past, to enable Julie to say hello to Rosa. But first the window display had to be applauded. Kate had designed a setting where the model wore a woollen cloak-like garment in shades of claret and black resting on padded shoulders over a matching costume.

Rosa had seen the girls approaching and greeted Julie warmly at the door. 'So smart,' she said, gazing approvingly at Julie's outfit. 'And the hat does wonders for your eyes.'

It was the first time that Julie had visited since they had moved to larger premises. Now she gazed about her appreciatively. 'My, you have come up in the world.' She smiled at Rosa. 'Very nice, too, I must say.' The pink-tinted mirrors and general air of femininity obviously went down well with the customers, for the shop was buzzing with talk as women admired dresses and the costume jewellery that had become so popular.

'I'm glad you think so,' replied Rosa. With a smug look on her face she gazed about her. 'I rather think we have done well. And your little friend, Kate, has helped enormously.' She smiled at the two girls facing her. 'And what plans have you two young ladies for the rest of your holiday together?'

The girls exchanged looks. 'We haven't decided on anything yet,' replied Kate. 'I guess we'll play it by ear, as they say.'

'Play it by ear!' Rosa shook her head at the idiosyncrasies of the English language.

Crossing the railway bridge, their steps echoing in the stillness, Kate said, 'I thought we might go to the pictures tonight. There's a good one on at the Dream Palace.'

Julie shrugged. 'Anything. Whatever you say, ducky.' She sighed. Did Kate's quest for entertainment reach no further than the pictures or that dreary club where everyone was bored out of their minds? She knew Guy was a member but from Kate's letters it wasn't all that much fun. She frowned as one of her high heels caught in a space between the iron steps.

'Bloody hell, isn't there another way to cross this blasted railway line?' She looked down at the scuffed heel, scowling.

'Not really. Only if we go round by road, which takes an age, or try to cross the lines.'

A memory of Kate's father came to Julie and she castigated herself for speaking so thoughtlessly. 'I'm sorry, love. Me and my big mouth. I wonder if I'll ever grow out of saying things I shouldn't?'

Kate grinned. 'Don't change, Julie. You're perfect as you are.'

Julie took her arm and they hurried down the iron steps and out into the clearing beyond. There was an air of excitement about Julie that slightly worried Kate. She thought of her friend's impetuousness, her almost passionate enthusiasm for anything new. She wondered who – or what – her latest fancy was. Julie wasn't tardy in divulging it. She began a long and involved story of a young man who had recently joined her father's staff and to whom she'd taken an instant liking.

'In fact,' she said, squeezing Kate's arm in an affectionate gesture, 'you could say I fell madly in love with him. I knew he didn't feel the same way about me – you can tell, can't you, if a man fancies you or not? Well, I wasn't going to let a little thing like that put me off and I went all out to get him.'

She paused, carefully negotiating an uneven part of the road where small potholes were filled with rain water. Kate said wryly, 'Personally, I shouldn't think any man has a snowball's chance in hell once you've set your sights on him.'

Julie smirked. 'How well you know me! Anyway, after a while he started to take notice, asking me out to dinner and a nightclub. We went to the Café de Paris where Snakehips Johnson has a band.' She shivered. 'Oh, now *that* was exciting. The next time you come up to visit we must go there.'

'Sounds fun,' said Kate. 'But what about the man? Are you seeing him on a regular basis now?'

Julie shook her head. 'No. I decided it was all wrong.' Actually, although she would never admit it to Kate, the man had dumped her after meeting somebody he liked better. It had been a blow to Julie's ego. But that was something else she wasn't about to admit to her friend.

'You must tell me all about Singapore,' Kate said. 'I bet that was lovely.'

'Fantastic! I had a great time.'

'What did you do out there?' Julie had written, of course, but there was nothing like hearing it first-hand.

'Played tennis and went swimming and in the evening was escorted by handsomely bronzed men to parties.'

'And you didn't fall in love with any of *them*, I take it?'

'No. I restricted that part of my life to having fun.'

Which seemed to be what Julie's life was *all* about, thought Kate, having fun. Then chided herself for thinking it. Wouldn't she do the same, given Julie's circumstances? If they had continued to live the easy life of colonial India, wouldn't her own existence have taken on a similar pattern?

They had reached the flats, which Julie viewed with her usual air of distaste. Coming from a background of luxury provided by her father's affluence, Paradise Buildings was as oppressing as ever. She wondered how Kate could bear to even enter into those dark, gloomy precincts, let alone *live* there.

They ascended the stone stairway, bringing back vivid memories of Paul Konig remarking, on that first occasion, how there were good ideas and there were bad ideas and this was definitely a bad idea.

An old man climbed the steps above them, bent almost double over his stick. His skin hung slackly from his face, and his eyes, behind the thick lenses of his glasses, had sunk deep into their sockets. He breathed in short wheezy gasps like a punctured squeeze box. He stopped to catch his breath at every landing and Kate remarked to Julie on how he lived in the next flat to her and how at night his coughing kept her awake.

'He's been trying for years to get a place down on the ground floor,' she told Julie, 'but it's like water off a duck's back. No one listens to people like him, even though he told me one time he went right through the war and was unlucky enough to be gassed in the trenches.'

Julie wrinkled her nose. 'Does he *have* to live here? Doesn't he have family who can help him?'

'I don't think so. I've never seen anyone visiting him. It's such a shame, he's a fascinating person to talk to. Led a most interesting life.'

They passed the man on the next flight of steps. It seemed that each time he paused for breath it took him longer to move on. Kate said, 'Can we help, Mr Barchester?'

He gave a gruff laugh that ended in a fit of coughing. When at last he could speak, he said, 'Nay, lass, not unless you and your friend can carry me the rest of the way.' And his eyes lingered on Julie's prettiness with a hint of mischief.

Kate felt Julie's fingers pulling at her sleeve, heard her saying under her breath, 'Come on, Kate. He *smells*.'

'Well, don't forget, if there's anything I can do,' said Kate and followed her friend the rest of the way.

Standing to one side, waiting for Kate to unlock the door, Julie said, 'Well, I must say you've got some charming neighbours! What does your mother think of him?'

'The same as you, I imagine.'

Kate pushed the door open and stood back to allow her friend to enter first. She didn't think she liked this side of Julie. She'd changed since their days at school together, when they'd been in agreement on everything. Joined at the hip, like Siamese twins, the nuns used to quip. But then people did change; just look at her mother and Aunt Norma! Who would ever have thought Monica would suggest going to stay with her sister and actually – but *actually* – seem to be looking forward to it?

Kate lifted the small suitcase which she had carried all the way from the station, and showed Julie into the bedroom. She herself would make do with the settee again. That wasn't a problem. She was used to it by now.

In honour of Julie's presence, a bedspread of heavy white cotton, with an exuberance of flowers embroidered in vivid silks, and which Kate remembered from her childhood in India, had been arranged over the blankets. Julie plumped herself down on the narrow single bed. Her mouth pouted unattractively. Hard as the proverbial old maid's heart, she thought.

Kate was saying, 'I'll put the kettle on, make some tea. Or would you prefer coffee?' She'd got the taste for coffee working with Rosa.

Julie stood up and went to the small dressing table, bending to look into the mirror. Carefully she removed the hat, patted her hair into shape and smiled at Kate in the looking glass. 'Coffee, I think. And a fag. I'm dying for one.'

She picked up her bag and rummaged inside. Producing a wafer-thin silver cigarette case, she flipped it open and offered Kate one of the slender black cigarettes inside. They had a narrow band of gold about the tip and looked very exotic. Kate, who had never really taken to smoking, shook her head. 'Not now, thanks. I'll just see to the coffee.'

Waiting for the kettle to boil, Kate thought, why should I feel so gauche with her, so stiff? She sighed as she remembered the episode when Monica had caught them smoking in her room on that very first visit of Julie's.

She looked at the pot of marigolds that had pushed through green shoots from their dank earth, and reached out one hand to touch them. No matter how many times they wilted and died, somehow, like a small miracle, they were there again as soon as spring showed. Brushing her palm lightly over their tops, she breathed, 'Everything changes, Daddy. Everything. Wouldn't it be nice if it didn't, if things could always stay as they are?'

They went to the pictures that evening and afterwards, at Julie's suggestion, popped into the Green Man for a drink. Being a week night it was quieter than usual, a blessing for Kate. To her surprise, Julie ordered a gin and tonic. 'Don't look so shocked,' her friend laughed. 'Try one yourself. It'll do you good.'

'I don't think so, thanks. I'll just have my usual orange juice.'

Julie shrugged. 'Oh well, can't please all of the people all of the time, as they say.'

They hurried back to the flat just as a spatter of rain started. Crossing the well-trodden path to the railway bridge, Kate could hear the wind sighing in the trees sheltering the old railway carriage. Thoughts of Paul came into her mind. Where was he now? What terrible thing could have happened that made it impossible for him to write . . . ?

She felt Julie take her arm as they hurried up the iron steps. Sensibly, her friend had put on flat walking shoes before they left for the pictures and they were able to run the rest of the way.

Kate had banked the fire before they went out and now she added more coal, giving it a good poke so that the cherry-red heart flamed brightly and tangerine-coloured shadows danced on the pale walls. With the table lamps that Kate preferred to the hard ceiling light, the room took on an air of coziness. To Julie's amusement, Kate made two mugs of hot cocoa and after handing one to her friend, she switched on the wireless. Music filled the room.

'Ah, Jack Hylton! I like him, don't you?'

Julie raised her eyes ceilingwards as if searching for patience, but she said, mildly enough, 'He's all right.'

'My mother loves him. She scoured Woolworths for his records, ending up buying them all.' Kate began to hum along with the music, 'Love is the Sweetest Thing', and Julie said, 'Tell me about your mum. How is she taking to living here?'

Julie didn't know the full story of Gerry Patrick or the awful room in Liverpool from which Kate had rescued her mother. Nobody knew about that, not even Rosa.

Kate sipped her cocoa and stared into the fire as she said, 'She isn't happy. I know that but there's not much we can do about it.'

'Maybe she'll decide she'd rather be with your Aunt Norma?' suggested Julie. She thought of her own mother, of the arguments over

271

some of the unsuitable – her mother's expression – escapades Julie had been up to since she left school. Her mother's one ambition was to get her safely married, once more off her hands.

Kate was saying, 'I worry about her. There's no communication between us at all. I can't play the part she wants me to play, therefore we have nothing of consequence to say to each other.'

'Isn't she trying to push you into marriage?' asked Julie.

'Oh, she'd love me to get married.'

'And you're not so sure? I thought you had a thing about Guy?'

Kate thought of the night in the back of the Rolls, of Guy's lovemaking. Although Julie was broad-minded and Kate knew she wouldn't be shocked, still it was a special thing, something to savour until the right moment came along. She thought again about how much they'd changed. At one time there would have been no hesitation on her part; once she'd confided to Julie every little thing that happened to her. Why should she be so reluctant now?

She shifted in her chair then looked at the mantel clock and said, 'It's late. Better get my bed made up.'

Julie made a half-hearted request to be allowed to take the settee, but Kate wouldn't hear of it. 'I'm used to its lumps and bumps,' she laughed. 'Besides, you're my guest, remember. Can't have a guest sleeping on the couch.'

The next morning they were enjoying a late breakfast when there was a knock and Kate opened the door to Ruthie, welcoming the girl with a wide smile. 'Well, isn't this a nice surprise. Come in, we're just having breakfast. Have a cup of tea with us.'

Seeing the other girl there, looking so sophisticated, clad in a silk dressing gown of the most gorgeous shade of royal blue, Ruthie blushed and said, 'I can't stay but for a minute, Kate. We've 'ad wot Mrs Konig calls a disaster in the shop and she wants you to come in for a couple of hours and sort it out.'

Kate frowned. 'What sort of a disaster?'

Ruthie went into a long, involved story of an infuriated customer, one of Kate's 'special ladies', entailing the colour of the beads that embellished the bodice of an evening gown and which the customer said should have been white glass.

Kate flushed. She distinctly remembered the woman, a haughty sort who liked to throw her weight about, vacillating over whether to have black bugles or the white glass, finally agreeing with Kate's choice of black.

Kate glanced at Julie, who was listening dispassionately, one of the thin black cigarettes between her fingers. 'Can't Mrs Konig sort it out?' she asked.

'She said she wanted you, Kate. Oh, I'm sorry, I reely am, you 'aving your friend 'ere an' all, but Mrs Konig was very upset . . .'

Julie gave a breathy sigh. 'Oh, for goodness' sake go, Kate. It wouldn't do for Mrs Konig to get upset, would it?'

There was a hint of scorn in the words and Kate glanced at her sharply. 'It probably wouldn't be for long . . .' she began.

Julie shrugged. 'Take as long as you have to. Lil' ol' me will find something to amuse herself with, I'm sure.'

Thinking of the bead work, if the jet bugles had to be replaced, Kate said, 'I know we went to the pictures last night but there's a musical on at the other place. Why don't you go to the matinée?'

Julie took a long draw on her cigarette and blew the smoke towards the ceiling. 'I might. Don't worry about me, I'll be fine.'

Kate reached for her coat, then gave the littered table a brief look. 'Leave the dishes, I'll do them when I get back. Now you know where that other cinema is, don't you? The far end of the High Street, down that narrow lane . . .'

'Don't fuss. I know.' She stood up and Ruthie's eyes popped as the loosely tied sash of the dressing gown allowed the full skirt to fall open and a completely naked Julie was revealed.

'Whoops!' Julie grabbed for the sash and tied it firmly. 'Naughty to shock the children!' She stretched languorously. 'I'll have a bath and do my nails and then if you're not back I'll think about what to do for the afternoon.'

Kate wasn't back and so Julie sat in the darkness on a warm spring afternoon enjoying Alice Faye in one of her singing and dancing roles. As she emerged on to the pavement with the throng of housewives still wrapped up in the excitement that their twice-weekly dose of the pictures provided, the sunlight made her blink. She stood hesitantly, wondering if she should walk down to Rosa's Boutique and see how Kate was getting on. But she might already be home, and even if she wasn't, Julie didn't want to seem inquisitive. She joined the stragglers as they hurried down the narrow lane towards the High Street. She'd have a look round Woolworths, and Marks and Spencer, and then go back.

Passing a fishmonger who displayed fresh fish on stalls on the pavement outside his shop, she decided to treat Kate to salmon for supper. Causing much amusement in the crowded shop, she asked the fishmonger how to cook it. Solemnly, he described the procedure, going into details that Julie stored away for reference.

She should have worn the walking shoes again. Her high-heeled court shoes weren't made for pavements like these. She stumbled across the rough grass where the road ended and the path leading to the railway bridge began. She heard footsteps coming towards her, clanging in the quietness of the sunny afternoon. As it had before, the heel of her shoe caught in a space between the iron slats and she fell headlong.

The footsteps hurried forward and she heard a voice saying on a note of concern, 'Are you all right?'

Feeling foolish, she struggled to her feet. The paper parcel of salmon lay a couple of feet away and the man who had approached her picked it up and held it out to her. The smell of fish was strong and he grinned, saying, 'I hope it hasn't come to any harm.'

'It's salmon,' she said, feeling even more foolish, 'fresh salmon. It's for our supper.' She felt with her toes for the shoe, still wedged in the space between the iron slats. The young man, good-looking, she saw, fair-haired and well dressed, bent to pull it free. Making a joke of it, as he slipped it on to her foot, he said, 'I don't often get the chance to play Prince Charming to such a pretty Cinderella.'

Julie felt herself blush. Something she hadn't done since convent days. 'Thank you,' she said, wriggling her foot firmly into the shoe. 'That's fine.'

He looked sceptical. 'You're sure? No sprained ankles or anything like that?'

She laughed, shaking her head. 'Sorry to disappoint you, but no sprained ankles or anything like that. 'Bye, and thanks.'

She was aware of him gazing after her as she walked away and she thought: Hmmm, now there's a possibility worth taking up!

Kate appeared not long afterwards, full of apologies. 'Did you go to the pictures? Was it good?' she asked, throwing her coat over the back of the settee. 'I'm sorry I was so long, but I really felt I had to stay and help Rosa.'

Julie shrugged and said yes the picture was enjoyable and that she'd bought a piece of fresh salmon for their supper. Kate exclaimed over the salmon, protesting it must have cost the earth.

Julie shrugged again. 'My daddy always taught me that if you want something badly enough you don't ask the price.'

Following the fishmonger's instructions, between them they managed to turn out a respectable version of poached salmon. Kate made a green salad and the girls tucked into the meal hungrily. 'How did the bead work go?' asked Julie as she lit her first cigarette after the meal.

Kate stood at the sink, beginning on the washing-up. Julie, she saw, had rinsed the breakfast dishes and they lay face down on the draining board. 'The customer conceded my point about black beads being smarter and just to soothe any hurt feelings, I added a few white artfully placed amidst the black.'

'Do you get that often, women being difficult?'

'Someone's always changing their mind and forgetting to tell us she's changed it and then we get blamed for the result. It's something you learn to take in your stride.'

Julie pulled a face. 'I don't think I'd be cut out for taking that kind of fault-finding. You must have changed quite a bit to put up with it so calmly. I remember one time you wouldn't have been so unruffled.'

Kate looked at her consideringly. On the tip of her tongue were the words: When you're on your own with no one else to turn to, it's surprising just how accommodating you can become. And she thought of Guy. The few times they had met since his return from New York, he had been in a hurry, pleading pressure of work, and there had been no time for real discussions. Either about their own future or his grandmother's overture.

She rinsed the dishcloth under the tap and wringing it out placed it to one side of the draining board.

Turning to face Julie she said, 'I almost forgot, Guy is coming to take us out tomorrow evening. Apparently he came here to the flat, but since there was no one in, he dropped round to the shop and caught me there. I didn't think you'd mind. We thought we could take you to that new roadhouse out in the country. I've been there before and in this nice weather it's a pleasant drive.'

Julie puffed at her cigarette and Kate, trying not to be too obvious, opened the kitchen window a little wider. 'Sounds super to me,' said Julie. 'Gives me a chance to wear one of my posh frocks.'

'Not too posh,' said Kate jokingly. 'I don't want to have to compete for Guy's attention.'

'As if I would,' murmured Julie, smiling.

Chapter Twenty-Nine

They took the tube up to Town, walking the length of Oxford Street, window-shopping, later deciding on a tea room near Selfridges for lunch. Kate hated the crowds, hated dodging the oncoming hordes of people, the overheated smoky atmosphere of the tea room. She wasn't to know that Julie was feeling the same. Julie, in fact, was thinking back to shopping in Milan where her parents had taken her for a holiday between leaving the convent and going to finishing school.

They arrived back at the flat tired and with aching feet. They took turns in the bath, Julie first, so Kate was still dressing in the bedroom when Guy knocked on the door.

She called out to Julie: 'That'll be Guy now. Entertain him for me for a bit, will you? There's a pet.'

Julie had changed into a sophisticated black crêpe dress with a low frilled neckline and see-through black chiffon sleeves. Guy's eyes sparkled when he saw her. They stared at each other and Guy said, 'Well, I don't believe it! The Cinderella girl!' Then, looking down at her foot, 'How's the ankle?'

'It's fine, thanks. Hello!' Julie could hardly believe her luck. So this was Kate's admirer! Only an admirer, she wondered, or had their relationship turned into something more lasting? She recalled Kate's letters, telling her about Guy, fantasizing about falling in love. She had to admit that Kate didn't seem like a girl in love. In fact, she'd hardly mentioned Guy except for the fact that he was taking them out to dinner that evening.

She realized he was still standing in the doorway and she took a couple of steps backwards. 'Sorry, do come in. Kate won't be a moment. She's just getting ready.'

He came in and sat down on the hard settee. Julie chose a straight-backed chair opposite. His eyes examined her with blatant curiosity. 'So you're Julie.'

For once feeling out of her depth, she replied, 'Yes, I'm Julie. Thank you for offering to take us out.'

He thought of his MG sports car and grinned. 'It'll be a tight squeeze but that will make it all the more enjoyable.'

Julie selected a cigarette from her handbag and he leaned across and lit it for her. 'How was the fish?' he asked. 'None the worse for its little accident, I hope?'

Coming into the room at that moment, Kate raised her brows and said, 'What fish?'

'The salmon we had for supper last night,' explained Julie.

Kate looked even more puzzled. 'How would Guy know about that?'

Guy smiled. 'I rescued your friend on the bridge when her heel got caught and she fell.'

Julie returned the smile, flirting with him, and to her dismay Kate felt a pang of jealousy.

'Yes, and quite the gallant he was, too. I couldn't have asked for a more chivalrous knight, with or without shining armour.'

'So you two have already met?' Kate said. 'Well, not forgetting my manners, I'd still better introduce you. Julie, this is Guy Ferris, and Guy, my friend Julie Johnson.'

Feeling gauche and inadequate, comparing her own appearance with Julie's – the chic black gown against her own fine cotton voile that Guy had seen a number of times – knowing her tone was too brusque, Kate turned and picked up the light woollen shawl from the back of the couch and said, 'Didn't you say you'd booked a table for eight, Guy?' He nodded and she went on, 'Hadn't we better get going then?'

The car was a squeeze, no doubt about that, but they managed. Julie tied a silk scarf about her head, worried about her hair in the open car. The countryside looked clean and fresh after the night's rain, as though everything had been specially scrubbed for their benefit. The car park of the roadhouse was full and Guy had to park towards the back, making him mutter under his breath. The girls' high heels twisted on the pebble-strewn courtyard and Kate gave a sigh of relief as at last they were seated at a table by an obsequious waiter.

They were handed large menus and Guy ordered for all of them. As the meal progressed, Kate watched and listened as Guy and Julie discussed places that were only names to her. Rome. Venice. Milan. At the back of the bar the shelves of bottles were backed by mirrored glass, and her reflection gazed back at her. So doleful and pale. She forced a smile to her lips; crazy not to be enjoying an evening out with her old school friend and her lover.

She felt herself blush at the word. Lover! How brazen that sounded! She hadn't yet told Julie all that had happened between her and Guy. Would it be tempting the Fates to do that just yet? Julie seemed to have taken to him without reservation. But still a small, quiet voice inside Kate warned: Not yet! Wait a while.

The plates cleared away, Guy took out a cigarette case and offered it first to Kate and then to Julie. Julie preferred one of her own exotic brand. Guy lit it and the waiter brought their drinks. When he had gone,

Guy, looking at Kate, said, 'All right, what is it? What's wrong?'

Kate looked uncomfortable. 'Why, nothing. What could be wrong?'

'I know you well enough by now to know that when you look like that, something is wrong. Didn't you enjoy the food? Or is your drink too strong?'

Seeing that Kate had ordered her usual orange juice, the question had to be a joke, one of Guy's subtly malicious jibes. 'The drink's fine. And the food was delicious.'

'Then why aren't you joining in the conversation? Why are you letting your friend bear the brunt of it all?'

'You sounded as though you were enjoying yourselves, talking about the sights and places you had both seen. I had nothing to contribute.'

Julie stubbed her cigarette out in the crystal ashtray and reached for her small black evening bag. 'I need to powder my nose. Coming, Kate?'

Kate nodded. She felt Guy's gaze on them as they walked between the tables to the ladies' room. In the sweet-smelling, pink-mirrored room, Julie touched up her lips with the scarlet lipstick she wore and fluffed out the ends of her hair with a small comb. Catching her friend's eyes in the mirror, she offered the tube of lipstick, saying, 'Here, use some of this. You look pale. Sure you're all right?'

Kate declined her offer. 'I'm all right.' She spoke more sharply than she'd meant to and Julie gave her an enquiring look. 'I'm sorry if I took over there,' Julie said. 'Your Guy Ferris seems to have vacationed in all the places I've been to with my parents. It was lovely, reviving memories of them all.' She looked contrite. 'I'm sorry, Kate. You won't hear a peep out of me from now on, I promise.'

'Don't be silly!' Kate smiled. 'He isn't *my* Guy Ferris . . .' Not yet, anyway, she reminded herself. His moods were part of him, she knew how swiftly they changed. She couldn't blame him for wanting to talk to a pretty girl over dinner about mutual interests. Goodness knows, she and Guy had very little in common – only that I love him desperately, she thought. And he feels the same about me, I'm sure he does. When Julie's gone back, we'll drive out somewhere, maybe that reservoir we visited once before, and talk about our future. And after they had been married for a while, maybe she'd let him set her up in a shop of her own. In another town, of course. She wouldn't want to poach Rosa's clients.

Julie gave one last pat to her hair and preceded Kate from the room. Over her shoulder she said, cheerfully, 'And if he's not *your* Guy Ferris, then it's open season on tall good-looking men with blond hair. Right?'

Kate laughed but didn't answer. They were almost back at the table, with Guy rising to his feet as they approached. If she replied, even jokingly, to Julie's remark, he would surely hear.

The possibilities for entertainment in the borough were limited, and after sampling the various walks and the shops in the High Street, Kate wondered what on earth they could do now. Julie gave her suggestion of borrowing a bicycle for her the thumbs down. It was ages since she'd ridden anything except the sleek chestnut mare her father had bought her one birthday. Besides, she hadn't packed anything that would be remotely suitable to wear, scorning Kate's offer of a full cotton skirt or shorts.

Strolling aimlessly along the High Street, they saw ahead of them a small crowd of people huddled outside Rosa's Boutique. Kate broke into a run, followed closely by Julie.

Breathlessly, Julie gasped, 'What is it? What's happened?'

Kate didn't answer. They had reached the edge of the crowd and inelegantly she pushed her way through, using her elbows to nudge people aside. The crowd by the window cleared and she came to a dead halt, open-mouthed, staring. The window had been shattered completely, shards of glass hanging dagger-like from the surrounding woodwork. The floor was covered with broken glass, the wax model leaning drunkenly to one side. Printed in red paint on what little glass remained were the words: Nazis Go Home.

Kate felt sick. She turned her back on the carnage and glared at the faces of the crowd, expectant, relishing the bit of excitement in their lives. 'What happened? Can anybody tell me what happened?'

Nobody answered. She saw Mrs Wells and her daughter's triumphant faces at the front of the crowd, and just behind, Mr Shipton. All three looked as pleased as Punch.

'Why, it do look as though someone chucked a brick through the window, don't it?' the heavy-set grocer's voice mocked. 'Showing 'ow we all feel about bloody foreigners 'ere.'

Kate was startled at the violence of the anger that stirred in her. If she'd been able, she would have raked those sneering faces with her nails. She took a step forwards, her hands coming up like claws, and it was only Julie's steadying hand on her arm that stayed her.

'Don't, Kate,' she heard her say. 'Leave it, let the police handle it.' Julie spoke quietly, with authority, urging Kate through the open doorway of the shop. Now, standing inside, surveying the damage, her thoughts were of Rosa and Ruthie, and, to a lesser extent, Sylvia.

In the little gilt chair used by customers, Rosa sat bent double, her face in her hands, sobbing quietly. Kate went to her and disregarding the broken glass, knelt beside her. Julie waited in the background, looking uncertain.

'Shhh, Rosa,' Kate whispered. 'It's all right, we'll soon have it tidied up. It's nothing we can't cope with.'

Rosa's sobs went on unabated, as though she didn't even hear. 'The police will catch the ruffians who did this,' Kate promised her, 'and, if I had *my* way, they'd hang them from the nearest lamppost.'

Rosa's hands came away from her face and Kate felt in her pocket for her handkerchief. Tenderly she wiped the damp cheeks, and Rosa smiled at the vivid picture Kate's expressive description conjured up. 'That would only lower us to the level of whoever did this,' Rosa said quietly. 'Violence is no solution.'

'Maybe not,' Kate replied grimly, 'but it certainly would help in this case.' She rose to her feet and gazed about her. 'Where's Ruthie and Sylvia? Are they all right?'

As if in reply to her question, the two girls came through from the series of back rooms. Ruthie, she could see, had been crying. But Sylvia was dry-eyed and met Kate's gaze with composure.

Ruthie burst into fresh tears when she saw Kate. 'Oh, I'm so glad you came, Kate. We was so frightened . . .'

'Did someone phone the police?' Kate enquired tightly.

'Yes.' Rosa rose from the chair as she spoke, straightening her shoulders, lifting her chin. 'In the meantime, we'll start clearing up.'

'I don't think you should,' Julie said. 'They will want to see the full damage.'

'I agree,' Kate said. 'How about if you put the kettle on, Ruthie? Make us all a cup of tea?'

Ruthie escaped from the scene of carnage, moving quickly, as though to block it from her mind. 'When did it happen?' Kate asked, glancing about her.

'When I arrived this morning to open the shop I found it like this,' Rosa said. 'I suppose we were lucky that we weren't burgled at the same time.'

'Whoever was responsible,' Kate said, 'wasn't interested in burglary. Only in an outpouring of hatred from their nasty little minds.' Since Rosa had moved to the larger premises, the old shop leased by Mr Shipton had remained empty. A sore point with him. And every time she came face to face with Mrs Wells or her daughter in the street the women glared at her with animosity. Still, unless someone actually saw one of them hurling the brick, there wasn't very much they could do about it. As Julie had said, it was best to leave it to the police.

As though her thoughts had conjured him up, a policeman on a bicycle arrived and parked his bike at the kerb. Entering the shop, he glanced about him, his brow furrowing. 'Hmmm, someone's got a grudge, I would say,' was his first comment.

Then, solemnly taking a notepad from his top jacket pocket, he licked the end of his pencil and gazed enquiringly at Rosa. 'You Mrs Konig?'

'I am.'

'All right, better tell me what happened.'

Behind Kate, Julie breathed, 'It took them long enough to get here, I must say. And *one* copper on a bike! What would they do if they had a murder on their hands?'

Kate shuddered. 'Don't even say it!' Resentment of foreigners in their midst didn't stop with grocers and some of their customers, it seemed.

While Rosa quietly answered the constable's questions, Ruthie carried in a tray of tea. Julie with quiet politeness declined a cup, and Kate said, 'I don't think there's any need for you to hang about, Julie. Why don't you get back and start on your packing?' Julie was leaving the following day and was more used to her mother's maid packing for her than doing it herself. 'I think I ought to stay here a while and give Rosa a bit of support.'

Julie hesitated. 'If you're sure . . .' She would never admit it but she was dying to get out into the fresh air and sunlight, away from this cruel scene of broken glass and red paint spouting its legend of hate and bigotry. And as though the special genie that looked after her was still on his toes, still granting her wishes, Guy Ferris came into the shop.

He had, he explained, been driving past and saw the crowd and the broken window. He looked so handsome, standing there with the sun glinting on his hair, turning it to ripe gold, his skin smooth and faintly sunburned from the fine weather, that Kate wanted to fling herself into his arms, to feel them close comfortingly about her. All this – the damage, the hateful words painted in red, Rosa's bewildered face and her distracted answers to the policeman's questions – all this she wanted to leave behind, to go somewhere quiet with Guy, to be cosseted and pampered. But, because she was Kate and had to show strength and integrity, just as the nuns had taught, she must stay and support Rosa until this terrible thing had been sorted out.

Looking about him, Guy said, 'Jesus! Sorry, Mrs Konig. But you must admit it does make one's blood boil. What happened?'

During the explanation, his eyes rested on Julie. When all had been clarified, he said, 'Perhaps it might be appropriate if I offered you girls a lift home? My car's outside . . .'

'Take Julie,' Kate said. 'There's no need for her to stay. In fact, we were talking about it just before you arrived.'

Guy looked at the other girl. 'May I? Offer you a lift, I mean?'

For the briefest fraction of a second Julie hesitated, not wanting to desert her friend but loath to pass up the opportunity of having Guy to herself. After tomorrow she might never see him again. Next time she visited Kate he could be married. To Kate? she wondered. Last night when they got home, she had felt that Kate was on the brink of telling her something. Something about Guy?

But she hadn't. Kate obviously didn't think of him that way. Guy was a philanderer. Goodness knows, she'd met enough of the breed to know one when she saw it. But Julie didn't mind philanderers. They were whole lot more fun than that German boy Kate seemed to think so much of, for all his intrepid bravery.

'All right,' she said and stepped carefully across the broken glass to kiss Kate and then Rosa on the cheek. 'Chin up,' she whispered to the surprised woman, then to Kate, 'I'll see you later, then.'

Kate nodded and watched them go, followed shortly afterwards by the police constable. There wasn't, he explained, much he could do. Not unless someone saw the perpetrator actually throw the brick. But he was sure that now this had happened, a watch would be kept on the premises, just in case it happened again.

'Now that it has happened!' said Rosa bitterly. 'For all his fine words, they will do nothing. I know. How much I wish my Pauli was here. On top of my anxiety for him I have now to face this alone.'

'You don't have to face *anything* alone, Rosa.' Kate looked affronted at the thought. 'We are all here beside you, Ruthie, me and Sylvia.' Could she include Sylvia? she wondered. But while she was working for Rosa, surely Sylvia would see on which side her bread was buttered and help all she could, regardless of her own thoughts on the matter? 'I know you're worried about Paul, I am too, but I'm sure he wouldn't want us to capitulate to thugs who know no better.'

Rosa dabbed at her eyes and then regarded Kate fondly. 'Such a girl!' she murmured. 'I am so lucky to have you to stand by me like this.'

Kate stayed until late in the afternoon, helping shovel up broken glass and drinking coffee and tea by the mugful. Ruthie swept everywhere she could reach with a handbrush while Sylvia, looking mutinous, used the yard brush. The shop carpet was bristling with shards of fine glass and Rosa feared they might have to get a new one. It was a fitted carpet so they couldn't take it up and shake it outside. Examining the window model, Kate saw that with very little effort it could be restored to its former glory. Making a lie of their first thoughts that there'd been no burglary, the claret-and-black woollen cloak and costume worn by the window dummy had vanished.

'Some bastard's nicked that,' said Ruthie. 'Shame, it were so pretty, too . . .'

Other things, small items of costume jewellery, even the wig from the model's head, were also missing. Ruthie scowled. 'If I see anyone around 'ere wearing it, Kate, I know what *I'll* do; I'll rip it right off 'er.'

Kate couldn't help but smile. Ruthie's words seemed, if only fractionally, to lighten the black mood that had hung over them all day.

'What, Ruthie, the wig or the outfit?'

'Both.'

'I think there's very little likelihood of that happening,' Sylvia said dourly. 'I can't see anyone wearing a costume like that in any of the places *you* frequent.'

For once, Ruthie stood up to her. 'Oh, and when was the last time you was invited to Buckingham Palace?'

'Oh, for heaven's sake,' Kate said, 'isn't there enough ill-will about without you two having a go at each other?'

She went into the kitchen to wash her hands, grimy after the cleaning up and Ruthie followed her in. 'Can I ask you somethin', Kate?' the girl began, twisting a long strand of hair about her fingers.

Drying her hands, Kate smiled. 'Why not? Go ahead.'

'Well, you remember that time I told you about 'ow my friend 'ad asked me to go camping with 'im?'

'That was ages ago – last summer.'

'Yes, well . . .' Ruthie looked uncomfortable. 'Remember Mrs Konig let me 'ave that week off in August? I didn't tell anybody but I went then.'

'Why, you little madam, you!' Kate couldn't help looking amused.

The girl's eyes brightened as though a candle had been lit behind them. 'It were lovely, Kate. 'E – my friend – was so nice and – and gentle. No one's ever been like that with me before.'

'And?' Kate prompted when the girl fell silent, a rapt look on her face.

'Well, my mum found out, didn't she, and last night in our 'ouse when Bill came to take me out – that's 'is name, Bill – there was such a carry-on I was sure she were goin' to throw a fit.'

'How did she find out? And after all this time?'

'I think Sylvia told 'er. Don't ask me 'ow *she* knew, but I'm sure it was 'er. She likes to bide 'er time, does Sylvia. Probably bin brooding on it all these months. When me dad came back from the pub he took 'is belt to me . . .'

And she lifted her dress at the back to show Kate the welts, red and angry, on her upper legs. Kate was horrified. 'For goodness' sake! Didn't your Bill do anything about it? Try to stop him . . . ?'

''E weren't there, my mum 'ad sent 'im packing before that. Just as well, I suppose. My dad would've knocked his block off if 'e'd still bin there.'

'But you've told him?'

Ruthie nodded. ''E was waitin' for me this mornin' as I left for work. We're goin' off together as soon as Bill's got 'is wages on Friday. I wanted to tell you, Kate, because you and Mrs Konig's bin so kind to me. I 'ate leaving her in the lurch like this, but I daren't stay, not now.'

'But there must be another way. Where will you go?'

'There ain't, Kate. My Bill's got relatives in Birmingham. 'E says we can go there.' She gave a self-satisfied smile. 'Me mum'd never find us there.' She looked up at Kate. 'I can't face Mrs Konig. Would you tell 'er for me? There's plenty of girls looking for jobs as'll be only too glad to take my place.'

And, being Kate, what could she do but agree?

Chapter Thirty

Paul saw a rabbit, grabbed at the dog's collar too late and missed. He cursed then looked up to where his father sat on a folding canvas stool, a paint-spattered canvas on its easel before him. The reeds here were as high as a man, water gurgling in the creeks, sunlight glinting on the smooth surface of the lake like those sequins his mother painstakingly sewed on other women's gowns. It was a scene of complete peace, another Eden, pure and unspoiled. Paul decided he never wanted to live anywhere else.

The dog raced across the grass, following the rabbit that twisted and turned effortlessly, and Paul called to his father, 'Five to one that he doesn't get it!' Then he heard his father's laughter and a voice – not his father's voice – said, 'On your feet, Konig. You're going on a little journey.'

And the gloom that settled on him was so black, so bitter, that he never wanted to open his eyes again. But he knew if he didn't move there would be a kick in the ribs, followed by other indignities. His captors weren't known for more gentle persuasive methods.

He opened his eyes and struggled to his feet. The burly middle-aged man who had been his warder all these months stood at the open door, glaring at him. 'Come on, haven't got all day.'

Paul stumbled before him into the long narrow passage. 'Where are you taking me?'

'Never mind where we're taking you, Konig. It could be to one of those nice health farms.' The warder's voice was sarcastic. 'You'll find that out when you get there.'

What was the use? Paul thought. They had never told him anything since that dark night when he was dragged away, Hilda's screams ringing in his ears. He'd tried to find out what had happened to Hilda, but to no avail. His one hope was that she had given them Hans's name and they had let her go.

He was pushed into the courtyard of the prison and ordered to climb into the back of a canvas-covered truck. Other prisoners were already there. They huddled together as though the slightest movement would bring disaster down on them. Nobody spoke. All were terrified. The sound of boots pacing the cobblestoned yard prompted Paul to lift the canvas, trying to peer out. The butt of a rifle was immediately thrust into the opening, catching Paul's face with a glancing blow, cutting his cheekbone.

'Next time you try that, my friend,' the guard growled, sounding not in the least friendly, 'it will be a bullet in your head.' He then proceeded to fasten the edges of the canvas, lacing them together with criss-crossing thongs of leather, leaving the interior of the truck in almost claustrophobic darkness. The journey was to be long and monotonous. Shut up in the back of the lurching, badly sprung truck, Paul could barely make out the faces of his fellow prisoners. They avoided his eyes, frightened to talk, to even move. Outside somewhere, a dog barked, reminding him of his dream. The dog in the dream had been the one who had had its throat cut, poor Bruno who had been left for his mother to find as she opened the door to bring in the milk. The dog barked again, a wild, joyous bark that reminded Paul that life was going on, would go on just the same long after he was dead and forgotten. His mother would get up in the mornings and go to work. She and Kate would discuss him over a cup of coffee and Kate would work willingly with his mother to continue making a go of the shop. In a year or two Kate would marry – please God not that rogue Ferris! – they would have their reception at some grand venue, and their laughing photographs would be in the weekly paper, together with a description of the bride's dress, made exclusively by Rosa of Rosa's Boutique.

And suddenly he felt an aching, terrible despair, so that to his utter shame sobs tore at his throat with a rasping noise that made him stuff his fist into his mouth. He knew he was crying for Kate, for what seemed to be the end of all his hopes, but that wasn't all. There was something else his tormented mind was weeping for. His ideals, his self-imposed mission to set the world to rights. For his mother and his dead father. The tears ran down his face and he groaned aloud.

Someone behind him reached out and placed an arm about his shoulders. A voice whispered, 'There, son, there! That's what the bastards want to see, grown men crying. Don't give them the satisfaction.' Paul turned and smiled at the outline of the white-haired man sitting behind him.

Some time later the man's arm slipped away and he fell asleep. Through gaps in the tightly laced canvas at the back Paul could see that the skies were dark, a full moon shining on an empty countryside. There were no features to distinguish it from any other part of Germany. No lights from farmhouses or the pink glow of a far-off town. He fell into an uneasy doze, hearing the snoring of other men all about him.

The screeching of brakes, the shuddering stop that threw them all forward, woke him up. Outside in the darkness there came the sound of men shouting. Risking the bullet he'd been promised if he tried again to peer out, Paul loosened the leather thong and pulled the canvas to one side. Pitch darkness met his gaze. The noise was all coming from the front of the vehicle.

He sat, crouching as close to the stretched canvas as he could get, listening to the shouted argument going on between, presumably, the driver of the truck, the accompanying warder and a third party. The old man who had tried to comfort him crept up beside him. 'What is it? What's going on?' His voice creaked with fear.

'I don't know. It sounds like we've run into something.' Paul sat listening for a moment, then went on, 'Nobody's at the back of the truck, all the action seems to be happening at the front. I'm going to try and make a break for it.'

Then, galvanizing Paul into action, the shouting stopped, the driver turned the ignition and the engine roared. With fingers that trembled he unlaced a further space of canvas, large enough for him to slip through. He had lost weight in prison and was thinner now than he'd ever been. He landed on the road with bent knees, stood upright and then was running for his life across the field bordering the road to where a thick clump of trees stood dark against the horizon. Thank God the moon had been covered by a cloud, he thought, offering up a silent prayer for it to stay there.

He crouched within the shelter of the trees for what seemed like an eternity, but in reality could have been only minutes. The adrenaline was pumping, the fear had gone, evaporated somehow into the dark night. Suddenly he felt invincible. He was going to get away, get home to Kate and his mother. His eyes were on the road, watching as the taillights of the truck slowly faded in the distance. Only then did he rise to his feet to turn and look about him. To his relief, he caught a glimpse of lights on the other side of the small copse. And where there were lights there were people.

He was so consumed with the thrill of his escape that it never once occurred to him to wonder whether those people would be friend or foe.

Kate was surprised to find when she got home that Julie hadn't returned. It was a nice day, maybe Guy had decided to take her for a drive. She put away the bit of shopping she'd purchased on the way home: cold meat for their supper, some nice-looking tomatoes, a jar of home-made pickled beetroot she'd seen and fancied in that new delicatessen recently opened in the High Street. Freshly baked rolls she'd bought at the bakery.

She'd have a bath and wash her hair and if Julie hadn't returned by then she'd know Guy was treating her to dinner out. The stab of jealousy she'd experienced before returned, worrying her. She ought not to feel like that. Letting her imagination run away with her, that's what she was doing. Wasn't Sister Devota forever lecturing her about that!

She pulled a face at herself in the mirror over the fireplace, ran widespread fingers through her hair and went into her bedroom.

Falsifying the promise of a fine night, the storm started while she was in the bath. She'd always had a fear of being caught in the bath when a disaster happened. Not that the storm was a disaster, but she didn't want Julie, perhaps still accompanied by Guy, drenched and shivering like a pair of drowned cats, ringing the doorbell when she was still *déshabillée*.

She slipped on a warm dressing gown, rubbed her hair with a towel, shook it back from her face, and then started on her own supper. She wouldn't wait for Julie. Glancing at the mantel clock, she saw with some surprise that it was past nine. She wished she was on the 'phone so that she could ring Mrs Ferris to see if Guy had taken Julie there. Although she didn't think it at all likely, still there was a possibility that he had.

Her concern for Julie wouldn't go away and finally she crept out on to the landing. She saw with relief that it was deserted and she tiptoed down to knock on Mrs Konig's door so that she could voice her worries. Women in dressing gowns wandered the building day and night, some not even bothering to get dressed until late afternoon. Kate prayed that, no matter how long she was forced to live in Paradise Buildings, she would never become like that.

Rosa, too, was in her dressing gown. She looked worn out. 'I was just on my way to bed, Kate.' She glanced sharply at Kate's face. 'What is it, has something happened?'

Kate felt a fool. She had no right to further unsettle this woman with worries of her own. Backing away, she smiled and said, 'No, everything's all right, Rosa. Forgive me, I'm sorry to disturb you.' If Rosa felt anything like she did after their horrendous day, then all she would want to do was slip into bed with a cup of cocoa. 'It's just that Julie's not back yet and I was worried.'

Rosa frowned. 'Do you want to use the telephone? Is there someone you could call who might know?'

Fleetingly, the white-haired elegance of Mrs Ferris came to mind. Was it fair to disturb the old lady too? If they *were* there, perhaps having a nightcap and a gossip, then it would seem like prying and that she wanted to avoid at all costs. No, better to leave it. She certainly did not have the right to tell Julie what time she should be in.

'Thanks, Rosa, but I guess I'm worrying unduly. I'll let you get to bed. You must be exhausted.'

'Well, let us say I have had better days.'

'Goodnight.'

'Goodnight, *liebling*.'

Kate crept back upstairs.

She fetched a blanket and wrapped it around her and finally fell asleep in the armchair. She had given Julie her mother's door key when she arrived and the rattle of it in the lock woke her. Daylight was not far off, soft pink streaks of dawn lighting the sky over the countryside. In Paradise Buildings, the dawn chorus of birds nesting under the eaves of the roof made a joyous sound.

Kate sat up, expecting to see Guy come in behind her, full of apologies for the night out. Something had happened to the car, it had broken down and they'd had to wait for it to be towed in. They would laugh and say, 'Gosh, what a night! Everything wrong that could happen did.'

But Julie was alone. She closed the door behind her and came forward, gazing down at Kate with heavy, slumbrous eyes. 'Don't tell me you waited up all night for me? You silly girl! You should have gone to bed.'

'I didn't know I was going to sit up all night,' Kate said with a hint of resentment. 'Where were you, anyway? I was so worried . . .'

'Worried?' Julie laughed. 'About lil' ol' me? Now that's a turn-up for the books.' She bent over Kate and kissed her on the cheek. She smelt of the exotic tobacco of her own cigarettes, gin, and something else. Something that brought back memories of the day by the reservoir when Guy had held her in his arms. The smell of the Brylcreem that Guy used on his hair.

Kate sat tight and rigid in the chair, watching as Julie went through to the kitchen. She heard the tinkle of glass, the tap running and Julie came back with a glassful of water. 'Do you mind if I go straight to bed, ducks? I'm pooped . . .'

'You haven't told me what happened,' Kate reminded her stubbornly. 'Did Guy have trouble with the car?'

Julie sipped the water. 'Weeelll . . . not exactly. We had dinner at that roadhouse and then drove on and found a quaint old inn where we stopped for a drink. Just as we were leaving it started to rain and Guy suggested we stay there for the rest of the night. It was quite late by then and knowing the sort of day you'd had we didn't want to disturb you. And I really thought you would grab the chance to sleep in comfort on the bed for a change.'

'It didn't occur to you that I might be worried?'

Julie frowned. 'Oh, come now! You're sounding more like my mother every minute. You must know how persuasive Guy can be. Besides, I was having such a good time . . .'

'Did you share the same room?' Unwittingly, Kate's voice rose. 'Did you sleep with him?' Hating herself even as she said it, thinking: Oh God, I'm the chump of all chumps. How could I think such a thing of my best friend? Abruptly she got to her feet, holding the blanket about her shoulders. 'No, you don't have to answer that.' She headed for the kitchen. 'I'm going to put the kettle on and make some tea. Want some?'

Julie followed her, standing behind her as she filled the kettle from the tap. 'But I think we ought to talk about it, Kate. Yes, I slept with him. It was a mutual decision. It never occurred to me that I might be stepping on someone else's toes. I thought you were just good friends. Although, looking back on it, I feel sick at what I've done. It shows such a lack of character.'

Kate pretended that shock waves weren't tumbling through her, making her hand tremble as she struck a match to light the gas. But her voice was steady as she said, 'Sexual attraction has nothing to do with character.' The nuns were big on character. But you couldn't blame your particular character for everything you did wrong. 'Guy is an attractive man. He knows it and doesn't mind going all out to get any girl he's got his eye on.'

'That should mean you. Would you have done the same?'

'You mean, would I have slept with a man whom my best friend was seeing? Never! I'd never do anything as heartless as that to a friend.' She kept her face turned from Julie, spooning tea into the brown glazed pot, reaching for cups from the high cupboard.

Behind her she heard Julie catch her breath. 'I swear I'll never see him again, Kate. Never.'

The tea brewed and poured, Kate turned and handed a cup to Julie. 'In a pig's ear! Besides, what's the difference? When you're around he doesn't even know I'm alive. Looks like he's taken a fancy to you.'

Julie looked miserable. 'What are we going to do?'

'I don't know.'

'You'll be glad to see the back of me.'

Kate reminded herself that Julie was going home that day, taking the train to Victoria where she would be met by her father's chauffeur.

'Why should I be glad to see the back of you? I enjoy your visits.' She sipped her tea. Hindsight made her say, 'Besides, if it hadn't been you it would have been some other girl.'

'You've got him all wrong, Kate. He's really sweet.'

'Sweet when he can get his own way, unpredictable when he can't.'

And the bittersweet memories of Guy seemed to wither even as she spoke.

Kate's air of restrained politeness saw her through until the train carrying Julie vanished into the distance. She gave a last wave of her hand, knowing she was waving away a joyous part of her past, wondering if Julie would ever come again. It was as if a heavy load rested on her shoulders and she tried to convince herself it was the result of her uncomfortable night spent in the chair. She knew that was partly the reason, but also partly Guy's betrayal with Julie. *Mostly* Guy's betrayal with Julie. She ached all over and had hardly slept a wink for the rest of the night. She felt deathly tired, and wanted nothing more than to crawl into bed and just sleep.

She hoped Guy wouldn't come fawning, full of excuses and explanations. She wasn't ready for that yet. At the moment she never wanted to see him or his grandmother again.

Rosa remarked on her paleness when she went into the shop. It wasn't open for business – wouldn't be open for business for some days, Kate imagined, looking at the boarding nailed across the space where the window had been. Inside, Rosa had all the lights switched on, creating at least a semblance of normality.

She fussed over Kate, instructing Ruthie to put the kettle on. 'Did your friend get back all right?' Rosa asked in a conciliatory tone.

'Yes.' Kate wasn't prepared to enlarge on the subject. Carrying her cup of tea, she went into the back room where the window mannikin stood waiting for a restoring hand.

Later that morning the police constable visited them again, asking questions, prying into Rosa's clients and acquaintances. 'Are you sure there is no one who has a grudge against you, Mrs Konig?' he asked. 'Nobody you've had a dispute with?'

'Quite sure, Officer.' Tight-lipped, Rosa gazed at him. 'My clients are all on good terms with me and my staff. I have few acquaintances and those I do have would never sink to such depths.'

When he had gone, Kate said, 'Why didn't you tell him what we all suspect? That it was either that Wells woman and her repulsive daughter or Mr Shipton?'

'We haven't a shred of evidence, Kate. It is just one more thing sent by the good Lord to try us.' Smiling, Rosa squeezed Kate's arm. 'I have been through worse and no doubt I will again, especially if our two countries are at each other's throats, as the newspapers seem to think they soon will be.'

Kate recalled Julie's words about how gas masks were being carried in Central London. Although their own suburb had been issued with them, few people bothered to carry them, thinking the square cardboard boxes ugly. The meetings between Mr Chamberlain and Hitler the previous year at the Führer's summer residence at Berchtesgaden had proved fruitless. A waste of time, everyone said. That piece of paper waved so jubilantly by the Prime Minister – 'Peace for our time' was the slogan on everyone's lips – wasn't worth a thing.

Just the other day there had been a report on the wireless warning the population that preparations were in full swing for the evacuation of women and children from London in the event of war.

And if the worst, the very worst, happened and war was declared, what would happen to Rosa? Kate felt sick. If only Paul was here. Please God, she prayed, let him be safe, don't let anything have happened to him.

Ruthie found her in a back room where she was busy restoring what she could of the window model.

'You 'aven't forgotten me going on Friday?' the girl began nervously. 'You promised to talk to Mrs Konig.'

'I won't forget, Ruthie. I promised, didn't I? Although I was hoping you'd reconsider and arrange a proper wedding here.'

'It wouldn't work. Me mum'd never give 'er consent and I'm under age still.' Deciphering the question on Kate's face, she added, 'You see, it's not that easy. I'm the only one bringing a wage in at 'ome and me mum and dad'd do anything to stop me marrying and leaving.'

Kate thought of the angry-looking welts she'd seen on the girl's legs and frowned. 'But won't you still need her or your father's consent wherever you get married?'

'Not if we go up to Scotland we won't.'

'All that way, Ruthie? So far from your friends and home!'

Ruthie shuffled her feet on the bare boards of the room, fixing her gaze on them as though she couldn't abide meeting Kate's eyes. 'I'll be all right, Kate. I'll be 'appy with my Bill. 'E'll take care of me.'

Kate went to her and hugged her tightly. 'Oh, I do hope so, Ruthie. I do sincerely hope so.'

Kate didn't relish breaking the news to Rosa on that Saturday morning when Ruthie didn't turn up for work. It was the day Rosa decided to reopen the shop. The replacement pane of glass sparkled in the sunshine, the newly cleaned carpet was immaculate. The model, resplendent in a blonde wig, curled and peroxided in the style of Jean Harlow, looked, as Guy remarked, popping in unexpectedly with a message from his grandmother, good enough to eat.

Kate, standing in her stockinged feet in the window, giving the last touches to the halter-neck dress with its bold abstract of black flowers on a white background, ignored him completely. Thinking she hadn't heard, Rosa pulled back the curtain that divided the window from the shop and said, 'Kate, Mr Ferris has just come in.'

'Really!' Kate murmured, fussing with the full skirt of the dress. She didn't even glance his way or show the slightest interest.

Rosa looked bewildered. What was happening to her staff? First Ruthie pulling a trick like that on her, and now Kate overlooking the grandson of their most important customer as though he didn't exist.

But there was a limit to the time Kate could spend in the window. Eventually, she had to emerge. To her chagrin she saw Guy reclining lazily on the small brocade-covered settee in the alcove, one of Rosa's special cups of coffee in his hand. Her cheeks flamed as he caught her eye. Angrily she swept the silver-blonde hair back behind her ears and bent for her shoes.

Guy's gaze was fixed on her feet. In a tantalizing drawl he said, 'Such pretty feet! Why haven't I noticed them before?'

'What do you want?' Kate didn't even try to sound civil.

'Mrs Konig was called into the fitting room, along with the delightful Sylvia, to attend to a customer. She asked me to let you deal with my grandmother's order.'

Kate snatched the folded sheet of paper from his outstretched hand and turned her back on him as she read it. In bold copperplate handwriting, Mrs Ferris informed Rosa's Boutique that she would be visiting them next Wednesday to choose a gown for a special theatre engagement in the West End.

She folded it again and thrust it into a file that lay on the counter top. 'You can tell your grandmother that we will be happy to see her.' She kept her head turned away as she spoke.

'But not happy to see me?' She heard him come up behind her and felt her muscles tense. 'Kate . . .'

'Go away!' She couldn't hide the anguish in her voice. 'Go away, you've done what you came to do, now get lost.'

'You're being very silly.'

'No, I'm not, I'm being sensible at last. I'm seeing you for what you really are.'

He took her shoulders and tried to turn her to face him. Stubbornly, she resisted, and they were standing like that when Sylvia came back into the shop. Her sharp dark eyes took in the scene and her mouth pursed up like an old woman's. 'My, my,' she said, 'in broad daylight and in the shop, too! What would Mrs Konig say?'

Guy muttered an oath beneath his breath. He strode to the door then turned to meet Kate's eyes, saying roughly, 'You haven't heard the last of this. Like hell you haven't. I'll be back and then we'll talk.'

Forgetting that Sylvia was still staring, that complacent grin on her face, Kate watched through the glass door as Guy roared away in his car. She thought: nothing defeats him. Things will always go right for him, because he has position, because he's a Ferris. But mostly because conscience, as most people know it, doesn't exist for him. His night with Julie had left no apparent trace of guilt.

One thing Kate knew now, was perfectly sure of, was that she hadn't fallen in love with him. It had all been a young girl's infatuation, a lonely searching for love.

Startling her, Sylvia said, 'Something to look forward to, eh? Looks like he means business.'

Kate sighed. 'Oh, Sylvia, if your brain worked as sharply as your tongue, you'd be a genius.'

Sylvia's dark eyes glittered with hatred. 'Well, thanks very much.'

Chapter Thirty-One

It was very quiet in Tom Marshall's Berlin office as he sat working through some papers in the light of a desk lamp. The door opened and his secretary, on the point of going home, looked in. 'Coffee, Mr Marshall?'

'Are you still here? I thought you'd gone home.'

'Just going.' The woman seemed to hesitate and looked over her shoulder. 'There's someone here to see you. That young man who used to work for you. Paul Konig.'

Tom Marshall looked up. 'Paul Konig? Good Lord, where's he been all this time? I thought he'd deserted us.' He gathered together the papers on which he'd been working and thrust them into a desk drawer. 'Is he all right?'

'He's pale and much thinner, but he seems all right.'

'Well, don't hang about, show him in. And bring coffee for two, eh?'

The secretary, who was secretly in love with Tom Marshall, smiled and held wider the glass door, at the same time beckoning Paul to go through. Tom stood up and leaned over the desk to shake hands. 'My dear fellow, we were all so worried about you. Where on earth have you been?' His sharp eyes took in Paul's appearance: the too-thin face, the longish hair. 'Looks as though you could do with a good meal.'

The woman came through carrying a tray on which two full coffee cups were set. She placed it on the desk and Tom Marshall waved her away with the words, 'That's all, Miss Schauer. I'll see you tomorrow.'

Seething with curiosity, the woman closed the door. She put one ear to its panels but the voices from within were only a murmur and she couldn't make out one word. Sighing, she struggled into her coat, adjusted her hat before the office mirror and went home to a mother who would be waiting in a wheelchair, full of complaints and accusations of neglect.

Earning her keep working for an English newspaper, dealing daily with the agent who represented it in Germany, she knew her duty was to inform the police about happenings of an odd nature. And what could be more odd than someone who vanished, then turned up four months later, quite out of the blue?

She considered herself a good German. Paul Konig was also a

German – whether good or not she had her own opinions, but nonetheless one of the master race. And Paul, describing what had happened to him over the lost months, was never to know that his life was saved by the fact that the dowdy, middle-aged woman was in love with his boss.

'The people who lived on the farm were friendly,' Paul was saying, 'and the next day they gave me a lift into the nearest town in time to catch a train to Berlin. They even paid my fare. Not wanting to incriminate them, just in case the prison authorities got on to them, I told them I was a soldier on leave and had been hiking and now had to report back to my unit. I was still wearing my original clothes and explained away their filthy condition by saying I'd fallen into some marshy ground, where I'd lost my wallet.'

He paused to drain the last of the coffee. Tom Marshall looked at the neat jacket and flannels he was wearing now and Paul grinned. 'Oh, I went straight home – or what has been home for me here in Berlin – and kept my head down for a couple of days. When I thought it was safe to emerge, I came to hand in my report.'

And he passed over the desk a sheaf of neatly typed papers. It was all there: the treatment of the young Jewish boys in the café before Paul's arrest, the conditions of the prison, the hundreds of pastors and leading churchmen who were imprisoned that winter and the hundreds more in the last couple of months. Paul had met them, hopeless old men with blank eyes and deeply lined faces, who shuffled round the prison courtyard, speaking to no one during their infrequent periods of exercise.

Tom Marshall's eyes scanned the typed words. 'The family you were staying with must have been relieved to see you,' he said. He nearly added, but didn't: We all thought you were a goner.

'Old Naldo Jenson, the grandfather – did I ever tell you he'd been an old flame of my grandmother's? – he collapsed and had to be given brandy. I suspect a lot of it was play-acting but he got his brandy in any case.'

Tom reached for his briefcase and stuffed the papers inside. 'I'll read these at home. Why don't you come and have a meal with us? The wife'll have it ready and there's always plenty for another one.'

Paul smiled. 'I promised the Jensons I'd be back for supper. But thanks. Maybe another time?'

Tom looked at him. 'Things have been quiet since you've been gone. I've been praying for something – something exciting – to happen.' He gazed down at the leather briefcase with the sort of look a fond father bestows on a beloved child. 'And by the looks of this, it has.'

On their way out of the darkened, deserted building, Tom asked, 'What are your immediate plans now, Paul? You can't stay here. It would be too risky. The Germans are on edge with all this talk of war. You'll have to get out, go back to England.'

'I realize that. I hate the idea, it'll be like running away.'

Tom frowned. 'I know how you feel, but if you don't get out soon it might be too late. If war should start – and from all my sources it looks extremely likely – we'll all have to get out. And if there was a war, would you want to be on this side of the Channel while your mother is on the other side?'

'Most definitely not.'

'Well then, we'd better do something about it.'

Three things happened on the Sunday following her encounter with Guy. Three things that were to change Kate's life. Guy appeared on her doorstep; her mother returned; and unknown to Kate, Paul arrived back in England.

Feeling the need for the consolation of the church – the shimmering candles, the blue-robed statue of Our Lady, the softly spoken words of Father O'Hanlan – that Sunday Kate took part in the mass with more fervour than she had ever done.

Rosa was there and together they walked back along the wooded pathway, across the stepping stones and towards the bridge. Rosa seemed quiet, reluctant to talk, and Kate respected her mood. They climbed the stairs in Paradise Buildings and parted when they reached Rosa's landing. But before she closed her front door, the older woman turned and said, 'Why don't you come for lunch, Kate? I've a nice shoulder of lamb and some new potatoes.'

Not wanting to hurt her feelings, Kate refused as politely as she could, saying that she too had lamb, lamb chops, and she'd better eat them up before they went off. Rosa smiled. 'Another time perhaps?'

'Yes, Rosa, another time. But thanks anyway.'

She wished she had accepted Rosa's offer when, halfway through her cooking, there was a knock at the door. Opening it she saw Guy. Grinning, as self-assured as ever, he elbowed his way past her and strode into the sitting room. The aroma of grilling lamb and mint sauce was mouthwatering. He threw back his head and sniffed like the waifs in the Bisto advert. 'Hmmm, something smells good.' And he looked at her so yearningly that she almost succumbed.

Stiffly, she said, 'It's my lunch. If you don't mind, I'm busy . . .'

Even after that night with Julie, he still seemed to think he had some kind of a hold on her. She avoided him as he made a grab when she passed on her way to the kitchen. 'Don't, Guy.' Her voice held a warning. 'I'm not in the mood for your silly games.'

'Would it help if I said I'm sorry? Did Julie tell you everything, the happenings that led up to our night together?'

He'd followed her into the tiny kitchen. Busy turning the chops under the grill, Kate didn't look at him. 'Julie told me all I needed to know. I'm not interested in any pathetic excuses you may have to offer.'

'You're going to listen, my girl, if it's the last thing you do. Did Julie explain how frightened she was when the thunder started – did you know she was scared to death of storms? No, you probably didn't. The rain was heavy and lightning flashed. I didn't dare drive in those conditions, not on the rough forest track we'd followed to find the inn. It seemed only natural to suggest we stay there.'

Sarcastically, Kate said, 'And I suppose they only had one spare room to offer and, knowing you, you jumped at it.'

'As a matter of fact, that's exactly what happened.' His grin widened. 'It's difficult to believe you two were educated at the same place, with Julie so modern and liberated and you . . .'

'Me so modest and reserved?' She'd turned to face him now, her back to the stove, her eyes luminous with unshed tears. Oh God! she thought, I'm not going to cry, am I? I mustn't allow that to happen.

'On the surface at least. Although I know that under all that maidenly sham simmers a passion that equals Julie's any day.'

Kate's lip curled in disgust. 'That's something you'll just have to dream about, isn't it?' The pot containing the potatoes boiled over, causing the gas beneath to splutter. Kate turned round to attend to it, feeling Guy's eyes on her back. 'You're a liar, Guy Ferris. I can't think what I ever saw in you. Right from our first meeting you've been rude and truculent. When I think of all that talk about honeymooning in a white villa, your grandmother going on about setting me up in my own business, I could scream. I wouldn't accept a penny from you or her.' She held the spatula, with which she'd been turning the chops, threateningly before him, as though it were a weapon. 'I really do think you ought to go. My chops will be overcooked.'

'You can't just break it off like that.' He sounded like a small boy denied his favourite toy. 'What happened with Julie is water under the bridge. Can't we start over from the beginning? I admit that when we met we got off on the wrong foot, and it's only now, after all this time, that we've finally fallen into step.' He moved closer, feeling the warmth of the stove on his face. 'The only thing I want now is to be with you. I don't want to say goodbye. We were going to get married, Kate, remember?'

She thought, if this were a picture, they'd start playing the really soppy theme music now. Or there'd be a view of the lovers walking hand in hand into the sunset.

Suddenly she despised him. Contempt welled up inside her. At this moment, more than ever, how she missed Paul. Never a day went by when she didn't think of him. She said, thoughtfully, 'You know, I don't think I've ever met such a sly, egotistical bastard as you. You are so wrapped up in yourself you just can't see any other person's point of view.'

'I made a mistake, Kate. You can't hold that against me for the rest of my life.'

'We all make mistakes,' she said bitterly.

Hope flared in his eyes. 'You understand, then?'

Only too well, she thought, loathing him. 'I suppose I should consider it a lucky mistake.'

'I don't think I understand . . .'

She gave a sigh. 'Oh, go and figure it out for yourself.'

His face flamed. For a brief moment she thought he was going to strike her. She lifted her chin and stared back at him.

'You bitch,' he said. 'You fucking bitch.'

Then, without another word, he turned and left her. She ran to close the front door after him, just in case he changed his mind

She didn't want to see him go, didn't want to set eyes on him ever again.

She didn't see him go, but Paul Konig, about to climb the stairs to her flat, did. He'd arrived home just after his mother had got back from church. Rosa had wept copious tears and produced the bottle of cognac she'd been saving for a celebration such as this. Stemming her flow of questions, mingled with fresh tears, Paul set the table while she continued with the roast. 'Wouldn't it be nice to ask Kate to eat with us?' he said, coming to stand behind his mother in the kitchen. 'How is she, by the way?'

Rosa thought of all the things that had happened to both Kate and the shop since he'd been away. Such a lot to talk about. But it would keep. Busy chopping fresh mint for the sauce, she said, 'I did ask her before but she was cooking her own lunch.'

'Well, she can warm that up for her supper,' smiled Paul, suddenly wanting to see Kate more than he'd ever wanted anything in his life. 'I'll go and ask her. She won't refuse me.'

Rosa didn't argue. As he stepped out on to the landing, he heard footsteps coming from the floor above. When he saw it was Guy Ferris, he ducked back into the shadows of the landing. So she was still seeing Ferris. Crazy to think she would be interested in anyone else when Guy was still around!

His mother raised her brows at his swift return. 'That was quick! Is she coming?'

'No, I changed my mind. I thought a nice, quiet meal together would be better. And we've such a lot to talk about.'

Eyeing his gaunt frame, the thin face, Rosa's lips tightened and she said, 'Indeed we have.'

They talked long into the night. 'Do you remember Hilda Steinberg?' Paul asked.

'Of course I remember Hilda. Did you come across her in your travels?'

Paul thought back to that night at the beginning of the year with the snow falling outside the lovely hotel and the Nazis celebrating their victories inside.

He told how he had met Hilda, but not of the man Hans. He didn't think his mother would be pleased to hear how the girl she had known for so long was now mistress to one of their enemies, staying with him for support and protection.

When he came to the part about the café and the drunken brown-shirts, of hearing Hilda's screams as he was dragged away, Rosa's face went a pasty white.

She breathed, '*Mein Gott!*' and a hand went to her throat. 'Was she hurt?'

'When I came back to Berlin, I went to find her, to make sure she was all right. She'd told me she was still living with her mother in the old house. I hung about outside. I could hardly go up to the front door and ask. Somebody came by and I enquired if a Hilda Jones lived there – I told you she had married that English boy from down the street, didn't I? – and I must confess to feeling a vast relief when they said she did.'

'Well, that's good. It would seem not every family has turned out as unfortunate as us.'

Again he thought of Hans, of the large hands and beer belly and he sighed. 'No, it seems it hasn't. But you shouldn't say that, Mama. You're not doing so badly from all accounts.' He reached for the bottle of cognac, pouring himself a liberal amount. He had never been one for strong drink, but maybe if he drank enough he would be able to forget the events of the past months, forget Guy Ferris as he came from visiting Kate . . .

Settling back in his chair, Paul smiled at his mother and said, 'It seems I've been doing all of the talking. Now it's your turn. How is everything going?' He allowed his gaze to roam the room. 'I was hoping you'd have found something a little more luxurious by now. Don't tell me trade has fallen away?'

'It's slowed down somewhat, what with all the war talk. But we're still kept busy. Oh, yes, we're still kept busy.'

Paul gave her a shrewd look, alerted by something in her tone. 'Well, that's good, isn't it?'

Rosa thought of the sight that had greeted her that disastrous morning, of the broken window and the hated slogan painted in red across what was left of it. She felt that he had had enough to bear over the last few months without heaping further troubles on his head. Still, if she didn't tell him, somebody else was sure to. One couldn't keep anything like that quiet for long. But she wouldn't mention the people whom she and Kate suspected. An investigative reporter like Paul would go all out to find the perpetrators, and that could lead to further trouble.

Giving him a stricken look, she began her story.

Listening, Paul squeezed his glass until his knuckles shone white. If he'd squeezed any harder the glass might well have shattered. 'Bastards!' he said between clenched teeth when she'd finished. 'Do they know who was responsible?'

'No, Pauli. Although I'm sure the police are doing all they can.'

He drained his glass and was about to reach again for the bottle of cognac when Rosa forestalled him. She rose to her feet and put it away in the sideboard. 'No more, Pauli. That isn't the answer.'

No, he thought. But what was?

Kate was washing up her dinner things when there was another knock on the door. Frowning, she went to open it. Sure that it was Guy, back for further discussion, the words 'If you want to argue any more, I don't want to know . . .' faltered on her lips.

Her mother stood on the landing, the suitcase she'd carried all the way from the station beside her. 'Well, that's a nice way to greet your mother after an absence of two weeks, I must say! I should have thought you'd be glad to see me.'

'Of course I'm glad to see you, Mummy. It's just that I thought you were somebody else.' She leaned forward and picked up the suitcase then closing the door followed her mother into the sitting room. 'Why didn't you let me know you were coming? I'd have met you.'

'It was a sort of spur-of-the-moment thing.' Monica gazed about her as though expecting to see traces of wild parties or such-like enjoyed by Kate while she was away. Everything was neat and tidy, only the litter of coloured crayons and sketch pads hinting that this was also a work-room.

'I've just finished lunch,' said Kate. 'But I can get you something if you're hungry.'

'I treated myself to a meal on the train. Expensive but very worthwhile.'

'A cup of tea, then?'

'A cup of tea would be fine.'

Filling the kettle at the tap, Kate called over her shoulder, 'Did you enjoy your holiday? How was Aunty Norma?'

'Your aunt was fine. She sends her love. And yes, I enjoyed my stay very much.' Monica thought of the elderly man who lived in the big red-brick house at the bottom of Norma's lane. She had met him in the local public house the two women had daringly visited one evening, and after assiduous questioning of her sister had learned he was a writer. 'Quite a successful one, I gather,' Norma had said, 'from the size of his house.'

Monica sipped her drink and looked interested. 'Anyone I should know?'

'Oh, way above our poor little heads I should think. All about medieval goings-on.'

Seeing the surprise on her sister's face, Norma laughed. 'Some people must like it. He seems to be doing well.'

Further questioning revealed that he was a widower and lived alone, apart from an ageing spaniel he took for walks every morning. His path, fortunately, taking him past Norma's front gate. Suddenly Monica displayed an interest in gardening Norma hadn't known she possessed. Every morning would find her on her knees, diligently weeding the flowerbeds nearest the gate. What could be more natural than for the man to stop, lean his arms on the top of the gate and discuss with her the events of the day?

Norma said her garden had never, since she'd moved in all those years ago, received such tender, loving care.

Monica reached for her bag, taking out her silver cigarette case. Kate wrinkled her nose as the pungent smell of the lighted cigarette filtered through to the kitchen. She opened the window above the sink a little wider, hearing Monica behind her say, 'I see you've still got those tatty marigolds on the windowsill. Why on earth don't you get something a bit more glamorous, like a gloxinia, for example?'

Kate's mouth set in stubborn tightness. 'I like marigolds. They were Daddy's favourite flower.'

Monica shrugged and stood aside as Kate pushed past with the tea tray. 'No accounting for taste, I suppose.'

Neither spoke as they sipped their tea. Monica listened to the loud voices of the neighbours, heard clearly through the walls, the screaming of children playing in the road outside. A world away from Norma's peaceful abode.

Kate wanted to tell her mother of the attack on Rosa's shop, about Ruthie running away to Gretna Green to marry her sweetheart. She knew her mother wouldn't be interested. And there was very little else to talk about. The distance between them seemed to have grown over the time Monica had lived here with her in Paradise Buildings.

With Ruthie gone, and, perhaps, Julie lost to her forever, who could she now share her thoughts with? All the dreams she had dreamed about Guy had come to nothing. In fact, looking back on the time they'd known each other, she wondered how she could have been so blind. Wasn't there an old saying that love *was* blind?

The thought of Paul Konig came into her mind. Suddenly she could not stop the memories from flooding back. Like the first time they had met, Paul standing in the shop, completely ignored by Mr Shipton; the afternoons spent in the old railway carriage, the sun shining on the tall grasses and wild flowers, making everything look like a picture out of a fairy tale. And Paul would be there to greet her warmly and pour sweet, milky tea from the old flask.

'Kate?'

She came back with a start. Monica looked at her and said, 'Daydreaming again! I sometimes wonder if you'll ever grow out of it.'

'There are a lot worse things than daydreaming,' Kate replied, trying hard to keep the sarcasm out of her voice.

Her mother shrugged. 'Here we go again! Derisive as ever.'

'I wasn't being derisive, Mum.'

Her mother fumbled for another cigarette. 'Weren't you? It sounded very much like it to me.' She lit the cigarette, puffing exuberantly, as though the cloud of smoke would somehow dull the sudden resentment between them. Her gaze rested on the litter of crayons and scraps of paper that covered most of the surface of the dining table. 'And just look at the place! I bet you haven't lifted a finger since I went away. I shudder to think what Julie must have thought.'

On the point of saying 'And I can't imagine why you came back from Aunt Norma's if you feel so strongly about living here,' Kate rose to her feet and went into the bedroom. She took her folded nightdress from under the pillow on the bed, collected the few items of make-up that belonged to her and went back into the sitting room. It would be the hard settee for her again, she thought. She wondered how long things could continue like this between them. 'I'll change the sheets later,' she said.

'Be sure that you do,' said her mother, sounding for all the world like the lady of the manor.

Chapter Thirty-Two

Kate was glad to get back to the shop the following morning. The atmosphere in the flat had become unbearable. She wondered how long it would be before a real bust-up ensued. What with her mother, and Guy, not to mention Julie's behaviour, everything seemed to be going wrong.

Rosa seemed to have a knack for sniffing out troubled souls, and during the morning she said, 'What is it, Kate? Something is bothering you, I can see.'

How she wished she could tell the girl of Paul's safe return. But he'd made her promise not to say a word. Holding up a restraining hand when she'd pleaded, 'But Kate, of all people, should know. I don't understand you, Pauli, I really don't,' he'd replied, 'I'll see her in my own good time, Mama. Just put it down to one of my little foibles.'

And there the subject had remained. Looking at the tired, worried little face now, Rosa had the greatest difficulty in controlling the almost irresistible urge to confess all.

A telegram boy earned a rebuking glance from Rosa when later in the morning he leaned his bicycle against the window and came into the shop. Blissfully ignoring the condemning look, he grinned widely and held out the yellow envelope to Rosa. It was addressed to Miss Kate Linley and rather apprehensively Rosa passed it to Kate. Rosa was of the generation that hated telegrams. The arrival of one during the war years would send women into hysterics.

Watching Kate's face as she read it, Rosa said, 'What is it, Kate? Not bad news I hope.'

'It's from Ruthie. Or rather, Ruthie's boyfriend. The marriage is going ahead, all is well, he says, and they are both very happy.' She glanced up from the printed form. 'He just wanted us to know so we wouldn't worry.'

'How very thoughtful of the young man,' murmured Rosa. Although Ruthie's abrupt departure, without even a goodbye, had disappointed her, she couldn't really blame the girl. From all accounts the parents had been a worthless pair.

'Any answer?' queried the boy. He'd had a good look round the shop, wondering what his mum would look like in one of those posh frocks, had winked boldly at Sylvia, who looked thunderous, and was now ready to go.

'No. Thanks.' Kate held the door open for him. Rosa followed him outside, watchful of the bike against the window. With exaggerated care, he pulled the bike upright, bowed from the waist to Rosa and cycled away.

'Young scamp!'

Sylvia caught Kate's eye and actually smiled.

'Young scamp!' Rosa repeated, closing the door behind her. 'Where do they recruit such boys from these days? Not an iota of manners to his name. Not like my Pauli . . .'

Aware of what she had been on the point of revealing, she pulled herself together, a warm smile transforming the frown as a client came into the shop. Discussing fabrics, colours, styles, she put all other thoughts from her mind except those of pleasing the customer.

After much consideration, she had decided what she must do. When she got home that evening she would ask her son's advice, sure he would wholeheartedly agree with her. It was something she had meant to do for a long time. Now some sixth sense told her the time was right.

'What I'm planning to do,' she told him over the cup of coffee he had waiting for her when she arrived home, 'is make Kate a proposition. I've felt for a long time that she would be an asset worth retaining. I'm going to offer her a partnership in Rosa's Boutique.'

Paul couldn't have heard anything that would have pleased him more. His eyes glistened. 'Mama, that's great! You couldn't have made a wiser choice.'

Rosa's eyes twinkled. 'I have to confess that I'm not being entirely altruistic. One works harder, and has more commitment, if one is personally reaping the rewards of that hard work.'

Paul laughed. 'Shrewd. But then you always were. And you won't find anyone who works harder than Kate.'

She gave him a look. 'Do you think she will accept? Will she, perhaps, consider herself too young to take on such a responsibility?'

Paul shook his head. 'I'm sure she won't. Kate's always had a yearning for her own shop. She's spoken to me about it many times.'

Rosa looked like the cat who had found the cream. 'All right, I'll discuss it with her tomorrow and if she is agreeable I'll instruct my lawyer to begin drawing up the necessary papers.'

As usual, Kate had walked home with Rosa and bade her goodbye at her landing. Kate was tired, the day was unusually humid and a slight headache niggled at the back of her head. Half expecting to smell the aroma of a casserole or even a meat pie which they could have with salad, she shouldn't have been surprised when only the acrid smell of her mother's cigarettes assailed her nostrils at the door of her flat.

Monica reclined on the settee, cigarette in one hand, an open magazine in the other. She looked up as Kate came in, the picture of an elegant woman to whom the mere idea of cooking was foreign. 'You're late,' she said accusingly.

'I know. A customer came in just as we were closing and you know Rosa, never turns anyone away.'

Monica dropped the magazine to the floor and sat up. 'I've had a perfectly horrible day,' she said, not in the least interested in late customers. 'That awful woman, that girl Ruthie's mother, came knocking on the door, screaming abuse.' She shuddered. 'The whole building must have heard her. The things she said, Kate. I swear I've never heard such words before. She hammered on the door until I was forced to open it and ask her to be quiet.'

'What did she want?'

'She went on about her daughter and how you had enticed her to run away with that man, and how Ruthie's wage was the only one coming in and they'd all most likely starve without that.'

'If anyone is to blame, it's her own parents. Did you know her father used to beat her? She showed me the strap marks on her legs after he'd found out about her and Bill last summer. That's her young man, Bill,' Kate explained. 'Anyway, with her gone, her father will have to look for work, won't he? Do him good. I have no time for either of them.'

'Well, whatever the reason, the mother had no right to come screaming abuse at me.' Kate's story about the beating had gone completely unnoticed. Monica was concerned only with her own bruised feelings.

'I tell you, Kate, I don't think I can stand living here again after experiencing the peace at your aunt's. It's like two different worlds. The noise goes on all day here, one can hardly concentrate. I don't know how many times I started to read an article in that magazine and never got further than the first few lines. It's not doing my nerves a bit of good. I shall have to consult Doctor Shearer again if this keeps up.'

'Mum!'

Monica ignored her. In full flow, she went on, 'You're young, it doesn't bother you the way it does me.'

Sighing, Kate said, 'I'm sorry about the noise, Mummy, but there's not much I can do about it.'

'You could move. Find another place to live. If your father hadn't been so foolish as to have tried to cross the railway lines instead of using the footbridge, all this need never have happened.'

As usual, when her mother spoke about her father in those derogatory tones, Kate felt her temper rise. 'I can't afford another place. If I could, do you imagine I'd still be living here? As for Daddy, well, you know he found climbing the steps difficult.'

'He shouldn't have been over that way in the first place. All that to buy another puppy. I ask you! He could hardly afford to feed us, never mind a dog. And the whole wretched thing ending up in us losing the house.' Monica always did like to magnify troubles. Kate couldn't help but to speak sharply.

'That's not true about feeding us, and you know it. We weren't doing too badly, with my wages and his combined. And if you'd been here, maybe some arrangement could have been made about the house.'

She wanted to rail at her mother, remind her that she had been the one to desert him. It was respect for the nuns' teaching that held her back, certainly not respect for her mother. She had little of that left. Monica would go on being the self-seeking, mercenary woman she had always been. The thought came to her: knowing her mother so well, it was funny that she hadn't recognized the same traits in Guy.

The next morning, hearing Kate moving about in the kitchen, Monica roused herself sufficiently to call, 'Will you telephone from the shop to tell your Aunt Norma that I'll be back sometime over the weekend? Tell her I'll get the bus from the station and see her at the cottage.'

Kate went to the bedroom door and peered in. 'Are you sure? Look, I'm sorry about our argument last night, and I don't want you to go off in a huff. I'm sorry it hasn't worked out, Mummy. Maybe later, when I'm able to afford a better place, perhaps another house, we could try again?'

Monica thought of the elderly writer, of the red-brick house with its lovely gardens, and smiled. 'It's best not to make plans, Katie. One never knows what is going to happen.'

She hadn't called her Katie for so long that tears came into Kate's eyes. Running to the bed, she bent and clasped her mother in her arms. 'Oh, Mummy, don't let's part with acrimony. I didn't want it to be like this.'

Monica smiled. 'And you'll be sure to keep me informed regarding your plans with Guy.' She'd wondered about him. In the short time she had been back he hadn't once come to the flat and she was sure Kate hadn't been out with him. A lovers' spat, she thought. Oh well, it happens to the best of us. It will soon pass. Jestingly, she said, 'Just be sure to send me an invitation to the wedding.'

Fresh tears pricked at Kate's eyes and she looked away. She held her breath until she had gained control of her voice. 'I'd better go. I'll be late for work.'

'Don't forget to telephone now. You've got the number? The old couple in the shop will run and get Norma, or you can leave a message with them.'

'I know.'

When Rosa asked her into the back room, saying she wanted to talk to her privately, and leaving Sylvia looking after them suspiciously, Kate didn't know what to make of it. Was Rosa going to say that she couldn't afford her wages any more? Although business had been slack – with all the talk of war, few women felt the urge to go out and spend money on new clothes – they were still doing pretty well. Or had Rosa received news of Paul? Something bad? She'd heard of people's hearts standing still. A line from a song, something made up by lyric writers. Now she knew it wasn't just that, but something very real. Her heart, besides standing still, actually froze.

Her face lost its colour, leaving the lipstick she wore standing out like a wine stain on a pure white table napkin.

'Oh, Rosa, what is it? It's not Paul? Please don't tell me something has happened to Paul?'

To her relief, Rosa smiled. 'Paul's all right, dear. It's not Paul.' She drew Kate towards two chairs used by the staff. 'I should have made coffee, shouldn't I? Or perhaps ordered a bottle of wine to celebrate. Never mind, that can all come later. Now, Kate, I want you to listen and tell me what you think of my plan . . .'

And, almost word for word, Rosa repeated what she'd said to Paul the previous evening. When she'd finished, she looked at the astonished girl with a raised eyebrow. 'Well, what do you think? Do you reckon you're up to it?'

Kate's expression was a combination of surprise and delight. 'Just you try me! Oh, Rosa, that's wonderful. I always planned to have my own business, but this is even better. I can continue to work with you.'

'So do we have a deal?' Rosa said, offering Kate her hand.

'We have a deal,' Kate agreed, shaking with her.

They stopped talking when Sylvia came in to take something from a drawer. Murmuring her excuses, the girl slipped quietly out. 'She's getting a little more friendly, I must say,' remarked Rosa. 'Quite an improvement.' She smiled at Kate. 'Have you been working your spells on her?'

Kate laughed, all the tension left from the quarrel with her mother finally disintegrating. Then she said, 'What did you mean when you said Paul is all right? How do you know he's all right?' Her voice sharpening, she added, 'Have you heard from him?'

The bell above the shop door jangled and Rosa stood up. 'Customers, my dear. Come and work your charms on them.'

309

When the customers had gone, Kate, remembering her mother's request, asked if she might use the telephone. Rosa waved an acquiescing hand and Kate picked up the phone. The elderly man who answered said that of course he'd be delighted to give Norma Kate's message. He hoped her mother had arrived back safely, they had all enjoyed having her visit their small village and it would be nice to see her again. His tone implied that he couldn't for the life of him imagine why anyone wanted to live in London or any other big city.

Kate thanked him. Unable to miss hearing every word Kate had said, Rosa looked surprised and said she hoped nothing was amiss. 'Not really. It's just that my mother dislikes living in Paradise Buildings, says it's far too noisy after the quiet of the country.'

Rosa knew of the antagonism between the two sisters but didn't think it was her place to comment on it. All she said was: 'Seems some things do change for the better, after all.'

Thinking of the wonderful offer made to her by Rosa, Kate's smile lit up her whole face. 'Oh, yes, you can say that again.'

It was Sunday again; Kate woke refreshed and eager to face a new day. Sleeping in a proper bed helped, of course, plus the fact that her future looked bright and promising. She decided to spoil herself and went into the kitchen barefooted, making tea and toast and boiling an egg for her breakfast. Carrying it back to bed on a tray, she thought she'd never felt so free and unfettered. Not a care in the world. Except, perhaps, the inescapable foreboding over Paul. What was Rosa trying to keep hidden from her? There was something, she felt it in her bones. She made a resolution that come Monday she would demand an answer to her question. She had to know. Didn't Rosa realize just how much Paul meant to her! The notion surprised her. If she wasn't careful she would begin to think of Paul in the way she had Guy Ferris.

Thoughtfully, she sipped her tea. She had thought she was in love with Guy. She knew she had been wrong, and now she was starting to think the same about Paul. Perhaps it was her age? Girls began to think of husbands and babies at her age. Perhaps she was at last growing up!

She smiled and putting the tray to the end of the bed, threw the bedclothes off. There would be no babies or husbands for her, not for a long time yet. She had a career to think about. Every ounce of her energy would be given to that.

Gazing through the kitchen window as she washed the few dishes, she decided she would give church a miss this morning. She was itching to sketch the designs that jostled in her mind. She smiled fondly at the pot of marigolds, and touched their bright petals with a gentle finger. 'How proud you would be of your little girl, Daddy,' she murmured, 'if you knew.'

Perhaps he did know. Maybe somewhere there was a place where he was smiling down on her, boasting to other parents of his brilliant daughter.

She made her bed, dusted and tidied things in general, then gathered her drawing materials together. The sun was delightfully warm on her head as she crossed the iron footbridge. Halfway across she heard the sound of an approaching express. The smoke engulfed her as it roared beneath and she was again reminded of Paul. She resolved on the way back to pop in to Rosa's and implore Rosa to give her a straight answer. She knew she wouldn't rest until she got one.

She wouldn't wait until Monday.

Summer that year had started early and already the playing fields of the Railway Club were busy. Elderly men in white flannels and straw hats were bending over their bowls. On the tennis courts a couple were prancing, with little shrieks from the girl each time she missed a ball.

Approaching the old carriage, Kate's steps slowed until she was sure Guy wasn't the man on the court. Then she hurried on, climbing into the carriage with a sigh of pure contentment.

As he trod the narrow path Paul thought the trees looked particularly lovely this year. The misty greenness of new growth had been replaced by an abundant lushness that pleased the eye, reminding him that beauty did not vanish despite the abominations of man against man.

Or would all this change if war should start? Would it all be dug-outs and bomb shelters, all this lovely greenery where he and Kate had spent so many happy hours, talking the afternoon away? And ahead . . . ?

He smoothed one hand over his hair. Ahead something was waiting for him. He only knew that the subconscious edge of his imagination, the part that still worked, was already filled with one person. A girl with bright hair and wide blue eyes. A girl who would partner his mother in the business. Her very being made everyday existence, for him, as intense and dramatic as it must surely be for any man who realized he was in love. You didn't know what was going to happen, but you knew that it would be a wonderful, tremendously exciting thing and sweeter, far sweeter, than anything you had ever felt before.

The sun shone down from a cloudless sky. Its warmth fell on the tall grasses, turning them to silver as they bent gently in the breeze. Wild mallow bloomed here. Cow parsley stirred in a drift of white lace, counterfeiting a scene that, by closing his eyes and letting his mind drift, he had re-created, along with Kate's laughter, when his captors were ill-treating him in that dank prison cell.

He climbed the two steps into the ancient railway carriage. Silently, he entered the compartment. Kate sat in the corner seat, engrossed in her sketching. So engrossed that she did not know he was watching. As he observed her, she pushed a long strand of the silver-bright hair from her eyes, tucking it behind her ear in that endearing habit he would always remember.

The combination of this delightful scene and his own euphoric frame of mind filled Paul with a contentment he hadn't felt since he couldn't remember when. He continued to gaze at her. It was as if a veil had dropped from his eyes. A feeling of pure love surged within him. He wanted to take her in his arms and hold her close, to look after her, protect her, cherish her.

He stepped forward out of the shadows and said, 'Hello, Kate!'

Kate lifted her head and stared at him in amazement, unable to believe that it was actually him.

'Paul!' she croaked.

'I knew I'd find you here. It's where you always came on a fine Sunday.'

'Paul,' she repeated and tears began to roll down her cheeks. With a muffled sob she came from behind the scarred wooden table and threw herself into his arms. They closed around her like a benediction.

'All the time I was away, I dreamed of finding you here,' he said, his own eyes moist. 'Even in my worst moments, I knew.'

'But . . .' There were a thousand questions she wanted to ask. Suddenly she realized that she was in his arms. What must he think of her, throwing herself at him like that? She gave a little push and he released her immediately. Going back to her seat, she tried to appear collected and calm, cloaking the tumultuous feelings that shook her.

'When did you get back?'

He came further into the carriage and sat down on the seat opposite her. 'I've been home a few days . . .'

'And you didn't let me know?' She stared at him accusingly. 'I guessed there was something funny going on when your mother let slip a remark the other day.' She leaned forward across the table, reaching for his hand. 'Why didn't you tell me, Paul? *Why?*'

Paul took a deep breath. 'I don't know. I'd been through a fairly traumatic experience and I guess I was still getting over it. I *should* have told you. I would have done, I wanted to wait for the right moment.' He didn't say it aloud but the name Guy Ferris hung like a spectre between them. 'Anyway, you first. What exciting things have happened while you've been away from under my watchful eye?'

Kate sighed. 'You are the absolute end, Paul Konig.' She released his hand and sat back. 'You first. You tell me first.'

The story he told made her catch her breath in distress.

'I was sure, when you didn't write, that something terrible had happened to you. Couldn't you have got word somehow? Your mother was so worried . . .' She reached out again and laid her hand on his. 'Oh, Paul!'

'Don't let's talk about it. It's already in the past.' He unbuckled the canvas satchel she remembered so well. Reaching inside, he produced the flask and a blue enamel mug. 'See, I didn't forget. I only wish it was champagne, but for the time being we'll have to make do with this.' He poured the steaming tea into the silver top of the flask, then filled the blue mug. Handing her the silver cup, he said, 'What shall we toast?'

Kate thought about that. 'Happiness?' she suggested. 'And peace.'

'Happiness and peace it is!'

They drank, and she was suddenly aware how close his face was across the narrow table. Only inches from hers. Time seemed to stop as they sat, the mugs of tea in their hands, eyes locked. Vividly, she was aware of her heart thumping madly.

'Kate?' he whispered.

'Yes?'

'I . . .' He trailed off, then seeming to find the courage, he said, 'About you and Ferris. Are you . . . ?' Again his voice trailed off and she smiled.

'Guy Ferris means nothing to me now. I should have listened to you in the first place. Your description of him, all that time ago, was pretty apt.'

He digested that. Hope flickered in his eyes. 'Then you're not . . . ?'

She sighed and said, teasingly, 'I do wish you'd finish a question. I never was any good at mind-reading.' Interpreting the look in his eyes, she urged softly, 'Nothing ventured, nothing gained.'

With a gentle sigh, he leaned forward and placed his lips against hers.

She brought a hand up to rest against his cheek and his kiss deepened. They broke off simultaneously, both confused at what had happened.

'This blasted table,' said Paul, rising and coming round to lower himself beside her. Taking her into his arms, he whispered, 'I'm in love and I've only just realized it. Isn't that crazy?'

'No more crazy than me realizing I'm in love with you.' She nestled against him, rubbing her cheek against his shoulder. 'Oh, Paul, I've been so bewildered. I hardly knew right from wrong. You being back has made everything all right again.'

He didn't answer but kissed her again. A kiss that made her melt inside. It seemed to her she had come home after a long and wearying trek going nowhere. When she pushed him away in order to get her breath, she said, 'I've been such an idiot, not to realize it was you I loved and never Guy.'

'I think we've both been idiots. But we can make up for it now.'

He kissed her again, this time strongly and passionately.

Later, like a bucket of cold water poured over their heads, the present intruded, and she said, 'What will happen if war should come? Will you have to go and fight?'

'I wouldn't object to fighting, although it's more likely that I – or rather we, my mother and I – would be interned for a while. I don't know what will happen, Kate.' He held her by the shoulders, looking intently into her face. 'You're not to worry about it, darling. We'll win through, you and I.'

She went again into his arms. 'Of course we will.'